The Gypsy Pearl

Full Trilogy Edition

Lia London

Copyright © 2015 Lia London

All rights reserved.

ISBN: 10:151433884X
ISBN-13:978-1514338841

A NOTE ABOUT THIS EDITION

THE GYPSY PEARL was originally published as a trilogy—three separate books with the subtitles, Book 1: Caren, Book 2: Craggy, and Book 3: Tye. This book combines all parts as if they had been written as one continuous story. The chapters have been reconfigured and any "reminder" paragraphs that had been in what formerly constituted books 2 and 3 have been deleted so as not to be repetitive. This edition is for those who want to read the whole thing at once. I hope you enjoy the journey.

CONTENTS

1	Caz and the Creature	1
2	Sentenced to the Surface	9
3	The Gypsies on the Ferry	15
4	Welcome to Lamond Reformatory	20
5	Meeting the Inmates	26
6	Dealing with Bullies	36
7	Alf	42
8	The Storm	50
9	The Woods	55
10	King's Crown	62
11	Three Worlds, Three Gifts, Three Powers	67
12	Fugitives	72
13	The Skimmer	79
14	The Wrap	83
15	The Viper and the Pyre	92
16	Gypsy Network Headquarters	101
17	A Rapid Education	108
18	The Fanep Cavern	114
19	A Dangerous Disguise	118
20	Flying in the Cargo Hold	126

21	A Good-bye	134
22	The *Ipko*	137
23	Enemies and Allies	146
24	Darkman	156
25	Going to the Capitol	167
26	The Tower in the Trees	172
27	Left for Dead	180
28	Secrets Revealed	191
29	The Sumayar	201
30	A Song and a Scream	213
31	Adrenaline	220
32	Climbing Away	229
33	Wandel Hav	235
34	Fishing	244
35	Scilly	253
36	Nathani's Purpose	262
37	Dabbling in Diplomacy	273
38	Altering the Course	286
39	Lapita	295
40	A Long, Lonely Night	306
41	People Change	310
42	Ikekane North	317
43	The Dive	326

44	It's All Over	333
45	The Gypsy Pearl	342
	Fun Trivia Facts about *The Gypsy Pearl*	348

OOO

1 CAZ AND THE CREATURE

"You're crazy, Caz! What if they come back?"

"They won't. They're on Deck 9 with the other gypsies from Tye." I don't know why Felly followed me, but I wasn't going to let her ruin my fun. Ever since Mom left, she's been trying to run my life, and after ten years, it's getting old. I'm fourteen. I don't need a mother.

I pulled my ponytail tighter and tried to walk calmly down the beige corridor. The grated flooring echoed beneath me, and the faint vacuum vents pulled at the cloth soles of my coversuit.

I'd timed it right. The guard was on break, and I'd be able to get into the docking area undetected. It had taken me seven tries, but it would be worth it. The only thing that broke the boredom on an Interplanetary City Station like the Arxon was when Surface dwellers docked to refuel and go through quarantine before travelling on to another planet. The Arxon's speed made it a popular ICS.

This time was special, though. A few weeks ago, gypsies had come up from Tye on their way to Caren.

Felly eyed the blinking lights. "What if they have an alarm system?"

"They're gypsies, Felly. Not ICS dwellers." I slid through the door. Several hangars stretched down to the right. Each craft had been docked with its aft facing out over the main cargo bay below, but the one I cared about lay right in front of me: a gypsy space buggy.

Felly followed me a few steps. "That thing's a heap," said Felly. "I don't know how it even flies."

I rolled my eyes at her superiority complex. Gypsies don't stuff themselves into all the rules of ICS dwellers, so they're free to come up with better ideas, including their spacecrafts. I've explained this to Felly before, but she thinks that being older means being smarter.

"I bet they never take this one down to the Surface so they don't have to worry about it burning up in the atmosphere." I walked slowly around the space buggy.

Felly bit her nails and watched the empty guard post. I shook my head. "No one's coming, Felly. I'll bet you my dessert no one will even care that we're here."

"The gypsies will care," said Felly. "And the security guard. And the Station Master." Felly frowned like Dad. "Have you no respect for order?"

I ignored her and ran my hand over the windows, trying to peek inside.

"I bet they've got amazing things in there," I said, but Felly never gets excited about Surface goods. I breathed in the smell of the metal—metal that had been all around the Granbo System. I'd eavesdropped enough to know that the gypsies who owned this craft were traders, not migrant workers.

"C'mon, Caz," said Felly. "We need to get out of here."

"I know. Haven't you figured out that's what I want more than anything?"

Felly folded her arms. "Caz," she said, echoing Dad's tone of voice, "You get to travel all around the solar system and meet fascinating ambassadors. If you were down on the Surface, you'd be living in primitive colonies. You should be grateful to live on the biggest and best ICS in the system."

She'll never understand me. Who wants to live in a space rest stop that's between the places people really want to go?

"Someone's coming!" hissed Felly, shuffling into a hangar two doors down.

I ducked behind the space buggy, clinging to the rear thrusters with my fingers. A false step would mean a twenty-meter drop, so I pressed up against the craft. Down below, the wide metallic floor was lit with red glowing strips to direct the caddies. Only a few workers monitored the area. One groomed himself in his reflection on the shiny metal support beams. Everything is shiny here. It's all I've ever known, but no one can convince me it's the natural order of things because I can't stay shiny for a whole day, let alone forever.

A woman turned in my direction, and I leaned back further into the space buggy. Suddenly, a small hatch opened under me, and I landed on my butt in the smallest cargo hull ever.

I peeked out cautiously. No one below had taken notice, so I relaxed. Enough light reached in to glance around, but I didn't see past the first thing I saw.

Wood!

A curved box—a really old piece. It smelled dirty and foreign ... and wonderful. The tiny ridges of the wood grain tickled my fingertips, and I rested my cheek against its dark beauty. An antique like this would bring an astronomical price with collectors. I twisted the old-fashioned lock made of some yellowish metal. A loud click echoed in the largely metallic chamber, and I winced. I checked over my shoulder for movement below, but the grooming guy was gone, and the other two were talking to each other.

When I turned back, a pair of bright yellow eyes glowed from under the open lid!

I screamed.

A creature—like a cat-sized human—emerged without blinking. It pulled its legs from the wooden box and leapt onto me, knocking me back onto my elbows. Its eyes narrowed, pinning me down with their intensity. The creature crouched on my stomach and started sniffing at my arms. Its mouth came open, and I almost screamed again. There were a lot of teeth in there. Sharp teeth.

"Don't eat me," I whimpered, looking at it sideways.

It wore a brown and green coversuit like the beige ones most of us wear on the Arxon. A thin layer of white fuzz covered its head, but otherwise its pale grey skin actually gleamed. It really did appear very human except for the mouth and eyes. That *should* have been comforting.

Exhaling slowly, I tried to shift to get some leverage to kick away. No luck. Sharp nails popped from the tips of its fingers like retractable claws. In a flash, the creature slashed my right shoulder. A burning pain propelled me into action. No longer worried about making noise, I scrambled back out of the space buggy, banging my head on the hatch in my haste. That disoriented me for a second, and I lost my balance. One leg dropped over the ledge and I felt myself fall!

The creature caught my arm with superhuman strength. Holding a tiny white ball between its thumb and forefinger, it spoke with a gravelly voice. "No one steals a Gypsy Pearl!"

"I didn't steal anything!"

With a violent shove, the creature crammed the ball into my wound and hurled me free of the space buggy and away from the ledge. It slithered back into the craft and closed the hatch behind it.

Panting, I crawled out of the hangar, feeling the grates of the floor dig into my kneecaps and palms. Drips of blood fell through the vents, and I wondered vaguely if some computer would analyze the debris and know it was me.

Exhausted from the adrenaline rush, I almost didn't hear the footsteps clanging down the corridor. "You!" called a guard. "What are you doing here?"

Cupping my hand over my shoulder, I rose awkwardly. "I'm sorry. I was just—"

"Oh, it's *you*, Caz," said the guard gruffly. "Go wash up, brat. And don't come down here again."

I hesitated because I couldn't see Felly.

"Mr. Lew will hear of this," he said, wagging a finger. "You're supposed to be on the family deck. Go to the rec hall like the other kids. Don't you know where you belong?" He waved me away, shaking his head.

I ran along the corridor and ducked into a washroom. An elderly lady glared at me disapprovingly, so I lunged for the sink, careful to avoid eye contact. My 'general disheveled nature' always gets scowls from the life-long ICS dwellers. They love to give me demerits for my sloppiness.

I worked quickly to rinse away the blood. The instant the fresh water touched my skin, I felt a relief from the pain.

"What the—?"

Not even a scar remained!

I ran my thumb over where the wound had been and felt a small lump under the skin. I stared at my shoulder, and then at my own horror-stricken face in the mirror. The sweat of exertion had made the edges of my hair curl, but otherwise I looked my usual tom-boyish self.

"You all right?" asked Felly, her reflection appearing next to mine.

The water faucet turned itself off, and the room became still. The elderly woman hurried out. I spun to face Felly. "Of course I am."

Her hand went to my stained, ripped sleeve. "I thought I saw blood—"

I jerked away. "Your eyes are old." I couldn't explain everything that had happened, so I concentrated on breathing normally.

"Caz."

"Felly, I'm fine." I rubbed my shoulder again, as casually as I could. The lump felt smaller now, as if retreating deeper into my flesh. What had the creature called it? *A pearl?* "C'mon," I said. "I promised you my dessert if anyone caught us."

We took a lift, neither speaking because there were others in the elevator with us. There always are. You're never alone on an ICS, even one as big as the Arxon.

I stepped out onto the resident deck, our tidy and stifling little world between the worlds. It's not as ornate as the deck for embassy families. They get carpeting and ambient lighting. We get hinged doors and painted walls for a 'Surface feel'.

The doors of the lift slid shut behind us, and I announced, "Level six, Paradise!"

"Stop it, Caz," said Felly, tugging me away. "Do you have to complain all the time?"

"What? I didn't complain. See how nicely someone arranged the fake plants. It's wild in here."

"Caz, you joke about it, but it *is* wild down there."

"So they tell us."

"Inhospitable weather, dangerous animals—"

"Felly, shut up," I said. "You will never convince me that life on an ICS is as good as life on the Surface." I stopped and slumped against the wall, my arms folded.

Felly waited for a small group of children to pass and then copied my stance on the opposite wall. "All right, out with it," she said. "You haven't given your speech for two days, and I want it over with before we eat, so I don't get sick listening to your ingratitude."

"Felly, you don't understand."

"No. I don't. Explain it to me. Again. Whine a little while you're at it."

"Felly—"

"I don't know how someone so smart can be so stupid, Caz. You got all of Dad's intelligence and none of his sense."

Maybe that's the part I inherited from Mom. I'd never know. No one would talk about her. Anyway, I hate it when she says stuff like that. I probably do make her crazy, but can I help it?

I growled in frustration just as a couple strolled by. They reacted with alarm and distaste. "Practicing my doggie speech," I said sweetly. "I want to be an interspecies diplomat when I grow up." They didn't respond.

Felly bit her lip to hide a grin. *Finally*, a spark of humor. But she blew it by saying, "You get to see all three planets every time we go around."

"I see them from *space*. That's not exactly thrilling." I shouldered open the swinging door to the cafeteria, smashing into a man carrying his dining tray.

"Take it easy, Caz," he grumbled, repositioning his cup before continuing.

"How is it that *everyone* on the Arxon knows my name?" I asked.

"Mr. Virgil says he learns the names of the best students and the worst troublemakers fastest because they make the biggest impressions."

I shot Felly an icy look. I wouldn't be a troublemaker if the Arxon wasn't so packed full of perfect people who do everything right all the time and bore me to death. Besides, if anyone admitted the truth, I was both the best student and worst trouble-maker in my class.

"Shut up if you want dessert," I said, picking up an empty tray and loading it with a plate and cutlery.

Felly followed behind me, careful to take napkins. Always clean.

I pointed to whatever rehydrated sludge I could identify until the light on the corner of my tray indicated I'd taken my limit of food as determined by weight. "Sorry," I said. "No dessert tonight."

Felly ignored me and asked the server for some leafy greens. By the time she reached the desserts, Felly's tray light had not gone on. She asked for a serving of ice cream. Still the light didn't go on. "May I have one more, please?" The server shrugged and plopped it on top of the other. "Thank you," said Felly. She's so annoyingly gracious.

Nudging me, she said, "You can have some of mine."

I closed my eyes and clenched my teeth. "I don't need ice cream." She treats me like a child. At the end of the line, I pressed my thumb onto the scanner pad. The old-fashioned turnstile rolled forward, and I scanned the room for a seat near the observation window. I found one in the corner. Felly sat next to me instead of across like she usually does.

"What're you sitting there for?" I asked. "I don't want to have to smell you."

"I thought you'd want to be able to see out instead of looking at me. We're closer to a planet than usual," said Felly.

"Yeah," I said, something sticking in my throat. Sometimes she's not a complete pest.

Filling the window, the giant blue-and-green ball hung in the black sky: Caren. It's the one that's supposed to be most like ancient Earth. Swirls of white clouds shrouded the edges of the continents I had come to recognize. I wondered if kids on Caren ever felt trapped on their planet and wanted to escape into space. Probably not. That would be dumb. There's nothing to do or see out here.

I slid the ice cream from Felly's tray. "Thanks."

Felly smiled, but said nothing. That's when I like her best.

OOO

"Caz, really? Again?"

Rolling over in bed, I glared up at Dad. "What? What did I do now?"

"You've been down in the loading bays again. I wish you'd stop—"

"I wish you'd stop worrying about me."

"Then grow up and follow Felly's example!" he snapped. He sighed and turned away. "Caz…" He sank to the edge of my bed on the bottom bunk. "We've got gypsies getting ready to go on the ferry to Caren right now."

"So?"

"So…" His face twisted in that way he reserved for talk of gypsies. "They aren't clean. They don't hold down stable jobs. They wander around the system with no direction."

"Sounds great," I said under my breath.

"It *isn't* great," he said sharply. "There's no order to it. It hurts families."

"Gypsies have families," I countered.

Dad rubbed the bridge of his nose. "I know." As if grasping for reasons, he blurted, "They keep faneps as pets."

"What's a fanep?" I asked.

"Dirty things. They resemble humans, but much smaller. Little rat men. They never take vaccinations, so they're full of diseases." His voice trailed off. "Do as I say. I'm trying to keep you safe."

"Yes, Dr. Artemus," I said saucily.

"Caz," he warned.

"Don't they need you in the infirmary?"

"As a matter of fact, they do. I'll be back by midnight." Dad left quietly, and a few seconds later, I heard Felly come in.

"Why do you have to be so rude to Dad? You know they work him extra hard when we're in ferrying range. There's always more sickness."

True. Travelers were exposed to the elements and germs on the Surface.

"So what?" I shrugged. "I'd love to be sick for once. I should go kiss a gypsy."

"Caz," said Felly soberly, "Dad has his reasons for not liking the gypsies. Think before you say stuff like that."

Felly always sided with Dad when it came to gypsies, and I could never figure out why. As she pulled her night shirt over her head, she said, "You always get this way when we're close to a planet."

I flopped the blanket away from my face with a grunt. "It's stupid, Felly. We shuttle round and round in an endless loop: Caren, Craggy, Tye, Caren, Craggy, Tye. But we never get to go down. The embassy people do. Why can't we?"

Felly gave me her 'compassionate' face. "We're unfit for full gravity. You know that. We're only at 80% pull of the densest planet in the system."

The conversation tired me already. "Are you coming to bed now?"

"Yes."

"Can you research something for me?"

"I'm not doing your homework," said Felly, stepping onto the bunk ladder.

"It's not for school." I grabbed Felly's foot. "Please?"

Felly stifled a laugh. "'Please?' Well, sure, if it's that urgent."

I pinched her toe, and Felly laughed out loud.

"Faneps," I said.

"Faneps? Ew."

"Please?"

"Okay." I knew she would. She loves studying things even if she doesn't have the right kind of curiosity.

While I waited, I prodded my shoulder. No matter how hard I pressed, I couldn't locate the thing the creature had called a pearl, but I could feel something inside the tissue of my arm. Something hot. Sliding out of bed, I stood in front of the mirror with my arm raised, rotating it so that I could see the back of it. My nose was pressed against the glass when Felly returned.

"You practicing kissing again?" teased Felly.

"Not kissing!" *One* time I practiced puckering, and she had to catch me. I changed the subject. "Tell me about the faneps. Where are they from?"

Felly started her nightly ritual of brushing her hair fashionably straight. "Faneps were the only really sentient life forms humans discovered in the Granbo System. Before humans arrived, they had a thriving civilization."

"Really? A civilization?"

"The reports said they had their own dwellings on the islands of Tye. Quite elaborate ones, actually. You'd like the images. They had agriculture and commerce. They also had a strong interest in exploring the System. But of course, they hadn't discovered space travel yet."

"So it was an impossible goal." I gazed dully at the ceiling.

"Gypsies—your fascination—first domesticated them over a hundred years ago. They were used like guard dogs because they were smart and understood commands even though they didn't speak."

"They can speak," I protested. *Oops*.

Felly continued as if she had not heard. "They're also supposed to be outstanding trackers. If they get a sample of someone's blood, they can find them by scent." She paused. "Good thing you didn't see one, isn't it?" she asked, her voice steady.

I rolled over, feeling sick to my stomach. "Good thing."

ooo

2 SENTENCED TO THE SURFACE

I settled back for a lecture on the need for civility in closed communities. Mr. Virgil gives this one every time one of us gets in trouble, so I mouthed the many familiar phrases as he paced. The boys on my left snickered. Mr. Virgil's face reddened, but he did not stop his monologue. When the chime sounded to end school, we bolted for the door, and he shouted, "I expect better from you!"

One of the boys slapped my back playfully. "If he's ever out sick, you could do his class. You've got him memorized."

"Don't we all?" I droned, but I couldn't hide my grin.

As I pressed the button to call the lift, however, someone punched me in the back. Jeroby. The tallest, dumbest boy in class.

"*I* don't think you're funny, Caz Artemus. I've had to take this course twice, and it's going slower this time because of you. Don't you have any respect for the needs of others? Where is your community spirit?"

"What are you talking about?"

"The class is going slower," he repeated.

"Maybe it's *you* that's slower," I said. That got a few laughs—my kind of community spirit.

"You better watch out, Caz," he said, stepping closer.

I stood my ground while others passed into the lift, suddenly quiet and keeping their heads down. So much for community spirit. The lift door closed behind them, and Jeroby's lip curled. "You think you're so funny," he said. "We got exams coming, and Virgil hasn't reviewed everything he needs to. It's your neck as much as mine."

"Not really," I said. "I know the stuff."

He shoved me back against the wall, but I jerked away so hard that he rocked forward a little. "You trying to fight me, Caz?"

"That would require my touching you. No thanks."

He advanced again, punching my arm. It hurt enough that I couldn't let it go. "Don't blame me if school's too hard for—"

His knuckles connected with my nose, and I saw stars. Hot blood poured down my lip and I felt a throbbing behind my eyes. I lashed back with a fist to his sternum. Jeroby doubled over, winded and in pain, and I took advantage of his position to elbow his ribs. Jeroby crumpled to the floor.

The lift re-opened. "Caz, do you have to bleed *every* day?"

Great. It was Felly.

OOO

That night, when Dad returned from his shift, he brought the Station Master. "Mr. Lew needs to speak to you, Caz."

"Good. I need to report a bully," I said, coming into the family common room.

Mr. Lew did not look pleased. "Caz Artemus, I need your help with something."

I fluttered my eyelashes and bit back a retort. "Station Master, sir?"

"I need you to help me decide what to do with you. At this point, there are two options. You can go into Solitary for the next fifty days—"

"What!"

"—or you can try a rotation at the Lamond Reformatory on the Great Rik Peninsula Colony of Caren."

That punch surprised me more than Jeroby's. My knees buckled, and I sat heavily on the nearest chair. I'd done Solitary once before. No recreation, no human contact, no variety in the food—and yet all the school work and the cleaning duties. It had been punishment for breaking a girl's tooth with a cafeteria tray. She had been teasing me for weeks, saying I looked and acted like a boy.

But the Great Rik Peninsula! I knew that one. The land mass attracted the eye from space because of its gold-green color and the mountain barrier that connected it to the main continent. I watched for it every time we passed the planet.

Dad sighed. "Surface time? That seems an extreme measure, sir. Isn't that for hardened juvenile delinquents?"

Mr. Lew's face reddened. "Dr. Artemus, do I need to remind you of Caz's record? She is repeatedly trespassing on the loading decks, she is disruptive in school, and she shows almost no respect for authority. Twice she has injured another child badly."

"She's fourteen, sir," reasoned Dad. "Mood swings—"

"Are you making excuses for her?" asked Mr. Lew, raising an eyebrow.

I'll give Dad credit for trying, even if it was the lame hormonal excuse.

"No, sir. It's just that…" Dad knuckled his eyes. "I hear most youth sent to Surface reformatories never return to their original ICS."

"That is not part of the Granbo System Charter, and no one would enforce such a thing. However, the delinquents are typically too ashamed to return to their own communities," agreed Mr. Lew. He ran a palm over her bald head and puffed out his chest. "Interplanetary City-Station dwellers should never flaunt their disregard for the rules. We must be uniform in our expectations if we are to have peace and order in a closed community."

Dad nodded grimly.

I'm guessing it's the *parents* who are too ashamed to take them back. I stared dully at my knees. "What did *I* do?"

Dad exhaled loudly. "Caz."

I couldn't keep the panic from my voice. "What? Jeroby? I was defending myself."

"He has two broken ribs and a bruised kidney," said Dad. "I know because I tended him myself. What in space did you hit him with?"

"I just punched him," I said, dropping my face into my hands.

"Your nose is swollen," said Mr. Lew. "Did Jeroby do that to you?"

"Yes!" I snapped back into the argument. "Is anything happening to *him?*"

"He'll be spending most of his disciplinary time in recovery, Caz. This is about you," said Mr. Lew. "So which is it? Solitary, or the Surface reformatory? We need to know right away because the last ferry for Caren leaves in two hours."

A fuzzy finger poked my brain and swirled something gently. *Lamond Reformatory is on the Surface of Caren.* "I'll take the Surface time!" I exploded cheerfully.

"Caz, no!" groaned Dad and Felly in unison.

Mr. Lew, however, straightened his stance and prepared to leave. "You get two standard crates. Be at Docking Bay 25 in an hour."

Before Mr. Lew could finish his hollow condolences to Dad, I slid into my room and stared at my reflection in the mirror.

"Enjoy your hair for a few more minutes," said Felly from the door.

"I bet they don't have mirrors at Lamond anyway," I said, running my fingers through my hair. I'd miss it when they gave me the 'convict cut'. It's thicker and curlier than most—different, like I am. But Arxon fashion is always to blow it into lifeless silky helmets.

I wriggled my nose painfully. "Just as well if there aren't mirrors. They'll put a tattoo on my cheek."

"That's only for killers. No tattoo for you." Felly stepped closer. "Why, Caz? Why not Solitary? We might never see you again."

"I'll come back." *Unless I like it better there*, I added silently. That wouldn't be hard.

"But a rotation is so long."

"The Surface, Felly," I said, stepping away before she could give me some smothering hug. "Don't you get it? I finally get to go down to the Surface and have the adventure I've always wanted."

Her lips trembled. "You'll be flat on your back dealing with gravity!"

"It'll make me stronger."

"What kind of adventure is that?"

"A real one. It's the *Surface*. I'll breathe real air and see real sunlight." I shrugged at her perplexed expression. "It's worth something. If I stay in Solitary, I get nothing. Just silver and beige rooms everywhere I go."

Felly looked at me so sadly that I felt sorry for her. Her face had aged with worry in the last hour, and now she was on the verge of tears. I tried to assure her, and myself. "I'm not scared." Before she could start crying, I said, "Now help me cut my hair off. I won't give Mr. Lew the satisfaction of doing it."

"You cut," she said. "I'll pack."

OOO

We arrived at Docking Bay 25 right on time. Dad set down my two crates and pulled a pair of syringes from his medical utility belt. He administered the vaccinations with stoic efficiency while Felly watched with red-rimmed eyes.

"I wish it didn't have to be like this," said Dad.

"So do I."

"You could still opt for Solitary."

"Dad, please." I tried to make a joke. "That didn't work last time, remember?"

He didn't laugh. He just lowered his chin to hide his feelings as he always did. "I shouldn't have to do this twice," he muttered.

Felly touched his arm and whispered, "She'll come back, Dad." When he rubbed his eyes, she moved to my side. "He's just worried. I wish you didn't have to go, Caz."

"I wish people were more understanding. That's what I wish." Dad turned back towards me, but stopped himself before making eye contact. Something was bothering him beyond my leaving. I didn't know what he meant by having to 'do this twice'. Had Mom been disciplined and chose the Surface, too?

Felly squeezed me tightly and stifled her emotion like a good Arxon girl. My own feelings were so jumbled up: excitement, anger, nervousness, elation.

"I understand," said Felly softly, answering my bitter remark. Her eyes told me she was trying, anyway. "Come home safe again."

For all her annoying perfection, she'd always been loyal to me.

"Thanks." I said it so hoarsely that she probably didn't hear me.

I drew a deep breath and stepped inside the ferry. It had been designed to break through the atmosphere of the planet and land on its surface. As I passed the cockpit, I searched for a place to stow my crates in the small cargo hold. My eyes fell on something unexpected. The wooden box from the space buggy! I think my stomach and liver switched places. Suddenly short of breath, I glanced into the passenger cabin. Several rugged gypsy faces stared at me, all with the characteristic curly hair and deep blue eyes. They all wore smock tunics over trim leggings, a style that only enhanced the impression of their strength. One, a tall, broad man with a tattoo on his cheek, gave me a wink that sent shivers down my spine.

An older woman wearing several colorful scarves tied around her neck nudged the man. "Maddy, can't you see the girl is terrified?" She beckoned me closer. "Come on in. We'll make room for you."

No one could make me stay near that wooden box. I entered the circular, windowless cabin feeling very small. Immediately, I could smell the gypsies. It wasn't so much a stink as a foreign smell. Nothing sanitized about it.

Five young men sprawled comfortably on the curved bench that lined the left-hand wall. The opposite curved bench held only the woman and the tattooed man, and straight ahead, a sliding door led to a small lavatory compartment. I placed myself at the end of the bench, beside this door. Worst case scenario: I could lock myself in there if things got ugly.

The man leaned forward and indicated a strap of thick material that crossed from his shoulder to the opposite hip and back across his lap. "You may want to fasten yourself in."

I found the mechanism to release the strap and tried to work it as if it were familiar, but I suddenly wished I'd paid more attention when travelers talked about zero gravity. I wondered how much of the trip would be like that, or if the ferry had any kind of artificial gravity.

Once settled, I let my eyes wander across the faces in the cabin. They came to rest on the man's branded cheek. An electric bolt shot through my stomach. *What was I doing on a ferry with a killer?*

"The 'A' stands for 'acquitted'," he said, pointing to the mark. He said it nicely, but it scared me to death. "The circle with the mountain peak shows I served my time on Craggy, but they put the green A over the top when I was acquitted."

I shifted my gaze to his eyes, bright and friendly. He winked again, and the edge of my fear softened.

"It was self-defense," he explained. "Someone tried to steal my treasure."

I gulped at the sensation of something small leaping within my arm. My hand moved instinctively to stop it, and I covered the gesture by whispering, "It's cold in here."

The woman nodded. "We're in space. No walls are thick enough to keep that kind of cold out. Here, why don't you lie down and sleep? You can use Maddy's blanket." She unfolded a shiny thermal blanket from her pocket. "It makes the ride go so much faster if you sleep."

"Thanks." I took the blanket and tried to find a comfortable way to recline while strapped to the bench. As an afterthought, I said, "My name is

Caz."

"I'm Ninetta," said the woman. "And this is my son, Maddy."

"It was self-defense for me, too," I said quietly.

Her eyebrows shot up. "You killed someone?" she whispered.

Shrinking into the blanket, I shook my head. "Broke his ribs."

"Well, that's a good start," chuckled Maddy.

Ninetta elbowed him. To me, she said, "The artificial gravity will be on until we push through the atmosphere. We'll wake you in time for the fun."

"I won't be having fun. I'm going to the Lamond Reformatory." I combed my fingers through the miserable remains of my hair.

"Things will seem different on the Surface," assured Ninetta. "You'll see. It's not as bad as everyone makes it out to be."

OOO

3 THE GYPSIES ON THE FERRY

A burning sensation in my right elbow woke me. I prodded my skin and felt the lump of the pearl. With a bolt, I sat upright. *How had it moved so far? Was it in my blood stream, or in the tissue? What if it got to my heart?* Suddenly, I missed Dad. Anatomy was the only subject he ever comfortably discussed with me. He would know if that little beast has sentenced me to death by shoving some 'pearl' in my arm. Why hadn't I told him? Oh yeah. We were arguing. *Again.*

The gypsies were all sleeping, so I untangled myself from the strap and blanket and stretched. The low ceiling crowded my head when I stood. The other passengers had probably entered the cabin stooped over. I slid open the door to the lavatory. Pressing the lever, I released a trickle of cold water in the sink and plunged my elbow into it.

Ninetta peeked in the door. "You're up," she said cheerfully. "Smart to use the amenities before entering the atmosphere so you don't lose everything the hard way."

"What?"

"You'll see," she said.

I wiped my arm on my coversuit and returned to the cabin. Sitting down, I hugged my knees to my chest instead of re-strapping myself. I figured I was supposed to talk now, so I said, "You're from Craggy?"

"We're gypsies," she answered. "We're from *everywhere*."

"But you lived on Craggy?"

"While Maddy served his time." Ninetta fussed with the blanket, tucking it back into her pocket. After a pause, she continued, "We prefer Caren because there's more plant life."

Maddy spoke though his eyes were still closed. "Craggy's just that: craggy. It's rocky and full of people who are hard as stone."

"I guess I timed my delinquency right to get the pretty planet," I smirked.

"You did, actually," said Ninetta smiling. "How long will you be there?"

I stared at the floor. "A rotation."

"That won't be enough," said Ninetta.

Suddenly, the whole cabin jumped. I fell forward, landing hard on my knees and wondered if I'd ever get through a day without hurting myself. The jolt roused everyone, and soon they all sat upright, holding on to their seats. I got back up and copied them, feeling my teeth chatter. Everything vibrated so violently that my vision blurred.

"This is it!" said Maddy, his voice wobbling over the rumble that filled the cabin. With a flourish, he released his straps, and the others followed suit. *Were they crazy?* My body slipped off the bench. I braced myself for a fall that didn't come. Though I still held the seat, the rest of my body floated upward. Over my shoulder, I saw that everyone in the cabin hung in the air as if they'd all jumped at once and then froze in time. Only I remained anchored.

"Let go," called Maddy. "It's more fun that way!"

One of the boys pushed away from the wall, his legs tucked. With a smooth motion, he summersaulted and kicked off of the opposite wall to return.

Ninetta hovered above the bench, her scarves floating like orange and gold steam.

I scrambled to get my limbs to cooperate without leverage. Suddenly my stomach summersaulted like the gypsy boy and I could almost feel my face turn green.

"Get back everyone," cried Maddy, pressing himself in place between the ceiling and the floor and scooting away from me.

I saw this and moved to copy him. "I can hold it in. I won't vomit," I promised, holding my breath.

The cabin shifted, as if tilting on its axis. Whereas the room had been cold, I now began to sweat. A whirring noise closed in around me.

"What's happening?" I cried.

"Wait for it," said Maddy.

The other gypsies watched the ceiling, still floating above the floor in the zero gravity.

"Is the ferry breaking up?" I shouted.

"Wait for it," said Maddy again, his voice quivering deeply with the vibrations. "It'll be right about … now!"

The room righted itself sharply again and the tug of gravity returned, throwing me into Ninetta. The others landed on practiced feet.

"We're here!" cheered Maddy.

"So fast?"

"Well, the parachutes have engaged. It'll be quite a while longer before the real ferry picks us up."

"The *real* ferry?"

"We'll have a water landing."

"In the sea?!" I could feel the color in my face flood to my toes. "Won't water get in the cabin?"

"No, no," assured Maddy. "This old ferry's air tight."

The pilot entered. "Get ready for splash down." He caught sight of me and said, "You'd better hold on to someone if this is your first time. In a few seconds the artificial gravity turns off and you'll feel the real thing. Walking will be hard, if you can even stand."

Even as he spoke, I felt my legs crumple beneath me, and I sat heavily on the ground. Maddy grinned down at me. "Welcome to the Surface, and real gravity! That's one law even criminals like you and I can never break."

I laughed weakly.

"You'll have to work your legs a bit harder to keep yourself up now." He extended a hand to pull me up, and I tried to bend and stretch. "There, you've got it," he said, squeezing my hand with encouragement.

Ninetta patted me on the back. "You did really well. Didn't get sick, and you're already standing. Not bad at all for a first-timer. You're a strong one."

A loud popping sound and a gust of air hit me simultaneously. I breathed in and almost immediately swooned. "Gas! There's something in—"

"It's the salty air of the sea," said Ninetta, obviously amused. "It's not air-conditioned," she went on. "And it'll come in unpredictable blasts, so mind your step if you go outside."

"Outside?!" Outside! *On the Surface!* I was actually here and actually going to be *outside!* My breaths came in trembling splutters, and I could feel my heart beat in my ears.

Maddy and the other gypsies stepped out of the cabin, and I squinted after them. A blinding light flowed in from where the hatch had been.

"Are we on fire?"

Ninetta laughed. "No. That would be sunlight. Nothing on an ICS can compete."

"Is there a platform out there?" I asked.

"They probably jumped in for a swim," said Ninetta.

What's a swim? I shrugged away the question. "Thanks for everything. You've been so nice."

Ninetta squeezed my hand. "Of course. Why wouldn't I be?"

"I'm a stranger. You don't know me."

"I do now," she said.

"No, I mean, if you knew me, you'd probably yell at me like everyone else does."

Ninetta lifted my chin with her finger. "I don't know a thing about you except that you're in a new world, and you need a friend. That's true of all of us at least once in our lives. Worlds come in all shapes and sizes, you know. And so do friends."

I hugged her impulsively, something I never do. "Maddy's lucky to have a mom like you." A mom. Is that what moms are supposed to be like?

"Come here," said Ninetta. "You need to see." We walked over to the hatch, with me covering my eyes against the sunlight and leaning on Ninetta for support in the heavier gravity. The ferry bobbed lightly, and I almost stumbled before grasping the frame of the hatch. Drawing one more deep breath, I gazed outside at the Surface for the first time.

My cheeks could hardly hold the smile that grew on my face. The sky shone pale blue, not black. I couldn't see a single star, and yet the blue seemed as deep as space. Pictures and holocube reports of 'sky' did not do any justice to the real thing. Though the brightness hurt my eyes, I didn't want to look away. Far in the distance, the pale blue met in a straight line with the ocean, and its shifting colors reached all the way back to us. The ground—or rather, the water that covered the ground—didn't lie flat and smooth. Air pricked at it, lifting little peaks that glinted with gold or white. I'd never seen water that color before, though I'd studied the oceans of Caren thousands of times from space.

I laughed even as I shuddered in the breeze.

"What do you think?" asked Ninetta. "Is one rotation going to be enough?"

"This is my punishment? I've never seen anything so beautiful!"

"Wait 'til we get to land," said Ninetta, pointing off to the horizon on our left. "That strip of yellow is sand, and the goldish green is the trees."

Far off, the gypsies seemed to be sitting on the water because I could only see the tops of their bodies. Eager to join them, I stepped forward and let myself slide over the edge of the ferry.

"Caz, no!"

Unlike the short slide in the Arxon's rec hall, this steep angle dropped me with alarming speed. I expected a fast impact, but instead, my whole body stung with an icy wetness. In the horrifying instant that I realized I'd fallen *under*water, brine clouded my eyes and salt water scraped into my lungs. Confused and engulfed in darkness, I tried to reach back up to the waning light above me, but still my body plunged downward. My lungs burned, and my ears hurt. My foot touched down on soft ground. Desperate for air, I panicked, taking in more salt water. Sensing mortal danger, I kicked against the bottom and rose so quickly that I almost forgot to take in air when I reached the surface.

Someone—the pilot, I think—grabbed my wrist and yanked me up again to lie on the floor of the cabin. I spent the next several minutes painfully coughing up water.

"You could have drowned!" Ninetta scolded, removing my wet clothing. She wrapped me in the thermal blanket from earlier and handed me a small heat disk. "Keep it on low and run it over your torso. You'll feel warm again in a few minutes."

"I forgot the water would be deep," I shivered. "It's not like the therapeutic baths." No wonder it looked dark. No light reached below. Like sinking into liquid space. No air. No light.

"Hush," soothed Ninetta. "I'll get you something for the brine in your lungs," she said.

I shook in spasms, still coughing, though no more water came out, but my breath caught in my throat when Ninetta bent over the wooden box in the cargo area. She poked into it with a scolding finger. "Hand it over. Oh no, you don't," hissed Ninetta, slamming the box shut without latching it. She stood and brushed herself off. In her hand, she held a small test tube of creamy white liquid. She shook it and examined it for a moment. Satisfied with whatever she saw there, she held it out to me. "Here, drink a sip of this."

"What is it?"

"A gypsy remedy."

"My father is a doctor. I don't take medicine when I don't know what's in it."

"Wise girl," said Ninetta, chuckling. "It's made from crushed pearls from the Karlis Ocean on Tye. It has many medicinal properties."

"Like what?" I asked, stiffening with sudden distrust.

"It strengthens the cells, rejuvenates them. If mixed with Earlie syrup from the timberline trees on Craggy, it can stop a heart attack, and if mixed with Rik leaves from here on Caren, it helps with memory loss."

I regarded the tube skeptically.

"Go ahead. Drink it. It'll help any damage to your lungs from the salt water, and—"

"Eeeeeeeeeeeeeeeeeeeeeeeee!" A green and grey blur of movement rushed toward us, and the fanep seized the test tube.

"King, no! Give it back!" said Ninetta firmly.

I screamed and Ninetta swatted at the creature with the back of her hand. Like an animal, it crawled forward and sniffed at my right arm. The knowing expression it gave me sent a wave of chilling fear through my body.

"King, come here!" said Ninetta, half cajoling and half threatening. "Give me the medicine."

The fanep—they named it King, like the dog on the Arxon?—put the tube between its sharp teeth and ran through the open hatch. Ninetta scrambled to her feet and chased after him, but to no avail. Her shoulders sagged in defeat. "That was my last batch!" She massaged her temples wearily, muttering something about lost revenue and time. Then her face softened and she spoke kindly. "I suppose you'll live without it. You don't seem so bad off after all. Just frightened."

"Don't you need that medicine?" I asked.

"We can make more," said Ninetta. "I still have one pearl left."

I glanced back at the wooden box and tried to ignore the burning feeling that had moved to my wrist.

ooo

4 WELCOME TO LAMOND REFORMATORY

The wait for the 'real ferry' took two hours, by which time I was back in my footed coversuit, squeezing the last of the dampness from my sleeves. My eyes had mostly adjusted to the brightness, and I could watch the water ferry fasten itself to the hull of the space ferry with magnetic tethers. A loading plank rose up to the hatch.

Before long, a woman called for us to come down the plank. Thankfully, Maddy piled my two crates on top of the wooden box and saved me the effort of carrying them down. I felt really heavy, and the movement of the watery surface below made me nauseous. Ninetta steadied me all the way down the ramp by letting me lean on her shoulders. I had no desire to plunge into the ocean again. The very thought of sitting in a small craft on the water made me cough with fear.

For the entire ride to shore, I buried my face in Ninetta's shoulder. Twice she had to pry her hand free from my sweaty grip to flex her fingers. She kept trying to say soothing things, but I could only hear the deafening rush of air as we sped toward the shore.

After a while, the jarring movements of the water ferry subsided. With my eyes still closed, I asked, "Are we there yet?"

"Almost," said Ninetta.

Maddy nudged me, beaming. "You didn't get sick once!"

I didn't know how to react. Before I could stop myself, I stared at his tattoo again. My mind went to what lay ahead for me. "Was it hard?" I asked. "The time you spent on Craggy?"

Maddy fingered the tattoo, and then touched my cheek gently. "The *people* were hard. But life doesn't have to be, if we don't let ourselves become hard, too."

"How long before you were acquitted?"

"Four rotations."

My stomach leapt with dread.

"Good luck at Lamond," he said sincerely. "Be strong, and enjoy the sunshine. It'll do your whole body good."

The loading plank clicked into tethers on a solid, grey platform and the gypsies got to the business of unloading. I took in my surroundings, too stiff and scared to move yet. Not far away, a long, wide stretch of yellow land rimmed the water. I recognized it as sand from pictures in holocube reports, but it was different in live color. Beyond the sand were dwellings of some kind, each much larger than the space ferry. Behind the buildings stood tall, frothy trees, hundreds of times taller than any potted plants on the Arxon. After a lifetime of silver, white and beige, I could almost feel the warmth emanating from the gold and green and red in the things of the Surface.

And everything was so big. Even the spaces between the big things were big. Conserving space probably isn't a priority with a whole planet available. It sure made me feel small, though.

On the platform, a tall, extremely thin man stood with his arms folded across his concave chest.

"That's the director of Lamond," said the woman who had piloted the water ferry. I hesitated, and she waved me on. "Come on. You know what to do. You've obviously been here before." Her tone squeezed my airways, tightening my chest with resignation.

I picked up my crates and turned to Ninetta. "Thank you," I croaked. It was strange to part with someone permanently. Not like on the Arxon where you see everyone several times a day whether you want to or not.

Ninetta nodded encouragingly.

I couldn't see the plank over the crates in my arms, so I shuffled my feet up the ramp to the platform.

"You are Caz Artemus?" asked the director, with a voice as sharp as his frame.

I swallowed and nodded.

"You will answer aloud when I ask you a question."

"Yes, I'm Caz Artemus," I said, more boldly than I intended.

He smoothed his already precisely groomed hair. "Come with me." He did not offer to help with the crates. With a brisk pace, he marched along the platform. I hurried to follow, almost dropping my crates. When he came to a full stop, I crashed into him. He stared down at me. "You are not tired?" He said it like an accusation, not a question.

"I'm ... not yet."

"You will be." The director pointed at a vehicle with the emblem for Lamond on the side. "Get in."

I hesitated, sniffing at the chill. "What am I supposed to call you, sir?"

The director's nostrils flared. "My name is not relevant." A sneer curled his lip. "But the inmates call me Nightmare."

OOO

The ride to Lamond was overwhelming to say the least. Because the vehicle had wheels instead of running on electromagnetic tracks, every flaw in the road jostled me until I thought my stomach might spill out of my mouth. I could also feel the weight of gravity taking its toll, and my shoulders sagged. The air, too, sickened me. It kept changing temperatures and would move across my body in unpredictable bursts. The sunlight spread across my lap, and I could feel its burning heat even through my coversuit. The Arxon cafeteria could not compete with the confusion of smells mingling around us. Most of them were completely alien to me. Perhaps in time I would be able to sift the scents apart and appreciate them, but for now, I took gulps of air in through the mouth and held my breath as long as I could.

But the excitement of being on the Surface overruled all discomfort. The whole concept of wide open spaces thrilled me. After a lifetime of narrow halls, the absence of walls made me feel free. The sun, too, intrigued me. It hung in a pale sky instead of piercing the endless black of space. I wanted to sit in whichever part of the vehicle allowed in the most sunlight, even if it meant squinting and feeling too warm.

"Do hold still," said Nightmare.

"I wanted to—"

"Do as you're told," he snapped. He sat facing me. Presumably, a driver in the fore section steered. I figured the director had to keep track of me personally because I'm such a dangerous criminal.

"Are we far from Lamond?" I asked.

"Not so far as you would wish," he said, closing his eyes and leaning back.

His pinched face lost its fright power when his beady eyes closed. I'm sure he said things like that to put on a tough show. All the same, I didn't need him hating me from day one. I waved my hand in front of his face. No reaction. I added a rude gesture. Not even a flicker of change. Satisfied, I slid to the side quietly and leaned out, soaking in the sunshine.

OOO

Nightmare stretched his legs and opened the door. "We're here. Get out."

I gathered my crates and stepped out after him and squealed at the unfamiliar feeling beneath my feet.

Nightmare spun around. "What's the matter?"

My toes tried to take inventory through the footed coversuit. Something wet and squishy.

"Oh. It's just mud," said Nightmare. "You'll be issued shoes in the morning."

Mud? Shoes? I stepped forward and lost my footing. With a crash, I fell forward onto the crates, bumping my chin hard and gouging my coversuit.

"Do your lying down in bed," said Nightmare derisively.

I stood, feeling rather than seeing that my clothing had been soiled. On the Arxon, except for sweat or spilled food—or, in my frequent habit, blood—nothing ever really gets dirty. The unpleasantness of the sensation pinched my stomach.

Grunting, I lifted the crates again and followed Nightmare up a very slippery path to a large building. My toe stubbed against something hard, and I stopped, biting back an oath.

Nightmare continued walking, rising with each step. He stopped and turned with his hands on his hips. His silhouette stood like some folding apparatus against the lit rectangle of an open door. "What are you waiting for?" he asked impatiently. "Climb the stairs."

"Stairs?"

"ICS dwellers," said Nightmare with contempt. "There are no lifts at Lamond. You'll have to *lift* one foot in front of the other to go up each platform. These are called stairs, and they require *work*. Get used to them."

Unable to see, I slid one foot up until I felt a ledge. Placing my foot on this, I pulled up the other leg. After repeating this action carefully several times, I reached the same level as Nightmare.

"Hm," he said, disappearing through the lit doorway.

What was that supposed to mean?

I followed him inside, but he was nowhere to be seen. Sighing, I put down the crates and flexed my stiff fingers. Although the building had walls, ceilings and corridors, it felt nothing like the Arxon. The interior, planked with wood, must have cost a fortune. At least it would in space. I guess wood is more abundant here.

"I'd say welcome to Lamond, but if you're at Lamond, it's more like badly-come," said a boy's voice drily. "You've been on the Surface before, haven't you?"

"What?"

A boy about my age with neatly-cropped black hair and large eyes stood yawning beside me.

"Where's Mr. Nightmare?" I asked.

The boy rolled his eyes. "*Mr.* Nightmare won't waste any more time on you today. It's past lights-out. Let's get you to your dorm room." He smirked down at my feet. "He thinks it's funny to stop the car in that muddy patch."

I looked down with horror at my feet. They had grown with a layer of brown-black sludge that resembled burnt stew.

"It feels really disgusting," I said, cringing a little.

"Yeah." His eyes lingered on my feet, almost as if he felt sorry for me. "Come on, you'd better step back outside. Otherwise you'll have to polish the floor for tracking mud all over it. You don't want that duty on your first day."

He led me back outside to the top of the stairs and instructed me to sit.

Then he trotted down the stairs lightly and returned with an extremely long tube that leaked copious amounts of water.

"What is that?"

"A hose." He shook his head at me, but not in a mean way. "Okay, hold still."

"What?" I threw my hands up to protect myself, but he placed his thumb over the end of the tube and forced the water in a hard stream onto my feet. The pressure surprised me, as did the cold, but very quickly, the clumps of mud dissolved and trickled down the stairs. He folded the hose tightly and the water flow stopped. With a lopsided grin, he said, "I should spray you down all over. You fell, didn't you?"

My hands went to the mud stains on the front of my knees and thighs. "Oh. Really?"

"No," he said, going back down the stairs. "You'd drip all over the stairs. Put the coversuit in the laundry chute by your bunk when you get to your room." A moment later, he came back from putting the hose away. "Do you know what shoe size you wear?"

"Shoe size?"

Before I could react, he'd come up right beside me and set his foot parallel to mine, his body pressed against me. I was about to punch him when he stepped back and said, "I'd guess a medium A will do."

I glanced down at his feet to see his coversuit tucked at the ankles into some kind of thick covering. He saw my gaze and waggled his foot at me. "Shoes," he said. "They protect your feet. Coversuits would wear out in a day or two here. Come on. Let's get you up to your room. We have a twenty-hour day here on Caren, and you'll need to be up and ready by 0600. It's 1930 now, so you need to sleep soon. Follow me."

"Wait. Who are you?"

"Call me Ruddie. I'm Captain of the inmates." He grinned and moved to the staircase. "Girls' dorms are on the third floor." I picked up my crates and climbed slowly after him. Ruddie stopped part way up. "Artemus, is it?"

"Caz. Call me Caz, please."

"Caz. You've got to alternate feet when you climb, or we'll be doing stairs until midnight."

I'd been leading with my right foot and pulling up my left behind it. Scowling with effort, I tried his suggestion and found it much easier. When I reached the place where the stairs stopped, my foot kept moving upward and I almost fell again. Ruddie caught my arm and then took one of the crates. Whispering, he said, "You're pretty tough. I'll help with the crate, if you don't tell anyone. It's better if you can see your feet."

I felt lighter in more than one way. "Thanks."

"Quiet. Second floor is boys' dorms. They get mean if they don't get their sleep."

On the top step, Ruddie set down the crate. "I can't go further, but it's that first door on the left. New inmates always get that room. You'll move down the hall closer to the washroom as you gain seniority. You have two others in there with you, so you'll probably have to take the top bunk. Stuff your crates beside the door for now and throw the coversuit in the chute. Try not to wake anyone."

"Thanks."

Ruddie gave a little wave. "Remember, be ready before **0600** so I can show you around. I'll meet you on the second floor. Don't be late."

I nodded and fumbled with the crates before sliding my wet feet to the first door. The only light I could make out came filtering through a window on the opposite wall. It was a night sky, filled with stars, but they hung differently here on the Surface. My tired muscles reminded me I need sleep, and I scanned the room. I could see the outline of a three-berth bunk against the right wall and shelves on the left. I set down the crates quietly and peeked into the bunks. The bottom two held shadowy lumps, so I'd have to climb to the top. I unfastened my coversuit and peeled it off gratefully. An oval chute like the ones on the Arxon filled the space in the wall between the bunks and the window. With relish, I shoved the coversuit into the gaping mouth, not caring if I ever saw it again.

In bare feet and underwear, I stepped lightly onto the edge of the bottom bunk. It screeched, and I dropped back down, holding my breath. Neither of the girls stirred. Moving quickly, I stepped up again and hefted myself up with both arms as hard as I could.

Crack!

My head hit the ceiling, and I fell forward onto the top bunk, my legs hanging down. "Huff!" I covered my mouth with one hand and the bump on my head with the other and wriggled the rest of the way onto the bunk. I don't think I moved again until morning.

25

○○○

5   MEETING THE INMATES

My eyes focused on a digital display above the door: **0548**. With a jolt, I sat up. Voices and light streamed in from the hall as the other inmates headed down the stairs. I took stock of how I felt. Tired, heavy, hungry and dirty.

Letting my legs slide slowly over the edge of the bunk, I lowered myself. Before I touched the floor, a hand grabbed my ankle and pulled hard. With a lung-emptying slam, I belly-flopped onto the floor. A second later, someone sat on my back and pinned my arms down at the elbows.

"New blood," said a girl with the distinctive lilt of the Selig ICS. "Check her crates, Petra. See what she's got!"

I tried to scrape together enough breath to protest only to feel my jaw smashed down. Beside me, I could see a scrawny girl rummaging through my crates. She probably looked better when she had hair covering all the sharp angles of her head.

"Look at this, Ora," said the girl, holding something up out of my line of vision. "That'll be worth some chores, don't you think?"

The girl on my back laughed cruelly. "Oh, I *do* think! Anything else?"

"Some real ICS food!"

The girl called Ora released me with a pinch to my bare shoulder, and the two girls ran out into the corridor with their stolen prize.

On my hands and knees, I crawled to the crates and pulled out a fresh coversuit. I fumbled in the shadows to put my scattered things back, and then pushed the crates to the base of the shelves. My hand hovered over the items stacked there.

"Don't even think about touching our things," said a voice behind me.

An overhead light came on, and the two girls, both older and taller than me, stood in the doorway gawking at my mostly naked self. The one called Ora had really pale yellow hair and an uncommonly puffy red face like she'd been exposed to radiation. She also looked as if she had been stealing food rations from the other girl her whole life.

I leapt to my feet. "Give me back—"

Ora punched me squarely in the mouth, sending me back down to the floor.

"Good one, Ora!"

Again, they slid out the door, apparently for good this time. I stood and wiped my mouth. A smudge of blood on my wrist made me double-check

O

HE INMATES

above the door: **0548**.
rom the hall as the o
how I felt. Tired, heavy

my teeth. They held firm. *I really can't go a day without bleeding.*

My lung capacity recovered gradually, and I peeked out of the door to the washroom at the end of the hall, hoping I would not find any other inmates. All clear. With my coversuit in hand, I tiptoed to the washroom and shuddered with relief upon finding it empty. Steam from showers still clung to the ceilings. I'd obviously missed all the commotion of the other girls getting ready. I'd been too tired to hear it, I guess.

A few minutes later, dressed and clean*er*, I returned to my room. Resting outside the door were the shoes Ruddie had promised, a welcome reminder that I had at least one potential friend in this place. The clock read **0559**. I jammed my feet into the shoes. They felt constrictive, and I feared I'd trip, but I hurried to the stairs. At the top, I clutched the wooden railing and moved steadily down with the same foot leading each new descent.

Ruddie stood waiting on the second floor. "You're late."

"I was detained."

"Nightmare isn't going to like it," said Ruddie, shaking his head.

I rolled my eyes. "Welcome to the story of my life."

Ruddie shrugged. "Come on." He led the way down the stairs, watching me struggle. "It'll get easier with time. The gravity won't bother you so much. Are you sure you've never been to the Surface before?"

"No!" I barked.

"Well, all right. Walk quieter, though. You sound like a thunder storm."

"A what?"

Ruddie smiled and kept walking down the stairs. At the bottom, he pointed left to the end of the hall. "That door leads to the gardens. You'll be assigned duty out there until you're strong enough to work in the orchard or duspy field."

"The what?"

He pointed to a closer door in the same hallway. "That is the library."

"Are you serious?"

"So you know what a library is?" said Ruddie, half grinning. "When we aren't working, eating, or sleeping, we're supposed to be educating ourselves, either intellectually or manually. It's part of our rehabilitation."

"No teacher?"

"No teacher. Just files and files of information on ancient electronic tablets."

"No holocubes?"

Ruddie laughed. "No holocubes. I hope you know how to read." He led me down the hall in the opposite direction, and his face took on a serious expression. "You were sentenced here for a rotation of the Arxon."

"Yeah, so?"

"For breaking a peer's ribs."

"I was defending myself."

"I know," said Ruddie. "I saw the vids."

"You what?"

"The whole incident and the reports afterwards were captured on the Arxon security monitors and sent here to Lamond." Leaning in, he confided, "You and I have a very similar story."

"You broke someone's ribs?" I asked. A secret part of me found that really cool.

"Collarbone. But *I* had to use a chair to do it." His face reddened with the recollection. "The kid had been beating on my little brother, and—"

"And *you* got sent here?"

"My victim was an ambassador's son."

"Oh. So your ICS is just like mine."

"Probably." Ruddie signaled with his head to follow. He continued speaking in a low voice as he pointed to various labeled rooms along the way. "Nightmare saw my vids, too. He knew my case and has been lenient with me, giving me some more clerical duties instead of the hard labor."

"So, if he saw my vids, he knows—"

"You had a record. He wants to see how you do here. He'll be watching you closely because he knows the incident that earned your sentence may have been unfair."

I filled in the unspoken part: "But he thinks maybe I deserved it for all the other trouble I caused. Isn't there ever a time you get your record wiped clean?"

"We need to get to the cafeteria. It's time for announcements."

"The girls in my room said something about chores."

Ruddie shook his head. "I don't know what to tell you there. It's Ora. The vids on her were clear. Dangerous." He pointed to my lip. "Don't get in any *more* fights with her."

"How did you know?"

"Stay out of trouble, and Nightmare will ease up on you. A rotation is a long time."

I followed him through the doors marked *Cafeteria*.

"Ah," said Nightmare with a loud voice. "The guest of honor has arrived!"

I surveyed the room with horror. About fifty teens sat at long tables glaring at me, not touching their food. Obviously, they'd been told to wait and were not happy about it. Ruddie faded into the crowd and sat down near a window as Nightmare placed his bony hand on my shoulder. I would have cringed, but it kept me from shaking visibly, so I mustered what I hoped passed for a confident stance.

"Inmates, this is Caz Artemus. She is here for assault and is deemed violent by nature. Treat her as such."

I tried to shift the lump in my throat while Nightmare recounted the loose details of my encounter with Jeroby. Of course he left out the bit about Jeroby being a complete idiot and a daily source of aggravation. His report concluded with a snide word of praise for my stamina on the stairs the first night. Lovely introduction: *Hey, everyone! Meet this vicious monster girl who's good at climbing stairs.* I'd have new friends lining up to meet me, like my charming roommates.

Raising both hands, Nightmare made a grand gesture. "And now you may eat," he said.

The room filled with the sound of clinking cutlery on bowls and plates, and I gazed out at a constellation of cropped haircuts. A few faces peeked up, some fearful, and some defiant. Ora and Petra sat to the left with their backs to the room.

"Mr...Sir? Where do I get my food?"

"You came late," said Nightmare. "You'll have to go without unless someone is willing to share." He strode off between the rows of tables leaving me standing by the door. It occurred to me that I hadn't eaten in about twenty-four hours, what with the time change from space to Surface. I didn't know what anything here tasted like, but it smelled good enough to make my stomach growl angrily.

At the nearest table, some girls sat eating with their heads down. They were a little younger, or at least smaller, so I decided to take a chance that they weren't killers. I walked over and sat on the very edge of the bench, not facing the table, and I concentrated on trying not to cry. I was physically and emotionally exhausted, and the day had just begun.

The girl closest to me, a petite specimen with all the right curves, ate quickly and quietly. Her short hair sort of fluffed instead of spiking in a way that made it hard to imagine she was the tough kid on her ICS. A slice of bread with something yellow smeared on it appeared at my elbow. I stared at this with surprise and then searched the faces of the nearest girls. They seemed determined not to look at me directly. I picked up the bread. Soft, not at all like ICS bread.

"It's real egg!" said the fluffy-haired girl without making eye contact. "Fresh. Not powdered."

I squinted at the golden goo and caught a drip with my finger before it splashed on my coversuit. Quickly shoving it into my mouth, I braced myself for the new flavor, but instead of being horrible, it melted on my tongue like warm pudding. The bread even tasted sweet, and it stuck to my teeth instead of crumbling. I vowed never to be late for a meal at Lamond again.

Leaning back, I spoke quietly over my shoulder. "I won't hurt you if you don't hurt me."

Out of the corner of my eye, I saw the girl nod.

OOO

Nightmare caught my arm as I filed out of the cafeteria. "You have fresh marks on your face. Have you been fighting already?"

Passing within earshot, Ora paused to eavesdrop. I shifted my weight to make eye contact with her. "No, I fell off the top bunk. I'm not used to having three tiers, and the gravity got me."

"Ah," he said, without emotion. Nightmare glanced at Ora, who moved on, head bowed. He folded his arms and stared at me until my esophagus squirmed uncomfortably. "You are either a very smooth liar, or a very clumsy girl. We shall see which it is soon enough. Toddy is waiting in the garden to instruct you on your morning duties."

"Yes, sir." I walked swiftly out of the cafeteria, then broke into a run down the hall. Suddenly Ora and Petra stepped out from the library.

"Petra, tell me again what you found in the new girl's crate?" lilted Ora.

"Something very valuable."

"Give it back," I said, wondering what 'it' was.

Ora clucked her tongue. "There's a penalty for leaving messes all around our room. You have to earn your things back." She gestured to Petra. "What do you think that's worth?"

Petra held up a silver egg-shaped object. "A comlink?" She let out a low whistle. "That's worth a month of cleaning at least."

"For today, the library shelves need dusting and the floor polishing," said Ora. "We'll supervise from outside." She jabbed me in the collarbone. "After lunch, you can do our morning duty for us. Just tell Nightmare you want to study."

I snatched for the comlink, but Ora blocked my hand, palmed my face and pushed. I fumbled backwards, narrowly missing a flat screen monitor on the corridor wall. "You'll get it back when the month is over if you do what we say," said Ora. She shouldered past me and down a hall to the back of the building. Petra followed, waving the comlink out of reach.

I watched them go, willing my fists to stay at my side.

OOO

Toddy was a boy of fifteen with crafty eyes. "You're late," he said. The other inmates in the garden watched us closely. He squared his shoulders. "I'm not afraid of you no matter how many ribs you've broken."

"Good for you. Were we supposed to fight? I thought you were going to train me," I said.

Toddy released a nervous laugh and turned to shout at the others. "Get back to work!" Seven inmates, including the puffy-haired girl from breakfast, stooped back into long rows of short, leafy plants.

"These are revo plants," said Toddy. "They're hard to dig, but they're very nutritious, and they show up in almost every meal. Each inmate is expected to fill two baskets—and I do mean *fill*—by the end of the shift." He pointed to open-topped crates made of a thin, woody fiber I didn't recognize. "You'll need to work hard to make your quota, so get moving." I could tell the whole do-your-part thing mattered as much at Lamond as it did on the Arxon.

I swept up a basket by its braided handle. It would have been worth something on the Arxon, but here it was used for chores. Strange again to think that my punishment was in such a luxurious setting, but I guess luxury depends on the person esteeming it.

The building hid the garden in a comfortable square of shade. I hadn't seen shadows much before with all the ambient lighting on the Arxon, but every now and then a bank of lights would go out and cast a swath of mystery over some unsuspecting furniture. This felt different, though. The brilliance of the sunlight contrasted so much with the darkness of the shade that my eyes took a lot of blinking to adjust. I strode down the row of plants, feeling cold droplets of moisture penetrate the cloth on my shins. The ground beneath me seemed to move slightly with each step, and tug a little at the shoes, as if the planet itself wanted to get my attention.

"It's my egg girl!" I said when I reached the farthest corner. The girl looked up wide-eyed. I knelt down beside her on the soft earth and immediately wished I hadn't. "Disgusting," I groaned, feeling my knees sink into the damp sludge.

"Everyone says something about the mud the first time," said the girl stifling a laugh. "It takes getting used to, but the revos are worth it."

Apparently we'd be doing a lot of laundry here at Lamond. I sighed and took the social plunge. "I'm Caz, but you know that already. You got a name, or do I keep calling you Egg Girl?"

The girl blushed. "I'm Sasa." Without speaking further, she demonstrated how to claw away the earth under the leafy plants until the top of a revo appeared. Sasa wrapped her fingers around it and wiggled it back and forth. This made a mess and explained how she had gotten so dirty in so little time.

I stared at the ground before touching it. "This is really, *really* disgusting."

"Work faster!" called Toddy.

I thrust my hands into the leaves, searching for a stalk. Touching the leaves released a sweet scent into the air, and I stopped to breathe it in. Tearing a leaf free, I held it to my nose and then my cheek. The softness tickled me, and I studied the specimen with wonder. Unlike the small potted plants on the Arxon that hung feebly under artificial lights, this leaf brushed thickly against my skin. Its golden veins almost pulsed. This plant was truly alive. I wondered if the Surface would transform me into something this hearty.

Sasa nudged me and jerked her head in the direction of the ever-scowling Toddy. Waving the leaf, I saluted him and then got to work. I found a revo and made a fist around the top. Exhaling to prepare for the pull, I yanked hard. The revo broke free from the ground with a shower of dirt and flew over my shoulder. It banged against the wall right next to where Toddy stood.

The nearest kids gawked at me and burst into laughter. "You've been to the Surface before!" said one of them.

Toddy stormed over. "I don't know what you're trying to prove, but you had better mend your attitude or you'll end up in Nightmare's office," he said.

"It was an accident," I said.

"Right!" he scoffed.

"It really *was*," said Sasa with the loudest voice I'd heard from her yet.

Toddy squinted at her for a second and then grunted. "Well do it like the others, or go to Nightmare's office!" he spat.

With exaggerated deference, I said, "Yes, sir!"

"Work faster!" he barked to the others. He marched back to his post.

"He's charming," I said, crossing my eyes. Sasa didn't answer, but she smiled. I wondered why she stuck up for me, or why Toddy believed her so quickly. Maybe she was the lone nice girl. But then, what would she be doing here at Lamond?

My hands had acquired a layer of dirt in that maiden effort, and I stared at them in surprise. Though slimy, it contained individual granules, and I rubbed these between my fingers, studying them closely.

Sasa hissed. "Stay on task."

"Sorry," I said, wiping my fingers on the edge of my basket. I found another revo. By rocking it back and forth, I managed to control the arc so that it merely shot down the row a few meters instead of going airborne. With her basket, Sasa crawled casually over to where it had landed, as if switching locations. She dropped my revo into her basket, but then tilted it slightly. With a wink she indicated the new target.

All right. So I do her work for her? Whatever. She'd helped me twice already today, so I didn't mind. In the next few minutes, I launched several more revos into the basket, and each time, she grinned, even as she kept digging the hard way. Before the shift ended, I had filled both of my baskets and one of Sasa's. "It's for the eggs," I said.

"I won't need as much breakfast with all your help," she said. "How can you work so well in the heat?"

"I don't know," I admitted. "I wish someone would set the temp controls and then leave them alone. One minute my nose drips with cold, and the next, my hair drips with sweat."

"Most of us got sick after the first couple of days," she said. "You might want to conserve your energy."

"Shift over!" shouted Toddy. "Bring in! Bring in!"

I wrapped my arms around one of my baskets awkwardly and stood. Only then did I notice that everyone else in the garden worked in pairs to carry one basket at a time.

"Oh," I said. These kids were serious about 'conserving energy'. Leaning over, I lifted one handle of Sasa's basket, balancing my own basket on my hip. Together, we waddled over to the wall and set down the baskets. When we turned around, everyone stood in star-like silence, watching us. I pulled my shoulder blades together in a stretch. "What's going on?"

Sasa whispered, "Have you been on the Surface before?"

"What? No. Why does everyone keep saying that?" I followed her over to our remaining baskets.

"You're as strong as a gypsy! I doubt Ora and Petra will be able to push you around," said Sasa.

"Have they been bothering you, too?"

Sasa nodded. "Nearly all of us smaller kids."

"What's the point of sending all the bullies down here to bully each other?"

"The Surface dwellers have no sense of order. Surely you see that. One man—even if it is Nightmare—in charge of so many of us? No guards nearby?" Her face twisted with disapproval. "There's no real discipline down here. Just dirty, hard work. They probably do it so we'll crave ICS life again and promise to be good."

"Tell me more about Ora and Petra—and anyone else who is dangerous down here. You can't all be thieves like Toddy."

"How'd you know he was a thief?" asked Sasa.

"What gets any kid in big trouble on an ICS?" I asked, trying not to sound too much like Felly. "Violence, thieving, and criminal mischief. He doesn't look strong enough for the violence, and he doesn't look smart enough for criminal mischief, so he must have stolen something and got caught."

"True enough," agreed Sasa grinning. "I'll tell you about the others at lunch. It's more comfortable inside anyway. Steady temp and no dirt!"

OOO

"That's very interesting," I said, entering the library to find Ruddie sitting with a tablet in his lap.

"What's interesting?"

"The conversation I had with Sasa."

Ruddie blushed. "I saw you talking to her."

"She told me all about everyone here. The only 'violent' people here are the girls in my dorm room, you and the big handsome boy."

Ruddie sank further into his chair. "Alf."

"Right. Alf."

Ruddie rolled his eyes. "Why do all the girls say he's so handsome?"

"Because he is," I said. "Of the forty-seven of us, six pulled too many major pranks, fifteen hacked into ICS computer programs, and the rest were thieves."

"You forgot the one who is here for blackmailing her peers."

"Sasa?"

"You're quick," said Ruddie, turning on his tablet. "She's a very good listener, and finds out lots of things other people don't want her to know."

"Did you want me to know that you two have a secret love thing going on?"

Ruddie groaned and covered his face with the tablet.

I sat opposite where I could see out the window. "Not very hardened criminals, are we?"

"I hear you're strong enough to defend yourself against Ora."

"Maybe," I said, spotting Ora and Petra outside. I ran my fingers along one of the shelves. "So how do these tablets work?"

"Each has hundreds of reports about the topic listed on its top edge. The tablets over there by the window are supposed to be great literature. Boring stuff, most of it."

"Stories?" I perked up at that. ICS studies rarely allowed for fiction. Imagination is disruptive after all. I casually pulled a tablet off the shelf nearest the window. Despite the cool showers we'd taken to clean up, I started sweating again. "It's hot in here."

"Open the window."

"They open?" I guess they could. No vacuum of space to suck me out to my imploding death.

"Grab that little metal loop and pull it up."

I did, and the window banged against the upper sill.

"Gently!" laughed Ruddie. "I think we're gathering evidence that you were really holding back when you only broke that kid's ribs."

"Jeroby deserved what he got and more," I said, resting my elbows on the sill.

"Don't forget our deal, new girl!" shouted Ora from below.

I eyed her steadily. She reminded me of a female Jeroby, and I mentally debated whether or not it would be worth another rotation to break a few of her ribs, too. "Hello, Ora! Hello, Petra!" I called musically.

Ruddie tensed. "Don't mock her, Caz."

I moved away from the window. "I'm not doing their chores. I'll have to steal my comlink back when they're sleeping."

"They took your—?"

Something grabbed my wrist. I screamed and jerked away from the window. Waving my arm, I knocked whatever it was away and it landed against the wall.

The fanep from the gypsies' wood box!

Had it tracked me here? "Get it away!"

The fanep recovered from its fall and scuttled up the book shelf. It perched near the ceiling and stared down with greedy eyes.

Ruddie sat frozen in his chair. I backed away, pressing into the wall. The fanep moved along clutching a tablet to its body. It let out a noise that sounded like a laugh. With its eyes never leaving me, it climbed down the shelves, carrying the tablet.

"Get away from me," I warned.

The fanep halted and slid the tablet across the floor. It came to a stop at my feet. I picked it up without blinking away from the fanep's face. The creature rubbed its own right shoulder with tiny hands. Then, in a blur of grey and green, it vanished out the window.

Breathing uneasily, Ruddie demanded, "What *was* that thing?"

"A *real* nightmare," I said. "And I don't seem to be waking up."

ooo

6 DEALING WITH BULLIES

"You didn't do your chore," said Ora, grabbing my arm on the way into the cafeteria for the evening meal.

"No, I didn't do *your* chore," I corrected.

Several inmates stopped to watch the exchange, and Ora steadied her voice. "Maybe you don't understand the deal we made."

"*You* made," I said. "*I* did not sign a contract."

Surprised laughter rippled through the room. Visibly flustered, Ora said, "You'll never get your comlink back now."

"I think I will."

Ora's face blazed even redder than usual. She raised both fists, but I grabbed her wrists and held them like human handcuffs. The onlookers inhaled, waiting. I spoke through clenched teeth. "You really shouldn't hit people, Ora. One of these days, somebody stronger than you might hit back, and it might really, *really* hurt."

"Let go of me!" she grunted.

I had to bite the inside of my cheeks to keep from laughing. The other inmates gathered a little closer. I'd never considered myself a bully, but then I'd never been one to let bullies get away with stuff, either. With a sugary voice, I kept my eyes on Ora, but said, "Petra, I believe you have something of mine."

"Is there a problem here?" asked Nightmare, striding into the ring of inmates. I let go so fast that Ora looked like she was reaching for me.

"I was asking Petra to return something she borrowed."

Nightmare raised an eyebrow at Petra, who questioned Ora with a glance. Ora walked away, leaving Petra to cower. Loyal friend, that Ora. Petra slipped her hand into her pocket and retrieved the comlink.

"Does that belong to you, Petra?" asked Nightmare.

She shook her head.

"Return it to its rightful owner," he said. "And then you and Ora should report to the library. I see that you have not done your chores today. It appears as if a wild creature has torn through it. Your meal will have to wait."

Everyone dispersed quickly, and I held the comlink triumphantly.

"I hear you worked well in the garden, and that you chose to study in your early afternoon shift," said Nightmare one shade more shrewdly than casual conversation.

"Yes, sir."

"How did that suit you?"

"I found something interesting to read."

"You read?"

"When motivated, sir," I said. Most of my friends on the Arxon relied solely on holocube reports, but Dad had made us learn the ancient art of reading. Reading and anatomy. Thrillingly useless most of the time, but coming in handy here at Lamond. "May I eat now?" I asked, leaning away from him without moving my feet. I didn't really want everyone associating me with him.

He extended an open palm. "Turn over the comlink."

"But—"

"Inmates are not permitted to contact any of the City Stations in orbit without consent from me, and never until they have served at least a quarter of their sentence."

"But the Arxon will be out of range by then." My voice trailed off with realization.

"Hmm," he said, unmoved. "You're right." Reluctantly, I placed the comlink into his palm. "Did any other inmates 'borrow' things from you?"

"I don't know," I said. "My sister packed for me, and I'm not sure what she included."

"Perhaps you should take an inventory after your meal and report to my office with your findings."

"Yes, sir."

Nightmare turned away to supervise the other diners, and I made my way to the serving line. No one scooped portions for the inmates, and there didn't appear to be any weight limit for food, so I piled my plate with anything that smelled good and went to find Ruddie or Sasa. I found them sitting together in a corner, whispering.

"Talking about me?" I asked, dropping the tray beside Sasa.

Ruddie smiled grimly. "We're trying to guess how soon Ora and Petra will get their revenge."

"They can't hurt me too badly, can they? Won't Nightmare punish them?"

"He may punish all three of you."

"So? How bad can that be? I'm already at a Reformatory. What else is there?"

"Solitary," said Sasa quietly.

"They do that?"

"It's not like on an ICS," said Ruddie. "You're out there." He pointed a thumb over his shoulder to the window.

"The garden? What kind of threat is that? It's beautiful out there."

"Not the garden," said Sasa. "The woods beyond the fields."

"What do you mean 'the woods'?"

"In the trees," said Ruddie, shuddering. "It's horrible. It feels like they're waiting to reach down and grab you. There are no walls or ceilings, but it's all closed in and dark. And sometimes there are wild animals."

Lowering her voice, Sasa said, "Nightmare thinks nothing reforms a wild child more than time spent in the wild. If hard labor doesn't mend our ways, he finds an excuse to get us into the woods." When I chuckled nervously, she added, "It's the reason he's called Nightmare. I heard even Alf cried when he went to the woods."

OOO

After the meal, most of the inmates stayed in the cafeteria for free time. They talked and played various games with Turbo Chips. Everyone spread out on the benches and seemed to become as wide as they could. Their body language clearly said, *Don't even think about sitting by me*. Ruddie and Sasa disappeared together, so I tucked myself under the tray shelf of the serving line and pulled out the tablet that the fanep had slid at me. It did not produce 3D holograms. A flat display appeared with a written list of reports. I hadn't practiced reading in a long time, so I ran my finger underneath the words only to find that this made them slide right off the screen. Once I located the list again, I avoided touching the screen, but I held it close to my nose so I wouldn't lose my place.

Mysteries of Karlis Ocean Life on Tye
1. Bulbous Squidworms
2. Giant Amoebas
3. Isopod Crustaceans
4. Predatory Sea Snails
5. Red Armored Oyster Pearls
6. Spiral Reefs
7. Translucent Sea Cucumbers

I blinked. *What in space…?* I tried again. Even when I deciphered them, I didn't know what most of the words meant. However, when I saw the word '*Pearls*', my heart switched places with my liver.

"Find something interesting to read?" Nightmare's voice surprised me so much that I banged my head on the tray shelf.

"What? Oh, I—"

"You failed to report to me with the inventory of your belongings. Am I to assume you are forgetful, or disobedient?"

I scrambled to my feet. "Uh, forgetful?"

Nightmare's lips formed a thin line. "So perhaps gravity affects your mind more than your body," he said quietly. "Come with me, and we will do it together."

He climbed easily, without tiring. Determined not to be ridiculed again, I kept pace right behind him, pulling myself up hand-over-hand so I wouldn't lose balance. At the top, he paused and studied my face. I panted a little, but otherwise stood strong.

"It usually takes inmates two months to climb the stairs as well as you do," he remarked. "Have you been to the Surface before?"

"No, sir."

"Were you particularly fond of the exercise rooms on the Arxon?"

"I don't know." I tried to remember how physical I'd been, but I felt like a million rotations had passed. "Felly didn't like to sweat, so we—"

"Who is Felly?"

"My sister."

"She's the one who packed for you?"

"Yes."

"You have no mother?" A flicker of concern warmed the lines beside his eyes. I didn't know how to answer. I had a mother, but no one knew where she was. She'd left us before my fourth birthday. Fortunately, Nightmare didn't press the matter. "I'll send word to your family about how well you are doing."

My lungs released a liter of air and the tears started. I croaked out a word of thanks even though I didn't know why it meant so much to me.

Nightmare walked to the door of my room and stopped abruptly, looking mildly alarmed. I came up behind him to see Petra standing frozen. Ora was perched on my bunk, staring down at us. Nightmare opened his palm to Petra. She handed him an object.

"My comlink!" I cried.

"How strange. I was sure I had placed it in the drawer of my desk," said Nightmare, his voice calm but his face furious.

Petra stuttered and appealed to Ora for help, but Ora said nothing. That seemed to be her way.

Nightmare cleared his throat. "Perhaps a night in Solitary will help you remember that thieving is not permitted at Lamond." The girls gasped, and Petra began to cry. "You remember Solitary?" he asked. "Good. There's hope for your mind to develop yet." He snapped his finger and pointed to the hallway. Petra shuffled out, and Nightmare directed his attention to Ora.

"Just helping the new girl make her bed," she said with an awkward laugh.

Nightmare folded his arms and studied her. "Take it all apart and start over so I can see how you do it." Ora protested, but then pulled the blankets and sheets off the bed, dropping them to the ground. "The pillow, too," said Nightmare. The pillow fell to the floor and a plume of pinkish dust rose. "Ah, it appears some ovling powder got onto her bedding," he said. "Itchy stuff, that. It's good that we caught it before she went to bed." Ora's face reddened. This guy was good at his job. I had to admire his style, even while fearing him a little. He wasn't spineless and mentally weak like Mr. Lew. "Shake the powder off of the bedding," commanded Nightmare. "Out the window."

Ora obeyed silently. As she reached for the pillow, she cast a bitter look at me. She turned away and beat the pillow against the sill. Beyond her, two crescent moons glared at her like angry eyes. "Oh!" she cried out, with totally fake surprise. "I dropped it!"

"How inconvenient," said Nightmare. "Caz will have to use your pillow."

Ora's gaze flickered to Petra's bunk, but Nightmare intercepted her. He snatched Petra's pillow and handed it to the sniveling girl in the hall. "Here. You might as well be comfortable in the woods." Petra hugged the pillow tight and sobbed into it.

Nightmare supervised while Ora replaced all of my bedding neatly, and I tried not to let a gloating sense of justice show on my face. I'd never had an adult stick up for me like this. "We have a few minutes to inventory your belongings before the signal sounds and everyone comes up for the night," he said.

I rummaged through my crate to see what, other than coversuits and underwear, Felly had packed. Tucked inside a pouch of grooming stuff was a small digiscreen. I thumbed through a few pictures, pausing on the one of Mom and Dad holding me as a baby. Though I couldn't really remember Mom, I liked her smiling face framed with dark curls. "These things are all mine, but I don't know if Felly packed more."

Nightmare gave me a knowing nod. "I very much hope there will be no further confusion caused by inmates in this room," he said, eyeing Ora. "You are all relatively new here, and need to get off to a better start if there is any hope of reforming you." He smoothed his hair with a tired sigh. "Wash up, girls."

Ora and I made our way down the hall to the washroom, avoiding eye contact with the weeping Petra as she trailed Nightmare back down the stairs. We remained silent while we showered in the small cubicles. I couldn't believe how much water we used here, but I had no trouble getting used to it. The whole time, I kept Ora within my peripheral vision, even as we aired ourselves dry under the hot vents. At last another inmate arrived.

"Where's Petra?" she asked innocently.

Ora stormed out. "How should I know? Ask the new girl." The girl turned to me, but I just shrugged and followed Ora out.

At the door, Ora stopped. In a low growl, she said, "Petra won't be getting any sleep tonight. You won't sleep, either, if you know what's good for you." She glared at me as if trying to melt me with radioactive eyes, but I smiled at the girls who walked by on their way from the stairwell to their rooms. No one dared stop or speak. Somebody really needed to cut this big idiot down a size.

"Thanks for the advice. Now let me in."

Ora braced herself against the doorframe and stuck out her chin. I shook my head, as if defeated, and lowered my head. Then I thrust my palm up sharply into Ora's solar plexus. She stumbled backwards, winded, and sat heavily on her bunk. It's handy having a father who makes me study anatomy. Bullies always go for blood, but I've found stealing their breath ends the fight a lot faster.

"Sleep well, Ora." I grabbed the tablet and pulled myself easily up to the top bunk. "Thanks again for making my bed for me. Real nice of you." I could almost hear her pulse throbbing in her ears.

When the lights went out by the automatic timer, Ora's bunk let out a few more cries, and then all became still. Lying on my stomach, I read the entire section on *Red Armored Oyster Pearls* from the Karlis Ocean of Tye.

> # OOO

7 ALF

I woke with the tablet sticking to my cheek. The morning alarm had kicked me out of an abusive sleep—the kind filled with such exhausting nightmares that I might as well not have slept. They were all about that fanep stalking me.

Quietly, I lowered myself and stood by the window. The morning sky had so many colors here, not just black. With a cautious tug, I opened the window a little and crouched to breathe in the outdoor air. It was unexpectedly cold, but fresher than anything an air-conditioner could spit out. It smelled like the dried fruits we ate on the Arxon.

From this vantage, I could see the paved area that Ruddie had called the 'court yard'. An enormous tree dominated the center. The edge of the area opened out on rows of taller plants, and beyond that, the woods grew. I tried to discern the horrors of such a Solitary assignment, but I could only make out the vague lines of the trees and the murky darkness between them.

"You'd better hope she didn't get hurt last night," said Ora from her bunk.

"What would hurt her?"

"The creatures in the woods," said Ora.

Unsure if she spoke truth, I faced Ora. "Have you ever had to go?" I asked.

"Why would I?" asked Ora sarcastically. "I don't break rules."

"Right. Ora, the model inmate." I moved to my shelf without turning my back on her. "I'll keep watching you so I can learn."

"You watch *out* so you can *live*," warned Ora. She punched the words as if trying to show how cleverly she'd played with my words.

I grabbed a clean coversuit and dressed while Ora stared at the bunk above her.

"How long have you been here, anyway?" I asked. Ora didn't move. "You're from the Selig, aren't you?" I mimicked the up-and-down cadence of speech Ora and Petra used.

Ora raised her voice. "Don't talk to me."

"Sorry. I didn't mean to confuse you with all the hard questions."

I freshened up in the washroom and tiptoed towards the stairs. For now, I had them to myself. The shoes still felt awkward, but I moved as quickly as I could without losing balance. Impulsively, I leapt down the last three steps at the first landing. I faced the next set of stairs with more enthusiasm. Gauging the distance carefully, I tried jumping down the stairs two at a time, three at a time, and even four at a time. In this way, I reached the bottom very quickly, and my heart pounded with satisfaction.

Nightmare stood with his arms folded. "You play like a Surface child."

I fiddled with my sleeve.

"I forgot to ask you last night: What were you studying?"

"Ocean life on Tye."

"Whatever for?"

Because some creepy little monster slid the tablet at me and I figured I might as well? "I couldn't find one on the oceans of Caren, but I really liked our water landing. I was curious."

"Hm." Nightmare gestured for me to hurry along. I don't know that I convinced him. Honestly, part of me wondered why I'd spent the night reading instead of sleeping or exploring.

I arrived in the cafeteria first and decided to take a place in the middle of the room to see what the other inmates would do. It quickly became apparent that they were as fixed in their routines as anyone on the Arxon. I had disrupted the order of their universe, and I watched with amusement as people walked past. Some looked like they wanted to be angry, but were too afraid.

A hulking form slammed a tray down opposite me. Alf, the violent offender. I gulped and flushed, but not in fear. He was too gorgeous, in a powerful way.

"I eat alone," he said gruffly. He had dark, forbidding eyes and thick yellow hair that had grown enough to show he had served a lot more time than any other inmate.

"Me, too," I said, trying to match his steady tone.

He leaned heavily on his forearms. "Don't cross me."

Gripping my tray to hide my shaking fingers, I said, "You're the one who sat across from *me*."

Our eyes locked for a long time, and my skin tingled with a ripple of teenage chemistry—painful and invigorating at the same time. Finally, he picked up his fork. Stabbing at a slab of meat, he grunted. "You're here for assault, yeah?"

"Just like you," I said, likewise stabbing a slice of revo.

He pointed the fork close to my nose, and my eyes crossed before I could stop them. "*Not* like me." He rested the tines of the fork on his own cheek. "See that? They started the tattoo, yeah?"

I stared at the half-circle of green on his right cheek that folded into a deep dimple. "Started it? What does that mean?"

"It means he was in critical condition, but pulled through at the last minute."

"Lucky for both of you."

Alf resumed eating. Through a mouthful, he repeated, "Don't cross me."

I glanced around and saw we'd been given a wide circumference of silent respect. I used the time to eat and steal glimpses at Alf's icy hot features. After a while, I pushed my fingers into my forehead, trying to remember the article about Red Armored Oyster Pearls. Streams of data had gone on and on about how rare they were. I had taken more interest when a footnote said gypsy divers were uniquely skilled at retrieving them. It made me think of Ninetta and her son. The reports had also speculated about the medicinal properties of the pearls, but most authorities agreed that ingesting a whole pearl could prove fatal. As I remembered that little detail, swallowing became difficult, and I washed down a piece of egg with some yellow juice that stung my throat.

"Don't plot anything dangerous without me," said Alf, almost smiling.

I gladly refocused my attention on him. "What?"

"You think a lot," he said, standing. "This is a place of action."

OOO

"No, she's been like that fifteen minutes. Trust me. She's out."

I could hear voices, but decided feigning sleep was my best option anyway. I'd dozed twice while digging revos, and Sasa had been more aloof. Now I could hear her and Ruddie whispering nearby. Otherwise, it sounded like we were alone in the library. Amidst giggles, I heard kissing. This made it harder to keep a straight face.

They murmured something I couldn't hear and then Ruddie said, "Let's give her time. She couldn't have known."

"Ora's going to use Alf against her."

"How?"

"She'll make Caz out to be the new threat—as Alf's ally—and sell protection."

Were things really that messed up down here?

Ruddie groaned. "Sasa, are you guessing this, or did you hear things?"

"You know me," giggled Sasa. "I hear things that help me guess, and I always guess right."

A long beat of silence followed. I opened my eyes enough to see Sasa slip her arms around Ruddie's waist and pull him away from the window. "We've got to warn Caz to stay away from Alf."

"I don't think warning Caz helps much. She does what she wants."

"At least she's not mean," said Sasa.

I made a show of waking up and stretching. "Did I fall asleep?"

Ruddie took a small step away from Sasa. "You awake?"

"I guess I got bored reading…" I looked down at the tablet screen. "Um, history of the Velmar Republic."

Ruddie's eyebrows climbed his forehead. "Reading up on Caren's great empires?"

I played along. "Yeah, well, you know. It's good to learn about where I am, right? One should always know who the powers are."

Sasa and Ruddie exchanged a frown. "Speaking of which," said Sasa. "We should probably tell you—"

"There you are," said Nightmare from the doorway. He pointed to Ruddie and signaled for him to follow.

Ruddie quickly went with him out into the hall, and Nightmare closed the door.

Sasa moved swiftly to eavesdrop. "I can't hear anything. Can you?" she whispered. I joined her, pressing my ear against the door. She gave up and stood fretting.

"…missing from the woods."

"Couldn't she have just moved further in, sir?"

"It seems unlikely. Petra has expressed great anxiety about the forest."

"So what's next?"

"The guards from the north and east towers—"

I snapped back at Sasa. "We have guards? What's a tower?"

"What's going on?" she pleaded, wringing her hands. I didn't know people actually did that. "Is Ruddie in trouble?" she whimpered.

"No, no. Your precious kissy face is fine. It's Petra who's missing."

Sasa stepped back as if winded. "Missing!" She gestured at the door. "What else? What else?"

I listened again. Nightmare's voice had dropped a few decibels and I could barely make it out. "…was her pillow."

"She took a pillow?" asked Ruddie.

"And it was shredded."

I covered my mouth and moved away from the door. A second later, a terrifying rattle at the window shook my intestines. I spun to see Ora pounding on the glass pane.

The door to the library opened again, and Nightmare re-entered with Ruddie. The director strode over to the window where Ora now backed away. He raised the window and called out to her. Cowering, Ora approached the building and stood below the window, tears streaming down her face. "What is the meaning of this assault on my window?" demanded Nightmare.

"Petra's not back. If something happened to Petra—"

"She will not likely be returning tonight," he said, sliding the window shut. He sounded more annoyed than worried. "Studying more oceanography?" he asked.

The change of subject confused me, but I recovered quickly. "History."

"Really?" he smirked.

Ruddie piped in. "Of Caren's Empires, sir."

"Perhaps your instructors did not challenge you enough on the Arxon."

"Perhaps not, sir."

"Come," said Nightmare to Ruddie. "I need you to make the necessary reports."

Ruddie and Nightmare left the library.

Grabbing the back of a big chair, I scraped it across the floor to the window so I could sit in the sunlight.

"What are you? A gypsy?" teased Sasa.

I made a face. It was a common enough insult, but after meeting Ninetta, it didn't rest well in my conscience to hear it. "Why does everyone say stuff like that to me?"

"Caz, you're so strong. Most of us lie in bed for the first week or two before we can even start to walk. You're like some superhuman Surface creature."

It made me blush despite myself. Flopping down in the chair with the tablet, I asked, "Didn't you ever want to come to the Surface?" I rested my ankles on the shelf below the window.

Sasa shook her head. "It's horrible here. Everything's so heavy, and I feel tired all the time."

I hadn't slept enough to gauge if my fatigue was Surface-induced or not.

"Twice I've had my skin burned by the sun," she continued. "My arms are getting darker. You can see how sunburned Ora is."

I examined my own pale hands and thought about the other inmates. "Alf's skin is darker, and I think it looks good on him."

Sasa chuckled. "Well, on him, sure. He makes *dirt* look good. But he's been here almost two rotations."

"Two!"

"Only inmate ever," she said. "He's really strong, too."

I thought about this as I gazed out the window. The library's silence calmed me. "Why don't more people choose the study option if they're trying to stay clean and conserve energy?"

Sasa snorted. "Because you never know when Nightmare's going to test you on what you said you studied, and if you don't know it well enough, it's Solitary."

I almost choked. "Ruddie didn't tell me that part!"

"Study hard," she said without humor.

OOO

I'd settled into a rhythm with Sasa, me pulling and her catching revos, when Nightmare's voice stabbed the back of my neck. "I'm reassigning you. Follow me."

Sasa's gaping mouth did not encourage my enthusiasm, but I trotted after Nightmare as he walked swiftly around the building, out of the shade, and towards the farm rows. He stopped before the grass faded into dirt.

Pointing, he said, "These duspy stalks need to be pruned and de-bugged. You will receive instruction from Alf."

"Alf?"

Nightmare smirked. "The girls are always so eager to meet Alf," he said. "But apparently you already did."

"Isn't digging harder work?" I asked.

"You can decide that when the shift is over. It's two hours of standing in the sun."

I drew a deep breath and stepped out into the dirt. Its depth pulled my feet down with each step. Much worse than the garden mud. I was glad to have the shoes.

The rows of stalks were another matter. ICS dwellers are rarely claustrophobic, but the confined spaces are still and silvery, not green and grasping. I felt my organs huddling together as I walked with the stalks so close that the leaves brushed against me. By the time I reached the end and broke out into the open space on the far side, I exhaled and shook the jitters from my arms.

Alf gave a lopsided smile, revealing perfect teeth. He really was distractingly handsome. "You get so you don't feel it anymore," he said.

"That's something to look forward to," I said.

"You're my latest victim, yeah?"

I took a step back. "What does *that* mean?"

"This is the hard labor camp," he said. "I'm here to break you in, or break you down."

Was he mocking me, or the labor itself? I stood taller. When he stared at me, still smiling, I grew uncomfortable. "What? Did my hair turn purple?"

"Your hands will. You want gloves, yeah?"

"For what?"

"See these things?" He grasped a cluster of about eight purple pods, each no larger than his thumb. "We pull off the extra leaves around it and make sure there aren't any insects in the fruit."

"Insects?"

Alf examined three clusters before finding something. "There. That little black thing with all the legs," he said, pushing it into my face.

I shrieked. "What *is* that?"

"A life form very common to the Surface. Has a nasty bite, yeah?"

"I'll take the gloves," I said.

"All right. But it's harder to prune with gloves on."

"Give me the gloves," I insisted. Even if I didn't get bit, I didn't want one of those things crawling on my hands.

He removed his own gloves and handed them to me with a grin. As I wriggled my fingers into them, I couldn't resist asking, "Why don't you smile like that back inside? Afraid all the girls will faint?"

He let out a soft laugh. "No."

"What then? Are you plotting my death?"

He laughed louder this time and covered his mouth with the back of his hand. "Not yet." Good. Keep him laughing. That worked on most boys. Well, boys other than Jeroby, anyway.

"Pay attention, yeah? This is hard work." He reached up and tore at the exposed leaves in each cluster. Then he dug between the pods with his pinky. He found another insect and held it up between his finger and thumb. "You'll see why this is our job." He crushed it with a sickening squelch and flicked it away over his shoulder. "We're dangerous killers, yeah?"

I grinned. "Yeah."

We labored in silence and pretty soon I felt the effects of the sun. Sweat trickled down my body even as I felt iron rising up within me, making me heavier—especially my arms—but I kept pace with Alf.

After a while, the questions in me burned more than the sting of my muscles. "Do the leaves in the woods grab at you like this?"

Alf froze with his hand on a cluster of duspies. "You heard I went to Solitary, yeah?"

"Yeah."

He leaned in so our foreheads touched. He smelled dirty and sweaty, and I could sense his strength. A knot of fear wriggled in my stomach. "Three things you need to know about that," he said slowly. "One: there are more than leaves grabbing at you in the woods. Two," he said, "I never cried. That's a lie."

We locked eyes and I saw his fierce courage. "And three?"

He whispered, "There aren't any fences around the forest."

"*What?*"

"After an ICS, with no space and too many rules, we have a whole *world* of space and no rules." His eyes flashed with excitement.

"There's nothing keeping us here? What about the guards?" I asked. "I heard there were tower guards, whatever that is."

Alf's arched eyebrow dismissed that concern.

I felt my scalp crawl with sudden understanding. "They're counting on the fear of the woods to stop us from going too far," I said.

"You catch on quick."

"But it must be dangerous in there," I said, pushing back the adrenaline rising in my ears.

He shrugged. "It is. But you're free."

"You're going to escape!"

His purple hand covered my mouth and held my head tightly in place. "If you tell anyone, I'll kill you." His grip loosened. "Don't make me do that. I don't want to."

OOO

8 THE STORM

I stared at the shelves, frustrated. Despite the shower and fresh clothes, I felt rumpled and weak, but I had to find the tablet I'd pretended to read in case Nightmare decided to test me. Alf might want to go to the woods, but I hadn't cast my vote yet.

"I can't believe Nightmare put you in the duspies. I think you might be the first girl he's done that to," Ruddie said from a chair behind me.

"It's hot out there," I mumbled in agreement, distracted by my search.

"Far left of the shelf directly in front of your shoulders," he said.

I checked. "How did you know?" I held the tablet up in an embassy salute. "Thanks."

"Next time, pick stuff you think you'll actually like."

I sat heavily. "You won't have to tell me that twice."

"Study," he said sternly. "Test tonight."

"Really?" My pulse quickened.

Ruddie chuckled and shook his head. "You never know."

After scanning the table of contents, I decided to focus on the most recent Empire on Caren, the reign of Queen Levia. A half hour passed in depressing silence. Apparently, fifty years ago, she had attempted to unite the entire Granbo System under one governance. Talk about hungry for power. And impossible. Even getting the various colonies spread out over Caren proved a counter-orbital waste of time. Mr. Virgil had never bothered with history outside of the ICS interactions with planets, but this report said that Queen Levia even tried to solicit ICS support. Still, she got further than any other person had, so she must have had something going for her.

"Did you ever study Surface history on your ICS?" I asked.

Ruddie roused himself from his tablet. "Hmm? A little."

"Did you learn about Queen Levia getting killed by her detractors?"

"Huh," said Ruddie, bored. "That must be Caren's version of the story. I heard it was an accident."

I tapped the tablet. "It says she was too friendly with gypsies and the fanep species for some of the colonies."

Ruddie barked a laugh. "Of course. That's disgusting."

I looked back down at the screen. A picture showed her standing in a long, flowing blouse worn over blue-green leggings. In her black, ornately braided hair, she wore a crown made of leaves. I grunted with surprise at the caption:

> *Queen Levia's tolerance of the gypsy migrant workers of the Granbo System initially earned her much criticism, but the gypsies became unusually loyal to her. Their labors brought additional revenue to the empire, and Levia's dissenters on Caren relented. The gypsies, as a token of esteem, gave her a crown fashioned from Rik leaves, which they claimed would make her wise beyond her years.*

I squinted in thought. The pearl mixed with Rik leaves helps memory. Hadn't Ninetta said that? Pointing out the window, I said, "Those are Rik trees in the woods, yeah?"

"You sound like Alf."

I snickered at myself. "Yeah."

The flat screen monitors on the walls lit up and flashed red.

"What's going on?" I asked. Until now, I'd never seen the screens display anything.

Ruddie waved me silent. "This must be important."

A man appeared on the screen standing in front of a swirling display of colors. It took me a second to realize that it was a satellite image of clouds that had been marked in green, yellow and red. "A severe electrical storm watch is in effect for the entire peninsula," said the man soberly. "Expect power outages throughout the region as wind gusts reach 80 kilometers per hour. Satellite connections may be disrupted and comlinks will be unable to reach stations in orbit for the duration of the storm. All residents are urged to shutter their windows and stay indoors."

The screen flashed three times, and the message repeated. Ruddie seemed concerned.

"What? What's a storm?" I asked.

Before he answered, Sasa ran into the room, red-faced. "Hurry!" she said, tugging at Ruddie.

"What?" My voice squeaked. "What's a storm?"

"Try to imagine a really long shower that fills the whole sky, and all the water is cold," said Ruddie.

"And it's as if the air vents go crazy," said Sasa nervously. "The wind blasts so hard and fast that it can knock you over. I hate it. Nothing like that could happen on an ICS."

"This one must have formed quickly," said Ruddie. "Usually we get more notice."

"When they come fast, they come hard," said Sasa. The buzz of voices filled the corridor outside and a surge of inmates moved towards the stairwell. We stepped out into the throng just as Ora broke through the crowd shouting, "Someone has to get Petra! She can't be outside when the storm comes!"

Nightmare's head appeared above the others, his hands raised in a useless calming gesture. "Everyone, report to the cafeteria for roll call. We need to be sure everyone is inside before we begin shut-down."

"Petra!" screamed Ora, turning on him. "Someone has to get her!"

Nightmare continued to usher inmates down the hall. "We will take roll, and then close all the shutters and check the power generators."

"No!" shouted Ora, tears streaming down her face. She grabbed inmates at random. "Someone help!" Pleading, she lunged for Nightmare, out of control. "Let me go find her!"

Nightmare jerked away forcefully, causing her to stumble backwards into Sasa. Her eyes aflame, Ora wrapped her arm tightly around Sasa's neck. "Let me go, or I'll choke her. I'll break her neck."

Sasa rasped and scratched at Ora's arms. Other inmates pulled them apart, and Nightmare grabbed at Ora. She raged and kicked him solidly in the groin. He doubled over in pain, and the inmates reacted with fear and surprise. Ora stood like a cornered animal. She hesitated and then charged with her head down into Ruddie, driving him into the wall. A flat screen slid off its mount and crashed onto him, the shards cutting his face and hands.

I saw the blood and felt my own boil within me. Diving at her, I took Ora by the collar with both hands and threw her down the hall so far that some of the inmates screamed.

Nightmare stood carefully. "Enough!" he boomed. I shook the anger from my fingers and returned to Sasa. "Get to the cafeteria," yelled Nightmare. He pointed at Ora. "I'll deal with you in a minute."

Ora rose to her feet, panting and crying. Weakly, she insisted, "But Petra—"

"Is most likely dead by now," said Nightmare. He cupped his hands to his mouth and shouted, "Roll call. Now!"

The fact that he had lost his perpetual calm spurred me down the hall at top speed. In the cafeteria, the inmates huddled at the windows. I was confused by what I saw. The sky had darkened into a solid grey, as if a giant metal dome had dropped over the grounds.

"Is that smoke?" I asked.

"Clouds," said someone to my left.

"But clouds are white."

"Not when they're full of rain," she said, her lip trembling. Almost as she spoke, the windows rattled. A few of the inmates pulled back, and several of them shouted.

"Rain!"

"I saw flashes of light!"

An explosive boom shook my nerves and the furniture. "What was *that?*"

"Just the beginning," said Ruddie.

The inmates grew quiet, but water lashed at the windows, blurring the view of everything but the large tree. It bent wildly back and forth in the wind, like a child throwing a tantrum. Every face in the room seemed younger than it had in the sunlight.

Nightmare called roll and scanned the crowd with urgency uncommon to him. "Alf! Where's Alf?" he demanded.

A cold chill gripped the back of my neck. *Had he escaped during the chaos?* "He went upstairs," I said without thinking.

Nightmare scowled. "Are you sure?"

"I can go check," I offered.

Nightmare shook his head. "No. Go shutter the windows in the library and then report back here."

In the library, rain slapped against the glass, and an eerie howl sounded from outside. It took me a minute to realize that the shutters were outside the glass, not inside like an airlock. I groaned and pushed open the window, then cowered back from the cold, wet wind. The storm roared. On either side of the window, long slatted boards banged against the outer wall. I fumbled to reach them, and as I caught the second shutter, something moved below the tree.

Ora! She was drenched. "I have to get Petra!" she cried.

A brilliant flash of light blinded me, and another bone-shaking boom filled the air. Both of us screamed. With a terrifying creak, a giant piece of the tree split free and pounded to the ground, pinning Ora to the pavement. Impulsively, I jumped through the window, landing on the wet concrete and slipping. I came down hard on my hip with a splash.

Ora called for help, her voice strangled by the weight of the branches across her chest. Scrambling over the branches, I felt my coversuit torn in many places by unseen hands. *Were there creatures in the tree?* Wiping the water from my face and trying not to think about the tree, I reached Ora.

"Can you move?" I panted.

"Help!" cried Ora.

I wavered. *Why was I out in the storm risking my life for—?*

"Please!" begged Ora.

I trembled uncontrollably with cold and fear. The maze of branches and leaves shook at me in the wind. Squatting into the weave, I wrapped my arms around two of the branches and stood. The heaviest part of the fallen piece came up, and Ora wheezed with relief. She squirmed out from under before I dropped it again. I untangled myself from the net of wood and reached Ora as she tried to stand up. A dark patch of blood seeped from the side of her abdomen.

"What happened?" I asked. But I already knew.

Ora put her hand over the wound and grimaced. "A branch..." The blood trickled over her fingers and mixed with the rain. A whistling gust of wind startled us both, and Ora toppled to her knees. Clutching for my hand, she wept, "Get Petra! She's not strong enough." Ora groaned and covered her stomach with both hands.

"I—"

"Please!" Ora stood up, but then crumpled into my arms weakly. "Please."

I watched the life seep from Ora's side with horror. The light in her eyes disappeared. I knew the look. I'd seen it once before when I visited Dad in the infirmary during a canflu epidemic. Out of breath and weeping myself, I lowered Ora to the ground and held her head in my lap. The tree continued to thrash at the clouds, but right around us was a sad stillness, as if even the rain dared not intrude upon her grief. I closed her eyes with my fingers and promised, "I'll find Petra."

In the minute or two that followed—or maybe it was an hour—the world darkened, both around me and inside. Whatever her crime, Ora had not deserved this. To die is one thing. To die feeling so helpless is another. In that moment, I admired her for giving her life in an effort to save her friend. She wasn't a perfect friend, but her death was somehow redemptive. Ora had done something right, even if no one saw it.

"Caz! Get inside! What are you doing?" Nightmare's silhouette waved at me from the rectangle of light in the library window. His voice panicked me, but I couldn't move. The tree with its deadly branches surrounded me. "Hurry!" he bellowed. "The winds are getting stronger!"

I stood, shaking violently with emotion and stared at the mass of branches that seemed to jump with life and bar my way. "How?" I cried.

Nightmare waved. "Back door! Hurry!" He pulled the shutters closed leaving me in the icy black rain.

Enormous fingers of blue light wrestled across the darkened sky. Heaving Ora over my shoulder, I edged my way around the tree's scratching claws. The air rumbled like the engines of a shuttle. Staring up, I could see no stars. The sky flashed again, and thousands of raindrops flew down at me like silver knives. I buried my face in Ora's side only to feel her hot blood on my face.

The back door opened, casting a column of gold light on the ground to guide me in. I ran, and windblown debris stung my arms and cheeks. Something clattered around me, sweeping my legs out from under me. Ora's body smothered me. Pushing to break free of the weight, I saw a blur of movement on the ground nearby.

The air erupted in high-pitched screeches, and something snatched Ora's body away. I rolled onto my stomach and came face to face with a row of sharp teeth.

The fanep! It stood with a large rock raised over its head and a glint in its yellow eyes.

○○○

9 THE WOODS

I was too sore to open my eyes. My body ached as if I'd slept all night on a pile of tether coils. I could hear a buzzing noise and faint whispers, but could not make out who spoke. Cold tightened my throat, and my skin crawled under a sensation of dampness. A creak nearby frightened me, and a strange musical whistle repeated the same three notes over and over. Trembling, I peeked through my fingers up at the ceiling.

But there was no ceiling.

I lay at the base of what appeared to be an enormous carved wooden support beam. It stretched up to a dizzying height and then burst into a fan of green. With a jolt, I sat up. It was a tree. *I was in the woods!*

I studied the looming shapes of the trees in the strangely filtered light, waiting for them to advance, but they did not. At last I exhaled. The tree, it seemed, anchored itself to the ground with great wooden ropes, and these had been my bed for the night. No wonder my sleep had been so uncomfortable.

Afraid to touch the tree for balance, but feeling light-headed from the heavy air, I leaned on my knees and breathed in the smells that mingled so freely on the Surface. A cool mist clung to the lower branches like the steam in a shower room.

The whistle sounded again, and something fell from the sky, swinging down and up in a fast arc, disappearing into the trees. I squealed, but quickly muffled my own cry, sensing a need for quiet here, as if the trees waited to speak, and had not yet decided what to say. A large drop of water splashed on my arm, and I flinched in surprise, recovering gratefully to find nothing had attacked me. The trees, still wet from the storm, gently shook themselves dry. I felt their watchful stare at my back no matter which way I faced, so I gave up and accepted their scrutiny.

My stomach rumbled, and this awoke a need to move. I needed to get back to Lamond. *How had I gotten here, anyway? Was I carried?* After scanning the spaces between the trees, I decided to head in the direction that admitted more light, hoping this led back to the open fields.

A few paces later, invisible strings wrapped around my face. I swatted at the sticky, wispy strands, shuddering and squeaking with fright. Breathless and weeping, I tried to comprehend a broken, shimmering net that stretched between the trees. On the side of this, an insect much larger than the ones in the duspy clusters scolded me with clicking jaws. I backed away and felt my foot kick through a pile of soft dirt. Looking down, I saw thousands of tiny insects scurrying over the wreckage my foot had caused. A few of them swarmed over my shoe, and I kicked wildly, leaping away. I reached down to brush them off only to find my hand covered in a gooey yellow substance.

Staring at this new horror, I screamed in earnest, holding nothing back for pride. I didn't care if someone heard me. I *wanted* someone to hear me! The noise rang out through the forest and instantly the branches above quaked and called back to me with shrill cries and more whistles. I tried to block out the sound, only to feel the stickiness on my ears and hair. Half blind with tears, I stumbled over the uneven ground, wincing at each snap or crunch under my feet. I rounded an especially large tree and tried to stop myself, but couldn't. The drop-off came steeply and suddenly. Landing hard on my butt, I slid down a green, slimy slope and came to a painful stop in a trench of knee-deep water. There, at sanity's end, I sobbed until all the adrenaline in my system evaporated, leaving me haggard and exhausted.

Calmer, I focused on my surroundings. The water, though flowing over dirt, looked clean, and at this point, I was too tired to worry about microorganisms. Plunging my hands into the water, I scrubbed away the yellow stickiness and the earth that stained my clothes. Splashing my face, I almost retched with revulsion to see blood sift into the water. The memory of recent events flooded back, and I stood, staring around me with unblinking eyes.

I remembered a purpose bigger than my own comfort. "Petra!" I called. "Petra, are you out there?" I climbed back up the slope awkwardly, all the while calling out for Petra. At the top, I heard a crack, and a second later, something small and hard pelted my shoulder. I spun so fast that I slipped and fell again. "Alf!"

"I told you not to make me kill you." The menace in his face was mixed with fear.

"What? I never told anyone, Alf. I even lied to Nightmare for you."

Alf relaxed a little. "Then why are you here?"

"Good question." I got stiffly to my feet. "The fanep?" I suggested.

"The what?"

"I think the fanep brought me here," I said, my voice trailing off with dawning realization.

Alf moved closer, his body tense. "What's a fanep?"

"Those little humanoid things that travel with gypsies."

Alf's mouth hung open. "Those rat men from Tye? They're here on Caren, too?" His voice cracked, and his eyes searched the leaves above us warily.

"One of them is," I said. "It's attacked me several times. Last night, I think there were more of them."

Alf grabbed my wrist. "We need to get moving."

"What about Petra?" I asked, resisting.

"What about her?"

"Have you seen her?"

"That weakling is dead by now, yeah?" he said bitterly. "Let's go."

I didn't like the idea of giving up the search for Petra, but I figured we'd be safer together, and I could always keep my eye out for her while I followed him. Besides, something in Alf's manner took away my fear of the forest, at least for now. We followed the course of the water through the trees, staying above the ravine, but the land slanted downward and the sound of the water increased. Alf helped me down to the edge of the rushing water. There was much more of it here, and the air moved with it.

"It's easy to cross here with the rocks, yeah?"

I stared at him. "Are you crazy? This water's deep." When he gave me a disapproving frown, I added, "I almost drowned once."

"On an ICS?" scoffed Alf.

"In the ocean, when the ferry landed."

That shut him up for a whole second. "It's like you're *trying* to die." He gauged the distance to the first rock before leaping easily to it. "It's dry," he said, calling over the rushing sound of water. "You won't slip."

"What if I knock you in?"

"I pull you in with me," he said.

I rolled my eyes. "I can jump that easy," I said. It was not a move I'd practiced, and I was pretty sure I would look ridiculous doing it. With a furious grunt, I launched myself over the water and landed beside Alf. For a delicious moment our arms tangled while we kept from toppling off. Then I broke free and smoothed my suit. "See? I'm not afraid."

"Never said you were." He grinned and jumped to the next rock.

I followed, surprised by the thrill that came with each leap. On the fourth rock, the largest of them all, I stopped and watched Alf continue on to the muddy edge of the water. I stomped my foot, feeling the solidity of the rock, like nothing on the giant, hollow Arxon. No echo. It had the weight of a planet under it.

"What are you doing?" called Alf. "We still need to get to camp." He took off running again.

With a burst of speed, I caught up with him and kept pace running beside him even as the land rose up before us. It felt good to run. It felt free.

OOO

The light changed, and we slowed to a walk, breathing in a new scent. The leaves above glistened a golden green, and the air tasted sweeter. *I could actually taste the air!* Away from the sound of the water, I heard the whistles again. "What's that noise?"

"Birds," said Alf, stopping to catch his breath.

"Birds? Really? Are they dangerous?"

"No. Pretty, though. There were some back in the gardens. The black and green things that fly."

We stepped into a treeless area where sunlight poured in. In the middle stood a crude shelter supported by short telescopic poles, like the "rooms" Felly and I used to build together.

"My tent," said Alf proudly. "I made it out of supplies I stole from the garden shed."

I rounded the tent, admiring his handiwork. When I came to the opening, I stifled a yelp. Petra lay curled up in fetal position with the fanep sitting next to her. The creature opened its eyes and looked straight at me. A curious smile spread across its lips, and it held up a finger as if telling me to be silent.

Alf stooped and grabbed a small rock to throw.

"Don't hit Petra," I warned.

With a flash of movement, the fanep rushed up and wrapped itself around my leg, as a toddler might cling to his mother. Then, it scrambled up my leg to perch on my shoulder. Before I could beat it away, it held something to my face so closely that it took me a second to focus.

"My comlink!"

The fanep leaped up into the nearest Rik tree, dropping the comlink at my feet. With what sounded like a laugh, it disappeared higher into the leaves.

I stared at Petra and, for a minute, forgot my purpose. "You stole my comlink *again*?"

Petra did not answer. She did not blink.

"How did you find my tent?" demanded Alf.

She seemed to be taking in the scene for the first time, as if in shock.

"Do you know where you are, Petra?" I asked, putting the comlink in my pocket. I kneeled down without moving closer to her. We made eye contact for a brief instant before she looked down at the ground. "Do you know *who* you are?" I asked.

"That's a stupid question," said Alf.

"Look at her eyes." When Alf didn't respond, I said, "My dad's a doctor. She needs a blanket or something. Hurry. She's in shock."

"You ordering me around?"

"Do it," I snapped, hoping he wouldn't get madder.

Alf crouched by the entrance to his tent. "She's not going to do something crazy, is she?" he asked, eyeing her suspiciously.

"No, I don't think so." I reached out a hand to her. "You want to lie down? Why don't you come over here to this patch of light? It's warmer over here."

Gradually, I coaxed Petra forward until she lay with her head on my lap. I shivered at the similarity between this scene and the one with Ora. Stroking Petra's short hair, I did my best to tuck the girl under a therma-pak blanket that Alf tossed at me. "Is there water?" I asked. "She'll need some, and I'm thirsty, too."

Alf frowned. "I only have supplies for myself."

"Just a little? Until she's strong enough to walk back to Lamond—"

"No!"

His cry filled the air with a new measure of tension.

"No...*what?*" I asked quietly.

"No one is going back to Lamond," he said.

"But—"

"No one is going back," he repeated. "I won't have my escape ruined. You're not going back."

"Or what? You'll kill us?"

"Don't make me," he said.

"You never killed anyone," I said, feeling my face flush at the risk of angering him.

"Almost," he said, pointing to the half-circle tattoo on his cheek.

"Were you even trying?" *Why didn't I shut up?*

Alf held his breath and sat facing me with hard eyes. "I almost killed a man," he said.

"When's the last time you actually saw death?" I asked, my voice hoarse all of a sudden. "Because I held it last night, just like this." I looked down at Petra. "I don't want to see death again, Alf, and neither do you."

None of us moved for a moment, though I could feel my veins throbbing with nervous energy.

"Who died?" Petra's tiny voice took me by surprise.

I couldn't bear to answer. Instead, I forced a smile and said, "You have some color. That's good."

Petra lifted herself up, wrapping Alf's blanket tightly around her shoulders. "Who died?" she repeated. She stared up at Alf, but he only shrugged. "Ora," she said dully.

All the emotion from the night before rushed back in through my gut and poured out of my eyes in a stubborn stream that I could not stop. "She was coming for you," I sobbed. "She ran out in the storm, and a piece of the tree fell on her. One of the branches pierced her body." I winced at the memory. "I lifted it—"

"You lifted the bough of a tree?" sneered Alf.

"I did!" I cried. "If a 'bough' is a big piece of tree." I glanced up at the nearest tree and understood his doubt. "I did," I insisted with a whisper.

"How did I do that? Must have been the adrenaline."

Petra sniffed. "She was my only friend." She rubbed her scalp with both hands, waking herself out of her stupor. "Everyone else was afraid of me."

"You were so tough on the Selig," said Alf sarcastically.

Petra stood and folded the blanket methodically. "My parents were the Station Masters." She sighed out her sorrow and offered the blanket to Alf.

"The boss kid takes up with the bully, yeah?" Alf groaned and swiped at the poles that held his tent. In a few short movements, the tent lay flat, and he rolled it up and stuffed it into his pillowcase.

"I didn't know that until later," said Petra. "Her family was new on my deck." She hung her head dismally. "Still, she was my only friend."

I could relate to that. Except Felly was my only friend. Actually, despite Felly's terminal niceness, she didn't have many friends, either. I guess people were afraid she'd report them or something. There she was stuck with me for company.

Alf shouldered the last of his supplies. He had packed them with practiced efficiency. "I'm moving on."

Petra and I exchanged a long look.

Shaking his head, Alf said, "You two *want* to get found?"

Petra's face drained of emotion as if too tired to feel any more. "What do you say, Petra?"

"I'd have to go back to the Selig when my rotation is over." Petra rubbed her eyes. "Ora is dead."

"Ora is dead," I said.

Petra nodded slowly. "I have nothing to go home to but shame."

I turned to Alf. "Are you trying to get home, or just escape Lamond?"

"Caren is my home now," he said roughly.

Where was my home? Would I ever go back to the Arxon? Would I ever want to? I sighed and ran my fingers through my hair. "We're going to need more supplies."

OOO

"We can't go into the town with our hair like this," said Petra, peering out at the homes that stood only twenty meters away. "They'll know we're from Lamond." She looked at Alf, and I could tell she thought he was handsome, too. "Well, you might get away with it. Your hair is longer."

I scratched my hair, curling now with sweat. We had walked for a couple of hours before stopping to sleep. Now the slant and color of the light had changed, hinting at a setting sun.

"What if someone sees us?" asked Petra.

"They send us back," said Alf. He stared at the buildings with a muddle of both anxiety and longing on his face.

I looked at the trees. It felt like we were in a big wooden holding cell with the door hanging open. Free, but not free.

"I smell smoke," said Alf.

I had slept a long time. "Smoke? Are you sure? Where would that be coming from?" I asked. On the Arxon, fire of any kind set sirens blaring and people running. Here, the stillness of the woods continued as if nothing was amiss.

Alf sniffed the air. "It smells like the bonfire they made last harvest when we burned all the duspy stalks."

"They started a fire *on purpose?*" squeaked Petra. "What's the matter with Surface people?"

Intrigued, I sniffed in a sweet, husky smell. "I'll go see if I can find it," I offered, torn between fear and curiosity. "It has to be nearby." I paused. "It can't consume all the oxygen, right? Because there's a world's worth of air?"

Alf shook his head. "On an ICS, you worry about the oxygen. Here, you worry about other things. Trees, buildings, people. Fire goes wild here."

I stood to go.

"Don't leave me with him," said Petra.

"Can I trust you not to kill her while I figure out where the smoke is?" I asked, heavy-lidded.

"I'll give you 'til the first star appears. Then I'm heading into town for food."

That was the best I could hope for. Staying inside the line of trees, I jogged towards the smoky aroma. A weighted shadow dropped from a branch above and landed in front of me.

The fanep! I swallowed a scream and held very still.

It signaled for me to be quiet and pointed in the direction I had been running. With an unmistakable gesture, it beckoned me to follow.

"Why should I follow you? You've slashed my arm and hit me over the head with a rock." It stared at me and waited. My hand went to both my arm and my head. Not a scratch or a bump. Did that mean officially no harm was done? "I guess you gave me reading materials and my comlink, too. So, you're not all bad." Gulping in courage, I lowered my stance, ready to run or fight.

The fanep made a chittering noise, like a baby's giggle.

"What in space…?"

Without coming closer, it gestured with such a pathetic expression that I felt myself laugh despite my terror. *Was this some kind of trick?* I felt a strong compulsion to go with it, so maybe I'd gone crazy. In a few hundred meters, we descended a slope into an open space between the trees.

"Well, look who it is!" came a woman's voice. "The girl from the ferry!"

OOO

10 KING'S CROWN

Less than an hour later, we Lamond inmates had joined the gypsies, Ninetta and Maddy around a campfire. Ninetta cooked food over small heat disks, but Maddy had also constructed a ring of rocks around a pile of small branches which he had set on fire. Bewildered and mesmerized, I stared at the flames and watched a dancing billow of smoke rise and replenish itself. Neither of the gypsies showed any concern about the size of the blaze, even though it would have been enough to set an entire deck on the Arxon into high alert.

Not far away, the fanep fiddled with a pile of leaves and sticks from the Rik trees. It was still too cunning and unpredictable to trust 100%, and it stared at me with an unnerving smile, like it could read my thoughts.

Alf and Petra had been willing to come with the promise of food and warmth, but now they huddled together, whispering.

"They don't seem to mind that you're an escaped violent offender, so why should you care if they're gypsies?" asked Alf.

"Do you forget who my parents are?" snapped Petra.

Alf snorted. "Parents of a delinquent, just like mine."

"I'm not—"

"We're outlaws now," he said. "No one can teach us better about how to live outside the law than the gypsies."

Petra stifled a sob, and I felt a surge of impatience. "What is your problem?" I hissed at her. "These people are nice, and they're sharing food."

Petra's eyes narrowed. "That man's a killer. He's got the tattoo."

"There's an A for 'acquitted' on it," I said, remembering my own fear on the ferry. "Quit looking down on them. They're good people. You can't tell me otherwise."

Alf knuckled his own cheek. "The rest of us should be that lucky—acknowledged for our innocence."

Our eyes met with understanding. "So you *weren't* trying."

He stared at the fire. "It doesn't matter anymore. Even my family believes I'm guilty."

Ninetta approached at that moment and offered him bread toasted from the fire. "It matters most what *you* think of yourself. Your actions will follow after," she said. "Other people will either love you or hate you. It's up to them."

Alf rolled his eyes, but I found the idea very liberating. I'd spent my life trying to live up to the expectations of others, wishing they'd give me the benefit of the doubt. The fact that their opinion of me was *their* choice was new to me. I don't know why, but it helped.

The fanep walked up to us slowly, like a kid playing at being an ambassador. It bent low and from behind its back, it brought forward a braided circle of the sticks and leaves.

"What's it doing?" I asked, leaning back.

"Some kind of game," said Ninetta. "I don't always know what he's up to."

The fanep gurgled and held the circle up to me, shaking it lightly.

"What's it *doing*?" I repeated.

Maddy glanced at Ninetta curiously. "He's made you a Levia crown."

The fanep chittered.

"A Levia...You mean like *Queen* Levia?"

Ninetta clapped her hands. "She knows her Surface history!"

"Only a little," I said, trying not to show the rush of pride I felt. "Wasn't she really smart?"

The fanep squeaked and hopped up onto my knees. I held still, except to curl and uncurl my toes. "What's it *doing*?" I whimpered through a plastered smile.

Alf snickered, "He's crowning you!" The fanep placed the crown of sticks and leaves on my head and pressed down.

"Ow!" I reached up to stop him. "I don't—"

"I wouldn't make him mad," said Alf. "Oh, too late. You're bleeding."

"I hate that little thing!" The fanep dodged my blow and pressed the leaves over the scratches almost tenderly before jumping back down to the ground.

"There now, all better," teased Alf.

I blotted the trickle of blood with my finger. *Every* day? I started to remove the crown.

"Ah-ah," warned Maddy. "I wouldn't take that off yet. That would be very disrespectful."

"*Disrespectful?* Do you have any idea how horrible this thing has been to me?" I muttered.

Ninetta patted the fanep's head. "What a nice gift you've made our guest." To me she winked and said, "Can you endure wearing it for now?"

The fanep grinned oddly at me, as if waiting for some response. I stared at it. "You are the strangest..." I sat taller. "Um. Thank you, Mr. Fanep, for your thoughtful gift. I've never had one of these before. It's ... really pretty." I made a face at Ninetta as if to ask, *Good enough?*

She shrugged a shoulder and checked the contents of a pot that had been burbling at the edge of the fire.

The fanep repeated the bow to me and moved a few meters away, sitting down and watching me. I guess I'd avoided offending it.

"His name is King, by the way," said Maddy.

"I've been crowned by a King," I quipped.

Ninetta chortled. "King does funny things, sometimes. He was by far the smartest fanep we encountered on Tye." She ladled vegetables and revos from a small pot into our mugs. "Eat. And then we'll come up with a plan for the three of you."

"How did the faneps become like pets?"

Ninetta pushed a leafy branch into the fire and it sent up a fountain of sparks before settling to burn more evenly. "Gypsies were the first to arrive in the system, but we were also the least inclined to settle in one place. The faneps had a quest to travel the three planets, so naturally, they took up with us as a way to get around."

Maddy shook his head sadly. "The irony is that space travel seemed to rob them of their mental faculties. They became like animals and lost the power of speech."

I shrank uncomfortably at the memory of my first encounter with King.

"It's too bad, really," said Maddy. "We could have learned so much from them."

"You've been to all three planets, haven't you?" I asked. "Didn't it—King—come, too?"

"He joined us on our last trip to Tye," said Ninetta. "We found him in a very large colony of faneps. When he saw Maddy diving for pearls, he swam down to him."

"How far down were you?" asked Alf, perking up.

"About thirty meters."

"Water that deep!" I relived my accidental dive with a coughing fit.

Ninetta smiled sympathetically. "Maddy's the best. Most gypsy divers only go half that. They can't hold their breath long enough, or endure the water pressure."

Maddy's gentle pride flickered with the firelight, and he resumed the original topic. "King found me down there by the oysters, and he's followed me ever since. Well, he did until you came along," he said without concern.

"Caz is prettier," said Alf matter-of-factly.

"Perhaps that's it," said Ninetta.

My cheek muscles twitched with a sudden joy. I'd never been called pretty in my whole life. Everyone called me the worst tomboy ever. But *Alf* said it!

"One never knows how much he understands," said Maddy.

I took a bite of toasted bread. "He seems like he *could* be intelligent, a little. He made this crown, after all."

The fanep's grin broadened so that his sharp teeth showed.

Alf pointed. "He understood that much, yeah?"

"He likes you," said Petra with a hint of Ora's sarcasm. "That's why he made you the queen of the camp. High honor."

"Well, the queen of the camp gets to haul water for washing up," said Maddy. "The stream runs by over there. Take this." He held up a large flexible, plastic sack that closed at the top with a sealable spigot.

"Only half full or it'll be too heavy," said Ninetta. "That's a big one."

I folded the sack over my arm and contemplated the darkness that had fallen everywhere but by the fire. Before I could think of an excuse, King appeared beside me.

"Follow him," said Maddy. "He'll keep you safe."

If he doesn't slice me open again, I thought.

King chittered and tugged at my pant leg.

Mimicking Alf's voice, I mumbled, "Don't make me kill you."

The fanep's mouth fell open as if laughing silently.

So much for intimidation.

No sooner had the sound of the camp voices faded than I heard the soft rush of water. The trees above parted to make way for the stream, and the moons lit the foaming current. King waded in a few steps. Though shallow like the first water I had found, this part of the stream moved much more swiftly. I fumbled with the sack and unscrewed the spigot. "All right, King, how do I do this? Don't tell me you don't talk because I've already heard you, you little beast."

King pulled the sack into the water and showed me.

"This water is clean?" I asked.

The fanep passed the sack to me and splashed some water on his face and arms. Then he rubbed his right shoulder and looked at me intently. I felt a knot in my stomach. I was bent low over the filling sack, and he touched my upper arm. Flinching, I said, "No you don't!"

But he didn't seem dangerous at all. His face became thoughtful, and his tiny hands wrapped around my arm gently. He placed his ear to the skin.

"What are you doing? That's not where my heart is."

"No one steals a Gypsy Pearl," said the fanep, its voice scarcely louder than a creaking branch. "Must be given."

I twisted my arm free. "I *didn't* steal the pearl. You shoved it into me, and it'll probably clog up my aorta or something, and I'll die." I screwed the spigot shut and wrapped my arms around the bulging sack as if holding a giant baby. As we walked, King danced around me in wide circles holding up three fingers on each hand.

"What are you doing now?" I asked, annoyed. But then I watched closer. His eyes glowed brightly, and his expression halted my steps. Again he held up three fingers, and then pointed up to the night sky.

I started walking again, thinking aloud. "Three? Three planets?" That seemed the most logical thing for him to talk about, given what Maddy and Ninetta had said. "You've been to two now, haven't you?" He made a happy sound, and I stopped at the edge of the clearing.

Maddy came up to me, his mouth hanging open with surprise. "How did you carry all that?" He took the full water sack from my arms, bending his legs to support the weight, and brought it over to where Ninetta stood ready to wash mugs.

I wiped my brow and felt the crown.

"Caz?" called Ninetta. "Are you all right?"

A completely random thought filled my mind. "Red Armored Oyster Pearls regenerate and strengthen cells, and Rik leaves are good for memory," I answered.

"Y-yes," said Ninetta. "That's true. Do you *need* some Rik leaf tea?"

I sat down right where I was and looked into King's eyes, all fear of him gone. "I don't think so," I said. King smiled at me, and I smiled back. "No, thank you, Ninetta. I'll be fine."

ooo

11 THREE WORLDS, THREE GIFTS, THREE POWERS

The air whispered of a fresh Surface morning, even though the darkness still slept around me. It took a moment to remember where I was. My mind swam with traces of dreams about every algebra, science, and economics lesson I had ever taken. I even remembered the strange sea creatures of Tye and the history of Caren's ruling empires. My head hurt as if I'd studied all through the night.

An unseen creature screeched, and I sat up. *I was alone!* Without the others nearby, I felt the forest's strangeness pricking my senses. Everything felt alive. The damp chill made my nose run, and I wiped it on my sleeve. I could feel the grubbiness in the cloth. A washroom and clean clothes would be welcome about now.

King appeared between the two nearest trees.

"Where is everyone?" I asked in a hoarse whisper, afraid that my voice would conjure more frightening company if overheard.

He turned on a ring light that emitted a soft green shaft, and waved me after him. Within a few minutes, we stood staring out at the dwellings I'd seen the night before. "Those are individual homes, aren't they?" I asked. "I guess there are no public washrooms in a Surface city." I rubbed my greasy hair. "My crown is gone," I said drily. "Have I been deposed?"

King shook his head and pointed to the sky. "Talk to stars."

"The stars? Is that a fanep thing?"

King scrambled up my leg in a way that had ceased to amaze me and delved his hand into my pocket. He pulled out the comlink. "Talk to stars." He jumped back down and stared up at the constellations with eagerness.

I considered the buttons. The Arxon might not be in range for a device this simple. Sitting down, I leaned against a tree and pulled my knees up to my chin. At last I switched it on, and the egg-shaped mechanism hummed to life. After adjusting the settings to locate Felly's comlink on the Arxon, I set it down on the ground and waited.

A minute passed, and I tried to swallow my disappointment. "I guess they're already out of—"

The comlink emitted a snapping sound, and a pale blue holographic image unfolded upward to form the life-size head and torso of Felly.

"Caz!" she exclaimed. "They told us you were dead!" Her face streamed with tears. "You're alive! This is amazing! Why is it so dark where you are? You look terrible, Caz."

Relief erupted as sarcasm. "I've been through a nightmare. What's *your* excuse?"

"I've been grieving," said Felly almost bitterly, her transparent blue elbows leaning closer. "What happened? They said you were attacked by faneps in the middle of an electrical storm, and—"

Felly shrieked as King positioned himself on my lap long enough to wave at her with both hands. Their two reactions surprised me so much that I rocked back with laughter.

"What is going on?" she demanded.

"I *was* attacked," I said, eying King. "It was terrifying, but I'm all right. Just really, really dirty."

"More than usual?"

"Much more than usual, Felly. Even *I* can smell me!" I held up my hands. "Real dirt, Felly. Surface dirt."

"Where are you?"

Oops. I didn't want to answer that yet. "How is Dad?" I asked instead.

"Emotionally destroyed! He's with Mr. Lew now, planning your memorial service."

"You think anyone will show up?" I asked heavily.

Felly's form shifted. "I need to go tell them you're alive—"

Now the dreaded tears came. "Thanks, Felly. I ... I love you, Felly."

Her eyes widened and then she broke into a sob, too. "And I love you, Caz."

"Sorry I never told you before."

"I won't hold it against you when you get back."

My whole being hesitated. "I don't know when I'll be back, Felly. Don't tell Dad I survived."

"What?!" I could tell she'd stopped moving. "But he's blaming himself for your death."

I steadied my trembling chin with my hand and pressed my lips together in thought. "I'll find a way to let him know before too long," I said. "But for right now, I don't want anyone following me."

"You *escaped*?" she cried.

"Not on purpose, Felly. I kind of went from one Nightmare to another." I laughed weakly at my own joke, but she frowned.

"Don't go off alone, Caz. You didn't want Solitary because you hate being alone. Go back to Lamond where you're safe."

"I'm not alone. That's the point," I said. "I need to find some friends I lost this morning." As soon as I said it, I realized I meant it.

"You're not making any sense."

"No," I agreed. "I'm not."

Felly inhaled and held it. "You have friends?"

I shared her wonder. "Yeah. I do."

The ghost-like Felly smiled. "Well, that's a start, I guess. It's better than gathering an audience or aggravating your elders. You'll come back reformed one way or another." Her face grew serious again. "But do come back, Caz. It's bad enough that mom went down to the Surface and never came back."

"Dad said she went voluntarily."

Felly's brows twisted with irony. "So did you."

I sighed. "I don't remember her," I said.

"Dad does. It hurts him that she left. Don't you hurt him, too."

She didn't say what we both knew: that I took after my mother, and that Dad had always held it against me.

"I'm not trying to hurt him," I said. "But don't tell him yet. Comfort him somehow, and I'll get word through. I don't know how yet, but it'll be soon."

"But—"

"I love you, Felly."

"Caz, you—"

"Save me some ice cream?" I pressed the control and broke the connection before I lost my nerve. Shuddering, I held the comlink to my lips, kissing Felly good-bye. I closed my eyes and let the tears fall for a long time.

When I raised my head again, King stood there holding the crown. I leaned on my elbows and regarded him. "Where'd you find it?" He gently placed the crown on my head. Too emotionally tired to object, I slumped back against the tree. He sat down with a solemn expression, and I felt the intensity of his gaze.

"What is it?" I asked.

He held up three fingers, claws retracted. With his raspy voice, he said quietly, "Worlds. Gifts. Powers." Again he held up three fingers.

I tried to make sense of the declaration, but couldn't.

He repeated the words, and each time, he held up three fingers. "Worlds. Gifts. Powers."

"Three Worlds, three Gifts, three Powers? Is that what you're trying to say?"

He beamed and pointed at me.

"Me? I don't know what you're trying to say. Three Worlds—Caren, Craggy and Tye?"

King gurgled encouragingly. He touched my right shoulder gently with one hand and held up a single finger on the other. "Gypsy Pearl Gift." Pointing to my crown, he held up two fingers. "Rik crown Gift."

"Two Gifts. You've given me two Gifts from two Worlds!" That was pretty amazing when I stopped to think about it, even though I couldn't exactly access the pearl to show it off to anyone.

King nodded vigorously and I felt like his eyes were reading the corners of my brain. He jumped to his feet in one move, crouching as if ready to leap. His hands moved excitedly from his arms to his head.

I stumbled through the words, guessing, "The Gypsy Pearl was a Gift from the World of Tye and it comes with a Power." My mind raced through the events of the last few days since the pearl had first touched my bloodstream. "It made me stronger!" King chittered, and I gained confidence. "The Rik leaf crown—*memory!*—from Caren. It made me smarter. Wait. I was already smart. But no, I definitely dreamed years' worth of memories in the night. Something mental has happened, besides the fact that I'm talking to you, I mean."

The fanep yelped joyfully and held both hands over his chest as if feeling his heart. Once again, he held up three fingers and croaked, "Worlds. Gifts. Powers."

"I need a Gift from Craggy, don't I?"

King pounded his chest with one hand and held up three fingers with the other.

"Chest? Lungs? Heart! Heart attacks. Earlie syrup from the timberline trees on Craggy! I can't believe I remembered that." I held my head in my hands, astonished. "Ninetta told me on the ferry. Is that the third Gift? Earlie syrup?"

The fanep spun in place and jiggled with obvious elation. I guess I had it right.

"So, where do I get the Earlie syrup? Do I have to go to Craggy?" I scanned the stars, trying to spot the silvery planet. "Maddy said it's a hard place full of hard people." A horrible thought occurred to me. "You gave me those things through my blood each time! The cut in my arm and the scratches on my head. Are you going to have to cut me open to pour in the Earlie syrup?" King squirmed nervously. "Never mind. I don't want to know." The scent of smoke caught my attention. "They're back!"

We hurried through the trees and soon found Maddy working over a newly lit fire. He smiled at me. "Oh good. You didn't wander away forever. Feeling better? You had a feverish night!"

Before I could answer, his eyes landed on King. Suddenly, his face darkened. "Where did you put them?" he demanded. "Have you sold them? Ninetta couldn't find it this morning." He moved toward King with a stick raised. "Where is the pearl and tube of powdered pearl?"

King cowered and pointed to me.

"What?!" I screeched. "I didn't take anything!"

Maddy tilted his head and eyed me suspiciously. "What do you know about the pearl?"

Unthinking, I blurted, "The fanep took the tube from Ninetta on the ferry when I almost drowned."

"And the pearl? The one we had saved aside?"

King stood as tall as he could and pointed again to me. This time he didn't cringe. His imperial demeanor unnerved both Maddy and me.

"Maddy, I need to tell you something about the fanep ... and the Gypsy Pearl."

OOO

After I told him everything, Maddy juggled his frustration with awe, fury, and child-like enthusiasm. "How could you—? This is amazing! What were you thinking? How does it feel? How *dare* you hide the fact that you could talk!" The unpleasant remarks were directed at King, but neither King nor I could keep from laughing. Finally, Maddy threw his hands in the air. "We can't tell anyone!"

"What? Why not?"

"Especially not Alf and Petra," he said. Maddy pulled his cheeks down with his fingers in exaggerated concern. "If word leaks out to the wrong people that a Gypsy Pearl is being cycled…"

"Cycled? What does that mean?"

He didn't answer. He buried his face in his hands, muttering things both thrilled and worried.

The fanep observed Maddy for a long minute, and then turned back to me. He pantomimed handing something to me with both hands. "Must be given." His voice grated like the morning chill.

Maddy and I watched reverently as King walked in a small circle three times, stopping at each rotation to speak a single word. First, "Worlds", then "Gifts", then "Powers." He held himself eerily still when he reached the last turn and repeated, "Must be given."

"Or it won't work," I said, knowing without knowing how I knew. "If people steal those gifts, they won't work."

OOO

12 FUGITIVES

"If you go back now," said Ninetta over breakfast, "Lamond authorities will be so happy you're alive, they'll probably forgive part of your sentences."

"How would they do that?" scoffed Alf.

"They can use express pods to get you back out to your ICS within a matter of weeks."

Petra squinted in thought. "I don't like the Surface. Everything's dirty." Though she bowed her head as she spoke, everyone saw the smirk she cast at King. "Do you really think they'll forgive my sentence if I go back?"

"You'll be a hero just for surviving," said Maddy.

"But if she goes back, she'll tell everyone about me," complained Alf.

"No, I won't!"

"Yes, you will. I'm not going back. I live on Caren, now." The sharpness of his voice soured the mood, and we sat like stones, listening to the breeze tell secrets in the leaves.

No one spoke or looked at each other for a long time. When buzzing insects lured the first swatting hand, Maddy broke the silence. "What about you, Caz?"

I shifted my gaze to King. *What if this thing with the Gypsy Pearl was real?* I didn't really know what it implied, but…"I'm not ready to go home," I said, standing and brushing myself off. "But I can walk you back, if you want, Petra. I remember the way."

OOO

Before the last morning mists had risen to the lowest branches, Petra and I had walked back through the forest over a kilometer in silence. Whirring in the back of my mind, past lessons about Caren's equator, its humidity and the frequent violent storms reminded me why I was supposed to hate the Surface.

But I couldn't. The birds gossiped back and forth overhead, and damp undergrowth squished under our feet. It was terrifyingly beautiful. When a lithe four-legged creature darted across our path, Petra screamed and then stood dry-heaving into her hands.

"Huff, Petra. What's the matter now?"

"I hate this place!" she screamed shrilly. "Everything is dirty and smelly and moving. I want to go home. *I hate the Surface!*"

"You'd rather live in a giant metal box?"

Petra wriggled her shoulders violently, as if trying to shake off the air around her. "How can you stand it here? We're all just waiting to get hurt, or sick … or killed."

I looked around with fresh eyes, admiring the way the morning slant of light changed the colors of the foliage. "I've seen scarier things than these trees."

"I suppose you think you *are* a scarier thing," said Petra bitterly.

"If you recall, when we first met, you were stealing my stuff while your friend shoved my face in the floor—"

Petra moaned and sank to the ground.

I swallowed and stepped closer. In a low voice, I spoke to Petra's shaking shoulders. "Huff, I'm sorry about Ora, but what kind of friend was she, anyway? One who took you away from your shiny little prison in the stars and taught you to be a bully? What good ever came to you through Ora?"

Petra spoke wearily. "I was alone."

"No one's alone on an ICS. You're always surrounded by the same dumb people every day of your life. You never get to be yourself because you always have to do what's expected. 'Small community, big responsibility. More people, more self-control.' Always the same lectures over and over."

I fell out of my tirade and stared into the space between the trees, smirking at myself. Ruffling my short hair comfortably, I said, "Some people need that kind of life, I guess. You must be one of them."

"So you're going to run off with Alf?" accused Petra.

I snorted. "I think we'll keep trying not to kill each other." We had reached the stream. As we approached the first rock for jumping across, I grabbed Petra's shoulder. "Please don't tell, Petra. Ora's dying wish was that you'd be brought home safe. I'm helping you do that. Please let me have my parting wish: a little freedom."

Petra said nothing, but eyed the current nervously.

A shiver of anxiety prompted my next words. "Promise," I ordered, "or I'll drown you now."

"No you won't," said Petra surely. "Ora's dying wish."

"Ora—"

"I promise," said Petra. "Now get me across this water."

OOO

"She really went back?" asked Alf.

"She really went back," I said.

Alf looked at me hard. "And you didn't."

Maddy and Ninetta smiled at each other, and Alf nodded.

"I was tempted, though, when I talked to Felly."

Alf seemed to grow larger with sudden rage. "You what?"

Ninetta and Maddy glanced up from their packing labors. "What's wrong?"

I backed away. "What? I comlinked to Felly." Pointing at King, I cried, "He told me to!"

"You idiot!" Alf flew at me swinging.

I dragged with fatigue, but I blocked a blow with one arm and thrust my palm into his rib cage. He coughed a round of curses at the pain, and looked up angrily. White terror seemed to grip his tongue, and we all spun around to follow his gaze.

Seven laser rifles hummed and pointed their long red fingers at the four of us. "Lamond security," announced a man's voice. "You're all under arrest."

As calmly as a mother tucking in her child, Ninetta addressed the officer who had spoken. "For this little scuffle? You know how brothers and sisters are. You're not seriously going to arrest a gypsy family for sleeping in the woods? Caren's laws in this territory permit it."

The first officer trained his weapon on me. "You from Lamond?"

Before I could think, a second officer stepped forward. "I don't think that's the right girl. She doesn't seem like a spacey."

"She's my daughter," said Maddy.

I followed his lead. "That's right. I'm a gypsy. Can't you tell?"

"Too pale for a gypsy. You haven't been in sunlight," said the officer.

My face flushed and I backed away, but another officer nudged me with the tip of his gun. "I don't know, sir. She seems pretty strong for a new spacey."

Alf breathed in ragged gasps. "She can beat you in hand-to-hand. That's no spacey weakling."

Unconvinced, the nearest officer moved to grab my arm. I bristled, but before I could lash back, King leaped onto my shoulder. The officer backed away. I patted King's back, and he curled into my arms like a baby.

"See?" I said. "I'm a gypsy."

Disgust registered on the faces of the officers, and they shifted their weapons a few degrees.

"What about the boy?" asked the second officer.

Alf watched them tensely. "I do migrant work with my Dad," he said with a strained voice, glancing at Maddy. When the guards turned to Maddy, Alf gulped in air, holding his side.

"He's dark enough for a gypsy. All the same," said the first officer, touching a comlink attached to a thick wrist band. "I need to call over—"

In a flash, King ripped the comlink from the officer's arm and disappeared into the branches above them. The officers shouted, and King replied with an eerie howl. My skin crawled from head to toe. Seconds later, the woods came alive with motion. Birds took flight, protesting the confusion and several faneps appeared, claws clicking. The ferocity of their snarls startled the security officers who pulled us into the field behind the houses. For a few seconds, I wondered which group presented the greater threat. In the chaos of limbs and lasers that followed, Maddy and I broke free and ran back to the cover of the forest, the faneps trailing after us.

Above the clamor, I could hear Ninetta's scolding voice. "Now look what you've done! My grandson is injured!"

We crouched low and watched the officers lead Alf and Ninetta into the town. Ninetta squabbled loudly. "My grandson needs a doctor!" The officers were clearly unnerved by what had happened. One fired off his laser rifle a few times, aiming recklessly behind him. The fanep swarm disappeared and only King stood by, tossing the officer's comlink back and forth in his hand.

Maddy sank to the ground. "King, you are a madman," he said appreciatively.

"Thanks for saving me, there," I said, gesturing to King. "I guess you owed me one or two."

"Give me the comlink, King," said Maddy. "I need to call Lamond." He winked at me. Activating the comlink, he held his hand over the display, thus blocking the transmission of his own face.

"Lamond," came a voice.

Ruddie!

"The inmates were not apprehended," said Maddy with a voice that mimicked the first officer. "The reports must have been mistaken."

"Actually, one of the inmates in question got back shortly after you left," said Ruddie. "Any sign of the other two? Or the creatures?"

"Ah. Yes. I mean, no. The inmates have not been found, but there were several of those *horrible* creatures." He rolled his eyes comically at me. "There was a carcass of some kind, quite gruesome. I couldn't tell if it was human. No skull. We fear the worst." Maddy chewed his lips closed and I pressed a laugh into the back of my hand.

A staticky pause followed, and Nightmare's voice came over the comlink. "What's wrong with the transmission?"

"We're hiding from the creatures, sir," said Maddy. "There were quite a few of them. We—"

"By all means," said Nightmare. "Shut off anything that would attract them. When they've moved on, search for signs of the bodies. We need some kind of confirmation to give the parents."

"Yes, sir," said Maddy.

"Can you give me your current position?" asked Nightmare.

I reached over and slammed my hand over Maddy's and the comlink, turning it off. "We've got to get out of here. Let's find Ninetta and Alf."

He combed his fingers through the thick, dark curls. "Hopefully no one recognizes Alf from the holocube reports." Maddy playfully poked my leg with the toe of his shoe. "We need to make you look more like a gypsy."

Hands on my hips, I said drolly, "What? I'm not dirty enough?"

Maddy rubbed at the stubble that all but obscured his tattoo. "Very funny. King, why don't you stay on Caz's shoulder? That'll stop people from staring at her."

King squeaked angrily, but obliged.

"That's pretty insulting, you know," I said. "I mean, he's got feelings. Just because he has terrifying claws doesn't mean he's a monster."

King gurgled.

"You *are* a gypsy," said Maddy fondly. "It's amazing how many people are afraid of faneps."

"After what we just experienced, I can see why. I'm just glad King's on our side."

King sat on my shoulders, his legs dangling and his hands gripping my hair. Maddy removed his shirt. "Here, put this over your coversuit. You know gypsies and their layered clothing."

He now wore only a thin open-chested shirt. "It'll keep the ladies' eyes off you. Women are more likely to recognize you from the holocube reports of the missing Lamond inmates."

"There were holocube reports?"

"Here in town, yes. The town officers always get alerted directly when an inmate leaves the grounds."

"We aren't exactly inconspicuous—you all bearded and bulging with muscles and me wearing a crown and a fanep. Or is that the point?"

Maddy walked casually, as if he'd passed this way every day of his life. "They will be so absorbed in what is *un*familiar that they won't recognize the faces that are." He pointed down the road. "Less than ten minutes in that direction, we'll come to a public house for travelers."

"You mean for drinking?" I asked, halting with concern. Intoxication of any kind was always punished severely on the Arxon. It's wasteful and irresponsible.

Maddy blinked slowly. "Yes, that, too." He caught my discomfort and slowed down. "I need to go inside and talk to a few contacts about how to get you out of the area."

"Won't people there know I'm from Lamond?"

"No. No one will believe you're a spacey with strength like that in your stride."

"Am I really that much stronger?"

"How many kilometers have you already gone today, and here you are keeping up with me? Yes, you are much stronger. Youth from an ICS droop by mid-day with the heat and the gravity. Their bodies can't recover fast enough."

A thought occurred to me. "This has to do with the pearl's regenerative properties."

King gurgled.

"There's your answer," said Maddy, waving to three women who stopped and stared at him. They blushed and hid their eyes, embarrassed. "See? Give them something to look at, and they'll look away." I couldn't decide if he was being conceited or clever, but either way, it made me laugh. As we neared the public house, however, Maddy nudged me. "Be on guard. These people will be watching strangers more carefully. Try to be nondescript."

"With a fanep and a crown?"

Maddy smirked. "Why don't you wait in the alley?"

"Alley?"

"The hallway between the buildings. I'll be out soon." I must have seemed worried because he punched my arm playfully. "What? You can take care of yourself that long, can't you?" He entered the public house. After a few minutes, I began to pace nervously and had almost decided to enter the building when Maddy reappeared carrying a metal box. He shouted pleasantries and promises to return over his shoulder and then jerked his chin for me to follow him. When we had gone a few hundred meters, he whispered, "Change of plans. We need to head north right away. It seems your little friend didn't keep her secret."

"How do you know?"

"Lamond guards never come into town until after hours, but they were in there. They're searching for you and Alf again—alive."

"What about Ninetta and Alf?"

"They'll be safe. I have a contact in there who'll get them out once Alf is tended. We'll need him at full strength for what lies ahead."

"What do you mean, 'what lies ahead'? What are you talking about?"

He stopped, his eyes flitting up to King and back to mine. "Do you want to get to Craggy, or do you want to stay here on Caren, like Alf?"

The air in my lungs chilled. "I don't know." Suddenly, I felt extremely vulnerable. I didn't know anything about local culture or how to get around. I needed Maddy and Ninetta. "I'll go wherever you go," I said, ashamed of the weakness in my voice.

"Do you want the third Gift?"

King chittered. "Must be given."

"Right. I can't take it, so he has to come with me. Or, I mean, I have to go with King."

"We need to stay together," said Maddy, calming me with a pat on the shoulder.

"If there isn't any Earlie syrup here on Caren, I guess we'll have to go to Craggy. Won't we?"

"Maybe. Maybe not. But north is where we will find either the syrup, or the way off the planet. Both are pretty rare. Let's go."

A whining hum rounded the corner coming from a vehicle marked with the Lamond Reformatory logo. Maddy backed into me, pressing my face into the wall of the building beside us. "We need to move faster."

Maddy and I walked swiftly, twisting and turning through the narrow streets. It felt like a childhood game of Chase the Comet, but without the fun. At last, we ducked into a doorway where a man dozed standing up. Maddy passed him something with a smooth shake of the hand. The man sniffed, but did not open his eyes. "The blue one. 50 kilometers max."

We located a small, oblong vehicle, like the carts in the loading bay on the Arxon, but more rounded. It had two seats, one in front of the other, and no walls or ceiling to enclose the passengers. He tossed the metal box on the back seat. "Sit on top of that and hold on. King, I need you to go back and make sure Ninetta and Alf get free."

"Wait!" I protested. "Now he's left behind, too? Don't I need him?"

"He can find you," said Maddy quietly. "He'll always be able to find you."

A chilly twinge of terror scraped the back of my neck at that thought, but then King smiled at me, and his face told me I had nothing to fear.

OOO

13 THE SKIMMER

Five minutes later, Maddy and I were several kilometers north of town and heading into a range of steep mountains. I clung to the back of Maddy's seat with the last of my sanity streaming from my eyes with tears in the wind.

"Slow down!" I cried.

"We're fine!" called Maddy. "You went faster than this in the Arxon all the time."

"There's no friction in space." This thing negotiated each bump with hostility. It couldn't be good for my internal organs. They were in revolt and heading up my esophagus.

Ahead of us, a great black tunnel yawned open in the mountain face, and the road disappeared into it like a concrete tongue. I stared up, amazed that the little ridges I saw from space could be so incredibly huge in person.

"Are we going in there?" I cried through clenched teeth, holding my crown to my head with one hand. I didn't want to be buried under something larger than the Arxon.

Maddy only laughed, flipped a small switch, and veered right, slowing down enough to avoid crashing into the rock face. "Better?" he asked.

The ride was much smoother now despite having left the road. Then my stomach lurched. "Are we *flying?*"

"Skimming," corrected Maddy. "This is a skimmer."

I squeezed my eyes shut and rested them on my white, numb knuckles. At least the shaking had stopped. The skimmer slowed, tilting at an upward angle, and my grip switched to keep myself from falling backwards. The air changed around us, growing cool and damp. I ventured a peek and sighed in wonder.

Maddy had found a long, sloping stream of water that tumbled down the mountainside in lazy leaps. Its path between the trees, wide enough for the skimmer, wound back and forth as it climbed. About half way up the mountain slope, Maddy touched the skimmer down on level ground next to a dark span of water. With the rush of air no longer deafening me, I paused to admire the serenity. The water itself nestled against a jagged, rocky wall that stretched straight up.

"This is where we get out."

"You can't be serious. We have to climb that?"

"We're not going that way," he said with a glimmer of humor. He pointed to the water. "We're going that way. Under that wall of rock is the spring of this stream and a secret place that only the gypsies know."

"A hiding place?"

"We'll wait in there for Ninetta and Alf. There are supplies and a place to rest. It's a cave."

"In there?" I stared at Maddy. "*In* the rock?"

"That's what caves are. Rooms under a wall of rock."

"Which is under the water." I took a step back. "I am not doing that again!"

"Gypsies are divers," said Maddy. "It's only about three meters deep—"

"Three meters!" I squeaked.

"You're scaring the birds."

"You're scaring *me*," I said.

"It'll be easy. With your strength, you'll be able to swim down to the bottom—"

"The bottom? Swim?" I threw my hands in the air. "I may be stronger than the average ICS dweller, but there are no rivers on space stations, you know. I don't know how to swim."

Maddy grinned. "Perhaps 'swim' is the wrong word. What you really need to do is sink."

I exhaled a few words that would have gotten me in trouble on the Arxon and squatted down, hugging my knees. "I've already tried sinking once. Almost killed me, remember? I'm not going in there. I'll sleep in the skimmer."

"No, I'll have to skim it back down to the base of the waterfall and hide it for Ninetta and Alf to use."

"But—"

"Neither of them is going to have the physical strength to climb this mountain. They'll need the skimmer."

I groaned. "Can't we make a camp out here?"

"Can't risk a campfire being seen. You're a wanted woman, you know."

I covered my face with my hands wearily. *How did I get into all of this?* Scratching the back of my neck, I stared at the water and thought. A couple of minutes passed in silence, except for the pounding of my heart and the prattle of the newly discovered water phobias in my brain.

"The water will feel cool. Like a fresh bath," he coaxed.

I half whined, half grunted. "You're going to leave me in there while you take the skimmer back down and then climb up? How long will that take?"

"I'll be back by nightfall," said Maddy.

"Which means nothing to me inside a mountain."

Maddy chuckled. "Trust me, Caz. I'll keep you safe."

"Why? Why do you even care what happens to me?" It came out more defensively than I meant it, but the sentiment was real.

Maddy rubbed his chin thoughtfully. "King gave you a crown. That means something. He placed a valuable pearl in your bloodstream. That means something, too. I want to see the end of this. I've been around faneps all my life, but this is new. Something big will come of this. Something bigger than any of us by ourselves."

"Something good?" I asked skeptically.

"We won't know until you drink the Earlie syrup."

I snorted. "Oh, King won't let me *drink* it. He'll slice me open and slather it on my liver or something."

Maddy laughed. "You're afraid of this pool of water, but not King cutting you open?"

Unable to argue that point, I stood. "Show me what to do," I groaned.

Maddy retrieved his heavy metal box from the skimmer and waded into the water. "Come on. Follow me."

I stepped into the water and shivered at a stinging pain that assaulted every nerve now under water. "You said 'cool', not freezing."

"You'll be numb in a minute," he said pleasantly. "It's waist-deep, and then it drops off a little before the wall."

"Well, that's not too bad—whoah, that's c-cold—if I get to w-walk most of the way," I said, inching in with rapid breaths that failed to relieve the cold.

"About three meters before the wall, I'll hand you the box. That should weigh you down to the bottom. Hold your breath—"

"What? How long?"

"Twenty seconds at the most."

I did a test run, holding my breath until Maddy wriggled his eyebrows at me and I exhaled with a laugh. "Won't the box hold me down forever?"

"No, because you'll put it down so you can rise again. Make sure that when you come up, you push forward so that you're at an angle to go under the wall."

"What if I hit my head on the rock?"

"Don't. That'll hurt." When I glared at him, he added, "Keep your hands above you."

"This is suicide," I said miserably.

"No, it just feels like it," he said. Maddy patted my shoulder. "You said you were a gypsy. Now prove it. Come on!"

I growled in protest, but waded further into the chilling water, feeling my skin erupt in new layers of goose bumps with each step. Even through the shoes, I could tell the bottom was slick. I held my arms above the surface, not ready to surrender my last warm limbs. Maddy, however, kept splashing the water on his arms and chest with his free hand while holding onto the metal box with the other.

"Ready for this?" he asked, handing me the box.

The weight of it pulled my arms down so far my chin splashed. "Haven't you ever heard of polynthex?" I spat. "It's lighter."

"But then it wouldn't pull you to the bottom," he grinned.

Adjusting the load, I stood tall again, but did not lift the box out of the water. "I take it this is sealed tight."

"Very," said Maddy. "The ground is changing soon. Take a deep breath and—"

My foot slipped and I plunged underwater, narrowly missing smacking my skull on the ledge I'd just gone over. The surprise left my eyes and mouth open. My feet touched down on an uneven surface, and a second later, my burning lungs urged me to kick upward. But the heaviness of the box and the pressure of moving water held me down. *Moving water?* In panic, I screamed into the murkiness and saw bubbles rise. Above, a dim blue glow beckoned. My ears hurt and I needed air. Dropping the metal box, I kicked again, remembering to keep my hands above me so I wouldn't hit the wall of rock with my head. Something obscured the blue glow from view, and I grappled with slimy rock back and forth before finding a way up. I broke the surface, coughing and crying.

I had missed passing under the wall and clung now to a tiny outcropping. If I let go, I would sink into the deepest part of the pool where the water churned like blood in the mountain's heart. Breathless, I called out, "Maddy! Help!" but he was nowhere in sight. I steadied myself and found another handhold, but the cold robbed my fingers of strength. "Maddy!" I peered into the water beyond my feet and saw a faint blue line of light. That had to mark the bottom of the wall and the entrance to the cave, didn't it?

Taking a deep breath, I shoved downwards against the rock. I dropped quickly, brushing the rock with my fingers on the way down until it stopped and the water before me brightened. I rolled over in the water to crawl on the rock upside down, like the insects on the duspy leaves, until I reached the other side. Using the bottom of the wall as leverage, I launched myself to the other side, arms outstretched.

Again, I felt the water push me back. A galaxy of bubbles spun around me, and I lost all sense of direction. My back slammed against something hard, knocking the last of the breath from my lungs, and I started to black out…

ooo

14   THE WRAP

"You got caught in the current of the spring," said Maddy. "There, now you'll be all right." He stroked my back. "I'm sorry. I forgot about that. Gypsy divers don't even notice." Strong emotion colored his voice, and I knew he'd felt a measure of my panic.

I lay on my stomach with my legs still dangling in the water. "Why is it so blue?" I leaned up on my elbows and pulled myself onto a stony platform. On all fours, I repeated, "Why is everything blue?"

"What? No thanks for saving you?" he laughed weakly.

I relented and threw my arms around him in gratitude. He hugged me back for a long minute and I tried to blink away the blue that covered everything like a film of stardust. Nothing helped, so I let go and took inventory of my condition. "I lost a shoe. *Why is everything blue?*"

"I'll be right back," said Maddy. He jumped feet first into the water, making almost no splash.

"Wait! Don't leave!" I let out a shrill wail and stood up, staring into the dark water.

Maddy surfaced holding the metal box. "Quick! Take it," he grunted.

I kneeled and picked it up from his hands. He immediately slipped underwater again. "Maddy!" I shouted. "I will drop this on your head if—"

He appeared again and pulled himself out of the water easily, my missing shoe between his teeth.

"How did you find that?"

He grinned. "I'm a gypsy diver from Tye. I dive for tiny little pearls. A shoe is easy."

I took the shoe and hit him playfully on the back. "Well, you get a thanks for that."

"Good," he said. Maddy spread his hands wide. "What do you think?"

"It's very blue. You want to tell me about that?"

"It's the etak crystals," said Maddy. "They're actually indigenous to Tye, but have been brought and grown on the other planets by gypsies."

"Growing crystals?" I examined the walls and ceiling. It looked like someone had taken piles of hexagonal plexiglass tubes and crammed them into the black mountain rock in random places, filling most of what I thought of as the ceiling and upper walls. Each crystal emitted a soft blue light so that the overall ambience had a hazy glow.

"What holds them up?" I asked, sizing up one and realizing it was almost as big as Maddy.

"Like I said, it grows from the rock. It has roots."

"It's pretty, but I can't help thinking one of those big pieces is going to slide out of its place and shatter."

"No, it holds. It's like coral, but it produces its own light."

"Is blue the only color option?"

"Yes."

"So there's no electricity in here?"

"No, but the crystals can draw the tiniest bit of light from the water and magnify it."

"Like refracted chemoluminescence?" *Where did* that *come from?*

Maddy gawked and then laughed deeply. "That would be the Rik leaves talking, and I'll take their word for it."

My hand went absently to my forehead. "I lost my crown again." I moved closer to the wall, measuring the space with my eyes. "Is there a fresh air source?"

"Yes, there are at least two small air shafts that I've found. You'll notice when it rains because they drip."

"Over there," I said, pointing to a worn circle of rock that slanted into the water.

"Yes," said Maddy. "All right, Caz. You're plenty intelligent enough for me to leave you alone."

"Wait, what?"

"I'll only be gone a few hours. Eight at the most, if all goes well." He unlocked the metal box with a few quick spins of a dial. "There's a heat disc in here, and some space food." He made an apologetic grimace. "Sorry. It's easier to pack."

I shrugged. "It'll taste like home."

"It won't get cold in here, so you should be comfortable enough." He walked to a dark patch in the wall that proved to be an opening to a smaller cave. "That's where we stow blankets and some other comforts. We've got clothes, food, gadgets, lights—not that we need them in here. They're out of sight in case someone ever comes in here accidentally."

"Right. All the divers in the area."

"Surface kids camping for fun."

"Surface kids are crazy."

"You're a Surface kid now," said Maddy. "At least until we get off-planet."

"I do want to see another planet, but one thing at a time. Let's get Ninetta and Alf."

Sighing, he said, "Eight or nine hours at the most."

"And if you don't come back?"

"I'll come back."

"And if you don't?"

"Wait two days and make your way—no. I'll be back."

OOO

I rolled over and pulled the blanket around me more for comfort than warmth. The only way to survive the next eight hours—or two days—was to sleep through as much of it as possible. I was certainly tired enough. The gypsies had stored sufficient gear and dried food in the smaller room of the cave to care for a hundred men. Since it was more comfortable and darker in there, I tried to nap, but I kept hearing movement. Whispers and clicks. At last I pulled the blanket over my head, and willed myself to count backwards from a thousand. Before I reached the eight-hundreds, my breathing slowed and hints of dreams filtered into my subconscious.

Tall trees, limbless for the first several meters, reached straight up with forbidding force. I climbed the trunks with long talons that sprung from my fingertips. Just as I reached the first, prickly branches, my claws became wedged in the wood, and I could not pull free. Something golden oozed from the bark and dribbled over my fingers and wrists. I squirmed and broke free, only to fall through the air in slow motion. But it wasn't air. It was water, and I could not breathe. A pale circle of light above me shrank as I plunged deeper into darkness. Silent screams escaped me, and I reached upwards even while falling back. The circle disappeared into a pinpoint of white light which then fell through the blackness into my palm. A pearl.

I peeked out from the blanket. Hundreds of glowing eyes looked down at me, like stars, winking in and out, but remaining constant in their positions. The whispers made no sense, and it felt too surreal to frighten me, until very close to my head, a row of glinting sharp teeth appeared. I screamed, and all the eyes disappeared in a clatter of sound.

Fully awake now, I tried to determine if it had been a nightmare or reality. I lay still, listening intently. No eyes appeared. No other sounds came through to my hiding place, so I shuddered away the fragments of the vision. *Just a dream.*

Wrapping the blanket over my shoulders, I crawled out of the space and into the blue light of the main cavern. It felt larger now, and eerie in its silence. Except that a steady flow of drops fell from the air shaft above, landing in the hollowed rock puddle and sliding into the pool.

I sighed and made my way to this source of fresh water, drinking from cupped hands and washing the sleep and fear from my eyes. I leaned back on my bent knees only mildly surprised to see King standing at the water's edge.

"I'm not dreaming any more, am I?" I asked.

King smiled at me with mysterious eyes. His gaze flickered over to the space where I'd been sleeping. He didn't answer but dashed to the hiding place in a blur of motion. When he emerged, he wore a new coversuit made of a soft blue-green fabric that seemed to shift and sparkle as he moved. It reminded me of ocean water.

"Nice outfit," I said.

King disappeared into the inner cave again and returned with a bundle of cloth and a small silver tube. This he held up to me.

Uncapping it, I sniffed its contents. "For cleaning?"

He nodded and made a great show of turning around and covering his eyes. I laughed. "Thanks for the privacy consideration, but I'm used to community washrooms." Even so, I sat at the water's edge and undressed, checking over my shoulder to see King holding his stance.

I braced myself for the cold water, but found that the soap had a warming effect that counteracted the chill. It also soothed the abrasions I'd somehow acquired on my arms.

"No chance that was Earlie syrup? It just entered my blood stream."

King chittered and shook his head, but did not turn around.

"No, of course not. That would've been too easy." Feeling clean and sweet-smelling, I unfolded the cloth to get dressed. It was like the bottom half of a coversuit without the feet, but it had two ridiculously long, wide strips of cloth. I put on the part I understood and held the rest in front of me with one arm. "King? Help, please?"

The fanep averted his eyes as he approached me with outstretched hands. I handed him the remaining strips of cloth. Gingerly, he poked my arms with a finger so that I would raise them. With formal care, he wrapped my shoulders and torso, leaving the lower half of my arms bare. The end result resembled an elegant blouse and leggings instead of a drab old coversuit.

"This will follow Maddy's advice of staying inconspicuous." I ran my fingers through my freshly washed hair. "Get me another crown and a big white blouse, and I'll look a little like Queen Levia in her leggings." I rolled my eyes. "La la la. All those L's. Look a little like, Levia—*Levia!*" I stopped and dropped to my hands and knees beside King. "Queen Levia was known for her wisdom, and she had a crown like the one you made me. Did she have a pearl, too?"

King sat down, his legs folded and his face serene. "A Cycled Pearl."

"Not a Gypsy Pearl?"

"Cycled touches Worlds."

I tilted my head in thought. "Levia had been to all three planets?"

"*Queen* Levia cycled," corrected the fanep.

"All right." I still didn't completely understand.

"Pearl has Power."

"But I'm not good and wise like Levia. I cause trouble wherever I go. Look at me."

King did look at me, but with confidence shining in his eyes in a way no human had ever looked at me. "Queen will know," he said.

"That doesn't make any sense. Which queen?"

King closed his eyes. "Queen will know."

OOO

Ninetta and Alf came up through the pool of water and pulled themselves onto the platform. A moment later, Maddy surfaced and shook the water from his hair. He caught sight of me. "Where did you get that?"

"Get what?"

"That—those clothes. Where did—?"

King jumped between us and held his hands up. Maddy's gaze fell to the fanep, and he saw the changed suit on the creature, too.

Maddy's jaw went slack. "Oh."

I glanced down at my blue-wrapped body and wiped my hands self-consciously. "What, 'oh'?"

Ninetta, who had just pulled herself to her feet, lowered herself slowly back down to her knees, staring. She looked at King and then back at me. I couldn't read her expression, but it was like a happy version of shock. She tugged at Alf's sleeve, trying to pull him back down.

He did not oblige. "What's going on?" he asked.

"Get down," she said. "She has on the ceremonial wrap. She has been chosen."

Alf waved a hand vaguely. "What, the blue?" He cocked an eyebrow at me. "You look like something from the Gwillon System."

I was inclined to agree, but then Maddy knelt and nodded his head slowly.

"Are you *bowing* to her?" asked Alf.

"A fanep has chosen a queen," said Maddy solemnly.

"Yeah, we all saw the crown," said Alf, his fingers wiggling in mock praise. "Who cares what the rat man thinks?"

Maddy's leg swung out from under him in a wide arc, catching Alf on the back of his knees so that he fell forward hard on the stone.

"A fanep has chosen a queen," repeated Maddy.

My focus turned to Alf, who grimaced with fresh pain. "Did you get help, Alf? Did they recognize you?"

"No. They filled me with pain medications and sealants to heal my punctured lung—"

"Oh!" I covered my mouth.

"The rib just has to heal."

"The guards did all that?"

Alf laughed derisively. "They barely touched me. *You* did this to me."

Tears sprang to my eyes and I dropped to hug him. "I'm so sorry, Alf. I didn't mean to."

"Don't get me all wet, yeah?" he said, gently pushing me away.

I slapped at his dripping clothes and spluttered with nervous laughter, then looked around at the others in the room. "Why are you kneeling?"

"My lady," said Ninetta, rising stiffly.

"'My lady'?" echoed Alf sarcastically.

"If my lady will make herself comfortable," said Maddy, "I think we ought to explain some things about what has just happened." His whole demeanor had changed.

"Yes, 'I think we ought'," I said, copying his tone.

Maddy's smile returned. "Yes, my lady."

Ninetta ushered Alf towards the storage place. "Come, let's get some dry clothes on you."

"I don't want anything like that," he said, thumbing the air towards me.

"Not to worry," said Ninetta mildly. "There is only one of those." They ducked into the small space and their voices faded.

I gestured a question at Maddy who sighed. King sat beside me and placed his tiny hand on my thigh protectively.

"My lady," began Maddy.

"Caz. *Not* 'my lady'. That's ambassador protocol."

Maddy paused, searching for the words. "What King has done, dressing you in this way, is not by chance. This is ceremonial clothing, and there are garments like this in most of the gypsy hideouts, but they have been largely forgotten." King chittered as if to urge Maddy to continue. "I don't profess to understand much about the fanep traditions, but as you know, they involve the connection between the three planets in the system."

"Right. "Three Worlds, three Gifts, three Powers."

"Yes. What I know of Queen Levia, and the few who went before her, is that they were given a pearl from Tye which was then cycled through the planets."

"Cycled," I repeated, still trying to grasp the concept. "Why have I never heard of any of this until I came to Caren?"

"It's the stuff of legends and myths," said Maddy. "In an age of science—especially on an ICS—I imagine they do not devote time to anything mystic or…magical."

"Magical," I said flatly.

"What else would you call your sudden strength and intellect? The pearl inside of you came from Tye and is now on Caren, where it has come into contact with the Rik leaves in your bloodstream."

"Through the crown."

"Yes, my lady."

I nudged King. "Why couldn't I just drink the powdered pearl?"

King shook his head vigorously. "Only in blood!"

"Can I drink the Earlie syrup?"

"Queen must not!" shrieked King, agitated.

"All right, it's bad for me to *ingest* the Gift ingredients," I said. "So, can we just find some Earlie syrup and inject it?"

King held up three fingers. "Cycle three Worlds."

"I have to go to Craggy and Tye, too?" Something from my recent studies bothered me. "Queen Levia never made it back to Tye. She was assassinated, according to Caren Surface history." I held my breath while mulling over this fact. "This feels like a very dangerous quest, politically. Queens with Cycled Pearls don't have a high life expectancy, apparently. Especially if they are connected to gypsies and faneps."

"True," admitted Maddy without taking offense. "It would be good to keep this cycling—and your status as a chosen queen—a secret until the process is complete."

I rested my head in my hands, massaging my scalp, wishing this wasn't all so complicated.

Ninetta and Alf entered and I looked up, grateful for a change of subject. "You make a good gypsy," I said, aware of the heat rising in my cheeks. The clothes totally transformed Alf, making the rough edges proud. He wore the loose clasped shirt of a laboring gypsy. Short leather boots blended into the leather leggings smoothly, creating an illusion of increased height.

"What would you like to do next, my lady?" asked Maddy.

I wriggled the tension from my limbs with a sudden burst of energy and groaned. "Don't you see how inside-out my whole life is right now?" My nerves crumbled with emotion. "A few days ago, I was making jokes in Mr. Virgil's class. My biggest complaint was not enough dessert. I was bored. Everything irritated me. I wanted out." Slumping, I hugged my knees and waited for someone to say something, but they all continued to watch me. "I'm just trying to survive life on the Surface, and now he—King—crowns me and wraps me in some ceremonial blue ribbon and you start bowing. Can't you see this is all very overwhelming?"

They murmured sympathetically, but it didn't help.

"Only Felly knows I'm alive," I said. "Or I guess everybody at Lamond does now, but if anyone catches me and sends me back, then I can't go on with this crazy quest to cycle a pearl so I can ..." My voice faded with misery. "Why am *I* in the middle of all of this? I'm just a kid! How am I supposed to know what to do?" Too drained of reason to deal with a single thing more, I only knew I couldn't do this alone, no matter how smart the Rik leaves made me. "Why me?" I asked weakly. "Why does everything happen to me?"

No one spoke for a long time. At last, I felt someone crouch beside me and put an arm around me. "We all feel that way sometimes." It was Alf. "But in your case, it's truer than most, yeah?"

I laughed weakly and leaned on his shoulder. "Yeah. Is there a chance the pearl or the Rik leaves are making me crazy?"

Ninetta chuckled. "Your mind has been strengthened, my lady. Not twisted."

"I had a dream that I climbed up a tall tree and goo—it must be Earlie syrup—ran down my arm. Then I fell through water, but I didn't drown."

"Were there faneps in your dream?" she asked.

"I thought there were eyes all around me."

"Hm," she said. She pointed up to a protruding shard of crystal, the largest one in the cave. "Did they look like that?"

That particular crystal sank into a patch of wall covered with the same glassy blue etak, but the surface was much smoother. From within the wall's shine glowed two eyes. I sat up with a sharp intake of breath. "Is that—?"

Ninetta spoke softly. "We think they are the eyes of faneps far away. Captives."

"Captives?"

"The eyes are always *behind* the crystals. We use crystals much the way holocubes are used. They can show us things."

It sounded too 'magical' to be real, and yet... "They definitely look like fanep eyes." I stood under where it grew at a sharp angle with its point hanging about a meter above my reach. Jiggling my ankles to loosen them, I focused on the shard. "Do you think it'd support my weight?"

"What are you thinking, my lady?"

I didn't answer because I guess I wasn't *thinking*. I was reacting to something inside of me that urged me to make contact with the eyes. Crouching low, I jumped straight up, reaching with my hands to grasp either side of the shard. With no holes or ridges to dig into, I swung my body until my legs wrapped around the crystal.

"My lady!" yelped Ninetta. Maddy, Alf and King awoke from their naps with a start and quickly gathered beneath me.

"Be careful!"

"Hold on!"

"We'll catch you!"

I hung upside down. "I'm all right," I grunted. With a few writhing moves, I maneuvered myself to sit atop the shard, my head now near where the crystal disappeared into the cave's glossy wall. The eyes within the wall blinked, and I placed my fingers where I imagined the fanep's cheeks might be. "Are you in there?" I whispered. "Are you trapped?" Another pair of eyes appeared, and another. All around me, bright eyes watched me, as if waiting.

I waited, too.

King stood inside the range of my peripheral vision and howled as he had in the woods. His cry echoed mournfully through the cave, and a clicking noise from within the crystal vibrated. It grew louder until I could feel the shard beneath me shaking with the sound. King was calling to them somehow, trying to tell them something. *But what?*

"Caz, be careful!" cried Alf.

The shard shifted, and I slid back a little. The eyes seemed to crowd against the wall even closer. I could see no faces, only the eyes. My hands reached to the wall and pressed against the eyes. *How do I help you?* I wondered. *Are you there in the rock? Or somewhere else?*

The shard broke and fell to the ground, shattering between Alf and Maddy, but I remained as if it still held in place. My body hung in mid-air, and I felt no fear. Only my hands still touched the crystal wall. At the point of contact, the eyes flowed closer together and disappeared in a growing white circle of light. When the last one faded, I felt a loss within me.

A deafening explosion shook the cave. All over the wall, the cracks between the crystals widened and split, and those on the side that marked the barrier to the outside rattled apart. Chunks of glowing blue splashed into the pool, filling it so much that the water spilled up onto the stony floor of the cavern. The cave rumbled to stillness again, now filled with dusty sunlight that poured in where the wall had once been.

I drifted downward like a bubble and landed beside them, dazed, but smiling.

"What just happened?" demanded Alf, shaking his legs free from the knee-deep rubble.

"I don't know." said Maddy, helping Ninetta up from a cowering crouch.

I turned slowly to face them all, my face warm with an exertion beyond my understanding. But I did understand one thing: the Cycled Pearl would help the faneps. It would restore them, free them somehow. I scratched my scalp, trying to locate the source of my sure knowledge. I don't know how I knew, but it was no longer just about me being a queen or obtaining some third Power.

I had to help the faneps.

ooo

15   THE VIPER AND THE PYRE

"Do you need help, my lady?" called Maddy from several meters above.

"I'll be all right," I said. I wore a heavy traveling pack strapped to my shoulders, as did Maddy and Ninetta. We had salvaged as much as we could from the cave, and now were making our way up the mountain on foot. Maddy had apologized for loading me up so much, but I really didn't mind. My legs, although thrumming with the effort, loved this mountain.

"Speak for yourself," said Alf, wincing. He alone did not carry anything because of his ribs. "Not all of us can defy gravity."

"Are you hurting?" I asked, feeling guilty.

"I'm fine," he groaned, crawling up to sit beside me. Some of the smaller rocks slipped away beneath his knee and he jerked forward. A string of angry words poured down with the rocks.

"Wish we were all as fine as you are," I said.

"Shut up, Caz," he grumbled. "My lady," he added with mock formality.

"Don't *you* start," I groused. "Now keep moving, or get out of my way. I don't trust this ledge to stay here much longer."

With a sustained yell, Alf propelled himself forward on his hands and knees, reaching a solid patch of stone.

I leaned into the rock face laughing and coughing at the dust he had kicked up. "Are you trying to start another landslide, idiot?"

"Come here and call me that," he said, rising cautiously to his feet and glancing back with a grimace of pain.

"Alf, are you going to be able to do this?"

"I'm already doing it."

"Don't be proud," I said. We locked eyes with a hard stare that softened into a smile. "I need a friend, Alf. Maddy and Ninetta have … I don't know."

"Then leave them," he said.

"You know I can't do that. I don't know my way around or how to get to Craggy."

Alf rolled his eyes. "You're the smart superhuman one."

"Please," I said. "They've been really nice so far. I like them, and … I need them. They're the closest thing to a family I have right now. But I also need you—to be my friend."

He ran a hand through his hair. "Yeah."

"Yeah?"

"I said 'yeah'."

"Good. Now keep moving or get out of my way," I teased.

We quickly reached the adults.

"Where's the rat man?" asked Alf.

I slapped his arm with the back of my hand.

Maddy pointed. "He went to scout the easiest trail. We need cover from the sun and searching eyes, so we need to get under that brush."

I looked at Maddy, taking in his stubble-covered tattoo and the weary lines on his face. "If this whole queen thing is real, and I really do get any authority, gypsies won't have to hide any more. They won't be outlaws. You should be free to move around. Some people need that."

Both Maddy and Ninetta exchanged the kind of suppressed grins that normally made me crazy, but it felt different coming from them. They weren't making fun of me.

A nearby bush rustled, and King crept into view, his blue garb far more noticeable than his former camouflaged attire. He stopped in front of me and bowed. When I groaned, he meekly stood up and pointed back the way he had come.

"Uh, I don't think we'll fit," said Alf.

King ignored him and chittered excitedly, nodding vigorously. Maddy and I tugged the branches aside and peeked into the foliage.

"This must be a game trail. Good work, King," said Maddy. A narrow path wound through the crowded shrubs.

"Good work if he's trying to kill me," grumbled Alf. "I can't go on for long if I have to keep bending over."

"Let's get it over with," I said, plunging into the opening on all fours. A second later, I let out an embarrassingly shrill scream, and stood shuddering and brushing at my face frantically. "Something grabbed—"

"Oh, it's just a spider web," said Ninetta, sifting stickiness from my hair. "You scared it more than—"

"Not a chance," I said, breathing heavily. "King, how long is this? I need to get out in the open. This is too much."

"It *is* dense in here," agreed Ninetta.

"There should be a pass coming up soon," said Maddy. "The tunnel would have taken us under this mountain and the next ridge beyond before coming out, but there's a shallow valley between the two sets of peaks. The next gypsy check point is on the far side of the valley."

"Check point?" Alf perked up.

"There are gypsy checkpoints scattered around this colony," explained Maddy.

I moved to the water sack and unscrewed the spigot. "Why am I always hearing how you live on the edge of the law? I see you living on the edge of *civilization*. What crime is there in that?"

Ninetta sighed. "Because we don't like to live in space or pledge allegiance to any of the colonies on the Surfaces, people don't always trust us. They don't trust, so they don't hire. They don't hire, so we don't have work or money. No money...?"

"You've got to steal," said Alf without judgment.

I eyed the various gadgets and supplies strapped to Maddy's back. "You got stolen things there?"

Maddy looked down at the ground. "Believe it or not, no. I'm a diver, and those pearls like the one in your arm can bring a very good price on the gypsy market because of the healing properties. We came here originally to make a sale."

I frowned and rubbed at the blue wrap that covered my limbs. "I've got your pearl inside me where I can't give it back. Sorry I've made things so much harder for you." My eyes misted. "I can't do anything without trouble finding me." I dusted off my hands and stood up. "Let's go. King, get us there faster."

In less than half an hour, we stepped out onto a wide ledge. Below us, a shallow, grassy valley lapped the edges of the two steep mountain ranges like a golden green lake.

Alf sighed with relief. "That'll be much easier."

"It's deceptive," said Maddy. "The grass is tall and sharp, and it's almost five kilometers across."

"And it's hot," said Ninetta. "Even at this altitude."

The way down proved treacherous. Rockslides evidently happened often here. Whereas we had experienced loose bits of rubble on the other side, here the boulders leaned against each other on the slope, threatening to roll if one of us put too much weight on them.

When we had descended about half way, I stopped to rest in a small shaded spot created by two boulders. Ninetta hoisted herself onto the rock next to me. "You coming all right, Maddy?" she called.

"Yes, right here," he said. "Ready for the water?"

"Roll it," I said, bracing myself to catch the sack.

As it reached me, a barking yell startled me, and I dropped the sack. It tore open and spilled water through the cracks of hard earth and stone.

"Viper!" screamed Ninetta.

"What—?" I stopped short, frozen in fear. A black, limbless creature the size of my arm had fastened its fangs into Ninetta's calf, but instead of tearing her flesh away, it just hung there.

The anguish in Ninetta's eyes sucked the air from my lungs. Her tongue flailed, as if reaching for something. Unable to shout for help, I signaled desperately to Maddy who scrambled down the boulder in time to see the black thing slither away. His face darkened with instant horror and he pulled Ninetta into his arms, rocking her and pleading that it not be true.

"What? What *was* that thing?" I cried.

"Viper!" coughed Ninetta.

"Deadly poisonous," wailed Maddy. "She … Oh!" He sobbed into Ninetta's shoulder, too weak to respond.

"Poisonous?" I wriggled out of my back pack and opened it. "Don't we have a remedy? An antidote? Anything?"

"The pearl powder would have been her only hope." Maddy choked back an oath and looked away.

I climbed back up on the rock worried that I would vomit as strange emotions punched my insides. I had just met this woman. She couldn't be dying. And it was my fault that she had no remedy. "What do we do?" I shrieked, searching the valley below. "Are there people down there? Can we—?"

"She's gone," said Maddy, his voice barely audible.

"What? No!" I cried. "King! Do something! Where's that pearl powder?"

"She's gone," said Maddy more firmly. "The poison is too strong."

Ninetta's purple lips hung open, and the whites of her eyes were tinged with green. She stared, unblinking at the sky. A trickle of blood ran down her leg, but just beneath the skin, it looked like something had exploded. Harsh black lines splayed away from the mark of the wound.

"She's gone," he repeated into Ninetta's hair, and his body shook with grief.

OOO

Traditional gypsy death rites involved cremation. Maddy, in his misery, would not hear of any other alternative.

"But the whole valley could go up in a blaze," said Alf.

Maddy was unmoved.

"All right, then," I said. I descended to the base of the slope where the grassland began. Dripping with sweat, I searched for a way to help. A way to give back. A way to make it right. Ninetta should have survived, but the saving pearl instead made me strong. Well then, I would use my strength to help honor her in death.

I scanned the boulders and blocks of stone and determined which ones would not cause a landslide if moved. These I lifted or rolled to form a giant ring on the grass. I filled the spaces between them with smaller rocks, blocking out the warm breeze so the sparks would not fly. Whenever I felt weak or helpless, Maddy's mournful cries spurred me on.

With the stones in place, I climbed all the way back up to the shrubs and trees, breaking off branches for the fire. It took me three trips to carry enough wood down to build a pyre of the sort I had only seen in ancient history holocube reports, and all the while I neither ate nor drank. There was no water anyway.

When only the sun's glow clung to the peaks on the distant horizon, Maddy brought Ninetta down and placed her carefully on the bed of branches. Using one of his many tools, he ignited the grasses within the stones. They withered quickly in a blackening wave, but the wood and Ninetta's clothing caught fire, and soon the bitter smell of death overwhelmed us all.

Alf and I waited outside the ring of rocks, blinking at the smoke. This was no little campfire, and we both marveled at the raging power of the flames. I wondered if anyone could see the smoke rising, or if we were far enough away from civilization here in the mountains.

Maddy stood on the largest boulder and watched Ninetta disappear slowly into the embers. Soot and ashes blackened his face except the lines of tears that did not cease to fall. Eventually, he slid into the ring and waded through the embers, oblivious to their heat, as if his sorrow had numbed the rest of him.

"My father is grieving right now," I said heavily to Alf. "And so are your parents."

"You think we should go home?" His voice held no anger.

"What are we doing to them? Do they hurt this much?"

Alf shivered involuntarily and nodded in the direction of Maddy. "I don't know. But what about him? We can't leave him alone, yeah?" He looked at me. "What about you? You're supposed to be queen of … something. Worlds."

"You don't believe that."

"Maybe I'm starting to," he said. "What you just did, building that fire. The floating in the cave with those eyes. I don't know. You're different, and it isn't just the Power, yeah? You have a heart for others. For the first time in my life, I wish I had someone to tell me what I'm supposed to do next, and—"

"Don't look to me for that, Alf."

"If not you, who?"

I flexed my shoulders and squinted at where Maddy sat murmuring to himself. Whether he recited a ritual, or talked to Ninetta, or had gone mad, I couldn't guess. His muscular body hung together with the last of his strength.

"Do you think there are any more of those black viper things around?" asked Alf.

"It's too cold for the reptiles to be active right now. Crazy how the sun sets and suddenly it's cold." I hugged myself tightly. "Besides, the smoke will have frightened them away."

Alf shook his head. "I'm so thirsty."

"You're so annoying is what you are," I said, shaking the stiffness from my legs. My joints scolded me for my earlier work. Peering into the falling shadows of night, I hissed, "King! King, where are you?"

The sharp grass parted beside me and the fanep bowed to me wearily.

It hadn't occurred to me that he would grieve, too, but he clearly felt something. "I'm sorry, King. Losing Ninetta is hard." I crouched down to his level. "Let's make sure we don't lose any more of us."

King nodded. His blue wraps, like mine, peeled away in places to reveal scraped skin beneath. The soot and sweat had blackened the cloth so that even in the twilight, I knew neither of us had retained our other-worldly splendor.

"Shouldn't we be moving on, King?" I asked, hating myself for having to be so practical. "With no water here, it would be better to travel at night while it's cool."

"Are you asking him, or telling him?" sneered Alf.

I licked my lips. "Consulting, I guess."

Alf buried his eyes in his palms. "You are so much stranger than when you got here. Who cares what the rat...?" He cut himself off. "Sorry."

"King, which of us should get Maddy? You, or me?" I hoped he would volunteer because I really didn't feel comfortable being that close to Ninetta—or what was left of her. Her death felt so different from Ora's, probably because I really liked Ninetta.

The fanep trotted through the grass and over the boulders.

"That's our answer," said Alf, standing up and shouldering one of the supply packs with a wince. "Let's get moving. They can catch up."

I hesitated, but followed with the remaining supplies slung over my back. "King can track us, even in the night."

"Are you sure we're going in the right direction?" asked Alf.

We had not walked more than a few hundred meters into the valley and already the vast darkness had swallowed us.

"I'm just walking to where the stars stop. I figure that's the mountains on the horizon," I said.

A tiny blinking yellow light appeared ahead.

"That star's not stopping," said Alf grimly. "It signaled red. It's coming in for a landing."

"Where? There's nothing out here." My stomach tightened. "Except us. Get down. Your blonde hair is glowing under these moons."

Alf covered his head with his arms and squatted. "Do you think they're investigating the smoke?"

"Probably," I said. I groaned with realization. "Come on! We've got to get Maddy. If they take him, we're lost. We don't know how to get to Craggy or Tye." I ran. Alf got to his feet and followed, bellowing oaths and holding his ribs.

The craft passed low enough overhead that I could hear a low rumbling engine and see the landing apparatus. Suddenly it slowed and stopped in midair, hovering not far from the pyre which now only glowed a dull orange above the line of rocks. Whirring, the craft dropped lower and landed. A door slid open, and a figure jumped out onto the largest rock. By the red flash of the landing lights, I could see he carried a weapon of some kind. He raised a fist and trained a focused light beam into the circle.

"What do we do now?" asked Alf through gritted teeth.

"How should I know?" I bolted as the man from the craft lowered himself to the charred earth inside the ring. Hurdling one of the lower rocks, I knocked into him, throwing him to the ground with a grunt. The man shouted out, but I pinned his shoulders and thighs before he could get leverage to escape. Heat rose from the ashes in visible waves.

Maddy rose slowly from where he'd been crouching over Ninetta's remains. He came over, as if breaking free from a trance, shielding his eyes against the glare of the craft lights. Gently, he pressed his foot over the fallen man's hand, blocking out the beam of light.

The man let out a muffled cry. "Maddy? Is that you?" He tried to roll beneath me. "Call off the fanep, Maddy. He's getting fat!"

Maddy's white teeth shone in the night. He wiped soot from his face and extended a hand down to the man. "Brade! That's no fanep. That's my friend, Caz."

My stomach buckled to hear him say that, and I slid to the ground, releasing the man called Brade. He pulled himself free and gawked at me. "She's a child."

"Your timing is good, Brade," said Maddy. "Was the smoke very visible over the range?"

"Enough that my boss had me come investigate. It's suspicious in light of the recent storm. When I saw the rocks, I realized what was happening. It's good for containing the fire, but they'll know it was gypsies. That's why I landed. We need to get you moving." He jerked his chin toward the ashy pile of debris. "Please tell me that isn't Ma Ninetta."

"It isn't," said Maddy. "It is only her bones." He put his hand over his heart. "She is in here."

Right as he said that, I felt it. As if Ninetta hugged me from wherever she was now.

Alf's head appeared over one of the boulders. "Everything all right in here?" he asked.

"Yes," called Maddy. "This is my friend, Brade. He works for the colony government."

Alf's eyes narrowed. "Friend?"

Brade raised a hand, "A lowly patrol pilot for the weather surveillance."

"Is that a friend, too?" asked Alf, pointing back toward the far mountain range.

We turned to see another craft approaching. "Uh, no," said Brade. "Maddy, you'd better hurry. That's a security patrol. Get everyone aboard." He glanced at Alf. "Aren't you the boy from the—?"

"Introductions later," I said. "Let's get out of here!"

Brade gestured for everyone to follow him. He grasped a tether by horizontal gripping bars and climbed into the craft. The rest of us followed with ragged haste, and Brade took his seat in the cockpit.

"Take us out," said Maddy. "And cut the lights."

The cabin went dark except for a small panel of pale blue control indicators gleaming below the window. With no seats in the aft section, Maddy, Alf and I sat against the wall opposite the door. King huddled between Maddy and me making nervous burbles.

Brade swore. "They're hailing us."

"They must have seen us black out," I said.

"They want to know if we're in trouble," hissed Brade. Slamming a button on the dashboard, he groaned, "We will be soon enough."

"Faster. Evasive maneuvers. You know what to do," said Maddy.

We were all thrown against the back of the cabin with the velocity.

"Sorry about that," said Brade.

King floated mid-air as the craft spiraled and banked away, his dazed eyes shining like the moons in the pilot's window.

"One more," said Brade. "Hold on tight!"

I screamed for only a second before King pounded into my chest, knocking the air from my lungs.

And then everything settled.

"I can get you as far as the next weather station," said Brade.

"And then he reports us," said Alf tightly.

"No," said Maddy confidently.

Brade pointed his thumb back at Maddy. "You should have known better than to light a fire. With heat discs so available on Caren, a fire is a dead giveaway for a gypsy."

Maddy's voice came hoarsely. "You know why it had to be a fire."

Brade sighed. "I know." He sat taller, focusing on something on the horizon. "We'll only have about three minutes at the station before someone will come out to the plane," he said. "Can you get out that fast?"

"What are you going to do?"

"I'll stall as long as I can. You need to get to HQ. I'll let them know you're coming."

"Let who know?" I asked.

"Brade," said Maddy. "You'd better tell them they've got a special guest."

"Who? The girl?"

"Tell who what?" I demanded, crawling forward to the cockpit.

Brade spoke without removing his eyes from his instruments. "The gypsy network, of course." His voice carried an edge that frightened me. "I'll lose my job if this doesn't go down right. Who am I risking it for?"

Maddy cleared his throat. "She's worth it," said Maddy calmly. "But she—we all—need to be hidden for a while."

"Don't worry. We'll keep you hidden. I don't want to get fired," said Brade. "We'll be landing now."

OOO

16 GYPSY NETWORK HEADQUARTERS

Alf and I crouched against the back wall of a darkened hangar, waiting for Maddy and King to return.

"How are your ribs?" I asked, turning on a ring light we had found in the cave supplies.

He lifted his shirt gingerly. "Don't say anything about the stink, yeah?" said Alf.

"Is it really blue, or is that just the ring light?"

"It feels blue," he said, exhaling and leaning back.

The cracks around the hangar door let in a faint line of light. I sat next to him and traced the line of the tattooed C on his cheek. "Alf, I'm so sorry. You wanted to run away and start a new life, and I've ruined everything—"

"Stop it, Caz. You're annoying when you feel sorry for yourself." He shifted his legs and flexed his toes. "If you were a bad person, you wouldn't care about other people."

"I never used to care. I wonder why I do now."

"Maybe because you need us," he said.

"Yeah."

"Sh. Someone's coming."

We held our breath. A door opened to the left and two men stood silhouetted against the blinking lights of the runway across the field. I recognized Brade's shape. He ushered in a man who wore the distinctive cap and coat of a security officer.

I grabbed Alf's hand instinctively. Alf cupped his hand over my ring light and turned it off. He froze when the stranger began striding toward us. The faint rectangle of light from the door did not reach all the way across, but it provided him a safe path most of the way.

"Are you there?" whispered the stranger.

The room went all but black again as Brade closed the door behind him. "They're coming. We have to hurry."

"My lady," said the man closest to us.

"Maddy?"

"Of course. Hurry!" Maddy turned on a ring light of his own. His face, worn with grief, seemed alien in the dimness. "We need to get you into a water tank. In a few minutes, someone's coming to load it on Brade's craft. They don't know you're with us. Please hurry."

"But won't they see you?"

"They won't see past the uniform in the dark, unless they see you two."

He led us over to a large water tank used to douse fires from the air. Alf maneuvered his torso painfully up to the top of it and wriggled through the metal rim. I followed, lowering myself awkwardly. My foot touched water. "It's full!"

"No, not all the way. Trust me," said Brade. "It'll keep you safer that way, and they won't detect you."

"We'll drown!"

"No," insisted Brade. "You'll have at least half a meter of air space, and the weight of the water will mask your weight."

Maddy nodded. I had no choice but to lower myself into the cold, dark water. Immediately, flashbacks of the sea curdled my throat and sent my pulse into high speed.

Maddy closed the hatch, plunging us into a black nightmare. The water was too deep to sit in, but if I knelt, my shoulders and head stayed dry, and I still had several centimeters of clearance above. At least he was right about the air space. I held myself still with my hands pressed against the inner walls.

Alf sighed. "It feels good for my ribs, anyway."

"I'll try to be happy for you," I said.

"Don't pee, yeah?"

"I wish you hadn't said that."

Something jolted the tank with a loud clang, and I covered my ears. The tank rocked from side to side, sloshing the water up to my chin.

"Sounds like a machine picked us up," said Alf. "Probably a forklift or crane—"

Suddenly, the whole tank tilted at a sharp angle, and Alf slid into me, pinning me underwater. Thrashing wildly, I searched for a feeling of *up*. My ears filled with a bubbling turmoil. Clawing at Alf, I at last broke into the air with a desperate gasp. Alf swore, and the tank rotated almost ninety degrees, rolling us before settling with a deep clunk.

"Do you think we're in the craft yet?" I coughed.

"Yeah," said Alf. The tank tilted again. "If he does 'evasive maneuvers' again, I'll kill him," breathed Alf.

"I'll help you," I laughed.

Within a minute, the tank leveled and only a vibration remained, muted by the water physically, but amplified in sound by the enclosed metal tube. I tried to find a comfortable position, letting my arms float, grateful that my knees, though sore, pushed against something solid that would not let me go underwater again.

"My eyes aren't adjusting to the dark. Are yours?" I asked after a few minutes.

"No light to adjust to."

"Right." As an afterthought, I tried the ring light. An eerie blue light flickered on and illuminated our hiding place. The dim metal and water bounced weak shadows around the tube, magnifying the sense of confinement. I inhaled a sob. For a second, the light resembled the last transmission I saw from Felly.

"What's wrong?"

"My sister." My mind flashed back, and I felt the need to share with Alf. "The night of my Sentence," I said, "we were in the cafeteria and she gave me her ice cream." I smiled at the irony of that particular memory.

"What's funny?" he prompted gently.

"She found me a seat where I could see Caren. She knew I wanted to go down to the Surface!"

Alf murmured his understanding.

"They gave me the option of Solitary," I said.

"Wishing you'd taken it?"

I listened to the sounds within the tank: our breathing, occasional drips of water falling from our hair, a metallic hum. "No. Even though this is kind of like it, isn't it?"

"We're not alone, though," said Alf.

"No." I couldn't see this as punishment. I had friends now. Alf had been lonely, too, then. I guess all the Lamond kids had felt that way. Maybe that's why we had rebelled. Maybe that was why we needed to get out of our flying metal boxes. For a long minute, I shivered in silence at the grief that crept into my mind for Ninetta, for my Dad and Felly, for so many years of feeling alone.

With a soft voice that echoed through the tank and into my heart, Alf said, "I'm glad you didn't choose Solitary."

OOO

The ring light eventually failed, and I lost all sense of time. Occasionally, the tank would tilt, but the darkness, the cold, and the weightlessness of the water wore on my senses by refusing to vary. Exhaustion had all but overcome me when I heard and felt the water slosh gently. Something on top of the tank, something not mechanical, thumped dully. The hatch scraped open, and I shielded my eyes against the light. A rush of cool air enlivened me, and I emerged, squinting at the dim panel of lights from the cockpit. Strange how even that amount of ambient light overwhelmed my eyes.

"Where are we?" I asked hoarsely.

"Inside a mountain," said Brade. "Welcome to GNHQ."

"Huh?"

"Gypsy Network Headquarters. Caren, North Mountain Chapter."

Alf half coughed, half laughed. "Are you kidding?"

"Did you think we were all wandering migrant workers?" asked Maddy pleasantly, helping him out and wrapping us both in warm, but coarse blankets.

Alf hesitated. "Uh…"

"Don't answer that," I teased.

Brade led us into a small hangar hewn directly into the mountain. I hummed appreciatively at the opening through which we had entered. "That's a small portal! This thing must really handle well."

"It's not a skimmer. That's for sure," chuckled Maddy. "Come on. Try not to drip so much. We don't want anyone to slip in your puddles."

"You know the way to the Council Room?" called Brade from the ramp of the craft.

"Yes," said Maddy with a wave. "Be off to fight those 'fires'. Thanks again, Brade!"

"You're leaving us already?" I asked.

"Unless you want the security patrols out searching for me," he said. "You're in good hands … my lady."

Maddy had told my secret. Hopefully his trust was well-placed.

Brade ducked back inside the craft and, in seconds, had retracted the landing gear and spun the craft around as neatly as if he simply turned a wheel. The craft accelerated down the short tunnel and into the dawning grey outside.

"I've always wanted one of those," said Maddy, echoing my sentiments.

Alf cleared his throat. "I don't mean to complain, but I'm freezing cold and wet. Can we get where we're going?"

Maddy laughed and ushered us towards a lighted sliding door near the rear.

"Elevators in mountains?"

Maddy shrugged. "Is it any stranger than a city floating around a solar system?"

The door slid open and we stepped inside. A lit panel revealed 40 possible level destinations. "An ICS is assembled piece by piece, but this! How did they make an elevator shaft in solid rock?"

"I think they used an old volcanic air vent," said Maddy comfortably, pressing the button for the top level.

Alf groaned. "Are we ever going to be somewhere that isn't dangerous?"

Maddy removed the security officer hat and jacket. "Not with her around," he said, winking at me.

The elevator stopped and the doors slid open to reveal a bright room paneled with pale yellow planks of wood so smoothly sanded that they seemed to be all one circular wrap around the inside of the room. It must have cost a fortune—just for a glorified hallway!

"Is that a chandelier?" I stammered. "I saw pictures in one of the tablets. Those are so rare!"

"Dripping," reminded Alf in a sing-song voice.

"Sorry. Washroom to your left," said Maddy, pointing. "You'll have to take turns. There should be towels and clothes already waiting for you." He bowed slightly to me. "We told them you were coming."

"You go first," I said to Alf. Truthfully, I couldn't see the entrance and didn't want to look like an idiot, but as he began walking towards the wall, a panel slid open to reveal a spacious washroom as clean as anything on the Arxon.

As he disappeared, another panel in front of us slid noiselessly open and a handsome woman with high-stacked braids strode out. "Maddy!" She held out her arms to embrace him. "I'm so sorry to hear about Ninetta. She will be sorely missed." Maddy mumbled his thanks, and the woman sighed. Glancing at the washroom door, she asked, "Is she in there?"

"No, she's right here."

The woman looked me with obvious confusion. "The *child?*"

Self-conscious, I let the blanket drop from my shoulders and fussed with my hair. Did I look *so* young?

"Oh!" The woman's gaze rested on the blue wraps and she stepped forward, stunned. "The fanep did this?" she asked.

Something about the way she scrutinized me—or rather, the way she scrutinized my soggy sea-colored garb—sent my heart quibbling with my lungs about how to circulate the oxygen to my brain. She was stately and elegant and terrifying all at the same time.

"Yes," said Maddy solemnly. "He crowned her, too."

"But she's so young!" The woman finally looked into my face. Raising three fingers, she traced a horizontal ring between us three times, all the while uttering noises that made no sense. She finished by bowing. When she rose, she said, "Forgive me if I seemed ... I am so pleased to meet you, my lady, our queen." She had one of those smiles that forced the corners of her mouth down so that she appeared more annoyed than 'pleased'.

I hugged the blanket tight against my shivering spine.

The woman indicated the washroom. "If you wish to ready yourself, I can send an attendant."

Her guarded expression told me nothing except to reveal intelligence. "Thank you," I said, slipping my finger between the loose spaces of the blue wrap. "I believe I just need King to help me." I stiffened. "Where's King?"

"He's safe," assured the woman. "He was taken from the craft before you were brought out of hiding."

Maddy leaned and whispered. "Some of the gypsies prefer to keep the faneps quarantined in case they've picked up viruses from other planets. Don't worry. Go tidy up."

That seemed weird, given how gypsies and faneps were famous for traveling together, but I remembered that Dad had said faneps never got vaccinations, so I guess there was a risk. Life here differed so much from the sterile Arxon that I really couldn't judge the practicality of such measures.

Alf emerged, clean and dry, and unusually striking in a white and gold patterned tunic with dark brown pants that came almost to his ankles. With a grin of encouragement, he said, "They've got everything in there, Caz. You'll come out feeling good, yeah?"

A hot shower with savory scrubs wiped away my worries and many of the blemishes of my travels. My muscles relaxed, and my breathing slowed. An attendant had carefully taken the blue wrap to be cleaned, so I donned a short-sleeved, flowing tunic of the same sea-like color. After years of form-fitting coversuits, it felt breezy and comfortable.

"Ah, you're ready, my lady," said the woman as I re-entered the circular room.

"You waited this whole time?"

"Not always right here," she said stiffly. "Please follow me to the Council room. The others are waiting."

"I…What's your name?"

"Saloma. I am the Presiding Councilor in Caren's gypsy network." She held her hand out to usher me through the door opposite the elevator. "Come in. Have something to eat in the Council Room."

I entered and felt my jaw drop open. This place beat all imagination. A long cluster of what could only be blue etak crystals burst upward from the center of a large hexagonal table like a massive, glassy bouquet. The table itself was made of a thick, polished slab of wood that must have been worth a small spacecraft.

Maddy and Alf leaned back in tall padded chairs showing the sleepy signs of recent feasting. Nudging Alf's shoulder, Maddy stood and bowed slightly to me.

Alf followed suit. "Took you long enough," he said. "Worth it, though. You look the part now."

My face must have flushed purple in the pale blue light.

Saloma indicated the seat beside Alf. "Please, help yourself, my lady. While you are eating, you can see what we've been able to pull up on the holocubes from the libraries. This is a very momentous thing. So rare." Dipping her voice, she added, "So needed. The gypsies have waited long for this."

I had no idea what she meant or why King crowning me had anything to do with the gypsies. Rather than answer, I reached for the nearest plate of colorful fruits.

Saloma nodded and clapped once. The light in the room dimmed. In the blue crystals, holographic images fluttered.

"Perhaps you will recognize these people," said Saloma.

I tilted to see a wider facet of crystal and squealed. There in the blue light stood Dad. He disappeared, and a new figure appeared. I recognized her from digiscreen pictures more than memory: my mother. For the first time in my life, I noticed something.

"My mother was a gypsy!"

OOO

17   A RAPID EDUCATION

Over the next two hours, Saloma lectured serenely on relevant histories, all the while displaying 3-D images in the etak crystals instead of a normal holocube image that floated uncontained.

My mother, Brita Artemus, was known well in the gypsy network. Apparently, since the time she had left us on the Arxon, she had tirelessly fought for more freedom for the gypsies under the Granbo System Charter. I had, of course, studied that great body of law, created to establish a balance of power between the colonies and the city-stations. Mr. Virgil had told us all about the equitable rules of conduct and trade throughout the System. Now, however, I saw it from a different perspective, and its value stood tarnished in my mind by the isolationism it had created. Everyone was supposed to keep to themselves. Each colony was largely self-governing as long as it abided by certain general principles. The same was true of the ICS system.

Gypsies, according to Charter authorities, had ruined everything with their frequent travels. They spread ideas and customs and created conflict. They 'cross-contaminated' the communities they visited, and that was why locals resisted them.

How was anyone supposed to unite all that under one voice? Why would anyone *want* to? It seemed like a really good way to get a lot of people really mad at you. Being a queen of all of this sounded like a horrible idea.

I retreated incrementally closer to Alf. The greatness of what I learned made me feel very small, and only Alf seemed to share my muted horror. Maddy could scarcely contain his excitement, and Saloma exuded cool efficiency.

When at last the lights in the room eased back on, I filled my fear-parched mouth with sweet juice and rested my head in my hands.

"Are you all right, my lady?" asked Saloma with steady concern.

I held up a finger, but continued to stare at my empty glass. "Let me be sure I understand this completely," I replied, with an edge in my voice. "I am only the fourth known person in the Granbo System to have had a pearl implanted in them by a fanep. The first two died as a result."

Saloma tried to brush it away casually. "They didn't know not to ingest the other ingredients orally."

"I'm not done yet," I snapped. "The third, Caren's own Queen Levia, got all three Gifts, but when she tried to get back to Tye for…"

"The Cycling Ceremony," said Alf drily.

"Right, the Cycling Ceremony," I said, finally meeting Saloma's eyes. "She was trapped in an airlock while transferring to the ferry."

"Intentionally trapped, or accidentally trapped?" chimed Alf.

Saloma cleared her throat. "It is unclear."

"She was obviously killed to prevent the ceremony from taking place," I said, pressing my hands onto the table. "And that happened because the colonies from all three planets opposed a regent who favored positive relations with the gypsies and the faneps?"

"Just certain factions, my lady," stuttered Saloma.

Silence weighted the room, and only Alf met my eyes. I'd acquired a death sentence, not just some happy little promise of being stronger and smarter. I swallowed and rubbed the bridge of my nose as I'd seen Dad do so many times before. With a sigh, I resumed. "*Factions* in the colonies assassinated Levia to prevent the Cycling Ceremony because … that's where I'm losing the logic. What difference does it make if one gypsy—and I'm only a half-blood—cycles a pearl and is crowned queen by a bunch of faneps. Faneps aren't included in the Granbo System Charter. Why does it matter?"

Saloma's eyes shone brightly. "The power you will wield, my lady, with a Cycled Pearl inside of you! You would have the capacity to bring the gypsies to power. They would no longer be outcasts and underlings in the worlds of the colonies or on the ICSs. They could rule."

"I'm all in favor of helping the gypsies not be seen as outcasts, but there are fifty-three colonies on the three planets. Why should they all follow me? I'm not going to bully people. Especially when I didn't ask for the job, and I'm so—"

"Young," said Saloma.

I frowned at her and she reacted to the visual slap by downing a glass of sweet juice.

"I was going to say that I'm so unfamiliar with the needs and cultures of their inhabitants. My youth won't matter much with the Cycled Pearl, will it? I'll be smarter and stronger than anyone else."

"Quite right, my lady," said Saloma.

"Why can't we just get some Earlie syrup here, give it to King to give to her?" asked Alf with a flair for the obvious.

I eyed Saloma sideways. She took the cue smugly. "That won't be possible. We've already run a planet-wide search, and there is none to be found on Caren."

"It's that rare?" asked Alf.

"It's very hard to retrieve. Harder than the pearls. Besides there is still the matter of the Cycling Ceremony," said Maddy. "That must take place on Tye."

"In the meantime," said Saloma, "we can pull up the reports and you can see all the Surface colonies, their customs, their leaders. You'll be able to consider how to unite them carefully, wisely." She reached for a touch screen panel near the base of the etak crystals.

"Who put all those reports together?" I asked.

"Oh, these archives were assembled by gypsies throughout the system," said Saloma proudly.

"So they're filtered through the perceptions of gypsies." I said. That met with an asteroid belt. "Or do they impartially show the histories of each colony? And what about the ICS network? I want to hear what people have to say from their own mouths."

Maddy chuckled softly. "She's a smart one."

"It's the Rik leaves," said Saloma under her breath.

"I don't think so," I said. "I've been interested in Surface life since I could walk and talk, but I am, after all, from an ICS. I don't want to change everyone's ways too much if they're already happy. People came to the colonies to start a new life. Who am I to tell them how to live it?" I squinted at the last flickering image of the holocube report. "A fanep did this to me. The pearl cycling is a fanep thing. This is about them, not us. Not gypsies, or anyone else."

"But every person they've ever chosen was a gypsy," said Saloma. "Of course this is about the gypsies, too."

"They chose gypsies because gypsies move around." I inhaled and stood up. "Human history is all about seizing power and ruling over the weak. This Cycled Pearl stuff is from the faneps, and they were here in the system first. I don't want to make any moves until I can talk to King."

Saloma shook her head. "I'm not sure where he is right now. The faneps are usually sequestered."

"Why? He wasn't sick."

"It's sterile there."

I stared at her. "You sound like my Dad. King isn't dirty. He's as clean as any gypsy, anyway."

Alf snickered.

"Bring King here, or take me to him," I said.

I cast a quick glance at Alf. His mouth twitched and he blinked slowly in approval.

"I'll see if I can find him." Saloma turned on her heel and walked out.

Maddy leaned back. "The most ancient of human texts say, 'a little child shall lead them'. That may not be received well by the various powers that be, but it may be exactly what the Granbo System needs."

I tilted my head at Maddy curiously. A sad smile creased his tattoo. How was it that I trusted Maddy and Alf when they were supposed to be so

Merry Christmas :)

im broke, this is my card :) anyways..
I love you!

-Rukia :D

dangerous? But thinking about all I'd just learned, I realized that ideas could be more dangerous than fists or weapons.

"Do you trust me, Maddy?" I asked.

His eyes shone deep. "I trust you, my lady."

"And you, Alf?"

Alf gave me the smile I'd seen in the duspy field. "The little rat man might be creepy, but he chose a good queen for that pearl, yeah?"

"But I don't want all that power so I can rule the Granbo System."

Alf grinned. "That's why I think he chose right."

Maddy nodded.

OOO

Half an hour had passed, and I had spent it studying holocube reports of when humans first encountered the faneps on Tye. "It's so sad," I said. "The vids of their cities are amazing. There's no way they could have built all of that and had codified rites without language."

"Why is there no sound on these vids?" asked Alf, drifting out of a lazy nap.

Maddy shrugged. "No one knows. Maybe the technician filming forgot to set the right controls."

"Maybe they spoke at a decibel or frequency the instruments couldn't pick up," I said. "But King understands our speech and can communicate a little. Obviously his capacity for language is still there. Maybe faneps haven't lost as much of their cognition as we thought."

Alf gingerly tested his ribs with his fingers and winked at me. "Who'd want to hear what they think, anyway?"

"Hear what they think—Alf, you're a genius!" I said. "Telepathy! What if they're telepathic?"

"Mind reading rat men?" asked Alf, laughing.

Maddy rolled his shoulders back and rubbed his hands on his knees. "Now there's an idea. But how would we test that theory if we're not telepathic?"

"Wouldn't that explain what happened back in the cave? When I saw them and understood them?" I jumped to my feet. "I really need to see King." I felt a lump in my throat. "But first, I need to talk to Dad and Felly. They need to know I'm safe."

Maddy and Alf both tensed.

"They'll keep it a secret. Please, Maddy. You said you trusted me. You know what it feels like to lose your loved one. Dad's suffering now because he thinks I'm dead."

His eyes welled with tears and he ran his fingers purposefully over the controls. "Enter the room code," he said, his voice clogged with emotion.

I reached over and keyed in the code to our common room. It occurred to me that I had no idea what time of day or night it was on the Arxon.

When the image bloomed on the crystal, I could tell it must be early morning. Dad had dressed for work, but hadn't finished his grooming. His voice cracked as he answered. "Dr. Artemus here."

"Dad, it's me." I leaned closer to the crystal, unsure of where the sensors might be.

He didn't respond except to blink.

"Dad, it's me, Caz," I repeated. "I'm alive, Dad. The reports you heard were wrong."

"Caz?" his voice sounded so far away. He raised his hand as if to touch me in the same way I had tried to touch holocube images before I knew they weren't real.

"Yes, Dad. It's me. I'm so sorry, Dad. I'm so sorry that … that I hurt you by my selfish actions. I'm sorry."

Tears blurred my vision, but I couldn't take the time to wipe them away. Grasping the etak crystal, I said, "Dad, I love you. I love Felly. I'm all right. I'm with gypsies."

Dad's eyes widened, alert now. "Gypsies! Caz! Are you hurt? Did they take you?"

"No, Dad. I'm fine. I'm better than ever, Dad."

Behind him, Felly appeared, ready for school. She saw me and her face broke into a wide grin. "Caz!"

"Felly! I told you I'd contact you again, didn't I?"

"Did you find your friends?" she asked.

Dad stared back at her. "What? You knew?"

"It's all right, Dad. I made her promise not to tell." I banged on the crystal, trying to get his attention while he and Felly argued quietly.

Finally he looked back at me, eyes blazing. "Can you get back to Lamond? I'm sure I can arrange for transport home."

"No, Dad. I think you'd better sit down."

His brows came together, but I could tell by the angle that he and Felly both sat huddled together and listened. And I told them. I told them everything that had happened, from trying to save Ora to arriving here. They didn't move. They hardly blinked, and I don't think I took very many breaths while I spoke, but when I finished, we all stared at each other in silence for a long time.

"Please, Dad. Let me do this. You wanted me to grow up and take responsibility."

"But faneps and gypsies—"

"Mom was a gypsy," I said.

My statement aged him in a second. "You know?"

"Yes, Dad."

"You know that Queen Levia was your great-grandmother?"

The skin on my head crawled backward and my mouth went dry, but I nodded. I knew now. Funny that Saloma had neglected that little factoid. "All the more reason, Dad. I have to finish what Levia started and what Mom is working to continue."

"You're in no position to rule a solar system, Caz."

"No, I'm not," I admitted. "But I can help the faneps."

Felly hugged him closer. "Dad," she said. "Maybe she can find Mom."

He held his folded hands to his lips in thought. Looking at me—through me, it seemed—he said, "Yes. Perhaps you can find Brita."

I touched the image of his face in the crystal. "I will, Dad."

Felly reached out her hand so it 'touched' mine. "I think you'll find yourself, too, Caz."

Her understanding warmed me. "Thanks, Felly," I said. "I promise to be good, Felly. Just like you. I love you, Dad. I love you, Felly."

"We love you, too," said Felly. "And we'll keep your secret until you've finished cycling the pearl."

OOO

18   THE FANEP CAVERN

"Come on, Alf. Let's go exploring."

Alf hesitated, raising an eyebrow at Maddy.

"Go," said Maddy, waving us away. "I'll wait here for Saloma. You know what level we're on."

At the door, I paused. Maddy already worked the touch screen. An image of a woman appeared in the etak crystals, surely Ninetta years ago.

In the lift, Alf surveyed the lit keys and picked something about half-way up. "Is that all right with you, your queenness?"

I snorted and back-handed him.

"So ladylike, my lady," he grinned. Then, with mock severity, he added, "And if you touch my ribs again, I'll have to kill you and make it look like an accident."

"That's not funny," I said, slumping against the back wall.

"No," he agreed. "This is…"

"Scary."

"Yeah."

I grinned at him appreciatively, tucking my hands behind me as I leaned. "Thanks, Alf, for staying with me."

"It's the other way around. You followed me in the woods, remember?"

The elevator doors swooshed open revealing a broad oval room with the lift at the narrowest end. It was like an empty rec hall on the Arxon except for the waterfall right in the middle of it. I guess they have something spectacular in the middle of every room: a chandelier, a big etak crystal monitor, a fountain of rushing water falling from the ceiling through the floor. We approached it with subdued awe.

"Must be some kind of subterranean stream," I said.

Alf gawked at me like I'd crawled off of an asteroid. "How do you even talk like that?"

"Rik leaves," I said, tapping the place where my crown had once rested. "But remember that it only helps with memory, which means I learned this stuff once before. Geology two years ago, probably."

He nudged me closer to the waterfall. A hole in the floor gave less than a meter's girth around the stream of water, and this was rimmed with tile.

"Careful, it's slippery," said Alf.

The power of the moving water called me forward, but I hesitated when I glimpsed the depth of the shaft through which it flowed. Or rather, the fact that I couldn't see the depth because it went down so *far*. It must have dropped for more than a hundred meters.

"Beautiful and dangerous," agreed Alf. "Like you."

His words evoked a hiccup. "I'm not beautiful," I objected. "I look like a boy and I'm dirty or bleeding most of the time."

Alf's lopsided smile made me dizzy. "You clean up all right, yeah?" He elbowed me playfully, and I slipped on the wet tile with a thud.

I sat with my feet dangling over the edge, mist from the waterfall seeping through my tunic. "You saying I need *another* shower?"

"Sorry, Caz!" He reached his hand to lift me up, but I tugged him gently down to sit by me. We wriggled our bare feet in the spray—they hadn't given us shoes—and enjoyed a moment of companionable silence. Why did this water soothe me when being underwater terrified me? I listened to the rhythmic white noise as if the water had a pulse. Resting my hand on his arm for balance, I extended one leg a little farther. I wanted to feel the stream of water, not just the mist. The force that struck my foot propelled me forward into the pounding column of water, Alf's arm still in my hand. We fell, unable to hear our screams over the roar of the water around us. My senses sped up, or slowed down, I'm not sure which. Though gravity pulled us down mercilessly, we floated in air and water that cushioned us even as it pushed. I tasted its sweetness, even smelled the freshness of it, new and ageless.

At some point during the fall, I let go of Alf. In an instant, the water closed around and plunged me into darkness. A giant water pipe? At the last instant, I remembered not to inhale. With my eyes squeezed tight, I felt my body pulled at great speed with the current, curving from side to side as the conduit changed angles and eventually leveled out so that I lay on my back, lightly bumping over ridges.

Suddenly, my face breached the surface. A second later, I heard Alf call out. The flow of the water slowed, but I still couldn't stop myself from sliding along with it. We seemed to be in a low tunnel carved into the mountain rock. We reached the light at the end, and Alf groaned behind me. "That did *not* feel good."

Able at last to pull myself to my knees, I noted that the channel had widened and the water now flowed only about ten centimeters deep. We huddled together and stared at the hole. A familiar blue light glowed beyond it.

"I guess that way is out," I said. I made my way forward on my hands and knees.

"Really, Caz?" he called after me. "Do I really have to crawl through that?"

I reached the end and gasped. "Yes, Alf. You really have to crawl through it. You've got to see this!"

The cavern, at least five times larger than any ICS, teemed with a bustle of motion. Faneps in every shade of green, blue or white moved purposefully through a multi-layered maze of gracefully constructed bridges and causeways that connected meticulously hewn buildings of black mountain rock. Etak crystals filled the walls and ceilings, shorter yet brighter than the ones in the gypsy cave.

Several of the faneps worked in perfect tandem, carving away at one of the outer walls to create a recessed balcony of sorts high above the other buildings. They chipped at rock and hauled away debris on small hovering platforms to be dropped in a pit of smoldering lava. Though they let the pieces fall from a great height, they never missed their target, and the molten rock absorbed them without a splash.

Through windows mid-way up, I saw faneps cooking or bathing, doing absolutely normal things. Their diminutive size only made them seem at a distance, but so human.

Down on the ground level, a triangle of very small faneps surrounded a larger one. They moved in seamless unison through poses that required superhuman balance and strength.

Pulsing through the entire space of the cavern, a counterpoint of sounds either led or followed their movements. The hum of the hovering platforms and the chiseling workers, the burbling lava and an unseen rush of water created the music of life here. The faneps pressed gently forward in an unhurried pace, and I blinked slowly at the hypnotic spectacle.

Alf poked me with a finger. "Wake up. What's the matter with you? Are you going to pass out?"

"Hmm?" My arms swished from side to side, and I moved, almost gliding, towards the triangle of small faneps. As I approached, my gestures mimicked theirs insofar as humanly possible.

"Caz!" hissed Alf. "What are you doing?"

"Dancing, I think," I hummed.

"They have sharp teeth and claws," he said desperately. With panic in his voice, he yelled, "Caz!"

In an instant, the whole cavern fell silent except for the rushing water and the bubbling lava. The larger fanep in the middle of the triangle turned to face us.

"King!" I felt an immediate and overwhelming joy.

The fanep grinned and resumed his dance. As he did so, everyone resumed the same steady labor. He continued to smile at me, his eyes never wavering, and suddenly I knew: King was not his name. It was his title. He was the King of the faneps. These were his subjects, and they followed him perfectly, eagerly. And he and I were supposed to work together to bring peace and cooperation between our species.

"It's all right, Alf," I whispered over my shoulder. "It's safe." I beckoned for him to join me, and he came up beside me, taking my hand protectively. I thought about the joke I'd made in the corridor of the Arxon—a week ago? A year ago?—about being an interspecies ambassador. *Well, wasn't I?* If nothing else, my family might have a reason to be proud of me. Maybe I could be proud of myself.

"Hello, children," I said, smiling at the small faneps sleepily. "May we join your dance?"

The triangle expanded with neat precision, each fanep child moving without instruction to a place that kept the symmetry and absorbed us at the same time. The dance continued, and I closed my eyes. "Thank you for letting me be one with you," I said. They sang their replies in a language I felt more than heard. "We're safe, Alf. This is right where we belong."

In my mind, I saw us as if from above, and we moved with the faneps, dancing as if we had done so all our lives. And when they balanced effortlessly on one hand, we likewise floated upside down, our fingertips grazing the ground for comfort, not support. I saw only blue and green and white swirling around me in fluid motion, up, down and around, with a guiding pale light always above.

"Like looking at the sky from underwater," I mused before settling on the ground to sleep.

Tall trees, limbless for the first several meters, reached straight up. I climbed the trunks. Just as I reached the first, prickly branches, something golden oozed from the bark and dribbled over my fingers and wrists. I let go, only to fall through the air in slow motion. But it wasn't air. It was water. A pale circle of light above me shrank. I reached upwards even while falling back. The circle disappeared into a pinpoint of white light and then fell into my palm. The pearl.

I opened my eyes. King sat beside me, glowing with peace.

"Queen knows now?" he asked.

His lips had not moved, yet I heard and understood.

I sat up, and King stood so that we were almost eye-to-eye. We looked at each other for a long, happy moment. "I know," I said.

And I did.

OOO

19   A DANGEROUS DISGUISE

"This is never going to work, Caz," droned Alf.

"It'll work," I said, tugging the clasps of my coversuit tighter across my chest. "My hair is shorter than yours. I can pass for a boy."

"Not so much." He knuckled his blonde stubble sheepishly.

I sighed and stared down at myself. *Why did those long-anticipated curves have to show up now?* I tried to loosen the cloth around the waist. I'd rather appear fat than feminine right now. "It *has* to work, Alf. They won't let me in the mining camp on Craggy if they think I'm a girl." I groaned and stomped my foot, causing Maddy to stir in his sleep on the bench.

Back in space for seventeen hours and already the sterile beige walls of the Ferry had compressed my temper to the popping point. Only Alf's smirk convinced me the last few weeks hadn't been a wild dream.

"Thanks for coming with me, Alf." I sat down so close our knees touched. "I need you to keep me safe."

He raised his chin without glancing up. "You're the one with superhuman strength and intelligence."

"The Gifts made me stronger and smarter, but…not wiser." Now I stared at the floor, feeling his gaze on my face. "King's more important than the Powers anyway. We've formed a mental link—"

"Lucky little ratman," muttered Alf.

I shrugged. "I know in my heart that cycling this pearl will help the entire fanep species."

"That makes no sense."

"I know. But I know it's true. Haven't you ever known something without learning it logically?"

"Trust," he said.

"What do you mean?"

"That's trust," he said, looking at me intently. "Trust is when you know—like I know it's a good idea to stick with you." His voice held a tinge of something in it that I couldn't place.

Feeling the heat rise in my cheeks, I changed the subject. "I don't know why Saloma and Maddy have it in their heads that this whole process will make me Queen of all the Granbo System."

"I know," he said, leaning back and draping his arm along the bench. Something jiggled my internal organs as I absorbed the nearness of him. "Your rule will bring gypsies into their rightful standing," he sneered, with a glance at Maddy.

"That's the part I don't understand, but I'll worry about that when I get there. For now, I just need to get that Earlie syrup into my blood, and that means getting to Craggy. Alf, you're the only one who understands what it's like to be from an ICS, an outcast that didn't grow up like a gypsy. I need you to help me be true to myself."

Alf shifted and looked at me in the same way that King often did. Maybe Alf couldn't read my mind like the fanep, but he could relate to it. He nodded, and a lop-sided grin crept up to deepen the dimple. My hand went to it, brushing his cheek with my fingertip.

"You'll never pass as brothers if you act like star-struck lovers," said Maddy, stretching awake with a suppressed smile.

Heat rushed through me like a bolt of electricity as Alf and I jerked apart. *Star-struck? We're not...*

"How much time left?" asked Alf, cool as ever.

"A few more hours before we dock on the Ivan."

"Isn't that the smallest ICS in the system?" The Rik leaf residue in my bloodstream must have remembered that because I sure didn't. "We'll stand out more in such a small community, won't we?" I thought of how everyone always recognized me and Felly on the Arxon. *What chance did we have to hide on the Ivan?*

"It's the smallest, but most transient," said Maddy, untangling his curls with rugged hands. "Besides, we'll be in the Quarantine Deck. Saloma checked everything out. We'll be safe there."

"Did Saloma check all the airlocks?" asked Alf.

"Not funny, Alf," I growled.

"You have something your great grandmother Levia did not," said Maddy.

"Right," I scoffed. "She was one of Caren's greatest queens—beautiful, famous, powerful—"

"Exactly," said Maddy.

I blinked. *Did he just insult me?* "Exactly *what?*"

"Queen Levia was too easy to recognize. Those trying to stop her could track her without any effort. You, on the other hand, are almost completely unknown in the System. Your anonymity is your shield."

Doubt wrinkled my forehead. "Wait. I just thought of something. She didn't live so long ago. Where's the rest of the royal family? If I'm descended from her, why am I *not* known? Why isn't my mother ruling the Empire now?" *Or did she run away from that like she did us?*

Alf let loose a single bark of laughter. "You mean I know something you don't?"

I scowled at him. "What?"

"A rotation on Caren taught me that much. The Empire dissolved about fifty years ago—I guess when Levia died—because all the local governors wanted more power. Her family faded into obscurity as they intermarried with regular people in the colonies."

"Levia made a noble effort to build unity," added Maddy, "but the factions divided up again when she died. Ninetta remembers, though, what it was like to be under Queen Levia." His breath caught, and he corrected himself. "Remembered." Grief over his mother's death showed raw in his eyes.

"Well, I probably wasn't in line for the throne anyway," I said, trying to kick away the sudden gloom. "And Mom married herself off the planet."

Alf forced a soft laugh. "It's good to be nobody, yeah?"

Maddy gave a half-hearted smile. "Yes, it is."

"We're just Alf and Caz Heywood now," said Alf, naming our aliases.

"Right," said Maddy. "Now cinch that coversuit tighter, Caz, and practice speaking with a lower voice."

OOO

The Quarantine Deck of the Ivan proved claustrophobic, even for a lifelong spacey like me. Maybe the artificial gravity provided a nice break, and it didn't have the constantly changing winds and temperatures of the Surface, but it felt like living in a box. No common areas broke up the monotony of the deck because that would spread germs, and travelers weren't supposed to enter each other's cubicles or cross the line that separated dorm sections by gender. Even our personal items were stored in a cargo bay devoted to those going through quarantine, lest they somehow contaminate the ship. King was there, tucked away in Maddy's ancient wooden chest. I hoped he would be comfortable until we could get to him. The architecture of the place managed to keep a hundred people isolated right next to each other.

Fortunately, the intake process was designed to keep us at a distance from all the staff, too. No point in getting them sick with the myriad diseases we no doubt carried from the Surface. I wasn't about to complain since it made it easier to hide my girl-ness.

Saloma had reserved us three cubicles in the same corridor: Maddy's to my left, a stranger to my right, and Alf on the other side of him. Apparently, we were to rendezvous with a cargo cruiser that would carry everyone in our row down to the mining colony of Garvey. No other drop location would bring us closer to the timberline Earlie trees that grew above the highest populated elevation. King would have to get some of the syrup—or sap—from a tree into my bloodstream somehow, but we hadn't discussed the particulars yet. These Gifts were not given lightly or received comfortably.

For those of us who had never been to Garvey, an attendant from the Ivan shared a short holographic presentation. As the blue shapes flickered before a semi-circle that included me, Alf, Maddy and another boy about our age, I willed moisture into my mouth. Even through the image, I could feel the dryness of the planet. Only a breathable atmosphere made it better than a giant asteroid. Solar panels, dizzying and blinding, covered all of the squat, hexagonal buildings. There were no bodies of water discernible from space, so all drinking water came from small subterranean streams. The temps at the mines would be at or below freezing most of the time. By the time the holograph faded, I wanted to apologize to everyone on the Arxon for ever whining about wanting to go to the Surface. Caren had been beautiful and lush, but this terrified me.

Nerves cracked my voice as I thanked the attendant, himself a native of Craggy. Fortunately, he credited this to a pubescent vocal change. "Voice drop. Good. Means beard grow soon."

At least I'm passing for a boy.

Turning back down the corridor, I whispered into Maddy's shoulder, "Why would anyone civilized want to live in such a barren wasteland?"

"Because no one civilized would want to live there."

"That makes no sense."

Alf poked me from behind. "No one civilized means no rules, yeah?"

"Oh, there are rules," said Maddy. "Only two, though. Don't get caught, and don't kill anyone who covers for you."

The boy who watched the holograph with us turned out to be in the cubicle between me and Alf. According to the pathetic progress of his facial hair, his voice had recently dropped. He grinned and rubbed his short black hair. "I guess I'm going to want to grow this so my ears'll stay warm. Pretty windy down there. My cousin Minster says they cover up good down there when they're outside and then take off all their clothes in the mines." He laughed and drew his first breath. Thrusting his right hand at me, palm up, he announced, "I'm Fizer. This'll be my first time on Craggy, but I need the money so I'm working the mines. I sure hope all my good marks in geology pay off. Who are you?"

"Caz Heywood," I said stiffly. I stared at his hand and swallowed.

Fizer grabbed my wrist with his left hand and then placed my hand in his right palm, wiggling it up and down lightly. "It's an ancient greeting custom. I like to study anthropology, too, but our learning center never had enough archives for me. It's called 'shaking hands'. I know we're not supposed to touch each other in quarantine, but I guess it won't matter since we're both coming up from Caren."

My ears followed a few words behind his rapid clip, and when my brain caught up, I nodded and shook his hand back.

"You got a strong hold. That's good," he beamed. "That's supposed to be a sign of honesty. I guess I can trust you."

My grip wilted, and I withdrew my hand into my blue-for-boys coversuit pocket.

"You planning on walking the halls for exercise? My cousin Minster told me to walk the halls a lot. It'll fight the boredom, too, I guess."

I smiled without answering aloud. Maddy, Alf and I could find a quiet spot in the halls to plan if needed.

"Well, I'll see you around." He pointed to my face vaguely. "Who knows? Maybe your beard'll come in by the end of the voyage."

I grinned wider. *He thinks I'm a boy, too.* With a shove to the release button, I opened the door to my cubicle and waved good-bye to Fizer.

OOO

Over the next four days, I bumped into Fizer at least thirty times while walking the halls for exercise. He could talk without breathing on two subjects: girls (which he knew nothing about) and geology (which he knew too much about). My bored grunts furthered my manly image in his eyes.

He caught up with me and Alf one morning after meal time. We'd been whispering about how much time Maddy had spent hidden away in his cubicle when Fizer rounded the corner.

"Talking about me, I guess," said Fizer almost self-consciously.

Alf restrained a sneer. "You guessed, you guesser, you."

Fizer stopped, uncertain, until I flashed a thin smile. The kid stood in visible awe of Alf's strong build, but he clearly viewed me as a fellow weakling and confidant. I didn't really care as long as the Rik leaves did their job and helped me remember everything he said about rocks on Craggy.

"Guess what?" asked Fizer.

"Couldn't possibly," said Alf.

"It's exciting this time. Even *you'll* want to know," he said to Alf. "I found a way into the cargo hold."

"What?" asked Alf. "You mean on the Quarantine Deck?"

Fizer bobbed his head proudly.

With a deep breath, I pushed aside germ containment concerns and focused on Fizer. "Huff, that's great. How?"

Fizer tapped the grated floor beneath us with the cloth toe of his coversuit. "I tripped and one of the grate panels popped up. I removed some screws and slipped through the vent system."

"Where does it come out?" asked Alf.

"Anywhere on this level, really," said Fizer, returning to his jovial clip. "There are ducts under the walkways about every five meters. They go up and down—the ducts, I mean—but not all the panels are loose, of course.

We'd have to bring along tools, and who brought those kinds of supplies? But I found another loose grate in the quarantine cargo hold. Guess they don't care too much about people tripping there. There were some—"

"You're brilliant," boomed Alf in the way he had discovered would silence Fizer without offending him.

Fizer licked his teeth and grinned. "I'm going in search of a girl! There's gotta be some on this deck, doncha think?"

I snorted and masked it with a fake sneeze. Back-handing him lightly on the shoulder, I said, "Germs! We'll get everyone on the Ivan sick if we climb in the vents!"

His face reddened. "Sorry. I wasn't thinking. I just…"

Alf shrugged it off. "She's just—"

I punched Alf's arm and grabbed onto his mistake. "*She's* just waiting for you, Fizer. Some girl can't wait to tie her lips to yours. Go find her and then tell us all about it!"

Fizer's face lit up again. "I'll find her. Better clean up first, though. Don't want to stink her up!" With a conspiratorial wink, he shut his cubicle door.

Alf gripped my wrist painfully. Through clenched teeth, he muttered, "What was *that* for? Punching me and winking at him?"

I pulled myself free. "I didn't wink. *He* did."

"What about the punch?"

"You called me '*she*.'"

Alf's face changed faster than Fizer's had. Terror and sadness melted his features downwards. With a hissed oath, he wrapped both arms around me in a tight embrace. "I'm so sorry. I almost ruined—I didn't mean to."

Surprise electrified my senses, and I felt as if I'd float away in his arms. "You'll cause more questions if you don't let go of me," I whispered.

He thrust me away so hard I banged into the wall opposite. Not hard to do in such a confined space. The door to Fizer's cubicle opened, and he peeked out. "You two fighting? I wouldn't recommend that, Caz. I guess Alf could probably hurt you bad enough for a Solitary sentence."

This time, neither Alf nor I bothered stifling our laughter. We each retired to our respective cubicles after Alf gave me a parting light punch to keep up the show.

OOO

"Dad, do you think the pearl is dangerous? I mean, physiologically?"

His blue holographic image floated over my comlink. "How do you feel? Does anything hurt?" he asked in his clinical tone, which always fit him better than the Father Figure. "Are you running a temperature? Got any rashes?"

"No, nothing like that."

"So what's worrying you?"

"I don't know," I whined. "There's a foreign object in my body. Isn't that cause for concern?"

He ran fingers through his hair. Even in the flickering image, I could see dark patches under his eyes. "People can go on for years with a projectile or piercing object lodged in—"

"Dad, it's moving around my body. It's not lodging anywhere. It's taking a tour!"

He chuckled. "I'm not worried unless you've seen any significant changes in your body."

"Actually, there is one thing."

His brows furrowed. "What?"

"My…uh…" I glanced down at my chest. "I'm rounding out rather rapidly."

"Gaining weight?"

"In two very select locations," I said, deadpan.

"Oh." The veins at his temple churned. "Well, you can thank your mother for that."

"Look, Dad, it's a problem if I'm going to pass as a boy."

"What? What do you mean?"

With a groan, I launched into the explanation that I knew would give him migraines for the next month.

"Tell me again why the fanep can't just go get the syrup and bring it to you on the nice, safe ICS? Which one are you on, anyway?"

"The Ivan," I said. "And I have to *touch* all three planets myself, Dad." I exhaled a steady stream of air. Talking to Dad always tied me in knots.

"The Ivan. That's good," he mused. "They've got some really archaic technology there."

"Why is that good?"

"You may be able to find a text tablet."

"Like the archives at Lamond Reformatory?"

"No, a communication device that sends information via text."

"No sound or image?"

"Just words. It's called a SWaTT—a System Wide Text Transmitter."

"Again, why is that good?"

He tilted his head sideways in a gesture usually reserved for confidential discussions with Felly. "Find one, and we'll be able to stay in contact no matter where you are in the Granbo System. They're powerful."

"But text?"

"Which you know how to read—"

"And most others don't," I said, catching on to his idea. The ICS system had shifted almost exclusively to iconic and numeric communications when not using audio, vids or holographs. "I'll look for one, but…"

"Quarantine Deck may not have them."

I suppressed a grin. "I've got a friend here who might be able to help with that." *Fizer. I might have to start being nicer to him.*

Dad described a SWaTT and insisted I send him messages in code. "Use anatomical analogies. Then, even if someone does know how to read, they'll think we're just talking about medicine."

My skin rippled with unexpected excitement. "What will we be talking about?"

"Anything and everything that will keep you safe until you've finished cycling that Gypsy Pearl!"

Tears filled my eyes. "Thanks, Dad. Thanks for being with me in this."

"I should have been with you sooner," he said heavily.

"I didn't have my comlink—"

"I mean, I should have been with you when you were *here* on the Arxon. If I'd been a present father, maybe you wouldn't have…" His voice dwindled, and I felt a surge of guilt.

Letting the tears fall, I said, "No, Dad. I'm half gypsy. Even if my brain didn't know it, my heart did." His sad half smile twisted something inside of me. "But I'm also your daughter, and I love you."

○○○

20 FLYING IN THE CARGO HOLD

The air in the ventilation system stung my nose, making it unpleasant to breathe. Beneath me, each panel had hundreds of holes just the right size for gripping with my fingers, except that the edges cut into my knuckles.

Fizer hadn't mentioned that the ducts often ran under the grated walkways for several meters in a row. The first time I emerged into one of these stretches, I almost screamed because two men stood in the hallway. I slid back down the way I'd come, hoping my dark hair would not be visible from above. The men seemed to be discussing a trade of goods. They stood close together, yet shouted everything in choppy half-sentences. If not for the fact that they looked at their feet as they spoke, I would have slithered beneath them, sure that their voices would cover any noise I could make. Instead, I remained crouched just out of sight, waiting.

After what felt like almost half an hour of bellowing baby sentences, they slapped each other's shoulders and clomped into their separate cubicles. I hesitated just a few seconds longer, listening for any movement, and then crawled with my arms pulling my cramped legs behind me. These spots just under the walkways provided less clearance, and I didn't want to risk bumping my backside on the grating and having it reverberate.

At last, I came up under an open space near a lift. The walls featured a slightly different shade of boring, and the vacuum beneath me tugged harder, probably to clear away all contaminants before someone changed levels. Halfway across the space, I heard footsteps and froze. If anyone looked down, they would see me. I groaned mentally and held my breath, not daring to peek up.

A light ring of vibrating metal told me that someone had stepped onto the panel directly above me.

"Do you have to go already? You just got here," said a boy's voice softly.

"I'll come see you soon," said a girl's voice. "I still have to unpack and go through orientation."

I glanced up and saw the back of a dark-haired boy in a blue quarantine coversuit. Some very feminine, yellow-clad arms wrapped around him.

Huff! Why did they have to kiss right here?

My torso and legs tingled from the suction of the vacuum, and I could envision the strange dots I would have all over my front when I got back to my cubicle.

The kissing couple came up for air, and the girl giggled. They seemed familiar. I rolled my eyes and pounded on the grate above me. "Hey Fizer! I see you finally found a girl!"

The couple turned, and the girl screamed.

I did, too—because it wasn't Fizer. It was Ruddie and Sasa!

She gulped back a sob, and I lay still, wondering what they would do. Their voices fluttered right above me. "Boy! Hey, you," said Ruddie tapping on the grate. "We know what you're doing, and we won't tell."

"For a price," added Sasa.

They hadn't recognized me. I peered up at her. "You seriously want to blackmail *me*, Sasa?"

Ruddie squinted down at me. "*Caz?* Is that *you?* You're alive? What are you doing here? What are you doing on the boys' deck?"

"I could ask the same of Sasa, but it's a long story. Get me out of here?"

To my surprise, Ruddie pulled a small tool from his pocket and began working the screws of the grate.

"Hurry!" urged Sasa, glancing over her shoulder at the lift doors. "Someone's coming!" She tugged at Ruddie's sleeve, and they darted away.

I scooted backwards as quickly as my arms could push me, feeling parts of my coversuit rip as they tore free of the vacuum holes. From the vent, I could see the lift door open and a man push a hover cart of cleaning supplies out. With a lazy pace, he walked across the grate and down the hall.

"Caz," hissed Sasa. "Go forward about twenty more meters. I'll meet you in the quarantine cargo hold."

OOO

After hearing their story, I shook my head at how much it didn't surprise me. Nightmare had been fired because Ora (and I) had died and Alf had escaped. Before leaving, though, he arranged for Ruddie's early release to the Ivan, which only proved he wasn't so scary after all. Sasa had then cashed in a string of "favors" and made it to the Ivan by express transit a week later.

Huddled behind a tall stack of crates in the least patrolled corner of the Ivan, they awaited my explanation. I decided not to tell them about the Gypsy Pearl, but focused on the story of becoming a miner on Craggy. I played up the adventure aspect and hoped they'd believe my restlessness had made me crazy enough to leave a perfectly beautiful planet.

"You'll make good money, but you'll never pass for a boy," Ruddie said, tossing his chin at my shredded coversuit.

Sasa grinned. "I don't know. She's stronger than the boys, Ruddie. Can't you get her another coversuit? You've made friends with the cleaning staff. I can't give her mine. It's the wrong color."

I hesitated. "I don't suppose you could find me a System-Wide Text Transmitter?"

His eyebrows shot up. "Do I want to know why?"

"No," I said.

"I do!" said Sasa eagerly.

Smiling as broadly as I could, I said more firmly, "No, Sasa. It's safer if you don't know."

"I'll find out some way." She winked and slipped back into the vent. From below, she whispered, "You seem to have a talent for danger, Caz. I won't believe any more reports of your death until I see the corpse myself."

OOO

My bladder nagged me, but I needed to find King. Cautiously, I stood, relishing the chance to stretch my legs. Scanning the walls, I located a door likely to lead to a lavatory on the opposite wall. Based on the lack of crates to my right, I assumed the three wide-paneled doors led to the docking bay. Normally, that would lure me with irresistible force, but I opted to go left instead. More crates meant more cover.

I padded quickly along the perimeter, grateful not to be in shoes. If I got caught in my shredded coversuit—a boy's coversuit—I'd have no explanation. I'd be punished severely for my fraud.

About halfway along the second wall, I came to a darkened room that held oddly shaped containers that could not be stacked in uniform towers like the crates. It occurred to me that Maddy's wooden chest must be stowed in there. With a glance over my shoulder, I slid into the darkness. I thought as hard as I could. *King? Are you in here?*

A faint tickle on the back of my neck crept up and around my scalp until I felt a distant answer. *I am here.*

"Where are you?" I squinted at the shapes, wishing the shaft of light that spilled in through the door offered more help.

Find my scent.

Frustrated, I reminded him telepathically that, although he could track me by the scent of my blood, I had no such talent. But even as I sent the thought, I picked up the woody smell of Maddy's ancient trunk. I dropped to my hands and knees and felt the different shapes until my fingers touched the familiar grain. A moment later, I'd released the lock, and King's yellow eyes glowed at me with that mixture of mischief and serenity that only he could manage. He wriggled out and clutched me in a childlike embrace. I squeezed him back, lifting him into my arms like a doll.

"How do you breathe in there?" I whispered.

He blinked slowly. Until his lips parted to reveal rows of sharp teeth, he looked like a tiny, harmless, bald man. "Lungs go slow."

"What?"

"Mind rules body."

Right then, my bladder reminded me of my original quest. "Uh, I don't think I can do that."

"With second Gift."

"The second Gift you gave me was the Rik leaf crown. Did that make my brain smart enough to—?" Even as I spoke, the pressure diminished. My mouth fell open. "Did I just…?"

King bowed. "Queen can control."

Impulsively, I hugged him tighter. Huff, I didn't really want to rule the Granbo System, but this—ruling my body! *Wait until I tell Dad!*

A noise outside startled us. I strained to listen for footsteps, voices, or the whirr of hover carts, but my heart pounded too loudly to be sure of what I heard. Just as panic wanted to grip me, my mind settled with a sensation of calm. *King.* I don't know how he did it, but he could reach into my nerves and muffle them with peace any time. I crawled with him on my hands and knees to the door.

A woman pounded on the door to the lavatory. "Are you still in there? Hurry up! You've spent half your shift in there."

A garbled voice responded, and the woman yelled again. "The Station Master will hear about this."

King pointed back to where I had entered the cargo hold. *Must not shout.*

"Huh? Why would I—?"

The next thing I knew, he had picked me up with his crazy, inhuman strength, and thrown me into the air. I flew—or fell horizontally—across the cargo hold, barely missing the ceiling. The trajectory took me right to the corner where I'd first entered. Before I could worry about the landing, it happened again, just like that day in the gypsy cave. I wafted to the ground like a bubble, landing without a sound on my cloth-covered feet.

I crouched low and peered back to the opposite wall. The woman stormed away from the lavatory, oblivious to our stunt, and a few seconds later, a scrawny man emerged and walked in the other direction. My eyes darted to where King stood concealed from the man's view. From across the room, King nodded and smiled before vanishing in a blur.

Sinking to the ground, I fidgeted with my coversuit, trying to poke the torn edges back into place. I'd have to keep waiting for Ruddie to return, but at least I didn't have to use the toilet any more.

I wondered what other bodily functions I could slow down or change. The idea that doing such things could backfire and cause kidney troubles pricked at me, though. So much so that I felt sharp pains up and down my legs. Maybe the toxins got into my bloodstream, or—

"Caz Artemus, you must be made of iron," hissed a voice beneath me.

Ruddie! I shifted to see him holding his screwdriver, poised to jab me again.

"I got you a SWaTT, but no luck on the coversuit. You'd better hurry back. The meals are about to be delivered. I'll show you a safer route to your section."

OOO

The attendant handed me a tray of food and squinted at me suspiciously. "Why are you wrapped in a blanket?"

I feigned a burp and lowered my voice. "Had a little nausea. My coversuit is ruined."

The man's nose twitched as if he could smell the imaginary vomit, and he took a step back. "Did you put it in the laundry chute?"

"Of course," I lied. No way would I throw that shredded suit where someone would find it and investigate the damage. I'd use it to pad my middle and make me more blobby shaped. "I'll need another size 6, medium tall."

He touched a control panel outside my door. A synthesized voice said, "Passenger 32, Garvey Colony, Craggy. Intake systems scan clean. Coversuit size 5 medium tall."

I grunted a low laugh. "That explains why the last one was so tight. Some idiot must have put in the wrong number."

"That happens if there's background noise when they record," he agreed, reaching for the hovercart stacked with food trays. "Someone will bring that by soon." He nudged the hovercraft onward with his knee and knocked on Fizer's door.

In my cubicle again, I placed the tray on the small bedside table and retrieved the SWaTT from under the pillow. It powered on like the outdated reading tablets I'd seen at Lamond Reformatory, but I didn't find a table of contents from which to select articles. Instead, I could enter the location to which I wanted to send a message, like on a comlink, except that I had to press little squares with letters and numbers on them. It was a bit tedious, but I managed to get the settings for the Arxon Resident Deck suite 254. If Dad had found a receiving device, we'd be able to exchange messages easily once the initial contact was made.

Now to compose a message. I sighed and took a bite of the spacey "bread" on my tray, wondering how King was getting food. Chewing gave me time to think how to explain what had just happened in medical code. *Why had Felly and I not used this as a game growing up? Oh, yeah. She didn't like games.* I took another bite and rubbed at the suction welts on my stomach.

Inserted sphere temporarily incapacitated patient's susceptibility to gravity under extreme test circumstances. No external injuries. Patient's urinary and pancreatic systems adjustable at will. Please advise if restraints should be used. I hoped he would understand and pressed the transmit command. The Arxon orbited millions of kilometers away, and I didn't know how long the transmission would take to reach Dad, or if he'd be able to receive it at all.

With nothing else to do, I stepped into the washroom section in the corner of my cubicle. It had a tiny toilet, a hand sink, and a shower nozzle that sprayed down over all of it. Steam soon filled the space, and I let the water fall on my stiff back and shoulders. My allotment of time under the weak stream would run out soon, but I couldn't make myself lather up. I just stood there. At the last second, I remembered to thrust my head in the stream of water. The flow stopped and I heard a faint high-pitched beep. I wrung my hair dry and looked out. There on my bed, a green light on the SWaTT winked on and off. I snatched it up and stared at the screen.

Report received. Advise of any further changes in the patient's status. Artificial controls of internal systems should be used with caution until further examination is possible.

The screen flashed white two times and a new message appeared. *Ultrasound indicates patient's right clavicle should adhere and be kept close to the cardial cavity. Evidence of investigative laparoscopic probe S/R. Advise if this procedure is safe to continue or should be aborted.*

My eyes glazed with confusion. Dad gave me way too much credit. The Rik leaves helped with memory and calculations, not decoding this kind of stardust.

I slumped onto my bed, shivering with a sense of futility. With the blanket, I started to dry myself off. Air dryers are too loud and don't work well.

A light rap sounded, and I heard the catch of my door release. I saw a familiar hand slide around it and quickly maneuvered the blanket to cover me.

"Huff, Alf!" I yelped.

He spun awkwardly and faced the door as it slid closed. "I'm so sorry! I didn't know." The back of his neck flushed, and he brought his fists up to his eyes as if to punch the vision of my wet self out of his brain. I laughed even as I maneuvered myself under the covers on my bed. "You can turn around now," I whispered.

"You sure?"

"Only my head shows." I sat with my knees folded up and the blanket pulled up to my nose.

He glanced over his shoulder. "You look like a mashed revo with eyes."

I giggled and smoothed my wet hair flat against my face. It had grown a little, but was still short enough to pass for a boy my age.

Alf took a step closer, still averting his gaze. "Sorry. I didn't actually see anything."

"I know."

"Where's your coversuit?"
"It's a long story."

OOO

"What's a clavicle?" asked Alf when I read Dad's message to him.
"Seriously?"
"My dad isn't a doctor, yeah?"
Stuffing the blanket under my arm to expose my shoulder, I indicated on my own body. "The bone there."
He ran his thumb along my neck and shoulder, and his touch on my bare skin sent shivers down to my tail bone. I quickly pulled the blanket back up. "It's really easy to break," I said.
Alf bobbed his head. "I did that three years ago. Couldn't use my arm for weeks."
"Yeah, it's one of those bones that seems useless, but it actually keeps the bigger stuff moving."
"Like Fizer," he smirked.
My jaw dropped. "Alf, you're a genius! Fizer! Fizer is my right clavicle."
"Yeah," he grinned. "Wait. What?"
"If I'm supposed to keep Fizer close to my 'cardial cavity'—"
"Is that the real word?"
"No, but close to my heart—"
"What?" he coughed. "You supposed to fall in love with him?"
"No, stupid. Just keep him like a close friend."
He grunted and crossed his arms. "I don't like it."
"Oh, come on. Fizer's not dangerous. Dad probably means I need to get information from him. He must trust Fizer. That's good, isn't it?" Alf didn't answer. Studying the SWaTT again, I said, "This laparoscopic thing has me worried, though."
"What's the lapro thing?"
"It's a more invasive procedure to explore internal organs or even do surgery. Kind of awkward and old-fashioned compared to what Dad would do."
"Who's exploring who?"
"That's what I'm worried about. It sounds like someone is trying to investigate me and is maybe being a little too obvious about it. But I don't know what 'S/R' means—oh, yes, I do!" I grabbed his arm, almost losing my blanket. "It must be Sasa and Ruddie!"
"What do you mean? They're back on Caren."
"No, they're here on the Ivan!"
"They are? Why—?"
The door rattled under a sharp knock. "Coversuit for you!" called a

whiny voice.

With a hoarse oath, Alf bolted into the washroom, making entirely too much noise.

I hesitated and wrapped my blanket tighter. Shuffling to the door, I released the catch.

"You all right in there?" asked the man.

"I tripped," I said, shrugging at my blanket.

"Oh, yeah. Of course." He handed me a neatly folded coversuit. "Well, this'll help. Hope you feel better."

I nodded thanks and slid the door shut. Alf peeked out of the washroom and I pointed my coversuit at him. Barely audible through gritted teeth, I hissed, "We have got to work on your stealth."

"Yeah?" he asked, chewing his lip. He tip-toed with exaggerated movements over to me and stood with his forehead nearly touching mine. "Better?" he mouthed.

My breathing stopped and my heartbeat a sporadic tattoo. "Much better," I whispered. "Now keep doing that all the way to your room. I need to get dressed."

He brushed past me, slipping out of the door. I exhaled a breath I didn't know I'd held. Something had happened to me physiologically that had nothing to do with the Gypsy Pearl. It was Alf. I couldn't say I hated it, *but did I have time for it now when Ruddie and Sasa might be inadvertently exposing my identity?*

ooo

21 A GOOD-BYE

When Maddy emerged from his cubicle, his whole being showed the strain of grief, and it made me hurt to see him. With forced cheerfulness, he asked if I'd put on weight.

"Does it look like it?" I asked hopefully. "It's a bigger coversuit," I said more quietly. "Does it hide the curves?"

He smiled. "Smart thinking."

"Walk with me," I said, heading down the corridor. "I have news." We turned a corner and I swiveled to walk backwards, running my hands along the walls to keep balance. In this way, we could keep our voices low while I told him everything I'd learned from Fizer's constant chatter, my visits with Ruddie and Sasa, and the SWaTT texts from Dad.

"So Ruddie and Sasa won't report you?" he asked.

"No," I said. "But I haven't told them the whole pearl thing."

"Can they help us?" he asked. I shrugged a maybe. "It sounds like we should listen to this Fizer kid," he said. "If we learn as much as we can from him, we can get promoted faster. The most comfortable positions go to the most knowledgeable."

"Right," I agreed. "And comfortable positions mean more access to transportation we might need to get to the timberline. Looks like we'll have to work there for a while."

"This won't be like a quick jog to the ICS commissary." Maddy chuckled. "Just make sure everyone thinks you're a boy, Caz."

I tried to laugh at that, but I had to tell him about my last visit with King. He wasn't going to like it. "King wants to stay with me when we go down, not you. I mean, if we end up getting separated." I winced at how cruel that sounded. "I think he's trying to protect me, but…"

Maddy stopped walking, his expression hurt, but he bravely squared his shoulders. "All right, then," he said.

"We might end up being together anyway," I said hopefully.

His lips pressed in a thin line. "I'll trust his judgment, and yours, my lady."

I wanted to comfort him, but I didn't know how. It felt like I was taking one more person from his life. He had repeatedly assured me that he didn't blame me for Ninetta's death, but the pearl in my arm could have saved her from the viper's poison if he'd had it in powder form. I hated the burden of that guilt, even if my rational side said not to carry it.

Before we could say more, an attendant with a hover cart of empty food trays appeared. His disapproving look spurred us down the hall.

"My lady, if I'm not needed to keep King or you safe, then I guess I'll go on to Tye and wait for you there, if you don't mind." He thumbed the tattoo on his cheek. "I've spent too much time on Craggy, anyway."

"In the prison," I mumbled. Right. *Why would he want to go back to that planet if he didn't have to?*

"It could be in a palace, and it would be too long," he said. "You'll see. Craggy is nothing like Caren."

My eyes blurred with tears and I threw my arms around him, squeezing him tightly. Maddy was everything I used to wish Dad would be: loving, adventurous, and—I admit it—focused on me more than himself. I shivered inside to think of facing a new, forbidding planet without him.

As if he knew what I was thinking, he placed his hands on my shoulders. "You'll be all right, my lady," he whispered. "You have been called to this, and you are more than capable. I'll go to Tye and tell the faneps and gypsies there you're coming." When I mumbled assent, he added, "I'll use the time to dive for more pearls."

Stung, I agreed, "We should always have a supply of powdered pearl on hand."

"Right."

I squeezed Maddy's hand. *What could I say?* He kept me alive and taught me so much, but now Alf and I would have to rely on King, Fizer and our own wits. At least we had allies in space. We wouldn't really be alone—just millions and millions of kilometers apart.

OOO

I lifted my crates. "Come on. Time to board the cargo cruiser."

"Right," said Alf. "It's Caz and Alf Heywood *returning* to Craggy, yeah? We'll talk like the natives, and we've been mining for two years over in Keene to the south."

"Right. No reason to doubt us."

He bent over to pick up his crates. "I sure hope Saloma's right about this."

I resisted the urge to nudge him over with my knee, and a few minutes later we came up behind Fizer and eight other older, hairier men all headed for the Garvey Colony via the cargo cruiser, Ipko.

"Oh good, you made it in time!" beamed Fizer. "I was getting worried. The transfer tube just locked in place."

I stared through the opening to see the black endless night of space. "Of course," I said, my voice cracking.

A second glance made my stomach lurch. The men in front of us floated into the stars. *Any second now they'd explode in the vacuum of space!* Then Fizer bounded unafraid through the hole that led to a transparent tube with no artificial gravity. Before long, his body rotated so that he looked upside down to me. Further down the line, others sprawled and drifted through the tube.

Alf exhaled loudly next to me. "Better act like we know what we're doing, yeah?" He gestured to my second crate. "He in there?"

I nodded, holding the crate tighter. King probably wouldn't mind the weightlessness. He'd been through it more often. Thinking of him reminded me of my control over body systems, and I wondered if I'd be able to use that to prevent nausea.

"Go," urged Alf, shoving his crates along the ground. A few meters out, they lifted off of the bottom of the tube and listed to one side, still going so quickly that they tapped Fizer's foot.

"Hey!" called Fizer. "Space out!"

With a snort of disgust, Alf launched himself into the tube, lying in the air with his arms rigid in front of him. He spiraled at least twice before bracing himself against the tube with his hands.

Figuring he'd pushed off with too much force, I controlled my strength. I set the bottom crate down and slid it with my foot into the tube, but I didn't let go of the crate that held King. Kneeling and crawling into the tube, I felt the pull of gravity end abruptly. For the first time in my life, I had Felly-like reservations about what I was doing. I hugged the crate tightly as my feet fell upward—and then I felt peace. Unlike the others, my body did not rotate. I glided steadily through the tube. In my heart I knew that King had something to do with the smoothness of my journey. While the others thumped and bumped against the tube walls ahead of me, we floated serenely onward. I closed my eyes against the enormity of the emptiness outside and trusted King.

WHAM!

My body jolted and the corner of my crate jabbed into my shoulder. I pushed up to see the door to the airlock close. The others stood safely inside the cargo cruiser, *but I remained trapped in the tube!*

OOO

22 THE *IPKO*

I pounded on the airlock door, but the force ricocheted me backwards through the tube. Scrambling for traction, I spread my limbs wide enough to catch myself and then maneuvered back up to the airlock.

"King!" I warbled nervously. "King, what do I do now?"

POP!

I pulled back, expecting to see him emerge from one of the crates, but instead a circle of light appeared around the rim of the airlock, and the door swung open. A man held on to a bar above the door and reached out to me. "Grab my hand."

He tugged me hard. Not thinking about the return to gravity, I fell in a heap to the ground at his feet.

"Oh, you're a smart one, huh?" he smirked. "Can't remember to put your feet down." He shook his head disapprovingly, and I wondered if Alf made the same mistake, or if he'd been able to learn from the others in front of him.

I stood and started to reach for my crates.

"Whoah. Wait, stupid. Grab the handle first." He folded his arms.

With a weak smile, I played up how dumb I felt, and used the bar as an anchor while I pulled my crates into the airlock. However, I forgot to curb my strength and ended up throwing them with way too much force against the inside wall.

The man heaved the airlock door shut. Regarding me with skepticism, he said, "Strong and stupid. Perfect for Garvey." He stood watching the door on the opposite wall, bored.

I thought I should establish my persona, so I practiced the stilted speech of Craggy in my manliest voice. "What cargo?"

He turned sharply, as if surprised. "I never ask," he grinned, but his eyes did not assure me of good will.

The door opposite the tube slid open, and I stepped through quickly, catching Alf's concerned look.

Fizer, still holding his crates, bumped his shoulder playfully against mine. "That's what you get for being at the end of the line. Only ten at a time in the airlock. What was it like? You feel all right? I almost vomited twice, but it seems like we all came through clean." He filed into the tiniest lift I'd ever seen and wagged his eyebrows at us. "See you next level!" The door slid shut.

Alf and I studied each other silently for well over a minute as we waited for the lift to return. When it reopened, he signaled with his head for me to enter. To my surprise, he squeezed in beside me, dropping his crates to the floor and gesturing for me to put mine on top.

The door closed us into the cylindrical lift, about as wide as the tube had been. Without moving his lips, Alf said quietly, "No surveillance in the lift."

"You noticed one in the hall?" *How had I missed that?*

"Not very trusting, are they?" he said bitterly. "And can we trust *them*?"

"I think so?"

"Thinking isn't knowing," he said grimly.

His pessimism chafed me, but I nodded again. I felt like I never spoke any more. Just nodded and grunted.

"The lift should have opened by now," he breathed through gritted teeth.

On cue, the door opened into a small command center. Panels of controls filled the walls not comprising the lift door. Two men in hover seats studied streams of data and a block of surveillance vids.

One of the men spun around and glided his hover seat towards us. "Hello," he said, cocking his head to one side. "Are you lost?"

"Must be," said Alf, taking a step back.

"I'm Captain Derven of the Ipko."

I nodded, and Alf grunted, "Yes, sir."

Captain Derven pressed his lips together and watched us squirm. "We've got three days before we reach Garvey. I would appreciate it if you did not abuse the lift by traveling two at a time. This is an old ship, and I don't entirely trust it to hold together."

"I'm sorry," said Alf. "We didn't…"

"No harm done," said Derven with a flicker of a smile. He spun back to his controls. "Get to level three for your tour."

"I'll go first," said Alf, quickly re-entering the lift. For a long minute, I watched the lift, willing my turn to come faster.

Derven broke the silence. "I advise you not to intoxicate yourself again."

"What?" I croaked. "I've never been intoxicated in my life!" I remembered too late that I hadn't spoken like a person from Craggy. He must have seen me in the airlock on the surveillance cam falling and crashing crates.

The silence that followed scared me. He took a deep breath without turning around. "Trust has to be earned. It's expensive, and I don't usually give a line of credit to a new face." The door opened behind me, but my feet remained welded to my spot by fear. "I don't take to liars," he said, almost looking over his shoulder.

"No, sir," I coughed. I stepped into the lift, squeezing my crates with white knuckles.

The lift descended way too fast. I tried to swallow a rush of emotion, but instead, bile filled my throat, preventing me from screaming like a little Felly. The overhead light flickered, and the background hum became a roar. The tiny cabin hit bottom, and my chin slammed into the crate with such force that my teeth sliced into my bottom lip.

"King, are you all right?" I hissed, licking away a trickle of blood.

Every part of me ached, and I twisted my head cautiously to find the ceiling of the lift folded into a sharp point not thirty centimeters over my head.

I whimpered, "King? You in there?" He didn't respond. Grasping for control of my senses, I shifted and kicked hard against the lift door. It buckled outwards slightly, but only opened a sliver of air about a centimeter wide. Even repositioning, I couldn't gain leverage to pull the door open, so I pressed my nose to the opening and screeched for help. "Alf!"

"I'm here!" he called. "Why won't the door open?"

"The lift fell," I cried through the line of light. "The door is—"

A loud metallic clang sounded, and the door dented inward.

"What's going on?" I yelled.

Amidst more banging and thudding noises, I heard voices shouting, "We'll get you out!"

"Wait!"

"We're almost there!"

With extreme effort, I tried to calm myself by focusing on a mental triage of all of my body parts to determine which ones hurt. King tickled my mind from within the crate letting me know he was alive and well. I tried to be happy about this, but my stomach overruled my mind, and I spewed all over the crates. It trickled down onto my legs, and I squealed, "Get me out *now!*"

Pressing my back against the wall, I shoved my leg with all my strength. Twisting metal complained back at me, and I stared at the gaping hole of torn steel. *Had I done that? How could I explain it?*

"Caz!" Alf pulled out the crates that blocked my way. Numb with fear, I crawled out and collapsed into Alf's arms where he knelt beside me. He held me tightly, and several seconds passed before I sensed onlookers muttering and swearing under their breath.

"No wonder he screamed like a girl," I heard Fizer say. "The cables snapped!"

Someone pulled the remains of the lift door fully aside. The crumpled cabin filled half of its usual space, and above it squirmed two lengths of sparking wiring.

"Huff!"

Others murmured agreement, and one man knuckled my shoulder.

"Cave-ins for mines, not lifts. You lucky no mountain over you."

I laughed weakly and stood up. They all slapped my shoulder or ruffled my hair grunting words of caution. "Danger everywhere."

"Adventure for strong."

"Garvey worse."

Their sympathetic tones implied I was too small for the mines.

Alf squared his shoulders and faced the miners. "Why cables break like that?" He pointed at me fiercely. "He's smallest boy in group. Not too heavy, yeah?"

Fizer raised a calming hand. "It's okay. Your brother's all right." He looked at me with concern. "You *are* all right, right?"

I stared down at my rumpled, vomit-smeared self. "Right." I wiped my hands and folded my arms across my chest in what I hoped passed like a manly way. Twenty eyes bore into me with surprise and appreciation.

"Little, but lucky," said a miner.

Alf peered along the upper corners of the room and found a security cam lens. Waving with both arms, he shouted, "The lift broke!"

An intercom speaker crackled from somewhere in the ceiling, and Captain Derven's voice came on: "Please wait there. I'll send my first officer down through another lift." Static followed, and then, as if in afterthought, Derven asked, "Was anyone hurt?"

I moved to face the camera, feeling a rush of stupid defiance. "No!" I barked in my best man voice.

My heartbeat steadied, and I reached with my mind to King, still concealed not far away in the crate. Clearer than any impression previously received, I felt King's words: *Queen has friends. Queen has enemies.*

000

Mr. Kinny, the first officer, assessed the damage grimly and ordered us all to our berths. I quickly snatched up my crates, hugging them—hugging King, really—to my chest with relief. With five tiny dorms available to house eleven miners, Fizer volunteered to bunk with me and Alf. I thought Alf would pop a blood vessel, but instead, he punched Fizer on the arm with a grin. "Good thinking, I guess."

Fizer rubbed the spot of impact with hesitant pride, and we soon stacked our crates along the wall opposite the built-in bunks. This allowed about half a meter of floor space.

"I can bunk with Caz, since you're bigger," offered Fizer to Alf.

"He's my brother, yeah? I'm used to his stink," said Alf. "We get bottom bunk."

I examined the narrow berth. We'd have to sleep on our sides to fit. Maybe I'd just slip onto the floor after Fizer went to sleep and hope he didn't jump down in the middle of the night to go to the lavatory.

"I'm going to change into a fresh coversuit," I said, indicating the stains. Bent over my two crates, I opened King's hiding space slightly, my body shielding him from view. I couldn't see his face, but he slipped his hand through and wiggled his fingers in a wave. A second later, he crammed a bundle of cloth out of the opening—a clean coversuit. "I'll be right back. I need to wash off," I said, stepping out into the hall.

Another miner jerked a chin at me. "Lucky."

My name now?

Consulting a floor plan diagram on the wall across from our door, I discovered I'd have to go up a level to all common rooms: washrooms, cafeteria, game room. With my coversuit under my arm, I trudged as heavily as I could, mimicking the gait of the Craggy miners. I turned the corner to find the man who called me Lucky holding the lift door open for me. This one could carry several passengers at a time, and I wondered why we hadn't been directed towards this one in the first place.

"Which way?" asked the man.

Considering all levels but the cargo bay lay above us, it seemed a strange question, but I didn't want to treat him like an idiot. "Up," I said.

He burst out laughing and punched the button to level 3. The door closed and he kept chortling. "Lucky, you right. You had a day!"

I assumed he referred to my crash and the vomit, so I smirked humorlessly, which just made him guffaw all the more. As the door slid open for our level, he slapped my back. "Up!" he repeated, heading towards the door at the end marked with the ICS icon for cafeteria.

Following a few steps behind, I ducked into the washroom. Inside, four shower stalls and four lavatories framed in textured metal meant I'd at least have privacy if I could do all my clothing changes in the tiny space without getting wet. I showered with my coversuit over the door, realizing too late that I'd forgotten to grab a towel. Turning off the water, I heard a noise that could only be a miner relieving himself, and shortly after, an air dryer roared and echoed around the room.

Air dryers. No towels. *Huff.* I had an unexpected twinge of homesickness for the washrooms on the Arxon where Felly and I showered and she tried to fix my hair. Although I fought it at the time, the idea of her making me prettier didn't sound so bad now. Being a boy was grubby work.

Kicking my soiled coversuit into the corner, I did what I could to shake water off my skin. Ruddie had finally found me two more size 6 suits in blue, and I now battled to pull one on over my damp body. It really knocked me out of orbit to think of all I had accomplished in the last month, and yet I still couldn't get dressed while wet.

Still tugging at the coversuit, I stepped back into the hall.

"How are you feeling, Heywood?"

I jerked my head up and almost crashed into Mr. Kinny. Wagging my head casually, I said, "Oh. Better. Not dead."

His face darkened with concern. "You were very lucky."

"Yeah, my new name. Lucky," I said as flippantly as I could while keeping my voice low. "I bet that'll give the captain another reason not to like me."

The un-Craggy speech slipped out before I thought about it, but the real surprise came when he cringed with me. "You're right," he said quietly.

A shiver went down my spine with his admission. "What? Why?"

"He is a very suspicious man." I nodded, unsure of what to say. Mr. Kinny put a hand on my shoulder, glancing up at the security cam. Tilting his head to block his face from the lens, he whispered. "Saloma knew that."

If he had kicked me in the stomach, he could not have ousted more air from my lungs. "Saloma?"

"She may have been counting on his nature." He waved back at the lift. "Accidents like that happen all the time when he's not in a trusting mood."

Saloma set me up to be killed by putting me with a dangerously paranoid man.

OOO

That night, after Fizer's full stomach finally weighed him down to sleep, Alf and I huddled in the bottom bunk as I texted Dad. Alf watched over my shoulder, trying to read along. His skills were barely half mine, and his lips moved as he tried to decipher the letters.

A moment later, Dad replied: *Medical reports only on this channel, please.*

Huff! In my haste, I'd forgotten to use our anatomical codes.

Another message flashed: *Base of the esophagus.* I squinted in confusion, and we waited for more. Nothing came.

I lay down on my side, and Alf draped his arm around me from behind. His touch made me tremble despite the warmth it provided, but I didn't move. Before drifting off to sleep, I remembered that the esophagus leads into the stomach where all the toxic acids are. *I'm at the base of the esophagus?*

OOO

Saloma wanted me dead. That meant I couldn't trust any aspect of the plans to get me to Craggy, and with Maddy gone, only two people with me knew the whole story—and one of them had to stay hidden. At least I'd been able to sneak King under my bunk and bring in food from the cafeteria tucked in my pockets.

I wondered how much Kinny knew about me. He did not acknowledge my gypsy connections in front of the other miners. Instead, he assigned Fizer and me to duty in the cargo bay. We earned part of our passage by working the ship.

"Check the temps on the outer rim crates," he said with a strange look in his eyes.

We took the larger lift down a level—equivalent to four levels because of the height of the cargo hold—and I flinched at every creak of the mechanisms.

Fizer and I stood in the central aisle of the storage area. Rows of towering crates branched off in either direction like bristles of a comb.

"What kind of cargo is so fragile temp-wise that packing it near the outer wall is an issue?" I asked. "There are layers of insulation against heat and cold."

"Something radioactive," guessed Fizer. He strolled along with the top half of his body tilted sideways so he could read the icons on the polynthex crates.

"Then there'd be rad-suits," I persisted, scanning the walls casually for security cams. I located four.

"Huh," grunted Fizer, crouching beside an unmarked crate near the back wall. He pressed the *Content Reveal* button, and a blue holographic image of the crate's contents appeared at our feet. "Small rocket components?" He frowned up at me with furrowed brows. "That's kinda strange for a mining company."

"How do you know what they are?"

"My friend's dad makes Surface-to-Air missiles for the security patrols on Craggy."

"I thought security patrols were the ones in the air," I said.

"Depends on the planet. Craggy people stay grounded with the heavy gravity. No good landing strips, either. Mostly only the criminals go airborne in contraband skimmers or small ships."

"Fizer, you are a never-ending source of fascinatingly useless information."

He beamed up at me and then crawled to the next crate, also unmarked. "They stacked this one wrong," he said, palming the exposed side in search of the *Content Reveal*. "But this *is* a temp-controlled crate."

I grabbed the corners and hauled it out into the aisle. This part of the cargo bay fell outside of the gaze of security cams, I noticed.

Fizer barked out a laugh. "You're stronger than you look, I guess. Maybe you could beat up your brother after all."

"You better believe it," I said, giving him a tough scowl. "Lean muscle mass."

Fizer chuckled and ran his hand along the edges until he found the *Content Reveal*. When he pressed it, we squatted and stared at the image with confusion.

"Liquids?" he asked. With another tap of the button, the image magnified, and we scrutinized it more closely.

"Half of the tubes are empty," I said. *Why would Derven be so concerned about empty tubes?*

"Maybe not," said Fizer. "Maybe they've got some kind of gas inside?"

"Good point. But why keep them in little tubes instead of a tank?"

A red tracking laser pierced the holographic image. "Because they're very potent," said a voice behind us.

We turned to find the guard from the airlock aiming a small laser pistol at us. His chin trembled as he spoke. "You two need to step away from that crate."

"Don't move," I said, grabbing Fizer's arm and holding him to the spot.

"What?" he hissed. "Are you crazy?"

"Move!" shouted the guard.

"*Don't* move," I repeated. "If he wants to kill us, he will. But if he fires at us with this crate right behind us, he risks destroying the precious cargo." I smiled at the sudden stiffness in the guard's jaw. "Maybe even the whole ship?" I added.

The guard gripped the weapon tighter, but shuffled back. "Come on. Move, or I shoot!"

I squared my shoulders. "I guess you'll have to shoot us here."

"What are you *doing*?" whimpered Fizer through gritted teeth.

"Fizer, this man wants to shoot us, and I'd like to find him a reason not to."

The guard shifted his aim back and forth between the two of us. "Captain Derven doesn't like industrial spies."

"We're not spies!" exclaimed Fizer.

"I…I don't like what you did to our ship!" added the guard, pointing at me with his free hand. "You wrecked the lift. How'd you do that?"

Fizer laughed uncomfortably. "How can you blame that on—?"

"Move, or I'll shoot!" shrieked the guard.

I raised my hand in a calming gesture. "You know you're not going to shoot us until we move, so you might as well relax." I lowered myself slowly to the floor and sat with my legs crossed. "See? I'm not going to run."

The guard wavered. "Who are you really?"

"It's probably safer if you don't know," said another voice.

The guard fell, stunned, to the floor.

"I don't know what you did to get on Saloma's bad side," said Mr. Kinny, rounding into view, "but you'll get on mine, too, if you're not more careful with the ship. First the lift, and now this." He indicated the crate. "Please return that to its proper position very carefully."

"We're not spies," whined Fizer. "We were just doing what you said."

"I know," said Kinny, watching me with narrowed eyes as I slid the crate back into place.

Glancing the way he'd come, I asked, "Aren't you supposed to kill us, too?"

Fizer, coming up out of his panicked stupor, shook me by the elbow. "Who is Saloma? Why are they trying to kill you? *Are* they trying to kill you? What's going on?"

Neither Kinny nor I spoke. I couldn't read his face. *Would he blow my cover?*

Fizer looked at me, his confidence visibly wounded. In that second, Kinny tazed him with a device he'd concealed in his other hand. Fizer collapsed in a heap.

OOO

23 ENEMIES AND ALLIES

I turned a steely glare on Kinny.

He raised his pistol and taser above his head to show he meant me no harm. "I didn't know if your friend knew your story, and we need to talk quickly before Derven suspects."

"Does Derven know who I am?"

"No," said Kinny, holstering his pistol.

"Do you?"

"I know that you could easily break my arm, but I'm going to ask you to come with me, and don't acknowledge the cameras." He took my wrist and gently folded my arm behind my back, not exerting enough pressure for it to hurt. "Make a good show, please, and don't let your lips move as we speak."

Ah. He had "captured" me, and I needed to play prisoner for the monitors.

"What about Fizer and the guard?" I asked, my lips in a loose, unmoving scowl. "Don't you think someone's going to notice bodies lying around?"

"They'll wake up in an hour with headaches. I'll move them before then and give them a cover story. Walk faster."

I shuffled down the main aisle, resisting the urge to peek at the cams.

"With all the damage you've done to the lift, it'll be hard to hide your …condition…from any familiar with fanep lore."

I halted, sucking in a sharp breath, which probably played well for the cameras. "You know?"

"Come with me. As crazy as Captain Derven is, he is safer than Saloma. She has been petitioning the faneps for years to be the one to cycle a pearl. It's no grand secret she wants the power that goes with it."

OOO

"I took the liberty of bringing your brother up, too." Captain Derven sat in his command chair. Nothing about him looked relaxed.

Alf stood in his ready stance, his arms hanging deceptively loose at his side, but I could sense his energy and his willingness to fight. If it came down to it, the two of us might very well be able to overpower Derven and Kinny, but then we would have a whole different level of trouble.

"Why are you two posing as miners?" asked Derven.

"We *are* miners," grunted Alf.

"You've never mined a day in your life," said Derven sharply.

"Gotta start someday," Alf countered with that amazing confidence he showed in tense situations. "This our first try."

Derven smirked. "Are you trying to convince me you're from Craggy with that talk?" When Alf didn't answer, Derven grabbed my face in one hand. "You two are from Caren. Your skin betrays it."

"So we're from Caren," shrugged Alf. "So's Fizer."

With a brusque flick of his wrist, Derven let go of my face. "You're too young. You can't have studied enough geology."

A rush of gratitude for Fizer restored the color to my face. "Ask me anything." Even as I said it, I felt the Rik leaves doing their magic in my mind. Facts about rocks, ores and mining bubbled to my temporal lobes.

Alf's jaw remained set. "He's top of the class, and I got hired for strength."

Derven gestured to Alf's cheek. "You have a tattoo on your cheek. Violent offender? Maybe the mines are the best place for you after all." He seemed to waiver, and I held my hope behind my lips. Alf's beard scruffed just enough to hide the fact that the circle mark of a killer wasn't complete. Good. Let them think he's dangerous. *Unless that made things worse.*

Mr. Kinny watched Captain Derven closely, but when I moved, he raised his weapon slightly. "Captain," he said. "What if we test all of the miners early? We have those ore samples. We'll be able to determine who knows what they're doing, and who is here for…other reasons." He gave me a stern look, but the tiny twitch of his mouth told me he'd just saved me for another day.

"Very well," said the captain, spinning his seat to face his panel of controls. "Have them all report in the morning to the game room. We'll run them all through the test."

OOO

I'm not sure how Kinny did it, but Fizer woke up in our dorm embarrassed to have "fainted". He didn't know he'd been stunned, and the moments leading up to the incident were a complete void in his memory. He absorbed the news of a test in the morning with a cheerful anticipation. "I always get top marks on tests, whether holographic or tactile," said Fizer. He had an endearing confidence about his career without being an insufferable know-it-all.

Now, Fizer lay snoring lightly above us. Alf leaned his back to the berth wall and his left arm draped lightly around my waist. His fatigue had finally beaten back his nerves, and I knew he had drifted to sleep by the sound of his breathing.

Gently, I rolled out of the bunk, landing quietly on my knees beside the crates. I unlatched the top crate and saw King's finger's slip out and wiggle at me. A second later, he stood noiselessly in front of me, his wide, luminescent eyes blinking slowly in the dark.

"Huff, huh?" I whispered. "Any chance we'll all pass tomorrow's test?"

Queen will know.

With a gesture to the top bunk, I asked mentally, *Will Fizer know?*

King nodded, giving another witness of his brilliance.

I turned my head and peered into the shadows at Alf's form. His hand rested near my head on the edge of the mattress. King looked back and forth between the two of us. *Stay with Alf.*

I promised silently, and gave King the food I'd retrieved from the cafeteria. Not until we had both settled back into our places to sleep did I wonder how to stay with Alf if he didn't pass and I did.

OOO

"Each compartment is labeled with the atomic number of the element it should contain, but the samples are incorrectly placed," explained Mr. Kinny. "Your job is to put them back in the right order. If you've studied your geology well and score higher, your assignment will be different. These mountains contain many different kinds of ore, often streaming together. They're still learning which veins run where. Scout digging is for the miners with the lowest scores, and then there are ore sorting jobs and on up to grade testing of samples for the highest scores." He smirked over in Fizer's direction. "The more you work with your brain, the less you'll have to work with your body."

The first man moved fairly quickly, switching pieces with confidence except for the last three. These he held up to the light one by one, squinting and sniffing and rubbing the edges with a thumbnail. At last he swore and tossed the last three without conviction into the final compartments.

The next few seemed mostly satisfied with what the first man had come up with, though each made at least one adjustment to the arrangement. As we got closer, Fizer watched with more intensity. All of the chunks had a dull silvery color, so that I would have thought anyone distinguishing them would have to know by the texture and weight. My gaze darted back and forth between his moving lips and the rock samples that the men held up, trying to decipher what he called each. Lithium, Titanium, Vanadium, Chromium, Cobalt, Nickel, Germanium, Niobium, Molybdenum, Cadmium, Indium and Terbium. Fizer nodded encouragingly at the man who had placed these, the same man who had laughed so hard in the elevator.

Reviewing the metals in my head, I recalled the Periodic Table of Elements I had studied two years ago, one of the vestiges of Ancient Earth science that still applied to the Granbo System. These samples were currently in order of their atomic numbers.

Mr. Kinny looked surprised, which I interpreted as meaning the miner had ordered them all correctly. I wondered how they could tell from that distance, but I understood a moment later as we moved closer. Kinny picked out all the samples and shook them in his cupped hands, as if rolling several gambling cubes. He then dropped them one by one randomly into the compartments. As he did so, I saw that each sample had a small painted circle on it, a different color for each piece.

As the man before him took his turn, Fizer pressed his lips together and watched. His eyebrows flew or flopped depending on the miner's choices, and when the man finished, Fizer gave me a "too bad for him" look. Then he took his place at the crate and lifted each sample, hefting it and rubbing his thumb along different sides and giving me a clear view of the colored dot. By the time he completed the test, I knew the order he used based on the colors, and by the look on Kinny's face, he had it right.

But Alf came next. Kinny again rolled the samples in his hands and dropped them into compartments. I stood close enough to see his moves, but couldn't find a way to help. My foot tapped with nervous energy, and I chewed on my pinky nail. I glanced at the enormous, calloused hands of the other miners and wondered how my pale, dainty hands would look after work in the mines. I thought of King's retractable claws and Felly's perfectly manicured hands…

Alf cleared his throat, getting my attention back on the test. He glanced at me with an unreadable cloud in his eyes. Feeling sick to my stomach, I realized I had not seen his final placements. *Had he gotten them right?* King's admonition came to me: stay together. *But did Alf pass?* I knew I could, but if he didn't… My mind welled with fear, and Derven's smug look felt like a laser through my heart. *Why didn't I pay attention to what Alf did?*

Numbly, I stepped forward for my turn. Kinny did not roll the samples again, which probably didn't bode well for Alf. Possibly Derven would kill him as a spy. And if I didn't pass, I'd be killed, too. *Then what would happen to King and the faneps?*

I studied the silvery lumps in the twelve compartments, knowing the colors to put them in order of atomic weight. With a finger, I nudged each sample enough to see the dot. He'd managed half of them right by chance.

Sucking in a lungful of courage, I picked up three of the metal lumps and rearranged them.

OOO

I sat on my crates with my head in my hands, willing my tears to dry up before they fell. Alf lay on his back in the bottom bunk, one arm covering his eyes. Fizer bounced in the doorway, his hands tapping the walls just inside as he surveyed the action in the hallway.

"I don't know what the score had to be, but you only missed three, Caz. That should be good. That was a pretty tough set of samples. They cut some of them funny so it was hard to tell how granulated they were. And I think some had been heated recently to blur the grooves." He glanced back at us with pity screaming from his grin.

"We're dead," muttered Alf.

"Not dead," said Fizer cheerily oblivious to our plight. "They might have you do some of the more hard labor stuff that isn't as skilled at first. Then you study at night. That's what my cousin Minster did. You'll be fine with that, I guess, being so strong," he added with a gesture to Alf.

"I guess," said Alf bitterly.

"They can't turn us *all* away," insisted Fizer. "Only two of us got them all right. Anyway, I think it's strange they did the test here instead of on the Surface, but maybe the Garvey staff is low and this gets us processed faster."

I wished he would stop talking. I wished the results would be announced so Alf and I could prepare for death.

The laughing miner who had aced the test stopped outside of our door. "Which way?" he asked.

"At my back!" beamed Fizer.

The miner slapped him on the shoulder with a good-natured chuckle. "Good! Good!"

Fizer turned back to face us, looking guilty for celebrating.

"What was that all about?" I asked.

"He wanted to know how I was."

"By asking which way? I don't get it."

Fizer stared at me disbelieving. "Which way? It's the Craggy way of saying 'How are you?' It's about the wind. Which way is the wind blowing? You answer 'at my back' if it's good, 'from the side' if you've been distracted or something, and 'in my face' if you're having a really hard time."

"Oh." *Oh*. I understood now why the miner had thought it so funny when I said "up". Wind up my rear would probably mean a *really* bad day. I almost giggled myself except the day ahead definitely would involve wind in all kinds of unpleasant places.

Ten minutes later, the miners all gathered in the game room again. Mr. Kinny stood with a small flat-screen vid monitor in his hand. "Will the following men please step forward?" he said stiffly. "Lahore, Gilgit, Fizer, Kargil, Bard, Skardu, and Karakoram."

"That would be the passers," I muttered. Apparently, the laughing miner was Bard.

Kinny indicated these men. "You will need to rearrange your dorms so that you can study together. The rest of you passed."

A collective gasp filled the room, and it hit me that Fizer's group had failed. My mouth fell open and I stared at Mr. Kinny.

"Please make the necessary room changes before the evening meal." He strode past me, pausing long enough to whisper, "They are right to call you Lucky."

A second later, Bard took a swing at Kinny. Without thinking, I blocked the blow with my forearm. Alf caught my other arm before I could swing. The miner backed away, shouting and rubbing his arm where we'd connected, and Kinny ran out of the room.

"Some first officer," jeered Alf. "Run away."

Bard glared at me, and I raised my palms in a calm-down gesture. "You hit first man, you go Solitary," I offered.

He nodded reluctantly. I turned away and leaned into Alf. "You check on Fizer. I've gotta find out what just happened." Before he could stop me, I jogged after Kinny. Jamming my thumb hard into the lift pad, I stood jiggling my legs, ready to jump when the door opened.

It slid to the side, and there stood Kinny. "I thought you might come after me," he said with a dark smile. He reached forward and gently pulled me in. The door closed, but he did not press any buttons. "I owe you one for saving me back there," he said.

"Apparently we're even. You know I didn't pass. I made sure of it."

His eyebrows shot up with surprise. "You what?"

"Fizer and Bard had it right," I said, rushing my words. "Why didn't you pass them? I faked a fail to stay with Alf."

"At the risk of your own life?" His face fell with amazement. "Your brother means that much to you?"

My mouth went dry, and I lowered my head. "Yeah. We watch after each other."

"You surprise me," he said quietly. He shook his head. "Saloma doesn't have half your character."

Still looking at the ground, I asked, "What about Fizer and Bard?"

"I had to flunk Fizer or Derven would suspect him. He was with you at the crates, remember?"

Right. The crates full of dangerous gases. "And Bard?"

"Scored exactly the same. I had to make it look like they'd both been wrong."

"So what happens next?" I asked, feeling the adrenaline crash.

"Those two will pass next time when they re-test at Garvey. In the meantime, stay away from Fizer so that Derven doesn't think you two are trying to conspire. He'll get over his suspicions in a few days. Just… try to blend in with the others."

"Which way, and all that?" I smirked.

He exhaled a knowing smile. "Right. All that. Craggify yourself. And one more thing." He grabbed my arm. "Make sure your brother studies hard. They will test you all again on site at Garvey, and…"

"Right." I slapped him on the back like the miners did. "Thanks, sir. You and I are even, but I still owe you one for Alf."

OOO

I opened my top crate and King came out. "At least you can move around now," I said, rubbing the white fuzz on his head with my palm. "Fizer's moved to another dorm."

King climbed up my legs and torso, landing on my shoulder with agility that still amazed me. Wrapping his skinny little arms around me, he hugged my head. "Queen safe for now."

Alf let out a single laugh. "You sound like you're from Craggy."

King chittered and zipped down to the door in a blur of movement. Reaching up to the catch, he opened it slightly and peeked out.

"What are you doing?" I hissed. "There are cams everywhere out there!"

He winked at me and began floating upwards as if the gravity had been turned way down. His retractable claws sliced out, and he gripped at the insulated foam ceiling. Hovering upside down under the ceiling, he crawled out into the hall, too high to be caught on the security cams.

Alf shuddered, standing behind me and watching through the slit of an opening. "That's so…"

"Brilliant," I finished. "The miners always walk with their heads down. They'll never see him," I smiled, closing the door and turning back.

Alf didn't move, and our bodies almost touched. One hand leaned on the wall behind me, and the other went gently to my chin. Tilting my face up, he looked at me. The dim sconce light behind him cast our faces in semi-darkness, but I could see his eyes glisten.

"Caz." His voice sounded raw. "How could you do that to me?"

I jerked my head back in surprise, knocking it against the door. "What did I do?"

The hand on the wall cupped the back of my head, and he gazed at me so intently, I blushed.

"You failed, didn't you?" he asked.

"On purpose, so we—"

"If Kinny hadn't been on our side, we'd both be dead right now. It isn't just your life you're putting in danger," he said. "Caz, if anything happens to you, I'll be dead, too."

"Alf, you're strong enough. You'd get through and get away."

"That's not what I mean, Caz. Without you…" He sighed and pulled away. "Never mind. You don't understand."

I reached after his back with my hand, my heart pounding in my throat. *I'm beginning to, Alf…*

ooo

Mr. Kinny assigned Alf and me to different shifts, so we almost never saw each other except at meals and at night when exhaustion overruled the need or desire to talk. A few times, I thought about telling Alf I understood what he tried to say, but then I'd have to explain how I felt, and I didn't know. He didn't talk much, but he would do little things when others couldn't see, courtly gestures I'd seen ambassadors do on the Arxon. He'd pass me things before I asked, slip me an extra bite of my favorite foods from his plate, or help me up to my bunk. All of this he did almost shyly.

On the very last day, minutes from our scheduled disembarking, Alf and I finally found ourselves together, hauling out tether beams from a storage room near the airlock. They acted as chutes like the one Felly and I slid down when we were little—except these were enormously long. Their half-pipe construction made it safe to drop passengers and certain supplies down to a landing platform on the Surface 40 meters below.

The first attached magnetically and with hooks to the airlock door. We slid subsequent ones down this hanging ramp, and Kinny used a remote control device to control the magnetism so that each tether piece glided slowly down before locking in place.

Alf surveyed the drop, shaking his head. "That is an accident waiting to happen."

Our eyes locked meaningfully, and I stood back from the opening, scanning the halls for any sign of Derven. No. Just Kinny, watching his controls carefully and nodding with satisfaction each time he saw a light flash to indicate the tethers had connected securely.

"It's really very impressive technology, isn't it?" asked Kinny as we brought out another piece. He watched us work. "You'll soon be off the ship," he winked.

"Not soon enough," said Alf.

With a grunt of frustration, Kinny grasped his control with both hands and frowned down the slide.

"What happened?" asked Alf, holding onto the bar above the door and leaning cautiously for a better view. Wind whistled loudly and bit with cold teeth when it reached our skin.

Kinny stared at his control. "It's jammed or something. It needs to go a few more centimeters to lock in." His face reddened as he tried again to work the controls.

"Can it be done manually?" asked Alf, squinting into the glare. Wind snapped at the cloth on his legs.

Alarmed, Kinny shook his head. "That would be very dangerous. There's still over a ten-meter drop."

"I could hold on tight enough not to slip," I offered.

Alf and Kinny both shook their heads at me. "No!" they cried in unison.

"I can do it," I insisted.

"*I'll* do it," said Alf firmly. He crouched beside the tether slide.

"You really don't need to," said Kinny, glancing at me as if I should stop him.

"I'll go down feet first on my stomach," said Alf. "It'll be all right." He got into position and let go.

"Alf!" I screamed.

His hands gripped the edges, stopping his descent, and he laughed. "You sound like a girl, yeah?" he shouted up. Locks of his thick blonde hair poked at his face, and he shielded his eyes in his shoulder.

Kneeling at the top, I scowled. "Don't do that, idiot!"

Kinny chuckled nervously, and studied Alf's position. Cupping his hand to his mouth, he shouted, "You have about four more meters to go. Slow down. Maybe you can just nudge it with your toes?"

Alf showed signs of strain now. He lowered himself gradually until his feet dangled just above where the last piece had stopped.

"Are you pushing?" called Kinny.

"I'm pushing!" he blurted. He had obviously been holding his breath with the effort. *If he fell now...*

"Push harder!" shouted Kinny, clutching his device.

Alf groaned loudly, and the last piece flew downward, spiraling to the ground. The impact clanged loudly even at this distance, and people on the ground scattered. I hadn't noticed them until now.

Kinny swore and Alf slid down further, part of his body now hanging off the end of the last tether.

"Alf!" I shrieked. I threw myself onto the slide, rolling to my stomach even as I fell.

"Caz, no!" yelled Alf.

I dug in with my fingers and stopped sliding. Instantly, I felt the icy attack of the wind on my knuckles. Peeking under my arm, I maneuvered myself carefully down to Alf. "Grab my foot!"

He hesitated, and I scooted a little closer. His grip surprised me, and I hoped it wouldn't cut off my circulation. My hands began to sweat, and I threw Dad's advice about controlling my body systems away. Willing my glands to dry up, I pushed up with my free foot. Alf encouraged me as we went, but after we'd gotten up several meters, he let go. I shrieked until I saw that he'd grabbed the sides to hold himself in place.

"I can get it from here," he panted.

We wriggled upwards, faster now. The wind tore at my coversuit and dried my tears in painful streaks at the corners of my eyes. In the hollow of the tether pipe, the sun's glare didn't reach me, but when I tried to look up at the ship, the brightness of the sky blinded me.

Pausing for breath, I called out to Kinny. "What will we do now, without that tether piece?"

He shook his head, putting his hand to his ear to show he couldn't hear us. We pulled a little higher, coming into the shade of the ship, and I caught a glimpse of him through my streaming eyes.

To my horror, I saw Derven beside Kinny. The Captain placed his fists on his hips and bellowed. "Kinny is right. You have much more character than Saloma."

What? He knew about—

"Too bad you don't have her money!" He laughed cruelly. "You've made this too easy for us with your selflessness."

He nodded to Kinny who pressed something on the control. The tether disengaged from the chute, plummeting to the ground with us still clinging to it.

OOO

24 DARKMAN

The wind shoved Alf's screams of terror right through my heart, and I gripped the tether tighter even as it toppled end over end. Hard rock and tiny moving people spun towards us.

The world slowed down inside my head. They say your life flashes before your eyes when you're about to die. Mine didn't. Only two moments came to mind: the gypsy cave back on Caren, and the cargo hold on the Ivan. My smile opened, letting icy air flap my cheeks. *I'm not going to die.* I knew it with certainty even as the first of the metal pieces hit the earth below us with a horrific clang.

The piece with which Alf and I fell rotated to block our view of the ship above, and we dangled directly beneath it. Alf screamed again and slipped, but I kicked out my legs and caught him. He grappled for a painful instant and then wrapped his arms around my legs.

Remembering what had happened in the cargo bay when King threw me, I shifted my thoughts from falling to floating down. I also concentrated on pushing up on the tether so that it would not crush us when we landed. Even as the shouts of men on the ground rang out, I felt the slowing— subtle, perhaps unseen from above. We landed, our legs buckling but not breaking beneath us, and I used the last of my energy to hold the tether higher. It bounced once and scraped on the rocky surface, hiding us in its hollow as we flattened ourselves to the ground.

"Are you all right?" I called hoarsely.

Alf's arms, still wrapped around me, tightened, and I heard a sob echo between the metal and stone. Trapped beneath the giant half-pipe and protected from the sun and wind—and for a moment at least, Derven and Kinny's view—I felt the cold grip me from the ground with icy claws. Craning my neck and shifting my body, I peered through the dimness. "Alf?" I urged again. A fumble of limbs followed and I found myself face-to-face with him. "Alf, are you hurt?"

He buried his face in my neck. "No, my lady."

My lady? I stroked his hair. His words brought another danger to mind: *King was still on the ship with Derven and Kinny!*

No one came immediately to check on us, though we saw boots at the end of the overturned tether. I felt no desire to come out into the open and risk further attack. From what we could hear, the first falling pieces had struck and killed two men on the ground, collateral damage for Saloma and her paid assassins. *What a perfect accident Kinny and Derven had created.* No one would question our deaths. No one would hold them accountable. I clenched my teeth against the bitterness rising in me.

A series of shouts and muffled crashes woke me from my depressing thoughts. From what I could tell, the miners and their personal items were still using the tether chute to disembark, but landing on some kind of makeshift platform that broke their fall.

Not until the angle of light shifted and we heard a great roar did we know the cargo cruiser had gone on. Through the roaring wind, we heard voices bark short commands. The edge of the tether lifted slightly and a hulking form with no face and giant glassy eyes peered in at us.

"Lucky here!" shouted the creature. "Lucky alive! Lucky! Lucky!" *Bard, no doubt.*

A moment later, a much smaller version of the same thing knelt beside him. "Lucky! Alf! You survived!" It was Fizer.

More shouts sounded, urgently happy instead of scared or angry.

"It's a miracle, I guess. Wait, don't come out. It's too cold and bright. Wait for us to bring overcoats and goggles. Close your eyes. This—"

"Fizer," I croaked.

"Really, Caz. Close your eyes. You'll ruin them in this light without goggles. Wait here. We'll get you some!"

The tether lowered back down, blocking the sunlight. Alf grinned. "I'm even glad to see *him.*"

"I know," I agreed.

"Caz, we're alive, yeah?"

"Yeah," I breathed, shaking violently now as the adrenaline wreaked havoc on my system. I didn't try to control it. I just held on to Alf and waited for Fizer to bring us coats and goggles.

I'm on Craggy, I thought. *Two Worlds down. One to go.*

OOO

Looking like mini mountains in our oversized coats, Alf and I shuffled after the others. Even with the massive protective goggles, I squinted at the glare. The coats doubled our girth with padding, yet the bite of the wind still reached my bones. Bracing myself against it, I immediately understood the idioms about the wind and why Craggy natives always walked with their heads down.

Still, I had to stop and savor my second planet! Years of dreaming, and here I stood on Craggy!

I thought I'd grown used to being on the Surface after my weeks on Caren, but this… Nothing felt the same. No beauty met my eyes, only fearsome, barren rock and the raw elements of wind and the glaring sun's fire. A cold fire. Was it the altitude, or did Craggy just repel life?

The mining camp—one of fifteen on the planet—made up a small part of the Garvey Colony. Apparently, somewhere to the east lay a city of several thousand people where the Governor resided and most commerce in the region took place. Landing there was impossible for a craft the size of the Ipko, so most cargo vessels touched down in the mining camp.

We had landed in a high valley shaped like a shallow bowl, except that one side of the valley had been blasted and chiseled into massive terraces. The far side stretched many kilometers away, and it boggled my mind to think of the explosive power required to form the artificial plateaus. On each of these steps, blast drills whined above the wind, and wheeled vehicles carried chunks of rock to a central area where the pieces climbed conveyer belts and jumped onto mounds. Workers, tiny in the distance, swarmed around the piles, presumably sorting valuable ore from rock debris. In at least twenty locations, I could see strange star-like clusters of buildings.

Beyond the ridges to the south, the stony mountain plunged darkly, endlessly to sulfur fields below. To the north, the grey rock kept climbing skyward in jagged leaps to where it stabbed the fast-gliding clouds. Somewhere near that altitude, snow fell enough to irrigate the land just below it. Up there, supposedly blending into the bleak façade, Earlie trees grew in a narrow swath, like a belt around the entire range.

At my shoulder, Alf leaned in and shouted over the wind. "That's gonna be a rough climb, yeah? I can't even see the trees."

I nodded, though I'm sure he couldn't see the movement through all the padding. Just walking the flats of this mining area sucked the air from my lungs. By the time we reached the shelter—a stout, hexagonal building gleaming with solar panels—my feet had numbed from the cold, hard ground. Alf, too, shifted back and forth trying to get circulation into his extremities. The other miners all wore thick boots. I hoped they paid workers often enough that we could find the commissary and purchase some more protective clothing.

As the men unpeeled their coats and scarves, I studied the faces of the workers who met us. I had heard about erosion in science lessons, but here on Craggy, it was real. The mountains, visible from space, had been sawed by the wind over eons. The faces of the people had been blasted, too. Their features were carved by the elements into hard, unmoving lines. Alf, Fizer and I stood out like babies in a school room.

The man in charge grumbled something and raised his hands at the commotion rumbling.

"We took test on ship," complained a miner.

Bard and Fizer exchanged nervous glances and I wondered what would happen now. More of the miners complained, and the worker roared,

"Don't get cracky!"

A hush settled, and I questioned Fizer with a shrug. He backed up and set his chin on my shoulder to whisper. "Cracky means mad. If you get emotional, it moves your face, and around here…"

Around here, movement would crack some of these faces. After allowing a little smirk, I decided to set my face in one position and keep it there until the ordeal ended.

OOO

Alf *almost* passed. So close. But I followed his lead, and the two of us accepted the intermediate assignment of sample scouting, deemed by Fizer to be a euphemism for rock crushing. Alf and I could practice with the ore samples in the Test Center for the hour before sunset each day. We could test again in a week. That wasn't horrible news, but I couldn't help wondering what difference it made without King being here. We'd have to survive until he could find a way back to us.

Because Garvey stood at the planet's equator, darkness and light cut each day in even halves of fourteen hours each. The winds and dropped temperatures prevented night work even though the mines underground ran hot.

Shortly after the test, we retreated to the barracks, which turned out to be the clusters of buildings I'd seen earlier. Networks of six hexagonal buildings much like the testing center joined at the corners creating a central area open to the air. The space provided a little shelter from the sun and wind depending on the time of day. The beds lined the inside of four of the six walls, and two walls opposite each other had doors that opened into the central common outdoor space, or to the camp outside. The ceiling of each room hung low, rising to a point in the middle where a thick window let in the natural light muted by filters. Bard, Fizer, and Alf would be my roommates until I could figure out how to get away to the timberline.

"No lights?" asked Alf.

"No need. Only sleep here," said Bard. Fourteen hours of work made you want to sleep for fourteen more? That didn't sound promising.

Below each bunk, someone had stowed our crates and a cylindrical tub with a lid which puzzled me until I saw Bard slide his out and relieve himself into it. Alf and I gaped at each other in horror. No washrooms. This place would stink really badly soon.

Only one of my crates showed up in the room, and no King. Without the SWaTT, I couldn't find out anything. I couldn't get Sasa or Dad to help. I'd just have to wait.

As I lay on my bed staring into the space in the middle of the room, the shape and the darkness brought back the haunting vision of Ninetta's funeral pyre. I pictured the boulders that I had placed to contain the fire that consumed her viper poisoned body, and I saw Maddy, black with soot, weeping and murmuring. An aching sense of loss stabbed me even though I'd only known her for a few days.

Blinking back the tears, I looked up through the skylight window. Despite its grubby surface, I could see stars. They arranged themselves differently here than I had seen from Caren or from the observation decks of the Arxon.

Were they really the same stars? Was I really in the right place among them? I closed my eyes and welcomed the exhaustion that took it all away.

OOO

A boxy vehicle with enormous wheels jostled us over land slowly while we learned that ours would be the task of chipping away at rock with things they called pickaxes. The officials hoped to locate a new vein of molybdenum to make heat resistant alloys for rocket thrusters or something. Four of us—two men, Alf and I—would be deep underground. After experiencing the collapse of rock at the gypsy cave on Caren, I did not like the idea of being inside of a mountain, but the open excavation areas had full staffs.

The heavy layers of clothing and goggles did little to block the press of the wind as we shuffled with our heads down from the transport to the squat shelter. Constructed like the other buildings we'd seen so far, it afforded a small eating space, a tub-like scale large enough to weigh hundreds of kilos at a time, and the desk area.

I backed my way into the room, pressed by the others until one of them grabbed my arms. "Watch down!" I spun to see a large hole in the floor, and a second later, a scraping roar sounded. Pulling off my goggles, I stared as a dirty yellow cage rattled up through the hole and two shirtless men emerged. Felly would have fainted on the spot at how filthy they were. One of the men from the cage grunted something at our driver who slapped the two miners with us on the back. They entered the cage with the dirty man, barely able to close the cage around them, and disappeared down into the hole.

The other man from the cage eyed us disapprovingly from behind a stony face. He looked as if he'd slept in the ashes of a gypsy campfire, but even the blackness of the grime on his body did not hide the stark contours of his muscles. He made Alf look like a weakling by comparison.

A line of off-white teeth cracked his face open, and he thumped his chest with his fist. "Darkman," he said. Before I could think of a response to this cryptic announcement, he punched me in the chest. "Pretty Boy!"

I collapsed back a step, gasping for air as Alf raised his arm to swing.

The driver caught his wrist and yanked him out of range. Gesturing with his free hand, he said, "Darkman your boss."

Alf stiffened. "Why you hit him?" he asked defiantly.

Darkman held a thick finger close to Alf's nose. "Stupid."

Alf started to protest, but the driver twisted his arm to deposit him next to me. "Darkman your boss. He name you Pretty Boy and Stupid." He turned to the door, laughing. "I come ten hours. No wait."

The cage screeched below us, covering the sound of my whisper to Alf. "Don't make this guy mad if we have to be with him for ten hours."

"If he touches you again, I'll kill him."

The ride down in the cage lasted for the longest two minutes of my life. Being packed next to Darkman's sweltering, hard body and feeling the weight of his soulless stare made my stomach drop much faster.

I also felt really hot. Tugging at my collar, I willed my eardrums to release the tension they'd inexplicably acquired. Alf unclasped his coat, and we followed Darkman, jumping down out of the cage into a rounded stone corridor. It had to be manmade, but roughly hewn. I turned back to see that the cage rested on a folded lattice of bars with some kind of power generator beneath it. Air-compressed power, most likely. The only light came from a disc on the ceiling of the cage.

"We bottom?" I asked, coughing at the dusty air.

Darkman nodded. "Tunnel 5 lowest." He pointed to me. "Hottest. No coat. You die."

Heat exhaustion for sure. I wriggled my already sweaty self out of the sleeves as Alf dropped his coat to the ground along the wall. Darkman nodded approval at this and scratched his chest. Alf unfastened the top half of his coversuit, letting it drop to the waist.

"Tie sleeves," said Darkman.

Alf obeyed silently, tying the sleeves in a knot. They turned to me, Darkman with expectation and Alf with thinly veiled horror.

Dropping my coat on top of Alf's, I shrugged. "Not hot." As if to spite me, a trickle of sweat ran down my back into the extra coversuit that formed my padding. If I perspired too much, the cloth would cling to me and reveal the unnatural folds of cloth that hid my shape. I wiped my moist upper lip and willed my body's cooling systems to stop leaking out so much liquid. "Not hot," I repeated, louder this time.

Darkman shook his head, growled, and walked down the tunnel a few meters to where it opened into a cavern lit by an enormous free-standing light. The space was not much bigger than our family room on the Arxon, and I had a feeling it would feel very claustrophobic once we started working.

Beside the light stood a large tub half filled with black rocks about the size of my head. Darkman lifted one of these and pointed out a silvery streak that colored about half of the chunk. "Molybdenum." He threw it back on the pile and jerked his shoulder in command to follow.

Stooping, he handed us each a pickaxe and pointed further down the wall. "Work three hours, then lunch." With that, he swung the pickaxe in a giant arc up then down, striking the sloped wall with so much force that a piece of the mountain rolled down. The noise of the metal on stone echoed painfully in the cavern, and the heat made me groggy, but I moved further down the wall to claim a workspace.

Alf looked at me grimly. "We'd better study hard tonight and get out of this job soon."

"If we survive," I said.

"Just like chopping wood," he shrugged.

"Except it's a mountain."

OOO

I had dozed off, but now lay in our dark room listening for any sounds of movement. Nothing but faint snores. Sliding off my bed, I grabbed up my coat and my portable latrine and headed for the door that led to the semi-sheltered area in the midst of the barracks. There in the enclosure, I pulled the coat over me like a blanket and disrobed beneath it, sitting on the latrine and leaning my back against the cold wall. I released urine and the pent-up sweat and tears as if my body could not hold water any longer. As the toxins left my body, loneliness and fear filled me. I wondered if I would ever see Dad or Felly again. Or King and Maddy. *Would I fail to cycle the pearl because I just wanted to go home?*

Despite the heavy coat, the air chilled the perspiration all over my body. I shivered uncontrollably and flexed my fingers, sore from the vibrations and friction of work with the pickaxe. Blisters had already turned to callouses thanks to the Gypsy Pearl. The sweat dripped audibly from my body, and my senses sharpened.

That's when I heard the sniffle.

I drew in a sharp breath and scanned the shadows that crouched beneath the small overhang at each wall. The starlight above seemed to fall straight down, leaving the edges in darkness.

An animal? How would it have gotten in to this enclosed space? No mammals were indigenous to this area according to the report on the Ivan. Straining to hear over the whistle of the ever-present wind, I reached down to my ankles for my coversuit with one hand, holding my coat in place with the other.

Could it be King?

"Who's there?" rasped a voice. Not King's voice.

I didn't answer, but quickly tugged at my coversuit. It stuck to my soaking body as if I'd just showered, and before I could fumble the coversuit all the way up, my coat slipped to the ground.

"Who's there?" repeated the voice, and to my horror, a heavily clad Fizer stepped into the pale starlit space. His mouth dropped open and he pointed. "Caz! You're a—"

I grasped at my coat and pulled it on, breathing heavily and searching my brain for an explanation. Fizer stumbled forward in a daze. I kicked my latrine aside and backed into the wall with a thunk and a whimper. "Please, Fizer… I can explain." *No, I couldn't.*

A second later, his gloved hands pinned me to the wall, his face so close our noses almost touched. "Don't let anyone know, Caz!" he hissed. *What?* "You shouldn't have come! You need to get out of here. It's too dangerous—"

I clamped a hand over his mouth and pushed him back a little. "You won't tell?" I whispered. He mumbled through my fingers until I let go.

"Caz, girls aren't safe here," he said. "What were you thinking? It's not worth the money."

"What do you mean?"

"Even *I'm* not safe…" His voice trailed off.

"What? What's going on?"

Fizer shook his head, his voice getting shakier with each word. "I'm too small for my age. I should have known to wait. It's only a matter of time before one of the men decides I'm his bully bag."

I took a step away and righted my latrine. The spill stank, but absorbed quickly into the thin layer of topsoil.

Fizer leaned a shoulder against the wall nearest the door to our barrack. "You're a spacey, aren't you? You're not from Caren."

My head drooped, and I stuffed my hands into my pockets. "Yeah."

"Got any other big secrets?"

I looked at him, tiny and dirty in a huge overcoat. With my bare hands, I could probably crush the life out of him, but right now both of us needed a hug. Still, I didn't move except to nod. "Yeah."

"Friends trust each other," he said.

"Alf isn't my brother." I looked Fizer in the eye. "Friends trust each other," I echoed back to him. "Can I trust you to keep my secret?"

Fizer shuddered involuntarily and nodded. "You can trust me."

OOO

The next morning, I ripped the sleeves from my coversuit, exposing my pale arms to the stares of the burly men. Two hours of labor coated me in a film of rock dust and sweat. I stood up to reach for a drink from my canteen and realized I'd left it with my coat beside the cage lift shaft. With a drinking gesture, I headed down the darkened tunnel towards the dim light of the cage. The faintest tickle of air came down the shaft, and I leaned against the cooler metal while I gulped down half of my rationed water.

With water so crazy scarce in the Garvey colony, I suspected kidney failure and lung troubles kept the mortality rate up in the mines more than industrial accidents. I couldn't guess ages of the miners based on their wind carved faces, but their muscles and gaits spoke of tired youth. They couldn't be much more than thirty at the oldest.

As I made my way back to the cavern, I heard Darkman's voice and briefly wondered if he'd earned the nickname from his rock-blackened skin. As I entered, Darkman stood back and wiped his brow. He took a moment to admire his own muscles. "Girls like me," he grunted proudly.

This inconceivable theme seemed to occupy most of his uttered thoughts, and I'd already grown bored by the subject.

"No girls here," grunted Alf in his best Craggy accent. For a heartbeat, I wondered if Fizer had shared my secret.

"No. But when I find, I take. Been too long." He sneered at me. "Even Pretty Boy look good."

My body tensed.

"Pretty Boy kill you," grunted Alf.

Darkman bellowed with laughter and resumed work.

Alf glared at his back and knocked loose a particularly large slab. It skidded to the ground between us, and he bent to pick it up. He used his path to the sample bin as a smooth excuse to nudge me further down the wall away from Darkman. My mouth dry, I retreated gratefully into the corner of the cavern.

OOO

Darkman finally declared it time for lunch, and the three of us grabbed our coats because the shelter above ground sometimes got chilly. Alf climbed in first, then Darkman. Squeezing in backwards, I fumbled with the latch.

With a pop of air, the mechanism heaved us upward, and just before we entered the narrow shaft, I heard a click, saw the cage door swing open, and felt a rough shove from behind. I landed the two meter drop awkwardly and crashed to my hands and knees. Alf shouted behind me, and I turned to see Darkman jumping down to face me as the cage disappeared above.

I rose quickly, my hands out in a calming gesture, but my voice cracked. "Which way, Darkman?"

With a frightening fire in his eyes, he merely walked closer, his hulking frame seeming to flex larger with every step. And then it grew very dark because Alf took with him the disc light of the cage.

Backing up, I tried to remember where I'd left my pickaxe. "What's wrong?"

"Don't get cracky," he scoffed. "We work deal. You stay. Break my rocks while I eat."

"Uh, is that legal?" I asked, my voice cracking. What sort of stupid question was that?

"This Craggy," he answered, and that pretty much summed it up. As if that ended the conversation, he walked back over to the lift shaft and looked up. He pressed the button to call it back down.

Tired and hungry, I stupidly came and stood beside him. Darkman must have felt me coming in the dark because he shoved me back hard. "Get working!" he roared. I pressed my back against the wall, holding my breath and hoping he'd lose me in the utter blackness, but his boot scuffed against mine. With an angry oath, he leaned his forearm against my chest pinning me to the wall.

"What the—?" His hand grabbed at my curves and squeezed hard.

I yelped with pain and thrust him back. The thud of his body on the opposite wall came with a string of curses. Scrambling back into the cavern, I ran my hand along the wall, searching for my pickaxe. His footsteps sounded, along with heavy breathing, and a moment later, the bright floor light blinded me.

"Pretty Boy!" he roared. "You a girl?"

"No," I said with as much gruffness as my trembling voice could muster.

"I beat you, boy or girl," he sneered.

"NO!" I yelled, swinging the pickaxe horizontally at him.

He caught it in his hands and used the momentum to twist me off my feet. I hit the ground and rolled. Still on my back, I raised a leg to kick if he came closer.

"Pretty Boy pay now!" He threw the pickaxe to the side and descended towards me.

I kicked as hard as I could, not aiming in my desperation. The crash that rang out terrified me, and I rolled to my side with my head between my knees.

Silence. The sound of gravel slipping. Silence.

I peeked out at the damage. Darkman lay slumped against the overturned sample cart, his eyes open but glassy, his hand weakly clutching his chest. He didn't move.

Cautiously, I stood and retrieved my pickaxe before approaching him. His gaze flickered to me, all the strength drained from them. Drawing a shallow, ragged breath, he whined, "Pretty Boy?"

And then he shifted almost imperceptibly to a new state: death. His lungs, no doubt, had been punctured by the force of my kick.

I stumbled backwards and fell to the ground in unblinking horror. My hand went to my mouth, as if trying to pull out words, screams. Anything.
I killed a man.

OOO

25 GOING TO THE CAPITOL

Alf's voice called me out of my stupor, and he lifted me into an embrace. "It's going to be all right," he whispered, "but we've got to work fast."

I nodded numbly, but didn't move. Instead, I watched Alf grab Darkman by the wrists and drag him over to his work space. Next he placed a larger sample rock on the ground and rolled Darkman onto his stomach over it. He threw Darkman's pickaxe down beside the body and then clapped his hands at me. "Caz, come on! Wake up!"

At the sample cart, he picked out a few larger pieces and tossed them onto Darkman.

"Alf, what are you doing?" I squeaked, moving for the first time.

"It has to look like an accident," he hissed. "He hit this part of the cave and a bunch of pieces fell on him, yeah?"

Spurred by a new burst of adrenaline, I righted the sample cart, tossing the remaining spilled rocks towards Darkman to form a heap. Alf and I surveyed the scene.

"It's no good," I said pointing to the cavern above Darkman. "That spot doesn't match the rocks here."

Alf handed me his pickaxe. "Take one good swing at it?"

I swallowed hard and looked down at Darkman. *How had this happened?* "Stand back."

A moment later, Darkman lay buried under a convincing rock slide. I leaned my face onto Alf's shoulder and just stood there, sure my limbs would disengage from my body if I tried to move.

"It was self-defense," said Alf after a long time.

"I know."

"We're on Craggy. You won't be prosecuted, Caz."

OOO

The man above believed our story after checking the scene. He ordered us to bring up the light, the sample cart, and the pickaxes. As we dumped the last of these, he shoved a handful of small square pieces of metal towards us across the table.

"What's that?" asked Alf.

The man shrugged. "Darkman's money."

"What?"

"From coat pocket," said the man. "You lucky. Extra pay."

His matter-of-fact chuckle sent a wash of chilling sweat down my back. No mourning. No sense of loss. Just money left behind. I wondered how much he'd kept for himself.

Alf slid the pieces off the desk into his open palm, and I stared down at his dirty hands. Not just mining dirty. Dirty for helping me cover my crime. He counted out my half and tried to hand it to me, but I just stared at it. With a gentle punch to my shoulder, he said, "You earned it, yeah?"

The man beside us snickered. "Darkman finally pay what he owe."

We stepped outside and moved to the shaded side of the building. Without speaking, Alf reached an icy knuckle up to circle my cheek tenderly. He meant it kindly, but I felt as though the green tattoo of a killer had been branded into my skin. Repulsed by what I'd become, I wondered how I could ever face my family again.

And how could a killer be a gypsy queen?

OOO

Fizer tugged off his goggles and sat gingerly on the edge of his bed.

"What happened to you?" gasped Alf.

Fizer fiddled with the clasps on his coat. His knuckles, less filthy than our own, bulged unnaturally like the swelling below his left eye and chin.

"You get in a fight?" I asked.

He folded himself in a tight knot, lying on his side.

"What happened?" I whispered. "Can you tell us?"

Fizer sniffed and looked at me with pain in his eyes. "Bard."

Alf tensed. "Bard attacked you?"

"No, Bard saved me," he gulped. "If it wasn't for him…"

"I can imagine," I said quietly. "Were they trying to get you to work their quota?"

Fizer snorted. "The opposite. The supervisor on the site wanted me gone. He said I was too little to act so big."

"What's that supposed to mean?" I asked.

"You don't act big," agreed Alf.

"No, he meant because I…" He gave a guilty look. "I knew the work better than he did. He said I was trying to take his job."

Alf barked a laugh. "You're too good for this, yeah?" He punched the air. "This place is crazy. You do your best, and you get punished for it?"

"Jealously does things to a man, I guess," said Fizer, glancing at Alf sideways.

This seemed to sting Alf, and he looked down at the ground evasively. "Yeah."

"Not everything that comes close to what we care about is a threat," said Fizer quietly, and I knew we'd changed subjects. *Was he going to let Alf know that he knew I was a girl?*

I redirected the conversation. "At least Bard was there."

"But I'll have to give him half my pay for continued protection," said Fizer miserably.

"What?!" Alf's cheeks reddened with fury. "You have to pay not to be beaten?"

"I'm too small. I never should have come," said Fizer weakly. "They always target the little ones." He grabbed my arm. "*You* never should have come."

"I had no choice," I said.

ooo

The camp foreman entered with an icy blast of wind that threw my covers back. Alf and Fizer grunted and leaned up on their elbows, squinting at the dim rectangle of light from the door. Bard just growled, "Too early!"

"Heywood brothers see Governor now."

Alf sat up straight. "What? Why?"

"Accident in mine," answered the foreman.

"But it *was* an accident," said Alf warily.

The foreman took a few steps forward. "Governor talk dangers in mines. Come now."

Bard sat leaning his elbows on his knees wearily. "Fizer go, too."

The foreman shook his head. "Fizer not summoned."

Bard stood up slowly, looming larger than the foreman by several centimeters. "Fizer know dangers. Fizer go, too." He slapped Fizer's back, and the boy moved for the first time since the foreman's entrance. Nodding meekly, without eye contact to the goggled beast in the middle of the room, he bent down and gathered his overcoat and boots.

The foreman shrugged and lumbered back out, leaving the door open to the elements. Barely audible above the sound of the wind, Fizer muttered his thanks to Bard.

ooo

After passing into the Colony Official Hub through a tunnel, I expected something more like the grand Council Room at Gypsy Network Headquarters back on Caren, but the Governor's office lacked any of the elegance. A bright shaft of sunlight from a small overhead window fell on a large uninhabited desk in front of us, but the majority of the room remained in the dark.

"You'd think the Governor of a colony could afford electric lights," said Alf.

I nudged him quiet, even though no one could hear us. We had discarded our overcoats before leaving the transport and taking the lift up, and I now stood with my arms folded across my chest feeling very small and exposed in my grimy, sleeveless coversuit. Even in the odd lighting, I knew we looked ghastly. On an ICS, all three of us would have been disciplined for lack of hygiene and grooming.

"I wonder what he's going to ask us," I mused aloud. With Alf and Fizer both in on my secret, I didn't force my voice low.

"I don't know what *he's* going to ask," said a lilting, feminine voice, "but *I* have several questions. The first of which is who are you *really*?"

A form emerged from the shadows to our left—a woman clad in a black coversuit of sorts and with thick, black hair framing her face. Her eyes gleamed a pale green from the darkness, like the cat on the Arxon that always unnerved me. She moved forward, almost slinking in silence, and stood behind the desk.

I could almost hear Fizer's heartbeat rising as he cleared his throat. "We came because Governor Jipps summoned us to discuss mining safety problems."

"Young ones should not be in the mines," she said. Her gaze swept over me from top to bottom, and she retrieved something flat from a drawer. Her unflinching gaze locked with mine before glancing over the boys on either side of me. Her lip curled slightly with distaste. "You all smell as though you could afford a shower before you meet in conference." She gestured to our right. "There is a private washroom. You two go first," she said, indicating the boys.

"But, we're supposed to meet with Governor Jipps," protested Fizer weakly.

The woman waved him away, and he and Alf disappeared into the corner where a door slid open. I soon heard the sound of water running. At this the woman turned to me and took a deep breath. "While I go order some clean clothes from the supply depot," she said, "you can see if this is still working." She handed me the flat item in her hand—*my SWaTT!*

I almost dropped it. "I don't know what—"

"Take it, Caz." She knew my name! "There was a message from your father, but it vanished before I could archive it for you." She knew my Dad?! Her demeanor warmed for an instant, and a smile tickled the corner of her mouth. "He's still using medical terminology as his code, I see."

Gasping, I took a step back, but she reached a hand toward me, not quite touching my shoulder. "Has it been so long? The sunlight here has marred my eyes, but I can still see you, Caz Artemus of the Arxon."

The room started spinning. *I'm caught!*

"Do you not recognize me?"

"I..." A glimmer of recognition collided with logic, and I shook my head. *Why aren't the Rik leaves helping me out?*

"Caz, it's me. Your mother. Brita Artemus."

OOO

26 THE TOWER IN THE TREES

"I came to Craggy three years after I left you…" said the woman, faltering. Her eyes held a soul-stinging pain.

"What? You work for Governor Jipps?" I gasped, still not fully absorbing the idea. "A gypsy working for a colony governor?"

"It's worse than that. I *am* the colony governor, Caz. I am Governor Jipps.

"What? That's impossible!"

"Why is it impossible?"

"Because…because we would have known. Dad would know you were the governor of a colony. You can't just hide that." *Can you?*

"Caz, I changed my name. I invented the name Jipps because it hid my real identity, but it sounds like gypsy."

"But…the news vids when you were elected…"

She looked at me with patient determination. "Caz, when's the last time you saw anyone on the Arxon take an interest in the affairs of colony politics?"

She had a point. Even Mr. Virgil, my teacher, never really talked about the leaders of the colonies.

"The colonies wanted local governors, not a queen, so I obliged. But I'm following in the footsteps of my grandmother."

"Ambitious," I said.

"I prefer to call it hopeful. We need to be flexible to get to a place where we can make a difference."

It sounded good, but I couldn't let her off that easily. "You're hiding who you are?" I accused.

She blinked slowly. "Sometimes we have to play a part, don't we, Caz? To advance a greater good?"

OOO

"You can give me your reports of what's happening in the mines, but let me tell you this: I know the one they call Darkman and his ways. His death is years overdue."

Air escaped from my lungs in a rapid burst. *Did she suspect that I'd murdered him?*

Governor Jipps—Brita Artemus, my mother—sat coolly behind the desk with her feet up and her hands in her lap. Because I'd showered right after the boys, I still hadn't told them she was my mom. The fact didn't make her any less terrifying to me. Nothing rational told me to trust her just because of bloodlines. After all, she had abandoned us over ten years ago.

My brain churned with questions: *Why is a gypsy the governor of a colony? Does she know about Saloma, and are they friends? Does she know about my escape from Lamond, or Alf's? Why was she acting so aloof? Will she try to stop me from cycling the Gypsy Pearl? Does she even know about it?*

I blinked away the doubts to hear Fizer explaining the conditions of the mines and how some miners targeted the smaller men for abuse. Brita flicked a finger in his direction. "Your black eye?"

Fizer lowered his head. "Yes, ma'am. But that was the worst of it for me."

"So far," she added grimly. "Caz? You?"

Trembling, I recounted what happened in the mine with Darkman. When I got to the bit where Darkman discovered the evidence of my gender, Alf and Fizer both gave me warning glances. Governor Jipps caught this, and swung her feet to the ground. Leaning forward on her elbows, she looked directly at me and said, "So they are in on your secret."

It wasn't a question. I nodded, unsure of what came next.

"You three are friends?" She stared at me pointedly. "You trust them?"

I glanced at both Alf and Fizer. "Yes. Absolutely."

With a grim look, Brita continued. "Good to know. Perhaps now you can explain the other thing of yours I found, Caz. It came with the other, in fact. On foot." She reached behind her for a cylindrical crate. Pressing a button, she released a magnetic catch and lifted the lid. The crate wobbled back and forth for a moment, and then tiny bony fingers appeared.

And then King's grinning face!

OOO

"I apologize for dragging you along with me," said Brita. "But given the circumstances, I'm not ready to send you back to camp, and you're safer with me." She cast me a sideways look, questioning. "And it gives us some time to get acquainted."

She'd received a call midway through our interview which angered her. Now, cramped into a small transport, Fizer, Alf and I sat with our knees knocking together at each jolt wondering what was going on. King, now well-fed and washed, curled into the folds of my overcoat and appeared to sleep, but I knew he took in everything around him.

"There has been some kind of trouble up at the closest watch tower, and I need to investigate personally, or nothing will ever get done right," she explained, blowing a stream of air through pursed lips. "On a planet where plant life—useful plant life—is so scarce, great care must be taken to protect it. All along the Earlie forest that rings this mountain range, we have towers placed to watch for fires or other problems. We can't afford to lose any trees."

My stomach bubbled with excitement. We were so close—and King was with me!

Alf and I exchanged suppressed grins, and he ran his fingers through his hair casually. "Can't you use surveillance satellites for that?" he asked.

"You would not believe how bad the satellite images are. The high winds disrupt signals, and we just can't get a close enough view of anything. But even if we could, that wouldn't mean there's someone on the ground who can take action. Views from space are never the same as views from the ground. We can mistake what colors we're seeing. This is one thing where human performance is better than machines. Well, except in this case. This man, Nagar, has been filing some suspicious reports."

"Who?" I asked.

"Nagar. Security breach," she said tightly.

Alf snickered. "Security breach? Someone running away with the trees?"

Brita didn't answer, but leaned back. "We've another hour at least yet. Get some rest. The climb up to the tower base is not for the weak or weary."

OOO

Bundled in our protective gear, we practically tumbled from the transport onto the rocky ground. I leaned back in and looked at King. He sat on a supply crate with his legs dangling.

"Should I leave the door open?" I asked with a knowing wink. "You could go out and, you know, look at the trees, or whatever you want." He could go retrieve the sap while we followed Brita on her errand.

King smiled and chittered, and I gently moved the door so that it all but latched shut. Hopefully the wind wouldn't yank it back open.

The angle of the slope made standing difficult. All around us, the ground appeared to move in swirls of white and grey, like ocean waves or a stream current flowing with the wind. It took me a moment to see that a very thin layer of something dusty followed every random gust of wind.

"What is that?" I asked.

"Snow," replied Brita with amusement. She pointed with a heavily gloved hand up. "Is this your first time seeing it?" she asked. Her face was hidden beneath the goggles and a scarf which explained why her skin remained beautiful.

"Uh-huh," I said.

She stiffened. "Well, I think it's more exciting than the first day of school, don't you?" Her tone softened my bitterness for a moment, and I looked up the slope.

About twenty meters away, a rocket-shaped building stood as if poised for launch. The sun's glare hid the top of it from view, but I could tell it stood much taller than any building I had ever seen on Caren or Craggy. The trees, however, were high enough up that the glaring sun forbade me a look. I'd have to trust they were there.

The short distance to the tower wouldn't have been so bad except that it was almost completely comprised of stairs carved into the mountainside, much more daunting than anything I'd seen at Lamond Reformatory. The swishing snow quickly dizzied me, and breathing proved difficult. The air, colder than a refrigerated case, lacked substance, as if thinner than it should be.

I tried not to think about this as I climbed. Instead, I wondered why she didn't tell the boys she was my mother.

About halfway up, I heard a yelp over the whistling wind, and turned to see Fizer collapse in a heap on the steps. Alf and I scrambled back down, and rolled him onto his back. Tucking my ear to his mouth, I tried to discern his breathing over the wind, but I couldn't. With his heavy coat and goggles on, I couldn't see the rise and fall of his chest or what his eyes looked like, but I figured he'd passed out from fatigue and thin air.

Brita stood above us in a stance that reminded me of Nightmare, the director of Lamond Reformatory, all business and no patience. I could read no expression behind her protective scarf.

Without words, Alf and I coordinated our efforts to lift Fizer to his feet. I knew I could carry him alone, but I didn't know if Brita knew about the Gypsy Pearl and the strength it gave me. Again my stomach tightened with distaste: *I don't know if I can trust my own mother.*

A few minutes later, Alf and I followed Brita into the base of the tower and shoved the door closed with our bodies. *More stairs?!* These spiraled upward and out of sight above us. Alf grunted and slumped to the floor, bringing Fizer down with him.

"Huff," I complained, jerking my head at the stairs. "No lift?"

"Can't risk a power outage leaving a worker stranded," said Brita. She removed her goggles and now stared disapprovingly up the steps as if she could see through the levels in between to something that annoyed her at the top.

"I gotta rest, yeah?" said Alf.

"Of course," said Brita, tugging open the clasps on her overcoat. "How's your friend?"

I'd removed Fizer's goggles and loosened his coat enough to feel his breathing, and as I worked to disengage him from his coat, he regained consciousness and beamed at me with a starry smile.

"Hey, you're pretty," he slurred.

My heart skipped, and then kicked when I saw Alf's immediate scowl. "Fizer, you're delirious," I said. "You have a head full of mountain air." I shook the remaining coat sleeve roughly until his hand flopped free.

Fizer's head lolled over to look at Alf at an awkward angle. "You're pretty, too," he added emphatically nodding. "But kinda prickly, I guess."

Laughter echoed around us as Brita sat down on the lower steps and shook her head. "That's the best one I've ever heard," she chuckled. "Oxygen dep does something funny to the brain, but…oh, that wasn't to say that you *aren't* pretty!" She closed her mouth, trying to regain her composure, and for a moment I saw a dazzling, warm beauty—one that I could imagine Dad falling in love with. Then it faded as she rolled her lips back into serious mode. "Are you going to make it to the top, Fizer? Or do you need to rest more? It's 260 steps to the top. Not for the faint-hearted. The spiral makes it worse if you're already dizzy."

Fizer hummed to himself and smiled at Alf questioningly. Alf waved a hand at me. "You two go on ahead, yeah? We'll catch up when he gets his stars aligned."

I glanced at Brita who shrugged and stood up. Hanging her coat, scarf, goggles and gloves on a large hook in the wall, she signaled for me to ascend. I shed my outer layers and followed, counting each step as I went and quelling the nausea that came with the tightly spinning path. The steps were less than a meter wide and shaped like extremely acute triangles, so I found myself pressing against the outer wall to have enough space for my feet.

"If you put your hands down on the steps above you, it'll help with balance," she offered. With that, she dropped forward as if walking on all fours except that her feet lagged a few steps behind.

Copying her, I concentrated on trying to climb with my eyes closed, wishing I could scamper on all fours like King. This worked very well until my head bumped into Brita's knee.

"Ow, sorry. I didn't see you stop," I said, rubbing my nose and settling my back end comfortably into the widest part of the step near the outer wall.

"You're not tired?" she asked, breathing audibly. Something that mimicked pride gleamed in her eyes.

Another flashback to my first encounters with Nightmare. He had been shocked that I could withstand the pull of gravity and climb stairs so well on my first day on the Surface.

"A little," I lied. I panted for good measure, but the knowing smirk told me fooling her would not be as easy as others. Well, Dad married her. She couldn't be a dunce. I glanced up to find her studying me with obvious interest. Still no affection, though. *What did I expect? That she'd be like Maddy and Ninetta? Had she been like that with Felly?*

"Can you hear that?" she asked, tilting her head as if listening to something above.

I held my breath and focused. Nothing. I yawned to clear the pressure from my ears. Sure enough, a muffled high-pitched whine spilled down the stairs. I nodded, and she smiled sourly.

"Let's go," she said, resuming the climb.

The sound grew as we got higher, and by the time we reached the top and staggered into the large circular observatory, I had to plug my ears. Brita stormed past a man who dozed with his feet up on a control panel and slammed her hand down on a yellow flashing button. The sound stopped immediately, leaving a startling silence.

Bracing herself against the control panel, Brita shoved at the man's chair with one foot, rolling it backwards into the wall where he crashed and tumbled to the ground with an angry yowl. "Hey, what's the big—?" His eyes met Brita's and he stiffened. A second later, he stood saluting.

"Your replacement is here. Report back to the Hub."

"Wha—?" He looked at me skeptically. "But...Is there a transport?"

"Of course there's a transport, idiot. Do you think I climbed the whole mountain just to see you?"

"No, Governor. I—"

"Go! Hurry up!" she ordered. "I'll be down within the hour."

"Yes, Governor." He snapped into action, gathering loose items of spoiled food into a compactor and retrieving a crate overflowing with personal items. "I'll be just a moment."

"The driver has four crates of food and a new water purifier. Bring those up before you settle in to gossip with him."

The man's face flushed brightly, even behind his unkempt beard. Within a minute, his fast-slapping footsteps retreated down the tower stairs.

A moment passed in silence while Brita looked at me, tight-lipped. I still trembled a little from the tension that she had caused by the abrupt dismissal. She seemed to sneeze into her fist, but it turned into a laugh. Her face brightened with mischief, and she let herself flop backwards loosely into the chair the man had vacated.

"What just happened?" I asked.

"The laziest man on Craggy just exerted more energy in one minute than he has all year!" she giggled.

I felt myself give into the humor, breathing out my anxiety. As Brita swiveled back and forth in the chair by rocking her heels, I took in a slow 360 degree survey of the room. Behind a wall that broke the round curve of the room, a closet housed a lavatory, a small sink, and a refrigerator of the sort our family owned on the Arxon. *Food and toilet together? Ew.* Near the staircase, a fold-down berth had been used for storage instead of sleeping since the man obviously preferred the rolling swivel chair. The control panels hugged the inside of giant windows made of something so thick that it muted the sunlight pouring in.

That's when I saw the view.

"Are those...? Is that the Earlie tree forest?" Hopefully King was out there right now, getting that third Gift.

Brita rose and came to stand beside me with her hand resting gently on my shoulder. "Yes, that's it. Interesting, isn't it? Named because of their altitude. They are the first to see the 'Earlie' morning sun each day."

"It's not at all what I dream—imagined." The trees in my dreams had been dark conifers.

"You hadn't seen pictures?" she asked glancing at me before squinting out at the mass of green. "They resemble cacti more than trees, don't they?"

I stared at the incredibly tall, green pillars before me. No brown or white bark like on Caren. Each tree grew straight up, featureless for many meters, a green stalk branching about two thirds of the way up into several smaller straight-up limbs. The whitish leaves, if they could be called that, sprouted like a mop of hair from the end of each of these branches and hung limply down. No majestic canopy of green latticework. It almost looked like an army of long, green forks standing in formation on the mountain, the tines combing wisps of cream clouds.

"No wind up there?" I asked, noting the stillness of the trees.

"What? Of course there is. It's worse up there."

I leaned as close to the window as the control panel would allow. "They must be really strong trees not to move in the wind. On Caren, a light breeze could move the Rik trees easily."

Brita stared at me as if processing several ideas at once. "Rik trees..." She peered out at the trees. "My eyes aren't what they used—you're right! They're not moving. I wonder how...?"

I put a hand down to lean on the counter and accidentally activated some kind of monitor. Brita's brows furrowed as she studied a computer-generated image of a cluster of Earlie trees rotating onscreen. Rubbing her neck irritably, she punched some controls and the same image now in blue formed holographically between us. The sunlight from the window illuminated it distorting the color to green.

I looked at the rotating image. Though the whole thing spun slowly around, the individual trees stood motionless. I gazed out at the forest of Earlie trees and then glanced back at Brita.

"The trees—!" she shrieked, pounding at several controls.

My gaze went back and forth between her and the unmoving trees outside. I heard her swear, and suddenly all the trees disappeared, leaving a snowy wall. The forest we'd seen was an optical illusion!

Brita's scream of rage rang out as she scrambled onto the control panel.

There she knelt, her palms pressed against the thick windows. The only green in sight glowed in her pale, tear-filled eyes.

ooo

27 LEFT FOR DEAD

"Excuse me, Governor Jipps?" Fizer's voice trembled behind us, and I turned to see Alf and Fizer kneeling at the top step where it entered the observatory.

Brita did not move from her perch atop the control panel.

Fizer faltered, so Alf took over. "Governor, the man who came down has left with the transport. Was he supposed to do that?"

"He what?!" she roared, on her feet beside him in a black blur.

Alf gestured over his shoulder with his thumb. "He came down and said he was supposed to take the transport. Are they coming back soon? I don't think they unloaded anything except the crate the rat man—King—was sitting on. They probably just wanted to get him out of the transport."

"King?" I gulped. He hadn't gone up to the trees because there were no trees.

The fanep's chittering voice echoed from further down the stairs, and I bolted towards him, hurdling the boys on the floor. I found him several spirals down and stopped before I fell onto him in my haste. He had been in the process of lifting a crate fully eight times his size step by step.

"C'mon, King," I said, hefting the crate onto one shoulder.

On all fours, he darted past me and up to the top. When I caught up, I found him holding one of Fizer's hands in both of his. Fizer babbled incoherently about the minerals test we'd taken and how he should be chief something or another. I stepped over him, careful not to knee him in the head, and slid the crate to the ground.

Brita immediately crouched beside it and snapped open the latch angrily to reveal hundreds of small packs of spacey food of the sort found in the ICS system. She released a heavy sigh of what I guessed must be relief. "Nagar left with the driver?" she asked quietly.

"Yeah," said Alf.

"Mom, what's going on?" The words came out before I thought about them, and everyone's eyes pinned me to my spot.

"*Mom?!* She's your *mother?*" hissed Alf. "When were you going to tell me that?"

"I didn't know," I said, still looking at Brita...Mom.

"Obviously, you did," he said. "I thought we were working on trust stuff."

"She didn't know until hours ago," said Mom heavily, dropping back down in the swivel chair. "It's not her fault." She held out a weary hand in my direction, and it took me a moment to understand that she reached for me. I stepped over the crate and slipped my hand in hers. She squeezed it and pulled me down to my knees in a very tight embrace. My resolve to be bitter dissolved, and I choked back a sob. Her eyes met mine and then she cried into my shoulder for a really long time.

OOO

"Can't you get another transport up here?" asked Alf.

"I could if they'd answer my hails. Either the solar panels are not charging properly to power the communications, or someone back in Garvey City is purposely avoiding my signal."

Alf and I exchanged a weighted look. "Saloma?" he muttered.

"Or Derven," I added. "Kinny… Huff, who knows how many—?"

"Did you say Saloma?" asked Mom, her brow knit with confusion. "Saloma—*The* Saloma—of GNHQ on Caren?"

King gurgled angrily, sounding almost like the dog on the Arxon when the children pulled its tail.

"What's a genie aychkoo?" asked Fizer wearily.

"G-N-H-Q," said Alf distinctly. "The Gypsy Network Head Quarters. Focus on drinking that protein mix, yeah?" He lifted the spacey liquid to Fizer's lips again.

Fizer squinted at Alf. "You're a gypsy? I never would've guessed that, blondie!"

"I'm the gypsy, Fizer," I said. "And the fanep's mine. My friend, I mean."

"Oooooh," he sang sleepily. "You're gonna get in trouble for that, I guess. No faneps on Craggy. Bad, bad, bad for the water."

"If it weren't for the fanep, you'd have nothing right now," said Alf, stuffing another packet of spacey food in Fizer's hand and standing up to stretch.

"Can we get back to the subject of Saloma?" droned Mom. "You know her? You've met? You're friends?"

"Not exactly," I said evasively. "If we can trust the people we know we can't trust, then we can't trust her, either."

Mom laughed without humor. "Run that report again?"

I looked from King to Alf, trying to gauge their reactions. King gestured that I should go ahead and tell her.

Alf shrugged. "If it turns out we can't trust her, I'm pretty sure that between the three of us, we can kill her, yeah?" He indicated King, himself and me.

"Alf!"

"No, he's right," said Mom, an unexpected glimmer of respect in her eyes.

"No killing," I said emphatically. "No more."

Mom's brows shot up, but she said nothing, waiting.

With a sigh, I explained what had happened on the Ipko with Derven and Kinny playing us and ultimately trying to kill us, supposedly under Saloma's orders. As I spoke, the surrounding silence got louder until it oppressed me. Everyone leaned in, alert and attentive, and everyone could feel the threat of danger, even if Fizer and Mom didn't really understand why. I had not yet mentioned the Gypsy Pearl.

Mom massaged her forehead with the tips of her fingers and exhaled slowly. "We really need to get back down to the city." She glanced at Fizer. "He's too weak to walk, so he'll have to stay."

"Without supplies? He'll starve."

"It can't be helped," said Mom. "This…mystery, development—whatever you want to call it—requires immediate attention. They're probably related to the disappearance of the trees, too, but I don't know how yet."

"No," I said.

"What do you mean, no?" she asked, stiffening.

"We're not leaving Fizer behind. Not until he's stronger."

"If we carry him down, it'll take us too long, and then we'll *all* die," she said, standing up and shutting down controls around the room.

"No. I don't care if you're the Governor. I don't care if you're my mother. I won't do it. No more deaths on my watch. *I* will die before I let anyone else die."

Mom scoffed. "Fizer isn't going to die, and Darkman had it coming."

"Darkman was an accident," said Alf, bristling.

"There were others I watched die," I said. "Ninetta. Ora." *They don't understand.*

"Ora?!" Alf barked. "What do you care about Ora?"

"*I* will die before I let another person die," I repeated quietly, shaking with emotion.

"But you haven't finished cycling the pearl," said Alf through gritted teeth.

King squeaked and nodded vigorously.

"So it's true," breathed Mom. Her pale green eyes studied me, an enigmatic expression on her face. "And you'd come here for the third Gift."

OOO

We agreed to wait on the subject of heading back down until we'd eaten and rested for the night. I could tell this didn't go over well with Mom, who obviously wanted to take care of the trees and her colony, but I had priorities and things to take care of, too. Fizer, the cycling—*who knew how big my role would be?*

"Queen will know."

"What?" asked Mom.

"What does that mean?" asked Fizer, showing marked improvement in his condition. "What queen?"

"Queen will know," said King serenely, his luminous eyes showing no anxiety. *Three Worlds, three Gifts, three Powers.* His three fingers drew a circle in the air three times.

I don't know, I thought back at him.

Queen will *know.* King beamed, sharp teeth showing. I was the only one in the room not startled by it.

As I got up and headed into the lavatory, I heard Fizer ask again, "What does that mean? What queen?"

Alf—steady, wonderful, loyal Alf—began at the beginning and told Mom and Fizer everything.

I came back out with a plan in mind. "King and I are going to go," I announced.

"You'll never make it down alone," said Mom.

"We're not going down," I said.

"What? Which way?" asked Fizer.

I snickered as I remembered Bard in the lift. Repeating it now gave it a different meaning. "Up." I tried to ignore the confused faces. "Well, not up so much as lateral. We need to follow where the forest should have been until we find the trees again."

"They didn't just wander off, yeah?" said Alf.

"I know. But is it likely *all* the trees are gone?"

Mom nodded. "It would be the only way to scout the real situation since I don't know if I can trust any of the other tower watchmen, either."

"You don't have to come," I started.

"Of course I do."

"Aren't you needed back down in the city?" asked Alf.

Mom heaved a sigh. "I suspect there will be chaos with or without me there," she said. "If Nagar or Saloma or any of those others are involved in some great plot, we just exposed one piece of it." She laughed bitterly. "It's safer to brave the elements to help a true leader than to go back down there and try to retake my own position." She stood and bowed slightly to King. "Lead on, fanep, as you did with my grandmother. May we find success this time—for the sake of the faneps, the gypsies, and all of the Granbo System."

Huff. This was big to have her on board with our plans.

King inclined his head toward her, and then faced me with a smile. "Lead on," he said in his gravelly voice.

"Me? How about you?" He looked at me unflinching. "Huff, we're a team. Let's do this together. Who's coming?"

It took us less than half an hour to pack and repack our supplies so that everyone carried what they could handle. We all followed Mom's example, winding cloth around our faces to shield them from the wind. It knocked out peripheral vision, but so did the goggles. King wrapped himself up thickly and sat on my shoulders. His mitted hands covered my ears and his body kept my head warm like a living hat.

From the base of the tower we decided to head west, figuring to travel with the sun at our backs for as much of the morning as possible to save our eyes the extra strain. When we'd marched along for a few hundred meters, a brightness flashed behind us, signaling the sunrise over the peaks. Mom turned sharply and threw her hands in the air as if shielding herself. A second later, we felt a hot blast and tumbled to the ground, rolling painfully until we could catch ourselves. Staring back the way we'd come, we saw the tower spewing forth thick black smoke and flames, worse than Ninetta's funeral pyre.

Someone had attacked the tower!

I choked, but not on smoke. I sweated, but not because of the flames before us. *These assassins are crazy—and extremely well-armed!*

Alf put a hand on my shoulder. "They'll think you're dead now," he said, his voice shuddering. "Maybe that's good."

King tugged my ears gently. "That is good," he rasped.

Alf nodded, fear pulling his face long. "Now maybe we'll be left alone to live."

Tears blurred my eyes as I turned and scanned the slope for Fizer and Mom. Both stood staring back at the tower, motionless and slack-jawed. Their packs had fallen to the ground beside them, packs that seemed very small all of a sudden. We'd be left alone all right. Left alone to starve or freeze to death.

OOO

We walked with our heads bowed as the sun came up. Mom and Fizer shared botany and geology notes in subdued tones, each clearly impressed with the other's store of knowledge. All around us, the charred stumps of Earlie trees stood like silent sentinels, unable to explain their dismal condition.

Emotion garbled Mom's voice more than the wind and her scarf. "They've taken so many."

"Why would they do that?" I asked, falling into step beside her.

"Money. It's always about money or balances of power, though I don't know what this is all about exactly." She shook her head and stomped a few paces. "People never think of what they're doing to a planet. They just…" She kicked her toe at the hard, cold ground. "It's Earth all over again."

Unsure what she meant, I looked away from her discomfort. "What's that down there? A path?"

She followed the line of my pointing finger. "Ah, good. We can follow that for a while until it starts going down," she said. As we all made our way down to a narrow plateau, Mom explained that during the few weeks when minor logging occurred each year, the cut trees had to be transported on wheeled vehicles with flat platforms. The paths needed to be level or the trees would roll off and tumble all the way down the mountain. I didn't care so much about that as I did about the relief my legs and ankles felt to walk on level, solid ground.

Fizer crouched down and poked at something on the ground with his gloved finger. We trudged over and stared at the head-sized lump on the ground that so captivated him.

"What?" I asked. "It's a rock."

"It's not a rock," said Fizer firmly.

"Yes, it is."

"It's brown," he countered.

"So what?" asked Alf.

"Caz, don't you see?" Fizer pointed to the lump closely. "It's feces. From an animal or something."

"What?" I kicked at it, and it rolled like any other rounded rock. "It's hard."

"It's frozen, Caz," said Mom. "This means there's something alive out here. Something big!"

"Couldn't it be human feces?" I asked.

Mom scoffed good-naturedly. "Not that size."

King jumped down from my shoulder and studied the sample, his face animated with sniffing. We all chuckled at this, and Mom pointed at the blob. "Caz, feces means life, and life means there's food out here. Food means plants and maybe water. We're getting closer to something good, hopefully the rest of the Earlie forest."

OOO

I found an outcropping of rock that provided a ragged triangle of shade and a little shelter from the wind, so the five of us sat pressed against the rock, avoiding the general glare of sunlight, and ate our spacey food. The wrapper of Fizer's nutrition bar flapped out of his hand, and he grasped weakly after it, showing signs of fatigue. Before I could stand to retrieve it,

King bounded after it. A second later, he appeared, eyes wide enough to show through the child-sized goggles. He chittered excitedly and gestured to follow.

Peeking up over the outcropping, I tried to see what he pointed at through the sun's bright rays, but I just saw the ever-swishing snow dust spilling in waves over the dark rocky slope. With my hands cupped over the top of my goggles, I squinted and saw where a growing patch of white climbed up the mountain. Either the rock had changed colors, or the snow lay deeper there.

I dropped back down, facing the others. "Does deep snow hold still?" I asked.

"Still*er*," said Mom. "Why do you ask?"

"Well, there's some ahead," I said. "Doesn't that require precipitation?"

Mom shrugged. "It happens, though there's rarely any new precipitation." She jerked her chin at the sky. "Not many clouds for starters, and the ones we have move too fast to drop much water or snow. Most of the snow we're seeing has been blowing around for eons. It doesn't melt. It's as close as water gets to being dry, which is why it acts like dust."

I stood back up and Fizer joined me, using his hands like twin telescopes to block the wind and sun. "There's something moving up there!" he cried.

"That would be wind, Fizer," I said drily.

"No, it's moving in the deeper snow."

"What? Where?" I searched the whiteness at least a hundred meters away and saw nothing but a cluster of dark rocks jutting out of the whiteness. "Nothing there but mounds of rock."

"Rocks don't move," insisted Fizer. "No matter how strong the wind is," he added with a grin. "I think those rocks are people."

The rocks definitely moved. Slowly, but steadily, they climbed at an angle not quite perpendicular to the slope, gaining altitude gradually.

"Hey, it's an animal!" yelped Fizer. "Maybe that's what left the feces we saw! This is great!"

"Great? Why is this great?"

"Maybe they know where the trees are! They'll know how to survive in the mountains, too, I guess. We should follow them! Maybe they're snow people or something?"

"Snow people?" I asked skeptically. "Fizer, do you not remember that someone just tried to kill us all by blowing up the watch tower?"

"But it wasn't them, right? It couldn't have been. Maybe they can help us. We'll need more supplies soon, especially with the tower gone. All we've got is what we're carrying."

"Or they could kill us." I groaned and returned to our rocky shelter to share the news.

Mom's face, now uncovered except for the goggles, showed a mix of annoyance and confusion. "How could an entire group of people have gone unnoticed? 'Snow people'? Don't you think I would have heard about them before?"

"No offense meant, Governor," said Alf, "but it doesn't seem like you could exactly trust your staff to keep you informed if they saw human movement up here."

She shook her head. "They must be gypsies. But..."

"But gypsies hate Craggy," I said. "Nothing much grows here."

"If they have an animal that big, they have a food source," said Fizer.

"Could they have been hiding in the Earlie forest all this time?" offered Alf.

I smiled. "Alf, you do have bursts of brilliance."

"Don't expect too much, yeah?"

"So, do we follow?" asked Fizer. "They're going to be out of sight if we wait too long."

What do we have to lose? I figured King and I could defend ourselves. And Mom wore a laser pistol strapped at her hip beneath the giant overcoat.

"If you're up for the climb, let's go. Maybe they'll lead us to the Earlie trees."

OOO

We followed the snow people, as Fizer insisted on calling them, for almost an hour, relieved to find that they did not move as quickly as we had been traveling before. I figured out why almost immediately. The deeper the snow got, the harder simple walking became. It didn't pull with the same tenacity as the mud in the duspy fields at Lamond, but the heaviness of the boots Mom had gotten us didn't make it easier.

King rode on top of my pack to avoid drowning in the stuff. When Fizer tired, I took on part of his packed supplies, too.

Mom stared at me. "You've been a spacey all your life, and you're climbing a mountain in high altitude while laden down with at least twenty kilos of extra weight, never mind the heavy clothing." She shook her head, whistling a puff of air through her scarf. "That pearl is potent stuff."

"Why don't more people use the pearls as a supplement? For strength, I mean?" asked Fizer innocently.

"They are exceedingly rare and hard to retrieve," she answered.

I could hardly explain that the Power only came if the Gypsy Pearl was "given" in a brutal manner.

Fizer, most likely because he felt weak and exhausted, insisted, "But with all the technology we've got, couldn't we—?"

"Couldn't we what? Ruin another ecosystem?" spat Mom.

Fizer flinched and stopped in his tracks. "I'm sorry. I didn't mean…"

Mom halted her climb and looked at him as if her coat and pack weighed a metric ton. "It's all right, Fizer. I know you're a good kid. You just don't know what people do to planets." She waved her arm helplessly at the barren slope. "This should be covered in trees, not stumps. People rape the land and don't think about the air we need, or the lives they take."

Alf cleared his throat. "Earlie syrup saves lives in a heart attack, yeah?"

"Only gypsies really know that," she said. "If everyone believed it, these trees would have been cut down years ago. They were rare enough before. In some ways, it was harder for us to get the Earlie syrup than the pearls."

Us. She talked like a gypsy now, not a colony governor.

"What about these Snow People?" asked Alf.

"Just one more mystery." Mom lifted her goggles and pawed at her teary eyes. *She* was the mystery.

"We need to keep moving," I said, changing the subject for her benefit. "Our mystery just disappeared into that rock face."

We followed the Snow People up to a narrow pass that looked as if the mountain had been chopped with a giant knife and the pieces left beside each other. The space between the walls was narrower than the corridors of the Ivan. We stopped just outside and peeked in. The dark, sheltered space held almost no snow, and only the tall line of light at the end proved it wasn't just a cave. Sound bounced off the walls, the acoustics carrying the noises of the Snow People back to us. As far as we could tell, they had not noticed us, and we didn't want them to detect us by the sound of our footsteps.

Sitting low in the dark mouth of the tunnel-like space, we removed our hoods, scarves and goggles and relished a fullness of sensory input. The unmistakable high-pitched giggle of a child rang out. I froze. *A child?* That meant a family. That meant women, or at least one. Given that men outnumbered women twenty to one in Garvey, this felt out of place.

Mom's pale green eyes gleamed with interest. *Big mystery*, she mouthed.

The Snow People disappeared into the glare at the far end of the pass, and we got moving again, placing our feet as quietly as possible. The terrain in this dim passage jarred our feet. I could rarely find a flat foothold large enough to fit my boot. Fortunately, we could brace ourselves against the walls on either side.

King jumped down and scampered ahead, negotiating the uneven ground easily. He reached the end about forty meters away and stopped, watching intently after the Snow People.

"He's like a dog," laughed Mom.

"A dog?" grunted Alf.

"A domestic animal. Didn't you have one on Caren?"

"Not from Caren," he said vaguely.

"King's not an animal," I said gruffly.

"Of course not," she agreed. "I meant the way he moves." She turned to Alf. "You're not from Caren?"

"No."

"Well, you're not from Craggy or Tye. Your skin betrays it."

"No."

"You're a spacey, too?"

"Kashmir ICS."

She grunted appreciatively and turned to Fizer. "You?"

"Caren," he said. "Rik Peninsula Colony."

"If we'd escaped into town, we'd have met you there," said Alf.

"Escaped?" Fizer pressed himself against the rock. "Escaped? From the Reformatory?" His jaw went slack. "Were you the ones who disappeared during the big electrical storm a while back?"

Mom's eyebrows shot up. "My daughter, the escaped...what? What was your charge?"

"Violent offender. Both of us," I said glumly.

Fizer's countenance darkened. "I thought we were friends."

"We are," I said, my heart skipping a beat with guilt. In the tense silence, King reappeared beside me, wrapping his arms around my leg like a child to its mother.

"Friends trust each other," said Fizer, his eyes on King. "How many more secrets? If I'm up here in this crazy wind and snow, risking my life to help you do some weird, mystical cycling thing, I'd like to know I'm not about to help a dangerous criminal get unlimited power."

His words echoed and faded into silence as we all stared at each other.

"Fair enough," I said, glancing at Alf.

With a deep breath, he nodded and pulled at his bearded cheek. "I got a killer's tattoo, or at least the beginning of one. The Station Master's son was our teacher, and he was trying to force a friend of mine to... He promised her better marks if she would..."

"Huff."

"I... I lost control of myself. She was crying out for help, and I... I almost killed him."

My legs gave out underneath me, and I sat hard on the cold ground. He had never told me the story. He wasn't a delinquent. He was a *hero*. Even Felly would say so. And yet if the Station Master's son had not survived, he would have been sent to Craggy's penitentiary facility instead of Caren's Reformatory.

Fizer's anger dissolved back into his former awe. "That's..."

"Yeah," agreed Alf. "And Caz busted a bully's ribs when defending herself. Not her fault she had the pearl's strength, yeah?"

Fizer and Mom both gave me questioning looks.

"That's the true story, and the last of my secrets," I said. "What about you, Mom? Let's hear your story."

ooo

28 SECRETS REVEALED

Mom looked to the end of the passage as if watching the Snow People depart. With a weary sigh, she repositioned her pack. "I suppose I owe you that much."

"Yeah," I said gruffly, signaling the others to keep moving, but lingering behind a little with Mom.

"I was born on Caren in the Tral Colony—that's on the smaller continent to the north—two years after my grandmother was murdered."

"Murdered!" gasped Fizer, tripping over a small rock in his distraction. "Are you people death magnets or something?"

"Queen Levia," explained Alf.

"Wait. You mean you're from the lost royal family?" he asked.

Mom nodded solemnly.

"My nanna talked about her," said Fizer. "About Queen Levia. She said she was good except for fraternizing with the gyp—"

Alf smacked Fizer with the back of his hand. "Caz and the Governor are gypsies, idiot."

"Half," I said, raising my hand.

"Less," said Mom. "My mother, Queen Levia's second daughter, married a gypsy, so *I'm* half. You're a quarter, Caz."

"Oh," said Fizer, as if to say, *That's better.* "Anyway, Levia was good until she died."

"Thanks for that," I said flatly.

"Yes, she was," said Mom, taking higher ground emotionally. "And she was cycling a pearl just like Caz. My mother told me all about it as I grew up, and we'd been waiting to see the phenomenon again. How amazing that it happened to the same family twice!" She flashed a smile at me.

"*Your* story, Mom. Not mine or Levia's."

"Right," she said. "So, my parents weren't sure if they'd targeted Levia personally, or the family at large, so my aunt—next in line for the throne—gave up." She threw her hands in the air with disgust. "Pearl or no pearl, she should have tried to hold the Empire together, but she was afraid. The Governors clamored for independence when they saw she didn't have Levia's wisdom or strength. Things just fell apart."

"Why didn't your parents step up?" challenged Alf, stopping to lean on the rock and watch us catch up.

"My father was a gypsy. Have you ever tried to pin down a gypsy?"

"Even to lead an empire?" asked Fizer, apparently forgetting his earlier objection to gypsies.

"No, they don't stick around for much," I said, bitterness greater than I felt dripping from my words. *Why was I acting like a spoiled child?*

Mom studied her boot. Swiping the back of her hand across her forehead, she sighed. "No, we're not good at staying in one place."

"Then why did you settle in Garvey?" I demanded. "You must have been here for a while in order to get elected Governor."

I could feel Fizer and Alf measuring the tension in the air, squinting in the dim light to see my reaction.

"Can I please put everything in context?" she asked, an acid bite to her tone. "I need to explain."

"Actions speak louder than words," I grumbled, reciting the centuries old cliché.

"And motives speak louder than actions, if you're willing to learn them," she countered. "Think of Alf. Judging by his actions on the Kashmir, he's a dangerous man, not a protector." She ran her fingers into the braids of her hair and tugged them loose. "Good people do bad things for good reasons, and bad people do good things for bad reasons."

"So fill me with reasons," I said.

"All right. I traveled with my family all over Caren, and occasionally we'd travel to Tye, too, but I never liked being in space."

I could understand that. Shielding my eyes, I looked at the bright shaft of light at the end of the passage. We'd almost entered its beam.

"Everywhere we went, we watched the decline of relations between gypsies and the locals. The Granbo Charter was written by isolationists, and the people who had been bred for years in confined communities in space now wanted confined communities on the Surface. They didn't want to interact more than absolutely necessary."

"Focus, Mom," I said, snapping my fingers into the space between us. "Your story. How'd you meet Dad? Why'd you leave? We heard from GNHQ that you were advocating for gypsy rights throughout the system. Saloma didn't even seem to know you were the Governor here. Or did she?"

"That's a lot of questions," said Mom.

"Questions are all I have any more," I said. "Strength, smarts...They mean nothing to me without trust, and I can't trust until I get some answers." I folded my arms across my chest and looked out into the sunlight. "Huff, they're getting away!"

We all swiftly straightened our gear and stepped out of the pass. With goggles and scarves back in place, we squinted out at a viciously steep drop-off. Just to our right, another steep peak stretched straight out from the one we'd been traversing all day. We'd come out in a corner between two colliding ridges and could see a narrow ledge that hugged the length of the perpendicular face as it descended into the distance. Nothing like the high valley we'd found on Caren, this one plunged with deadly drops. But at least we'd be going downhill for a long time.

I nudged Mom's elbow. "We're not done with this conversation yet," I said. Beckoning King back up to my pack, I signaled for us to follow the small trench in the snow that marked where the Snow People had recently walked. The wind here was much lighter, but it still sifted the top layer of snow enough that I feared the trail would be lost if we didn't keep up.

The snow on this side of the mountain piled itself more deeply. Even placing our feet into the footprints we found meant that bits of snow occasionally crept over our boots. The instant sting of melting ice penetrated my coversuit and dripped down to my feet. No doubt due to the Rik leaves I remembered the risks of frostbite and willed my body to fight off the coldness at least in my feet. That effort quickly drained my energy, and before long, I came to a stop.

"We need to get somewhere dry," I said, my voice as mushy as my coversuit.

"I think these footprints lead to that dark patch over there," said Alf. "No snow there, yeah?"

"Must be a cave," said Mom. "Keep wiggling your toes in between steps. The faster we move, the better the circulation, and we need that now. Hurry."

Sure enough, we found a cave. It looked like someone had decided to open a bleak little room in the side of the mountain. The footprints we'd followed did not stop here, but continued down the slope. However, the wind dropped to a mere breeze, and we felt confident that we could pick up the trail later, after another rest. *Besides, where could they go but down the narrow ledge?*

This time, we spread out and ate. I removed my boots and rubbed my feet. Mom and Alf unpacked heat disks, and rather than use them for cooking, we all sat with our feet absorbing the warm. Alf and Fizer shared one, so I sat opposite Mom.

After several minutes of quiet, Mom knocked one of my feet with her toes.

"What?"

"I met your father when he worked in the Quarantine Deck of the Arxon. He wasn't the chief medical officer yet, but he was well on his way."

Leaning back on my palms, I nodded for her to continue. This part of the story mattered more than I'd let myself believe. I glanced over at the boys, who both lay back, dozing. It didn't really matter if they overheard the conversation, but it felt more private.

"What happened?" I prodded quietly.

"It was my first time traveling without my parents. I was nineteen, and feeling independent. While taking my vitals, he kept smiling at me funny. I finally asked him why, and he asked me if I was part gypsy."

"Wasn't that a common question for travelers?"

"No, he asked if I was *part* gypsy. He could tell I wasn't 100%."

"So?"

"So, it led to a discussion about mixing cultures, and how it worked for my parents." She shrugged. "After that, he just seemed to check on me more than necessary."

"He liked you."

She blushed—*my mother blushed*—and looked gorgeous doing it.

"The next time I had to make a planet transfer, I purposely waited for a rotation of the Arxon—"

"In case you saw him again—"

"And I did, and… well. I decided to stay on board for a while after I'd finished Quarantine."

"You got married," I prompted, picking King up onto my lap to hug now that I felt all snuggly and lovey.

"And Felly came within a year." She sighed and pulled her knees up to her chin, grabbing her ankles with her slender hands. "The confinement got to me," she admitted. "And everywhere I went, it seemed Arxon citizens slurred my name. Half-gypsy was too much for them. It was hurting Dag's career, too."

Dag. My dad's name. I'd known that but never heard anyone call him that. "Why?"

"Gypsies are filthy, don't you know?" She grimaced at her own statement. "Doctors shouldn't be around them."

"That's ridiculous!"

"Yes, it is. But that's how they felt. Dag and I got so fed up that we tried some time on the Surface just to get away."

"Dad's been to the Surface?"

"Yes, of course. Caren. He met my family, who were then in Jammu Colony, and we stayed a rotation." She winked at me. "That's where you were conceived, you know."

"On Caren?! Why on earth would you go back to space to have me?!"

"Better medical facilities. And the old Arxon Station Master resigned. The new one wanted Dag back."

"So I had to be born in space." I mirrored her tucked position. "Maybe that's why I never felt like I belonged there. I should have been born on Caren."

"Worked for me!" piped Fizer without moving.

"You were listening?" I complained.

He leaned up on one elbow and smiled sheepishly at Mom. "I'm sorry what I said earlier about gypsies. Hearing it from your side… Well, they don't teach that in anthropology class, and it's…"

"Yeah," agreed Alf, sitting up and reaching for his boots. "Gypsies, spaceys, Surface dwellers. We all need to orbit together. Too many divisions."

"You forgot Snow People," said Fizer.

"I didn't," I said, getting stiffly to my feet. "Let's go find them."

OOO

"Latok! Spantik! Get back!"

A shrill voice met my ears just as I stepped out of the cave. Two children in furry-looking coats stared at me from under wide-brimmed hats and scarves. For a moment, we gawked in mutual wonder, and then they turned to run down the trail towards a man leading a shaggy, brown, four-legged beast. Atop the animal sat the woman calling out shrill warnings to the children, along with threats, pleas and promises. If I hadn't been so surprised, I would have laughed.

Alf and Fizer flanked me as Mom stepped past to greet the Snow People.

"Hello there!" she called, waving a friendly greeting. "Come warm yourselves in this cave. We have heat discs that are still—"

"It's *our* cave, woman," screamed the woman. "Get away from *our* cave!"

"Now Ganchen," said the man, his voice deep and slow. "How could they know? They're obviously lost." He halted a few meters below us, and the children gathered behind his legs. The woman and the beast snorted. However, the man raised a hand in greeting and boomed, "This is Sumayar Territory. What brings you so far?"

"Sumayar Territory? What is that?" asked Mom. When the man said nothing, she continued, "I am Brita Jipps, Governor of the Garvey Colony. Who are you?"

"Don't listen to her!" squeaked the woman called Ganchen. She looked about Mom's age, yet wrinklier.

"Children, get Ganchen into the cave and tend to her ankle." The children, neither taller than a meter, helped the fussing woman to the ground, unafraid of the docile animal with enormous, soft eyes.

As Ganchen hobbled past us, leaning on the children, the man dropped the rope that circled the animal's neck and patted the side of its very fluffy head which hung as high as his own.

Fizer couldn't resist. "What *is* that thing?"

The man came forward. "She's a kangra."

"That's no kangra," protested my mother. "She's too woolly. Too big."

The man smiled. "The kangras of Caren are smaller and sleeker, but she is seventeenth generation Craggy stock. Bred for life in the Sumayar Territory. The kangra here have grown each season since my people transferred the first pair." He looked closely at Mom. "I am Pathankot. Are you lost? The Garvey Colony mines are far from here, back the way you came." His eyes narrowed under his wide-brimmed hat. "Or are you scouting more timber?"

"*More* timber?" Mom blurted. "Were there scouts out here before?"

"We're looking for the Earlie trees," I said, glancing at King. "But not for timber."

"We just discovered they'd disappeared," Mom said, her voice trailing off in recognition of the strangeness of her claim.

Pathankot stiffened. "You 'just discovered they'd disappeared'? How did you not see it happen?"

"Don't listen to her!" came a shrewish cry from within the cave.

Mom and I glanced at each other. *Which of us should explain?* I decided to go for it because a youth might seem less likely to lie to an adult.

"We—I wanted to see the Earlie forest, and my mother took us up to an observation tower at the forest edge. When we got there, the trees were gone. We never saw them being harvested. Do you know when it happened, or who took the trees?"

"Was no one supervising the harvest?" he asked.

"We have no use for the trees," said Mom. "I mean, except to protect them for the air's sake. We allow only minimal cutting at specific times each year."

"Then those men have stolen your forest," he said grimly.

"How?" asked Mom, wilting with visible discouragement.

"We saw an air ship firing lasers back through the pass up there. It felled hundreds and hundreds of trees, and then men with long steel cords came down and lifted the trees up into the hull. That was weeks ago." He shook his head and called into the cave. "Ganchen? How's the ankle?"

"Is she injured?" I asked.

"Yes. Not sure how badly yet."

"May I see?" I asked. "I'm medically trained." *Sort of.*

"I don't want some outsider looking at my leg," bleated the woman. But Pathankot waved me in, and I set to work. Once I came near her, she seemed to freeze up. The children stepped aside—one girl and one boy—and watched me remove her long boot and ascertain the extent of the injury. It proved to be only a bad sprain.

"I'm going to need something to splint this with. Something about this long," I gestured with my hands, "and another about this long. And, do you have any rope or thin stripped cloth?"

Alf jumped to work. "We've got bandaging in the first aid kit in my pack."

Within ten minutes, I'd created a secure splint out of an eating utensil, a folded rod of aluminum from the frame of one of the packs, and the bandages. Adding some snow in a polysac to bring down the swelling, I sat back on my knees and declared the work done. King hovered just beside me and hummed his approval.

"If you're willing to take this pill, it will also help with the pain," I offered from the medical supplies in Alf's pack. She shook her head vigorously, lips tightly sealed, but her eyes had lost the scathing look.

The cave felt cramped with all eight of us inside and the kangra filling in for a fuzzy door. Neither the animal nor the people smelled too good, either, but that seemed the norm on Craggy. No water means no showers.

However, my service to Ganchen had made everyone friendlier, and now we sat contemplating the next move.

Pathankot and Ganchen's primary dwelling lay at the base of the mountain they'd been descending, but the injury required attention and rest. She couldn't ride the kangra for long without wearing him out.

"Why do you use a kangra? Why not a hover craft of some kind?" asked Alf with a gesture at the floating fanep.

Latok, the girl, giggled, and Pathankot shook his head. "Hover tech is useless up here. The paths are too narrow and the drop-offs too steep. A single gust could sweep us down into the abyss in no time. We need something heavy and grounded. A kangra works perfectly." He gazed out at the beast and smiled. "And she gives us milk."

"Milk? Real milk? I haven't tasted that in a long time, I guess. Not since I left Caren," said Fizer, bubbling with excitement. Pathankot noted this and moved to the beast. He retrieved a bowl from the packs tied to the animal. Reaching under the kangra, he fumbled for a moment and then yanked at some dangling appendage. A loud stream of white liquid splashed against the rock. Pathankot held the bowl under the animal and pulled again, this time catching the milk in the bowl. Two more squeezes and he let go, wiping his now damp glove on the kangra's side.

He walked heavily over to Fizer and handed him the bowl.

"It's on fire," I mumbled.

Alf snorted. "It's steaming. It comes out hot. It's been inside a living being after all, *doctor*," he teased.

Fizer held the bowl with two hands and tipped it to his lips. Chewing my lips shut, I held back all the spacey germ paranoia that accompanied the idea of drinking something that sprayed straight from an animal's undersides into an unwashed bowl. But Fizer's pleasure shone instantly in his smile, and he thanked Pathankot profusely.

"How many people live in the Sumayar Territory?" blurted Mom, and I realized she'd been containing her curiosity since the arrival of the Snow People.

Pathankot stretched his shoulders back, settling into a wary stance. "I think we number more than the miners. Maybe three times as many."

My question fell out before I could trap it. "Why don't you talk like the other people from Craggy? Are you gypsies?"

The children chirped back their surprise.

"We aren't speaking against the wind down in our valley," said Pathankot evasively.

Alf wouldn't be put off. "*Are* you gypsies?"

"We wander locally now," said Pathankot gruffly. "No planet jumping for a generation or more."

"Gypsies!" I laughed with delight before I remembered that Saloma was a gypsy.

Pathankot frowned. "I can't say being a gypsy means what it used to. They used to take care of the environment and live at peace with nature. But now, after those gypsies from Caren came…"

I stiffened. "What gypsies from Caren?"

"*They're* from Caren," warned Ganchen, gesturing at us. "They're probably in on the deal."

"Deal? What deal?" demanded Mom in her Governor Jipps voice. "Gypsies came here with a deal?"

"*Who* did you say you were?" challenged Pathankot.

"I'm Governor Brita Jipps of the Garvey Colony."

"Not a gypsy?"

"I am that, too." she said. "In fact, I am that more."

"A gypsy governor?" sneered Ganchen. "Who do you think you are?"

I could almost hear my mother's intestines clinch up, but she spoke with measured control. "We simply came to find out what happened to the trees. The Earlie trees. There used to be a considerable forest along the timberline, and now it has disappeared. We came to investigate."

"A gypsy governor and three kids? What kind of an investigative team is that?" Ganchen didn't trust us any farther than she could kick us with her bad ankle.

"A gypsy governor and three kids, yes," said Mom. "It's a complicated story, but we mean you no harm."

At that, Pathankot gave a quiet, bitter laugh. He pointed at King. "Like we meant no harm to the faneps when the humans entered the Granbo System? Like the miners meant no harm when they began tearing the mountains up? Like the gypsies who were just going to harvest a few hundred square meters of Earlie timber for medicinal development?" He pointed a thick finger close to Mom's face, and his tone bit like the cold outside. "Spaceys don't care what happens on the planets as long as they get what they want. People from Caren feel superior because they have the most natural riches, and they don't care if they strip the other planets of their few resources. You can't trust anyone but your own kind."

He ended his tirade by grabbing up the now empty bowl and throwing it towards the back of the cave. Spantik shrieked and Latok whimpered. My breath shuddered out in a ragged wisp, revealing the temperature drop as night began to fall outside.

King placed his hand on my arm so gently that I almost didn't feel the pressure through the coat, yet I felt a rush of warmth. With a chitter, he trotted into the darkest recesses of the cave and returned with the bowl. Stone dipped in molten silver? It showed no sign of damage, and King held it high in the air, offering it to Pathankot. The man merely tugged the kangra further into the shelter of the cave. King tried again to give the bowl back, first to Ganchen and then to Spantik.

Spantik, the closest in size to King, took the bowl and wrapped it into his stomach protectively. King bowed to him solemnly, as if thanking him. The boy, uncertain of this new creature, mimicked the bow. King gurgled cheerfully, keeping his teeth hidden, and stepped back.

From the mouth of the cave, Pathankot said, "You move your people to the back of the cave. It's warmer, and you don't have kangra wool coats. Besides, that way we can leave in the morning without disturbing you."

As the four of us and King curled up together for warmth, I found it strange that a governor, the king of an entire species, and me—destined to rule the entire system—all cowered before a brusque, kangra-smelling man in a cave. But we were in his territory.

OOO

Something shook my arm. I blinked and looked up again. King floated there, shrouded in shadow.

My elbow jerked again. "Lady, your fanep wants you. Wake up!"

I rubbed my eyes with my gloved knuckles and looked at the arm that kept shaking. Spantik stood eagerly trying to get my attention. "Your fanep!"

"Ah, you're awake." Pathankot's voice held none of its earlier rancor. I rolled to my side, careful not to knock my shoulder into King. Light streamed in from the cave entrance, and silhouetted against the brightness sat Pathankot and my mother, cozy like old friends.

"I thought you were leaving in the morning without us," I said, my voice hoarse with cold.

"Come on, Caz," said Mom, with a look that told me to stop being argumentative. "Try the flat bread and the sito."

"What's sito?"

Mom held up a tall mug with a lid and a stick in the top. She put this to her lips and sucked. Seeing my confusion, she explained, "It's a straw.

Drinking with it helps prevent chapped lips with the cold and the wind. Come try it. It's warm."

"Repeating: what's sito?" I asked.

"It's made from kangra milk."

I stretched again and accidentally knocked King backwards. Spantik shrieked with laughter, and I heard a collective groan coming from all the others who, apparently, had still been asleep. I walked stiffly over to them, absorbing the silence of the morning and thinking I never wanted to sleep another night on the rocky ground.

Pathankot glanced at me, dipping his head in a polite nod. "I apologize, lady, for my earlier conduct. I have not many reasons to trust outsiders."

My hands went to my hips and I tried to melt my mother's cool expression with a stare. "*Lady?* You told? My confidences were not yours to break."

Mom started to speak, but Pathankot raised a hand to silence her. "It isn't her fault. Not entirely. You see, I do know what faneps are, and I recognized that this one is unlike the others. Larger, greyer. Smarter. And if he is with you?" He shrugged pleasantly. "I made some educated guesses and pried the rest from Brita."

My hand went up to grab King's feet where they dangled in the air over my right shoulder. I tugged him down into my arms "He's their king," I said. My heart swelled with the significance of that. "He deserves our honor and…to be treated with dignity."

Despite myself, I giggled at the silliness of what I'd just done, yanking a regent from the air and holding him like a baby. Mom and Pathankot smiled, too.

"I agree. The faneps were here first," said Pathankot simply. "The Sumayar made a mistake in transplanting the kangra to another planet, but the stars have been forgiving, and the kangra have thrived despite the harsh climate. But our people have learned to respect the world on which we live. We adapt to the world instead of making the world adapt to us."

His last statement elicited a huge grin from Mom, and I saw again her beauty. "We can trust him, don't you think?" she asked hopefully.

I yawned, weary by all the newness and the weight of cycling the Gypsy Pearl.

Pathankot took this as an editorial comment and burst out laughing. "I shall not take offense, lady," he wheezed. "But I do think you are safer to retreat further into Sumayar territory than to go back to the camp. Your enemies no doubt believe you are dead, so no one will follow you there. It may give you time to plan."

OOO

29 THE SUMAYAR

For three hours, we descended the mountain on the narrowest and rockiest of winding trails, often entering steep crevices to pass under snow-packed fissures above us. The thin air finally got to Fizer, and I had to pack him onto my shoulders and let Alf take King. That was the first time Mom *really* saw the Power of the Gypsy Pearl working in me, and I could see her rolling it over in her mind. Something in the trudging soothed me, though. My heels hurt with the hard strike of each step, yet the solidity appealed to me. I really did like the feel of rock beneath me. Solid.

In the children's eyes I saw that these forbidding natural features were trusted friends. They skipped along, running their woolly mitted hands along the rocky cliff walls lightly even as Alf, Mom and I practically hugged them, hoping not to tumble from the ledges. Fortunately, the trail itself did not have much snow, just gritty, dry dirt that crunched like gravel.

The kangra impressed me, too. Sure-footed and sturdy, it plodded forward, unhindered by the grumbling Ganchen on its back. If it understood her constant complaints about aches and pains, it did nothing to make the ride smoother. I held back laughter at times because her streams of negativity matched Fizer's declarations of wonder. As he bombarded Pathankot with question after question about the geology of the mountains—not from a miner's perspective, but from a scientist's fascination—the man warmed to the conversation and revealed an extensive knowledge of all things natural. Whether he had learned them from experience or study, I couldn't tell, but it passed the time informatively, and I trusted the Gypsy Pearl to do its work in the recesses of my memory if I ever needed it.

Meanwhile, Alf and I fell into companionable silence, letting all the others make their noises to the wind and each other. On this side of the mountain, in all the tight passages, we had plenty of protection from the sun, so the goggles rested on our foreheads just in case we saw a patch of sunlight ahead. The temperatures hovered above freezing, and exertion kept our cheeks flushed with warmth. Alf eventually removed his gloves and flexed his fingers, coughing at how musty they smelled. I followed suit, stuffing my gloves into the cavernous pockets at my hips. The sleeves of my coat hung long enough to protect them from the chill.

The path eventually widened and became shallower in its downgrade so that we could walk side by side. Fizer begged to be let down and trotted to catch up with Pathankot.

Alf and I now lagged further behind, and he playfully elbowed me and pointed ahead to where Latok and Spantik had left the trail and entered a wide snowy patch. Latok bent low and scooped a pile of snow into her hands. Patting it with her mittens, she formed it into a sphere which she promptly tossed at Spantik. It exploded in soft white powder against his back, and he giggled. Returning fire in like manner, he grazed her leg. I waited for Pathankot or Ganchen to admonish them for aggressive behavior, but Ganchen actually chortled for the first time. "He's no baby anymore, Latok! He's got his papa's aim!"

As if to confirm this, Pathankot formed a snowy missile and struck Spantik solidly on the chest. The distance had been four times as great as the children's throws, and they all cheered with amazement.

"This is play?" I asked incredulously.

Mom grinned. "Give it a try, Caz."

"What?"

"Get your goggles on so you don't get hit in the eye. Go on. It's fun!"

I turned to Alf with a questioning shrug. King floated upward from his shoulders and signaled for us to try. Alf donned his goggles and plunged forward, dropping to his knees. Seconds later, I had a face full of snow. It trickled down, failing to sting my already cold-numbed face.

Roaring like a madman, I raced into the whiteness, instantly sinking so deep that snow chilled my thighs. Everyone laughed, Mom the loudest of all. I couldn't help thinking that even Felly might find this a worthy amusement. It wasn't dirty, after all. Although I felt like I couldn't walk fully upright with the tug of the snow, I dragged myself in circles, trying to duck away from all the incoming balls of snow. I became the target of choice. Delving my fingers into the snow, I gritted my teeth against the cold and formed a ball as I'd seen the others do. But I couldn't throw it. Instead I stared at it. *What a miraculous thing!* Snow—frozen particles of water—combined to make something semi-solid, and yet I could still distinguish individual crystals of ice. Holding it high, I pulled my goggles off to examine it more closely. Alf approached, his hands empty and in the air, gesturing to the others to cease fire.

"You're supposed to throw it, yeah?" he said, puffing out a wisp of steamy breath.

"It's too beautiful," I said. "Look at it."

He tugged his goggles down so they hung around his neck. Snow frosted his beard and his ruddy cheeks glowed. With sparkling humor, he made a big show of studying my creation. "Yes, Caz. Very beautiful. A nice white ball. Now launch it."

I couldn't resist. With both hands, I stuffed the snow into his face and pressed it into his skin. He let out a yowl of surprise. His hands came up to hold mine in place on the side of his face, and he bumped his forehead against mine playfully. Even in the cold, heat shot through me in a deliciously frightening way, and I wondered how all the snow around us didn't melt into a river.

OOO

We reached the settlement before sunset, and I stood in awe of the spectacle before me. "How did no one know about this?"

"It's pretty inaccessible for men who cling to modernity," said Pathankot with a wink. "Nothing local can safely fly over those mountains. Too tall and too windy."

"Right," I agreed. "But what about satellite vids?"

Mom shook her head, her mouth open in wonder. "Winds again, I bet. It's small enough that it wouldn't show with the resolution they can get. Especially with this patchy cloud cover blocking the view."

I gave an exasperated gesture. "Yes, but... This!"

We looked down on a narrow, deep valley of frosty green and white. Less than a kilometer away, the color ended abruptly at the base of a sheer cliff that rose at least that high up in one bound, disappearing into a haze of light clouds. It almost looked like someone had built a wall in the middle of an ongoing valley. Nestled against the cliff, about twenty manmade structures ringed an area of light brown ground. Between this tiny town and the slope on which we stood, hundreds of kangra roamed in the lowest part of the valley right down the center. On either side of them, four large rectangles of varying hues of green marked crops.

"You have agriculture here?" asked Mom, astonished. "How do you water anything?"

Pathankot's face pulled into a lop-sided grin, pride evident on his face. "You can't see it from here, but there's a waterfall that trickles down the cliff and feeds a little wading stream that runs through the valley. It dips below ground just over there, but it's enough for us to water the fields."

"It's warmer than it looks, too," said Ganchen. "Doesn't usually drop below ten degrees Celsius."

"That's blistering hot for this planet," grinned Mom.

Glee tickled a laugh from my throat. I started walking faster, almost breaking into a run. King, Latok and Spantik quickly passed me, rocketing down into the lowlands. A moment later, the kangra galloped past me with a grousing Ganchen clinging to its back. I stopped and laughed until the others caught up. Then we all burst into a sprint, racing to a place I somehow knew would feel like home.

The ground changed from the gritty rock of the mountain to snow-dusted grass unlike anything I'd seen on Caren. The blades in the mountains of Caren grew sharp and tall, but this ankle-deep greenery swished softly under our feet. Watching the others run ahead, I saw a sparkling dust rise up in their wake, like the tail of a comet except that it drifted, glittering to the ground. Thinking it was snow, I caught some up in my hands and saw that it was made of hundreds of the tiniest flowers I'd ever seen, each with four little white petals and a silvery center.

"What is that?" I asked Pathankot.

"Suma flowers. They are flowers and seeds in one, and they keep the valley replenished with grass all year long." He gestured to our right and changed course slightly. "Here's the stream. We call it the Mayar. Hence the name of our people, Sumayar. Suma flowers, Mayar waters. Flower Water."

"Not Snow People," said Fizer, gulping air through his happy grins.

Pathankot laughed pleasantly. "Well, we feel like that, too. But the snow doesn't keep us alive. The flowers and water do."

We resumed our walk towards the settlement, and Mom fell into step beside Pathankot. "You live on the flowers?"

"We have a bland and unvaried diet," he conceded. "We use the grass here along the stream for a flat bread. There are other plants that grow up against the cliff, lichen and such. We have the four fields, one side planted half a year after the other to ensure a steady harvest: a strain of rapa wheat on the east side and revos on—"

"Revos!" I clapped my hands. "Revos, Alf!" My first assignment at Lamond had been to dig the root vegetables up in the garden. They'd been served in at least one meal a day.

Pathankot looked pleased by my response. "They grow smaller than on Caren because there is less moisture, but even so, they are hearty and filling. Also, we transplanted some fruits from Caren generations ago. They are cultivated in the Greenhouse. Our scientists have found ways to make them thrive. I am told they are not as sweet, but they have the vitamins we need. We are not even a hundred in this settlement, so it is enough to sustain us."

"Do you ever eat the kangra?" asked Alf.

Pathankot's eyes darkened. "When a kangra dies of old age, we roast it over a fire and then partition the meat to be eaten right away or dried in small pieces. We save those for times when someone falls very ill and needs extra nourishment. The kangra's strength becomes their own."

Alf's lip curled with amusement. "It sounds like a superstition, yeah?"

The line of Pathankot's mouth tightened. "Most in the Granbo System make the error of thinking that science is the only way. Technology and chemicals. What they forget is that science is only trying to discover and replicate what Nature already knows. Sometimes we become so advanced that we hinder ourselves."

Mom removed her goggles and looked at him steadily. Whether moist with tears or the soft breeze washed them, her pale green eyes filled with discernible emotion. I could feel her respect for Pathankot and the Sumayar people, and I could see her happiness.

"You belong here, Mom," I said, surprised that I'd voiced it aloud.

She took a long, deep breath and smiled down at the lively stream. "It definitely has more appeal than an ICS." Mom shook her head in wonder. "Part of me wants to tell the Worlds about this, but people would come and destroy it." She frowned. "Like the Earlie trees. Pathankot, are there any more? What will happen to Craggy without them?"

"I don't know. But the children helped me gather seeds from the burnt stumps we found. Perhaps they are salvageable. I'll have the botanists examine them. If so, we could plant them there." He pointed up to the slopes on either side of the valley, above the line of the crops.

"I'll help plant them!" I cried. "Put me to work."

Pathankot's features twisted with confused amusement. He glanced at Mom. "Your daughter does not fit the mold of the legends."

"No, she does not," said Mom proudly.

I crossed my arms over my chest. "Are you calling me moldy?"

They burst into hearty laughter, and Pathankot waved broadly. "Come on. Spantik and Latok will have shown your fanep to the others by now. It's time to speak to the Council."

OOO

I counted eighty-six Sumayar people, plus the four humans in my party. We all sat on kangra wool mats in a semi-circle. Here in the shelter of the cliff, no one wore goggles or hats. The natural acoustics of the stone made it easy for us to hear each speaker, and there had been so many of them that my buttocks tried to take root in the soil. A Caz tree would sprout next month.

Pathankot reported the loss of the forest and the seeds he'd gathered. Another woman reported the birth of a healthy new kangra calf and a discussion followed to decide which family would take responsibility for it. The botanist proclaimed a new fruit vine to have previously undiscovered medicinal properties that would help infants with rashes. A man asked if anyone had unused silver that could be melted down and reshaped into needed cutlery. Alf, Fizer and I exchanged raised eyebrows at that. *Precious metals for forks?*

My gaze wandered to the rock wall just beyond the circle of buildings. It shimmered with water. Unlike the waterfall I'd seen on Caren that foamed and bounced down a slope, this cascade glided down from the great misty heights, rippling almost imperceptibly against the blackness behind it. Yet as motionless as it appeared, the glinting sunlight caught it in a few places consistently, making it seem like a night sky with glowing constellations.

It reminded me of a view from the cafeteria on the Arxon, but no homesickness bloomed. When all of this ended—if we could even finish the quest to cycle the pearl—how would I tell my father that I never wanted to live in space again? *How could I return to a place of so many rules when I had killed a man?*

"Caz, return to orbit," whispered Alf.

I refocused to see everyone staring at King hovering in the middle of the circle. Retraining my ears from my inner thoughts to the sound in the Council circle, I heard a cacophony of voices, mostly excited. Like when an ambassador or ICS dignitary would visit Mr. Virgil's class on the Arxon. A novelty of profound interest. The fact that no one seemed repulsed by him encouraged me greatly.

King clapped his hands in a slow, steady beat, and before long, others joined in, patting their knees, tapping their feet. The sound reverberated like a mountainous heartbeat, and my mind flew back to the fanep cavern on Caren where a whole underground city of the creatures worked in rhythm with each other—with King.

And as in the fanep cavern, King began to dance. Sometimes he touched the ground, and other times he hovered in poses no human could recreate. All the while, the beat continued, and as I watched, I understood. His dance, his movements. *Was I feeling it telepathically? Were the others? Could they see what I saw?* He was telling a story.

The planets share an orbit around a star.
One is green.
One is grey.
One is blue.
The blue one is alive with creatures that dwell in the sea.
Fires under the water push mountains to the surface.
The mountains sink again, leaving circles of land.
Some creatures climb up to the circles of land.
They live in two worlds—land and sea.
They see a third world—the sky.
Three Worlds.
Each has gifts that help the creatures.
Stars fall into the sea with new creatures.
The new creatures have come to live and to take.
The new creatures carry the old into the third world—the sky.
The old creatures see their three worlds repeated on three planets.
Each has green.
Each has grey.
Each has blue.
Each has water, land and sky.
The old ones leave their homes and begin to die.

They cannot see each other.
They cannot hear each other.
They are captive to their loss.
They want to go home.
The new creatures travel the planets.
They live.
They take.
They hold still.
Only a few continue to roam the stars.
Only a few live and give.
One of these must visit the three Worlds of the star.
One of these must visit the three Worlds of each planet.
One of these must receive three Gifts.
One of these must gain three Powers.
This one will bring the captives home.
This one will live and give all.

OOO

We retired after the meeting to a building they called the Inn. Kangra wool mats hung from the seam of the ceiling, covering the walls with warm insulation. Exhausted, I entered the sleeping room and lay on a mattress of sorts that felt like it had been stuffed with dried grasses, itchy but sweet smelling. Three more mattresses were stacked on the opposite wall. I removed my overcoat and boots, and yet I felt warm in my coversuit. On a small stone table stood a silvery bowl in which a liquid burned with a low flame. It provided a comforting glow of light much like the gypsy campfires, yet it contained no wood. *Animal fat oil?* The stuff of spacey legends. I wished I could show Felly.

Feeling a little light-headed, I dozed briefly. When I awoke, King lay near my feet and folded the corner of the blanket over himself. I watched him, wondering why he had danced his dance and told his story. I wondered if I truly understood it well.

Careful not to wake him, I slid to the ground and stood up. From the door, I saw Ganchen placing a silver-stone bowl on a low square table in front of Mom and the boys who sat on pillows. She glanced up and almost smiled. "Just in time to eat."

This room, much like the sleeping room, had small shelves between the hanging mats. They held eating utensils, blankets and other things I couldn't identify. Atop each of these shelves sat a flaming bowl. Seven flames danced, and clearly the one in the sleeping room belonged in the eighth shelf. I retrieved it and placed it in its spot, careful not to spill the oil or let the flame touch me.

Less than a rotation ago I'd been terrified of fire, and now it mesmerized me. Experience dispels so much fear.

The others delved into plates of steaming mashed revo with a creamy sauce on top. It smelled like bliss must taste, and I sat down on the remaining pillow. "Thank you so much, Ganchen!" I said sincerely. "This is wonderful. Will your husband be joining us?"

"My husband's been dead two years," she said gruffly.

Mom and I both stared at her. "Pathankot is not your husband?" Mom asked.

"No, he's my little brother."

"But...whose are the children?" asked Mom.

"They're his, but his wife died giving birth to the little one."

I gasped. "Oh! I'm so sorry. I wish I'd been here to help—or my father, or..." *Two deaths in one family!*

Ganchen's eyes softened as she studied my face. "You're a good little doctor," she said, shaking her ankle at me lightly. "But death comes. It's part of life and not to be feared." She smoothed her dark hair back from her face. "Not to be chased after, but not to be feared."

My mouth fell open. For a moment, she sounded like Ninetta. A grumpy Ninetta. "Well, thank you again for everything. I do hope you'll put me to work planting the Earlie trees."

Ganchen smiled wryly. "Oh, you'll all have work to do. It's the way of the Sumayar."

OOO

Pathankot took Mom to meet with the elders in the morning. Five men and women made all the major decisions for the settlement, the sorts of complicated things that couldn't be determined by common consent. Mom wanted to consult with them about what to do regarding the trees and also whether or not their presence should be made known to the outside world. Mom had essentially abdicated her governorship by not revealing that she had survived the tower explosion, but worry for the condition of the Garvey Colony clearly lingered in her heart.

King, likewise, seemed preoccupied. When I asked him about it, he said something unintelligible about faneps crying.

"You miss your home?" I asked.

He didn't answer, but folded his hands over his heart and sighed.

"Why don't you go see the waterfall or the stream? Maybe the water will feel like home?"

King smiled sadly and trotted off towards the cliff wall, buzzing with a melancholy, tuneless hum.

When the scientists learned of Fizer's geology expertise, they led him away to the Laboratory—a building reserved for research in all things natural. He went willingly, brimming with curiosity and enthusiasm in perfect Fizer style.

Alf and I laughed to watch him go, and then followed Latok, Spantik and six other children out to the revo fields. They could not contain their delight that "grown-ups" would be getting dirty with them, and they swung their kangra wool sacks in circles over their heads, cheering and singing the whole way. Singing.

Music on the Arxon came almost exclusively from digital data bases that recorded live music made on the planets by instruments carved from wood. With no trees in space, the luxury of owning a real instrument fell to the wealthiest of traders.

Here in the Sumayar territory, the children didn't wait for a computer or an instrument to play a melody. They simply used their voices, moving up and down in clear tones to sing the strangest of rhymes. The tunes all had an ordered feel to them so that I learned to mimic the rise and fall of the notes after a few repetitions.

Children sing, flowers dance
Kangras and the elders prance.
Babies cry, old men die,
And no one ever answers why.

"That's a cheerful little message, yeah?" smirked Alf, playfully slapping his sack on Latok's back.

She didn't seem to mind, and a moment later, she stopped on a small rise in the land where water poured out of the fount of the stream.

"Wait," I said, looking back the way we'd come. "The waterfall. Where does the water go?"

"This is it," said Latok. "The Mayar goes underground by the cliff and then shoots back out here. Where did you think we got the water for the lavatories and the showers? It pipes in from under the meeting place."

"Showers?" My body tingled at the very idea of being clean. "You have showers?"

"At day's end, silly. So you don't stink up the bed."

"Lavatories?" asked Alf.

Latok's hands shot to her mouth and she squealed. "Ew! You pottied in your room?"

"No, just outside," said Alf, winking.

Latok and the other children couldn't make up their mind whether to be amused or disgusted, but they ran down to the left of the stream and headed into the rows of revos.

I backhanded Alf. "That's really foul, Alf."

"Just because I can't control my body systems like you can," he said amiably. With a more serious look, he added, "Which you should stop doing. We don't know what that will do to you in the long run."

I nodded sheepishly. "Huff, all right. But outside? Really, Alf?"

He punched my arm. "Of course not. I used the lavatory. Nice stone and silver work. It's impressive what these people can make."

Whacking him with my sack, I darted after the children singing, "Alf pottied outside! Alf pottied outside!"

Because of the light cloud cover, the sunlight in the revo field was not as harsh as in the mining camp, so we wore wide-brimmed hats like the children. We'd also been given kangra wool coats—dyed red in berry juices—that came to our waists, so we could move more comfortably. Dropping to my knees beside Spantik, I noted immediately that the dirt didn't yield like the garden at Lamond Reformatory. Even so, I determined to do a repeat performance of my first revo harvest. Sifting through the fat leaves, I worked my hands into the ground, feeling for the round root. Rocking it back and forth as Sasa had taught me on another planet, I tugged hard.

Whoosh! It flew into the air, soaring so far that it splashed into the stream almost a hundred meters away.

The children exploded with laughter, rolling back onto their bottoms and pointing to the stream. The tallest boy cheered, "That's a great idea!"

"What do you mean?" I asked.

"Well, we have to take them to the stream to wash them anyway. Why not just do that?" he suggested.

"Because none of us can throw that far," said a girl sarcastically.

"Because they'll float away," added Latok.

"Will they?" I asked. "Sorry! I didn't mean to throw it quite that far."

"But if you can, do it again," insisted the tall boy. "A few of us could wait down by the Mayar and pick them out of the water. I bet they'd already be clean. It could save us more time to play."

The last word motivated all of them to run down to the stream at full speed, trailing their sacks behind them. At the water's edge they wandered a bit until Latok and the tall boy organized them in a long line with a few meters between each child. Then they waved at us to throw.

"Just you and me, I guess," said Alf, mimicking Fizer.

"I guess," I laughed.

"You know I can't throw a revo that far."

"That's all right, Alf. I love you anyway." It slipped out of my mouth and we stood staring at each other breathlessly, stupid wide grins on our faces. My heart pounded at the freedom I felt just from speaking what my whole being knew.

OOO

The journey back to the settlement took longer because the children dragged full sacks of revos behind them. Alf and I offered to help, but they declined saying that they wanted to do their part. *Do their part.* An old ICS thing that used to grate on my nerves, but I saw it in a different context here. These willing children *wanted* to contribute to society.

As we passed through the outer buildings into the packed dirt of the Meeting Place, the children stopped abruptly.

"Aw, the baby kangra died," said Latok, pouting. "Look, they're getting it ready to burn."

"I thought it was born healthy," replied the tall boy.

"Momma says there's always a chance in the first few days," said another girl.

Without a word, the children pulled their sacks into a large pile where we'd stopped and then spread out, fanning the edges of the clearing. Each picked up one or two stones the size of their heads that rested against the walls of the buildings. Other adults and youth were doing the same, all bringing the stones into the center of the space. They placed them carefully, forming a paved, circular area. Two other adults knelt over the inert kangra and lifted the beast onto this pile of rocks.

"A gypsy funeral pyre," I murmured. "Like Maddy did for Ninetta."

"Like *you* did," he corrected gently.

Memories of the kind woman flooded back into me and poured out through my eyes. Burying my face in Alf's shoulder, I relived all the grief I hadn't been able to process fully since the event. Sobbing, I cursed death for taking so many. *Could I have helped the baby kangra? Did I know enough medicine?* No, I knew nothing of animal anatomy, and the Gypsy Pearl could not help me remember things I'd never learned.

Alf squeezed me tightly. "It's all right, Caz. Just a kangra, yeah? They have lots of them."

I shuddered and stilled myself, turning to see the pyre. The children placed handfuls of grass between the stones and a man now sprayed something over the kangra from a round crate with a hose.

Mom appeared to watch the spectacle, too. "A special oil that actually keeps the heat controlled. They won't burn it to ashes. They will roast it."

I nodded, remembering what Pathankot said. This little kangra would provide food for others and sustain life.

"Did you do this with animals on Caren?" I asked, realizing that I didn't know much about her life as a gypsy.

"No," she said. "It's an older tradition. But the Sumayar came here so long ago that they have kept the older ways."

"How is it that there are not more of them if they have been here so long? Do so many of them die?" I asked.

"Ganchen says there are more settlements deeper into the mountains to the north. All small like this one."

I turned my attention back to the pyre and wondered where King was now. The Sumayar gathered around at a safe distance, laying down their mats and sitting to watch. We moved closer, joining Fizer and the botanist on a mat near the back. Five elderly people came out from a building to our left and raised their hands as they walked in a slow circle around the pyre. Everyone raised their hands, too, silently watching the elders space themselves evenly around the pyre. As one, they each tossed something onto the pyre, a spark. As wisps of smoke arose from the grasses and ignited into flames, the five elders raised their hands again, reaching out as if to form a circle around the kangra.

"From death comes life!" they shouted.

The Sumayar cheered back, "From death comes life!" All lowered their hands and watched in pensive silence as the fire grew and enveloped the calf. The elders stood there with their hands clasped behind their backs, like sentinels. I scanned the faces and saw no sorrow or distaste, just acceptance and trust. A strange ceremony in every way, but somehow beautiful, too. With the others, I watched gold and red and orange waves dance across the pyre to the imperceptible music of the breeze. This pyre did not frighten me like Ninetta's had.

Something moved on the far side of the pyre. King. He held something in his hands which he showed to each of the elders in turn. Then he stepped up onto the stones of the pyre, their heat not affecting him at all. Carefully he stooped over and placed something between the stones where the grass had been. He did this in several places, moving lithely along the rocks. At last he faced the kangra and lifted his hands. To my astonishment, the kangra rose from the pyre, spiraling slightly. He stood beneath it as it floated higher and higher.

And then it exploded into a floating fire ball!

The Sumayar screamed and pulled back, but the fire ball drifted back down gently, dropping ashes as it went. By the time it came to rest above King's head, nothing more than a cloud of black dust remained.

He brushed this from his fuzzy short hair and began to cry. *King cried!* His tears flowed in streaks down his sooty face and fell to the pyre.

In awed wonder, everyone drew nearer. A few mumbled complaints about the loss of meat, but most just gawked at the residue of the spectacle. I pushed through the crowd and leaped recklessly onto the rocks, feeling the heat through my boots.

"King! King, are you all right? Are you hurt?"

He gazed down at the ground, weeping silently. Only then did I look and see. In the crevices between the stones, pale green stalks spiked through and reached for the sky.

Earlie trees!

OOO

30   A SONG AND A SCREAM

"I will never call him rat man again!" roared Alf jubilantly, practically skipping around the table in the Inn. "That little man is cosmic! Did you *see* that?"

"Yes, Alf. Very impressive." I didn't mean to sound flippant about it, but my mind still reeled from all the things King had done, and the pyrotechnics felt like sugar—wonderful, but useless. Instead, the last lines of his earlier dance story echoed between my ears as if the Rik leaves deemed them of utmost importance.

One of these must visit the three Worlds of the star.
One of these must visit the three Worlds of each planet.
One of these must receive three Gifts.
One of these must gain three Powers.
This one will bring the captives home.
This one will live and give all.

No doubt about who the "one" could be, but I didn't like how the story ended. Visiting the three worlds of each planet—as in the earth, water and sky? What constituted a visit? Did I have to plunge into the ocean or a freezing pond on each planet like I did on Caren? *Not ready for that!* And what did that mean—"give all"?

At that moment, my mother burst into the room and slammed herself down next to me at the table. "Caz, you'll never guess what the scientists had in the Lab!"

"You're right. I'll never guess," I said, rubbing my temples and wondering why everyone insisted on being so terribly cheerful when we'd just watched a baby kangra blow up. Somehow the presence of Earlie tree sprouts didn't lift my spirits yet because it would be months before they produced any syrup.

She pulled something from her pocket.

"My SWaTT!"

"Not *your* SWaTT. Your SWaTT is in my pack."

"What? We could have used it all this time!"

"And give evidence that you're alive? Not so wise under the circumstances."

I stared at her, frustration melting to admiration. "Good thinking, Mom."

"You didn't get *all* of your intelligence from Dag."

"He's book smart. You're pragmatic."

"Right. And I'm also good at the persuasive arts. It got me elected, and it got you three texts to whomever you think can help us right now."

"What do you mean it got me three texts? That's nothing."

"Caz, this thing is extremely hard to come by. They only last so long. They've retrofitted it with a solar panel for powering, but it's not good for infinite texts. I convinced them to give you three transmissions, so think hard who you want to contact to get what information we need."

"Why me?" I asked.

"You're the one cycling the pearl. Time to learn to make the kinds of decisions that come with leadership."

"Mom, if this is your idea of making up for lost parenting time, I'm really not—"

Her look slapped me silent. Even Alf stopped moving.

"Sorry," I muttered.

Her face reddened unattractively. "I can never make up for the lost past," she said quietly. "But I would give my all for your future."

OOO

After deliberating almost all night, the five of us in the Inn decided the number one priority right now involved figuring out what Saloma and Derven had planned. We could ask one transmission's worth of questions, and then receive one answer back. Hopefully both parties would be thorough.

"But who will you contact?" asked Fizer.

"Not your father," said Mom. "He can't get access to that kind of thing."

My stomach sank. "I wonder if he and Felly think I'm dead again."

Mom's eyebrow arched and Fizer squinted. "Again?" they both said.

"Long story, yeah?" said Alf.

King touched my hand gently. *Queen will know.*

I wish you'd stop saying that, I answered silently.

If he heard me, he didn't react. His serene smile drove me crazy sometimes, and yet I knew the answer.

"Sasa."

Alf snickered. "The blackmail expert."

"I think she prefers the title Information Broker," I said with a wink.

"Who's Sasa?" asked Mom.

"A kid we know from Lamond," I said, already trying to figure out how to access the Ivan ICS directory.

"A kid?" Mom's skepticism quickly evaporated when Alf, Fizer and I all squared challenging looks on her.

Letting out a steady stream of air through pursed lips, I worked the controls, trying to be as clear and concise as possible. I closed with an admonition: *We get one transmission, so leave no room for follow-up questions. I'm trusting you.*

Mom peeked over my shoulder and nodded. "Good. Can she read?"

I sagged with hesitation. "Alf? Do you know? Come to think of it, I never actually saw her reading. Just kissing Ruddie in the Library."

He shrugged. "If she can't, Ruddie will help her. They're together, remember?"

"Don't they need a SWaTT to receive the message?" asked Fizer.

"It'll show up in their room's comlink with a special symbol for text. They can either transfer it to a monitor or read it in the blue."

"How will they write back?" asked Alf.

I breathed out a laugh. "It's Ruddie. He can find any supply he needs. The two of them will find a way." As I spoke, I adjusted the controls to connect the message to the residence listed for Ruddie and Sasa Carlow. I punched the button to send with my thumb. "Now we wait."

"Now we wait," agreed Mom.

"And sleep," suggested Alf.

Fizer snored in agreement.

OOO

In the morning, a green light flashed on the side of the SWaTT. I snatched it up from beside my mattress. The oil light had long since been extinguished, and I could hear the steady breathing of the others from where they lay around the perimeter of the room. By the time I turned on the screen, King sat at my elbow to watch.

I hadn't written in code because they wouldn't have understood, but Sasa (or Ruddie helping her) responded instinctively with a cryptic numbered list.

1. Survival contradicts prior news received.
2. Harvest intended to monopolize medicinal resources for maximum profit.
3. Efforts to retain all ETs extant by S to force negotiations with subspecies.
4. Depletion of Craggy's resources not of concern due to mandatory evacuation planned. D to gain exclusive contract for all cargo relocation.
5. Missing Garvey governor is maternal unit.

The last point made me laugh aloud. Sasa had figured out who my mom was when Dad couldn't! But then the rest of the message boiled my insides. King reacted with distress, screeching and jumping in place. That woke the others, and we all reviewed the message again. Ruddie and Sasa had outdone themselves, and if I ever made it out of this cycle alive, I would find a way to pay them back. They'd been so good to me from the very first time we'd met. I'd never known friends like that on the Arxon.

"Saloma's out of control," said Mom grimly. "If she's gathering all the Earlie trees—meaning the syrup—in the system, she's desperate for the faneps to choose her to cycle a pearl. She really doesn't understand how this works."

"She thinks they might because she doesn't know I'm alive," I pointed out.

"Right. She must not find out you survived," said Mom.

"Who does she think she's going to petition for the right to cycle a pearl if King is missing—I mean, as far as she knows?" I looked at King. "Will one of the other faneps give her what she wants?" I asked.

King shook his head slowly. "Must be given."

"I know, but she could make them give the gifts to her."

He shook his head again. "Gift from here." He touched his head and chest.

"From the mind and heart? The Gift has to come—like you mean it, not forced?"

He nodded. "Saloma not chosen."

Alf barked a victorious laugh. "Saloma will end up going through all that trouble for nothing!"

"Let her try," said Mom. "As long as she thinks Caz is dead, we have time. We'll have to find a way to stop her."

"What about the forced evacuation?" asked Alf. "Can they do that without your approval?"

Mom knuckled her eyes wearily. "I need to get back to the Hub and find out what's going on."

"Don't go alone, Mom. It's too dangerous."

She nodded. "Maybe I can get Pathankot to take me back."

"In the meantime, we have to keep those Earlie trees alive," I said.

Fizer perked up. "I guess I could see what they have in the way of fertilizer that would be best for it. Maybe we can match the minerals they would have in their original location."

"I'll go talk to the elders," said Mom. "Fizer, head over to the Lab and see about that." She pointed to me. "You and Alf should probably figure out who gets the next transmission."

I watched dubiously after them as they left.

King levitated beside me. *Queen will know.*

I turned, heavy-lidded, and knocked my forehead into his. "I'm not the queen *yet!*"

Alf could not hear King's thoughts, but he looked at me with a smile.

"Yeah, you are."

OOO

The next most pressing question was how many of those involved in the Gypsy Network on Caren—or throughout the Granbo System for that matter—subscribed to Saloma's self-serving mindset. If the whole network had been corrupted, it would make finding anyone willing to be loyal to the faneps or the cycling process really difficult. I had one gypsy on my side: Maddy. He had been the first to find King, or maybe it was the other way around, and they were friends. I just hoped that the Ivan ICS hadn't reached Tye's ferry range yet so I could find out what Maddy knew. I sent a message indicating his former cubicle in the Quarantine Deck and asked for it to be forwarded to his room if he hadn't disembarked yet.

Mom opposed me using one of my three transmissions for a person who may or may not even be able to receive the message, and it occurred to me after sending it that I didn't know if Maddy could read. Too late to regret the move now, though. I just had to wait. Alf and I easily decided to join the children in the revo fields again, and we labored for about an hour before pausing to rest.

The air here in the Sumayar valley felt crisp and alive. Sound carried far and echoed happily back and forth between the rocky ridges that held us safe from the outside harshness of Craggy. If I'd not seen the mining camp, I would never believe this planet had been deemed the most hostile in the system. Sure, the chill nipped at us constantly, but we kept moving, and our bodies soon acclimated to the normal temperature range.

Other Sumayar about our age worked on the opposite slope, and the children explained that harvesting the wheat by hand had to be done with great care, so only those tall and responsible enough could work there. They clearly considered it a privilege and wondered aloud why Alf and I would opt to stay with them in the revos.

"Because you sing so well!" I said. "Why aren't you singing?" I waved my arms to encourage them, and soon we all bent to work again, singing a different song this time.

Cold can be kind, or cold can be cruel.
Watch for the sun and store plenty of fuel.
Everything's good—everything's grand
Work with your mind and work with your hands.

Dig way down deep to the heart of the mount.
Water will come from the clouds and the fount.
Everything's good—everything's grand
Work with your mind and work with your hands.

This song made infinitely more sense than the last, and Alf and I joined in, our scratchy, untrained voices both offending and amusing the little ears. As we finished the refrain, Alf stood tall and placed his dirty hands on his chest, pealing forth a high, dramatic tone as if to finish the song with a flair. He held the note so long that the children began to giggle, and then one of them screamed.

I looked to see which one, but they all had smiles.

"Can't you hear that?" I asked.

"Hear what?" Alf shrugged.

Scanning the fields for the source of the scream, I felt a pounding in my head. I dropped to my knees, suddenly exhausted. Still the scream rang out. I covered my ears and turned to Alf for help. He watched me, perplexed, and showed no sign of discomfort, or of noticing the sound at all.

A second scream joined the first, a long wail. This time everyone turned sharply and stared back towards the buildings.

"What is that?" called one of the children.

"Someone's hurt!" cried another. Dropping their sacks, they took off running towards the settlement.

I tried to follow, but a stabbing pain closed my eyes and I fell. Alf caught me before I hit the ground, but I could not see him, and I could not hear anything but the screams…

OOO

I awoke for the second time from some kind of faint, this time lying on a mat beside the sprouting Earlie trees. King wrapped himself around my leg and held on, shivering and visibly sweating despite the cold. I disentangled his limbs and pulled him into my arms.

"What is it? What happened?" I asked.

King didn't respond, so I asked silently. He gave no response, as if his mind had shut down.

"Are you sick? Hurt? What's wrong, King?" Even as I asked, I felt dark corners encroaching upon my vision. Nearby, I heard the elders in consultation. "Please!" I called. "Do you know what happened to him?"

They seemed as if they wanted to answer, but couldn't. One of them, a woman with long silvery hair, came to the edge of the mat and looked down at us with great pity. "We don't know," she admitted.

"Caz!" Mom's voice rang out across the open space as she ran towards us, holding up the SWaTT. The expression on her face did not bode well, and the zing of heat rocketed through my eyes and into the recesses of my skull. Breathing heavily, she handed me the device. "I think you'd better see this."

I grabbed it and fumbled with the controls. The message from Maddy explained King's scream: *North Mountain fanep colony exterminated when would not reveal new king to Saloma. More divided loyalties. We retain hope in my lady and her small escort. May your journey be swift and safe. Meet on Iki-kane South Tye within a rotation.*

My voice joined with King's in a mournful howl. *The faneps—all the ones I'd seen on Caren—were dead!*

OOO

31   ADRENALINE

King placed his hands over his heart. *Faneps are crying.*

I shuddered. "Did they cry out for help?"

Cry for me. Tears welled in his eyes, and he crawled like a scrawny, tailless dog, to the edge of the pyre.

I followed, heedless of the cold ground penetrating my coversuit and stinging my ungloved hands. He sat on one of the rocks and studied one of the Earlie tree sprouts. Scarcely ten centimeters tall, it looked more like a flower than a tree. The very top, however, had the funny wispy white strands hanging down. King fingered these delicately with the point of one of his claws.

"How long before there's any syrup inside of the trees?" He didn't answer, retracting his claws and folding his hands together sadly. "King, we really need to get to Tye and finish this cycling. Can we bring it with us in a pot or something? Let it grow along the way?"

He seemed to consider this for a moment, but instead leaned over the sprig of green and wept some more, his tears watering the tiny plant.

I felt a large hand on my shoulder and turned to see Pathankot. "The elders want the SWaTT back now," he said gently.

"But I still get one more transmission, don't I?" I said, gripping it tighter.

Mom let out an uncomfortable gurgle. "About that… I-I sent a transmission already, so we've used up our three—"

"What?!" I roared, standing to face her. "How could you do that?"

"I called Dag," she said desperately. "I-I thought he and Felly should know where…"

She appeared weak for the first time since the windows in the observation tower, and my anger relented. "What did you tell them?"

"That we're waiting for the syrup, and we're safe in the mountains."

I embraced her in an effort to comfort both of us. Speaking over her shoulder, I admitted, "That's all I would have said anyway. I was going to send my next transmission to them."

"I thought so," she said quietly, sounding more apologetic than smug. "You miss them?"

I nodded. "Yeah, even though I never know exactly how to talk to Dad." I let go of her and she nodded almost imperceptibly.

Pathankot cleared his throat, and I held out the SWaTT. "Will the elders let me know if Dad responds?"

"Of course," he said. Glancing at King, he whispered, "What can we do for him? He seems very upset."

"He is." Understatement of the galaxy. My eyes swept the open space around us. "Where is everyone?"

Pathankot looked nervously at his feet. "I think his screams scared many indoors."

"What about the children?"

"I believe your friend took them back out to get the revo sacks they dropped."

"What about Fizer?"

A grin spread across Pathankot's face. "Our silversmith is showing him the forge. Your friend knows a lot about the ores found in these mountains. He's very useful."

"Yes, he is. I probably wouldn't have made it this far without him."

"You have surrounded yourself with good friends," he said. With a polite nod, he walked off to one of the buildings with the SWaTT.

Mom gave me a sideways hug and we watched King for a moment. "I think I'm going to rest," she said wearily. "All of…everything is catching up with me."

"I know what you mean," I said, feeling the roiling emotions of the last several days well inside of me, draining me of energy.

Mom kissed my cheek in a surprisingly tender way and wandered back toward the Inn. I watched her go, absorbing that moment. Finally I turned to find King. He was still on the pyre. "King," I called in a hoarse whisper. "What are you doing?"

He beckoned me over and pointed to the tear-drenched plant. *It had grown!*

"What've you got in those tears, King?" I balanced on a rock beside him, my knees folded almost to my chin. King fingered the wisps again and seemed deep in thought. I couldn't imagine what he must be feeling with the loss of so many of his people.

Abruptly, as if frustrated, he yanked the tiny sapling up by the bottom so that it dangled wiry roots.

"What did you do that for? It was growing so well—"

With comet speed, he kicked at one of my knees so I toppled backwards. Standing on my chest, he flicked open the claws of his free hand.

"King! What are you—?

He swiped at my chest, slicing through the thick red kangra wool coat—and all the way to my skin! Blood spurted and struck him in the face even as I felt him thrust the Earlie tree into my sternum area. I thrashed and fought to get away, but all strength drained away at the sight of his eyes narrowed in determination. Gulping in air, I stopped fighting and lay still, tears streaming down my cheeks. The struggle ended, and I saw him break the sapling in half and squeeze it over me. I gasped at the cold sting and my hand went to the burning wound.

King's face softened and he touched the back of my hand gently, holding it in place on my chest. I concentrated on breathing and trusting. King wouldn't hurt me. I mean, not permanently. The pain was one thing, but the damage would not last. This had to be done to cycle the pearl. I had to get the Earlie syrup in my bloodstream. I accepted and trusted.

He let go and jumped lightly off of me. Sitting up, I looked down, prying apart my torn coat. There on my pale bare chest…nothing. Not even a scar.

OOO

I pulled the blanket up to my chin as Fizer walked in brandishing my coversuit, cleaned of blood and sewn with the crude stitches of a child. He set it grandly on the bed over my hidden knees.

"I did a good job, I guess. Stitched it with a needle made from kangra bone. Hard and sharp, that stuff. I was a little uncomfortable with the idea at first, but that's all they have here, so I might as well learn. Very fascinating culture here, you know. This is like the best anthropology lesson ever. And you should see their Lab. It's really very impressive, all the things they've done. I could learn a—what?"

I shook with silent laughter, trying to keep my lips closed. "I'm sorry, Fizer. I'm really glad you're having such a great time here."

He puffed his chest out happily and beamed. "I love it here, except for the cold, I guess."

"Yes, the cold. I'm feeling it, Fizer. Any chance you could send your happy self out into the main room so I can get dressed?"

"Oh!" He blushed and practically tripped over himself getting out of the room.

I let the blanket fall and I looked again at my body. In the flickering light of the oil candle, I could see no sign of injury, and I felt great. Better than before. Humming the children's song, I tugged on my coversuit and fastened it. *What was the third Power, anyway?*

I padded out into the main room to find King and ask him. Fizer sat beside Ganchen sewing something else red by hand. King was nowhere in sight.

"Anyone mind if I take a shower?" I asked, combing my hair with my fingers. I could always find him once I was clean.

"Good idea," said Ganchen, distracted. "It'll be time for the evening meal soon. Oh, you should go find the elders. There was another SWaTT message for you."

My stomach tightened. "Not more bad news?"

She shrugged and muttered at the needle.

"It's the building three doors to the left," said Fizer, throwing a hand towards the outer door. "Tell us all about it at dinner."

"Can I borrow your coat?" I asked, taking his red kangra jacket from the hook by the door.

"Sure. I'm still mending yours," he said proudly.

I stopped, touched by his innocent kindness. "Thank you, Fizer. You are a good man."

He spluttered, but Ganchen smirked. "Yes, that girl in the Lab thinks so, too."

"Ooooh! Fizer's got a girlfriend!"

"Go check that message," he said, his voice cracking with embarrassment.

I stepped outside and almost collided with Alf. "Hey," he said, rubbing his shorn chin.

"You shaved?"

"Bone razor. Alien, yeah?"

My hand cupped his tattooed cheek. "You look all right."

"There's a message for you," he said stiffly.

"So I heard. Walk me there?"

"Yeah. Where's King?" he asked, pushing his weight off the wall where he'd been leaning.

"No idea." I'd forgotten to grab a hat, so I squinted across to the pyre. "Is he over there?"

"Not since earlier. Did he really rip you open?" he asked, his jaw tight.

I sighed heavily. "He really ripped me open. But there's no harm done."

Alf looked at me, tears brimming in his eyes. "I'm glad he's done putting the Gifts in you, yeah?"

"Right. Now the biggest dangers come from gypsies who want to kill me." My airy voice didn't convince either of us.

With a grunt, he walked into the elders' building. Customs here didn't require knocking or alerting anyone through an intercom. Friendly but a little strange. The interior looked a lot like the Inn except that in lieu of so many hanging mats, doors led to small sleeping rooms. In the center of the room stood a table, and on the table lay the SwaTT.

"I guess they left it for me to check," I said, gesturing to the green blinking light. Activating the controls, I saw that it was from Dad. Leaning against the table, I cradled it close to me, afraid to read it.

"How bad can it be, Caz?" asked Alf. "Your mom didn't even ask anything. Just let him know you're alive."

"You're right." I studied the screen and could feel my blood pressure rising.

Medical communications on this line only, please. Patient must forego third treatment. Repeat: must forego third treatment. Further study shows that having 25% G-blood concentration affects body systems differently. Combination of medications safe only when 100% G or S/S. Otherwise, any stress or health factor that releases adrenaline could bring about paralysis. Please return patient to my sick bay immediately.

"Huff!" My stomach clenched and my mind raced as I tried to chase down all the implications of this news.

Alf expressed it perfectly: "What has that rat man done to you? He's going to kill you!"

The tingling in my left arm could have been psychosomatic, but I didn't want to risk it. "Stay calm, Alf. I-I can't let my adrenaline rise. If..." I collapsed into a chair, not from paralysis of body, but of mind. I would be under constant stress until I could get to Tye, and yet elevated adrenaline could paralyze me?

What *had* King done to me?

OOO

It's hard not to feel all fight-or-flighty when you know you could be paralyzed if you get that way. It's even harder when the creature that put you at risk acts as if nothing is wrong.

It took Pathankot, Mom and Fizer to keep Alf from doing something horrible to the fanep king, and all the while, I lay on the kangra mat breathing deeply and forcing my mind to make an inventory of happy thoughts: *I'd found my mom, and she was a decent human being. I had family and friends who loved me. Alf...yeah, those are happy thoughts, but maybe not ones to keep the blood pressure down. We've been safe in the Sumayar territory. The Earlie trees have been saved, sort of. The children are cute.*

I winced at the panic fizzing in my throat and took a deep breath.

The main room of the Inn fell quiet, and a form darkened the door. Mom. "How are you feeling, Caz?"

"Do I have to answer that?"

She sighed heavily. "I can only imagine. Listen, King wants to come in."

Tears welled and spilled from my eyes instantly, but I nodded, willing my heart to keep a steady pace. Trust and fear are hard to balance.

King entered slowly and came to the foot of my mattress. As he had done all those weeks ago on Caren, he held up three fingers, moving them in a circle parallel to the ground. "Three Worlds. Three Gifts. Three Powers."

"Right, I'll be happy to see that third Power any time soon. I hope it has to do with being able to bring myself back from the dead."

"Power best seen on Tye," he said in his gravelly voice. He probably spoke aloud for Mom's benefit because she stood watching us.

"And how does she get to Tye without danger?" she demanded. "This whole adventure is laden with risk, and with risk comes fear and adrenaline rushes."

"Queen will know."

"Shut up, King," I snapped.

"Queen must trust." King smiled. Kneeling at my feet, he trilled, "Must trust Queen."

I stared up at Mom. "What does *that* mean?"

She shrugged, relaxing her stance. "Maybe just that. Trust yourself?"

Inhaling slowly, I decided to work with that idea. *Could I know what to do? Could I trust myself to stay calm even in danger? Could I rely on my other Gifts to get me through this?*

OOO

"Brita, Caz… You'd better come quickly. There's trouble heading into the valley!" Pathankot's whole being urged us even as he stood in the door waiting.

My eyes locked with Mom's in horror. *I must not panic. I can do this.* Standing up, I imagined breathing air down to my toes and anchored myself to the ground mentally. "I will not move with fear. I cannot. I must trust myself," I said softly.

Mom took my hand and we walked quickly after Pathankot. Through his portable telescope, I could see a group of seven men in heavy coats and goggles and packing laser rifles. They had stopped to rest in the pass that entered into the valley.

"You're one hundred percent sure they're not Sumayar?" I asked.

"They don't look right," said Pathankot.

"Someone has betrayed us," I said darkly. "How else would they know we're here?"

"Could they be exploring?" asked Mom doubtfully.

"With rifles?" I shook my head. "Someone knows we're here…" I didn't want to think of who it could be. *Someone we sent a SwaTT transmission to? One of the Sumayar?*

"How? Why? They can't think we survived!" protested Mom.

"No matter," I said. "We're going to have to face them."

"No we're not," said Pathankot. "I will not let them harm our settlement as they did the forest. We must evacuate."

"Evacuate? How? They're blocking the way!" shrieked Mom.

Pathankot turned and looked back at the cliff wall.

Mom followed his gaze. "We can't climb that! It's straight up!"

"There are tunnels."

"But they'll destroy your settlement. The Lab, the Forge." Mom's voice rose with each word until I reached out and grabbed her by the shoulders.

"Mom, I need you to stay calm."

Her face darkened with intensity. Through clenched teeth, she said "Caz, you must get to Tye. Go now. The elders will find a way to get you out. I'll go meet those men. They came for me anyway."

"No! Mom, you can't! What if they kill you? They might be looking for me!"

"Then I will delay them," she said with all the force of her governor tone. "Go." She questioned Pathankot with a look.

"I'll come with you," he said. Bowing slightly to me, he said, "Go, lady. The elders will show you where. Tell them what is happening, and they will start the evacuation."

"Where's King?" I asked, realizing I hadn't seen him for a while.

Mom hugged me so fiercely, I could hardly breathe. "We'll find him. Get to Tye."

OOO

In minutes, the whole settlement mobilized. The elders directed the work, and a line of Sumayar disappeared into an unseen crevice behind the shimmering waterfall. Fizer went with them even as Mom and Pathankot headed out into the valley with weapons and provisions.

Ganchen came to me with one of the elders. He held a backpack and two metal sticks in each hand. These he handed to me and Alf. "There is no escape through the tunnels," he explained. "It is a place of refuge in times of severe bad weather."

"I'm so sorry," I said. "I didn't mean for them to follow me here."

He and Ganchen fastened the pack to my back as he spoke. "We don't know who they are or what they want, but you must go to Tye either way." He pointed to the dark, forbidding corner to our left where the shaded side of the valley crashed into the cliff wall. "There," he said, "the rock is softer and the ascent not quite as steep. It may be possible with your strength..."

"What are these for?" asked Alf, holding a metal stick in each hand.

"Climbing spikes," he said. "Ganchen will go with you to the wall and get you started."

Ganchen?!

"She is one of our best vertical climbers." He grimaced at Alf. "Are you sure you want to try this? You can go with the others."

"I'm not leaving her."

"But if you fall—"

"I'll make the climb or die trying," he said firmly.

"If he falls, I'll fall after him," I said, remembering my ability to resist

226

gravity.

"Don't fall," said the elder, unaware of my Power.

I looked around, trying to quell the fear rising in me. "Where's King? He needs to come with me."

Ganchen pointed to the far end of the valley. "I don't know, but you have to hurry now. They'll be at the suma field before we get to the climb site at this rate. The kangra is waiting!"

The kangra?

As if I needed another new experience for the week, Ganchen led us behind the Forge to where three kangra stood meekly chewing nothing in particular.

Grasping its thick mane with one hand, she leaned forward and tossed a leg over the back of the kangra. She sat up straight, straddling the beast comfortably and looking at us like we were doomed idiots. "Get on!" she rasped. "We don't have time to waste!"

Alf, without a pack to carry, tucked the climbing spikes into his overcoat pockets and pulled his goggles on. "Here goes crazy," he muttered, copying Ganchen's move with moderate success. He got the first part right, but stayed on his stomach. The kangra took a step forward, and the movement jerked Alf into a sitting position. He shook his arms in victory until the kangra took another step and he toppled off.

The comedy of it felt like a calming gift, and giggling, I worked on mounting. The Gypsy Pearl put a turbo boost on my jump and I actually hurdled the kangra on the first try.

Ganchen laughed this time, and then sharpened her voice. "We are all going to die if you two don't get on *now!*"

With that, she flopped her legs against her kangra's hide and it broke into a run.

"Huff, she's leaving without us," I grumbled. *Where was King?!* My second try worked better, as did Alf's, but then we sat dumbfounded, unsure of how to make the animal move. We grimaced at each other, and Alf patted the neck of his kangra. "You can go now, yeah?"

"Yeah, yeah, yeah!" I added, ruffling my kangra's fleece. Nothing. In frustration, I slapped its shoulder.

Adrenaline spike! The kangra took off running after Ganchen, and Alf's thundered after. My body would have been frozen in fear either way, so I couldn't tell if my fixed position leaning forward and holding on for dear life hand anything to do with Dad's warning. I did know that my buttocks would be beaten clean off my backside by the time we got to Ganchen. I could smell kangra sweat, and its pelt flicked into my nose.

"Just get us there safely," I grunted through gritted teeth.

And it did. Fast. Breathless as if I'd done all the running myself, I rolled sideways off the beast and landed just in time to see Alf's kangra bumbling to a stop. He slid off, landing on his feet and rubbing the back of his thighs.

My pulse stabilized, and I felt my fingers flush with blood. No lasting paralysis for that jolt.

In the back of my mind, I wondered where King was. In the front of my mind, I figured climbing this rocky slope meant suicide one way or another.

OOO

32 CLIMBING AWAY

Ganchen's demonstration had been brief and discouraging. Basically, our lives depended on our ability to shove the climbing spikes into the rock above us one at a time, removing them as we went. Supposedly our feet would find traction because of the boots, but the motion required to pull the spike out tended to throw us off balance.

"So grip harder with the anchored hand," she said. "And don't let your gloves slip."

Before we'd gotten even five meters up, Ganchen and the kangras had disappeared back to the settlement and into the tunnels. I had to hope King knew where we were and would follow, tracking me if he had to.

Below me, Alf grunted loudly. I looked down between my limbs to see him tearing off his glove with his teeth.

"You'll freeze your hands," I called.

"I'll fall if I can't grip it right," he countered.

The climb was not quite vertical, but telling our muscles that was not convincing. However, Ganchen had been right about the footholds. We quickly discovered that our feet needed to do most of the work, pushing us up, or our arms and abdominal muscles would cramp. I could feel sweat pasting my coversuit to me. My muscles ached and I worried for Alf. He didn't have a Gypsy Pearl to strengthen him.

After what must have been about half an hour, I paused. "How are you doing down there?" I breathed heavily into the rock, letting it cool my forehead. When Alf didn't answer, I called again. "Alf?"

He groaned slightly. "Caz, I love you."

My heart skipped. "Uh… I love you, too, Alf. What brought on that declaration at this very moment in time?"

"I'm going to die here," he said weakly.

"No, you're not, Alf," I said, fighting the tremble in my voice.

"I can't keep going. I'm so tired."

"You have to, Alf."

"I can't."

"You can't die on me, Alf. Not after all this." I exhaled, steadying my emotions. "You just need to rest."

He barked an angry laugh. "How do you rest? If I let go, I fall."

"Hang on," I said. "I have an idea."

Pulling a spike from the rock, I maneuvered myself back down gradually until I hung a little below him.

"There. Put your foot there. Now pull up. See how I've got these two close together? Sit on them like a kangra. They won't run."

"Will they hold?" he asked even as he shifted his legs.

"If not, I jump down after you. Try it."

He pulled and twisted himself up to straddle on the spikes that stuck out about ten centimeters from the rock.

"Wait. What about you? How did you—?" He stared at me where I now held on to his old spikes.

"Don't ask. I probably shouldn't do it again." I had fallen slowly enough that I had time to grab the spikes. With the pack on my back, I couldn't turn around and face out like Alf, but I managed to get myself sitting sideways on two parallel spikes, one digging into my rear and the other propping up my left knee. My right leg hung down, and my left arm sort of rested up the wall. I snickered. "Huff, we look like we're already dead!"

His dimple deepened, but he didn't turn to face me. Instead, he gazed back at the settlement. "I don't see any movement down there. Maybe your mom and Pathankot were able to turn the men back."

Because of the angle at which I sat, the far side of the valley lay behind me. I dreaded to think what might be happening there. Mom had just come back into my life. I couldn't lose her again. Not like I'd lost Ninetta.

I slid my arm down the wall and removed the glove to flex my hand. Then, I reached to Alf. He carefully tucked his right hand into mine, smiling.

"I won't let you die, Alf. We have to get to Tye, and I want you with me more than anyone right now." *Except I wish King was here, too.*

Alf leaned his head back against the rock. "No matter what's happening below, or up on the mountain, we stick together, yeah?"

"Like a tail to a comet."

He gave my hand a squeeze and loosened the grip so that our fingers intertwined and dangled against the cliff wall.

OOO

Through some miracle, we slept like that for a short while until I woke up. "Alf!" I yelped. "The paralysis set in! Oh, huff, my leg is numb!"

He jerked awake and leaned back with a gasp, realizing how high up we perched. "Uh, not just you. Me, too."

Flexing my upper body, I cursed myself. "Oh. The spikes cut off our circulation." With a wild twisting swing, I dropped to hang by my hands on the spikes, letting my legs knock against the rock. "Yeah, here comes that horrible tingle of limbs waking up."

"How am I going to turn back around?" asked Alf, his voice wavering.

"Gimme a second," I said, kicking my leg back and forth until I could feel it better. I extended my right leg against the rock so that it formed a ledge beneath his dangling feet. "Step on me and turn around."

His dubious expression faded into an accepting smile and he gingerly lowered himself to stand on my leg. He turned to face the wall and that's when I got the idea.

"Let me follow behind you," I said. I'll keep my spikes just below your feet so you can stand on them—just stand on the ends so you don't crush my fingers."

"Are you sure?"

"Yeah, it'll make for better footholds so your feet don't ache. It'll be like stairs."

And so we wiggled our way up the mountainside, grunting, sweating, scraping, and trying to remember to breathe. We paused three more times before the sun disappeared behind the mountains, each time eating a little from the provisions in my pack. About the time I began worrying about dehydration, I noticed the skin on my ungloved hand had frozen to the spikes. I closed my eyes and worked on those happy, calming thoughts again, afraid to use the Gypsy Pearl's Power to heal my skin.

"How are your hands?" I asked as casually as I could.

"Starting to stick to the cold metal," he answered. "How much farther do you think?"

"I don't know. The clouds block the view, and it's getting dark anyway."

"Can you see anything back at the settlement?" he asked, craning his neck.

"No fires or explosions at least."

"Wait, what's that?" he exclaimed, his voice cracked and raw. "Those lights—are they *flying?*"

"A patrol plane?" I asked, thinking of the ones I'd seen on Caren.

"I thought no one dared fly because of the wind."

"They'd have to be crazy," I agreed. "Speaking of which, we're going to be back up in the wind when we reach the top. I bet it's bad up there."

"I think I'd rather take my chances with the wind than whoever's in that plane," Alf replied.

The lights of the flying craft drew nearer and slowed.

"Huff, now what? Do you think they know we're here?" I asked. "How could they possibly see us against the rock?"

The craft answered for itself, switching from a horizontal to a vertical course directly above us. Whoever piloted that thing knew how to fly. A search beam blasted us, and I wrangled my goggles into place with the spike still stuck to my hand.

"They've seen us!" yelled Alf.

"Caz Artemus, please stay where you are!" boomed an amplified voice.

Nothing could stem the flow of adrenaline. *We're caught! Will they kill us?* I couldn't feel my right hand. "Alf!" I cried. "Alf, help me!"

The lights brightened as the craft drew parallel with us, hovering so that its wing was almost within reach. "Caz Artemus, do not move!" came the voice from the plane.

I can't!

And then I fell and could not even flail my arms and legs. My voice wailed, "Alf!" even as my body flipped end over end.

I'm going to die a splattered mess at the bottom of a cliff!

No. I need to trust in myself. Trust in my Powers.

The falling slowed, stopped. I could not move the individual parts of my body, but I could suspend myself in the air. I lay as if on my bed, looking up at Alf and the plane. *Could I do more?* I willed myself higher. "Alf!"

"Caz! You didn't fall?" He couldn't see me in the darkness below the craft.

Instantly the craft dropped a little lower until it hovered with its wing right beside me. And then a man appeared on the wing, tethered with a cord to the chassis, but making his way out to me.

"Don't touch her!" bellowed Alf, dropping onto the wing from his spiked hold in the cliff. In my peripheral vision, I saw him slip and regain his footing, arms wide for balance.

"Take my hand!" said the man tethered to the side.

"So you can throw me?" scoffed Alf. He reached precariously for me, grazing the cloth of my coversuit leg.

"We need to get Caz safely inside!" yelled the man urgently. "We don't have much time. What's wrong with her? Why isn't she moving? Is she hanging by ropes or something?"

Alf caught hold of me and pulled me through the air so that I hovered between the two men on the shaking wing. "Stay away from her!" warned Alf.

"Look, boy. I don't know what you're trying to do, but I'm trying to save my lady, Caz."

Alf spun me upright and clutched me to his chest. He pivoted me around to face him, his legs bent to brace himself. Pressing his lips to my ear he whispered, "Do you trust him, or do we jump together?"

"Let me see him," I said. He obliged, carefully shifting so I could see the man's face. Even in the darkness, he looked familiar. In fact, he seemed familiar *because* of the darkness.

"Is that Brade?" I gasped.

"Yes, my lady," he said, his white teeth gleaming in the night. "Maddy sent me."

Maddy sent Brade! The fearless pilot from Caren's Gypsy Network who had rescued us once before when we were with Maddy. *But…*

"Saloma didn't send you?" I challenged.

"My lady, why aren't you moving? Are you hurt?"

"How did you get a plane?" I asked, my head spinning with doubt. "Aren't they contraband here?"

"My lady," he said soothingly. "Please, let us get you aboard where you won't fall."

I couldn't move, but I could feel Alf holding my hand in the darkness, and soon I lay inside the tiny craft's cabin, strapped to a bench for safety. I almost doubted the need for this this until I remembered how fast Brade flew. The memory sent a shiver through me and my lips went numb.

Whimpering incoherently, I tried to get Alf's attention above the roar of the engine, but he was busy trying to fasten himself in place as Brade checked the instruments on his dashboard. I could see nothing but the silvery ceiling above me and some unidentifiable gear hanging on the wall just next to me. These blurred with tears, and I felt panic swell within me.

And then Brade accelerated the craft and the straps cut into my torso and arms, straining to keep me in place.

All at once, Alf's arms were around me, his upper body pressed against mine as he hugged me to the bench against the force of the speed and vibrations rattling my bones. He stank, but I welcomed the sensory input. As the cabin shifted, tilted and then leveled out, he loosened his grip and slid his hands to my cheeks.

"Caz, are you all right? Do you hurt?"

Huff. I had no voice, and the two questions had different answers. Although I could not see his expression in the shadows of the cabin, I could hear the urgency in his words. "Caz, I won't leave you. We'll get you to Tye. Maybe the gypsies there can heal you with something. I won't leave you. I won't…"

I managed a gurgle which evoked a breathy laugh from him.

"I love you, yeah?" he whispered, kissing my forehead and resting his cheek against mine so lightly that his stubble tickled. Closing my eyes, I relished his closeness, and when his hand found mine again, I had strength enough to give it the minutest squeeze. He pressed my palm to his face and held it there, his hot tears rolling over my fingers and giving me hope that I would recover from the paralysis at least a little.

The plane sped away to the south as I lay thinking of all that had happened in the last weeks. From the horror of Darkman's death to the joy of Alf's love, and all the enigmatic things in between—most notably, Mom and King. I focused on what I knew: the cycling was almost over. I'd done what I came here to do. Only a ceremony remained. The faneps would somehow be freed by that, and although King had put me in danger, a piece of me understood why. His entire species—at least those whom Saloma had not exterminated—needed him. And he needed me.

But after that?

I sighed and felt a flutter of relief that I could do so.

After that? Run away with Alf? Return to the Arxon with Dad and Felly? Become a Gypsy Queen like Maddy hoped? Rule the Granbo System?

Huff. I'm just a child in the cosmic scheme of things. King always says *Queen will know.*

But maybe I can't know it all at once. Maybe I'll have to know the galaxy one constellation at a time.

Maybe it's time I know myself.

OOO

33 WANDEL HAV

If this is death, it sure feels cold. With a groan, I rubbed my clammy forehead and yawned.

"Caz!"

"She moved!"

Two faces appeared above me, and my heart leapt. "Maddy! Alf!"

Before I could sit up all the way, they smothered me in a group hug, laughing and tousling my hair. Then suddenly it was just Alf squeezing me with surprising energy.

He let go, and I grinned. "Well, good morning to you, too! Don't kill me with kindness, yeah?" I'd mimicked his characteristic tough tone, but my insides felt all jiggly with happiness at his enthusiasm.

A glance around the space confused me. It looked snowy except for the bed on which I sat bundled in thick blankets. Several dome lights appeared to be spiked into the glistening ceiling above us.

I turned to Maddy. "When did you get to Craggy?" I asked

"My lady?" His brows furrowed.

"Oh don't start that again. What is this place? It looks like we're inside of a freezer."

Alf looked at me funny. "Don't you know where we are?"

"You mean I'm not the center of the universe?" I teased. Pulling back the blankets, I swung my feet to the ground.

Alf and Maddy exchanged concerned glances but didn't answer.

"Aren't we in the Sumayar caves?"

Alf, clad in a thick, kangra-wool coat, sat beside me and wrapped his arm around my shoulder. Maddy crouched on the ground in front of me. They both studied me for a long moment until my smile faded.

"What? What's going on?"

"Caz, we've been in express transit for two weeks," said Alf. He gestured at the room. "This is Tye."

I blinked. "What?" My mind balked at the notion. I jerked my legs back up to the bed, wrapping my arms around my knees.

Maddy shifted. "We kept you sedated for a lot of the journey, but you were awake when we left. Don't you remember when Brade rescued you from the cliff?"

"What?!" I tried to stand, but my legs felt like rubber bands. "Why would you sedate me?"

"Your dad suggested it." Alf held my gaze. "He thought if you could calm your heart, you might get your body back. You know, from the paralysis."

Suddenly, it all came back to me. I nodded, grateful they'd been able to contact Dad. Grateful I could nod.

"Dr. Artemus is quite a genius," said Maddy.

I flexed and curled my fingers. "Well, whatever he said to do worked. I feel weak, though. Groggy."

Alf grinned, his C-shaped tattoo sliding into the dimple on his newly shorn cheek. "That's from lazing around all day while the rest of us work."

He winked, and my insides warmed up a bit. "I thought Tye was a world covered in water. How did you build a cave out of snow? Won't it collapse with the heat of day?"

"Not where we are," said Maddy, smiling.

I willed myself to warm up a little. "So where's King? Did Brade get him, too?"

Maddy sighed. "No. I'm sorry. We don't know where he is."

The last of the fuzziness in my brain cleared away, and I pushed myself to my feet, all business. "So? What's the status?"

"I searched all known channels for information," said Maddy. "I don't know if King stayed on Craggy, or somehow got off the planet, but if he's alive, he'll find a way here. He'll find you."

"All right. Let's assume the Ceremony is still on until we hear otherwise."

"Yes, my lady."

I arched a brow at him. "It's *Caz*, please." My stomach chose that moment to growl loudly, adding sound effects to my grumpy look.

Maddy laughed. "How about you wait here with Alf while I get you something to eat."

"And another layer of clothing?"

His head dipped in a slight bow, and he disappeared through a low doorway. I watched him go and then let my eyes wander around the tiny room. No angles here. Only smooth curves, as if the snow leaned in to accommodate our needs.

At last my gaze fell back on Alf. His pale blonde hair fell in shaggy wisps around his face. His eyes, so dark and forbidding when we first met on Caren, now gave me a sense of belonging.

"You all right?" he asked, the corner of his mouth creeping up. "You look a little shaky."

"It's just cold in here," I said. My fingers went to his cheeks, gently caressing a full smile from him. "I can't believe you're still with me." I sifted his hair, relishing its fullness. "You were going to run away and be a fisher on Caren, sailing the seas."

Alf chuckled. "Tye is one big ocean, Caz. I'll get plenty of fishing and sailing done here."

Maddy returned with a steaming mug of soup wrapped in a cloth so I wouldn't burn my hands. "Drink up. It's fortified."

Alf watched me closely with a twinkle in his eye that tickled the back of my neck with a blush. I took a sip, hiding my face behind the mug while I looked at them.

"Did you two put on some serious weight?"

"It's the bulky coat, yeah?"

"It's your butt, yeah," I said.

Alf spun comically as if to examine his own rear end and then laughed knowingly. "Oh, you'll get your bump, too, as soon as they bring you the overpants."

"My bump?"

Maddy chortled. "It's the height of fashion around here."

OOO

"I could pass for Stationmaster Lew's wife." On wobbly legs, I gave my rear a shake, and Alf snorted with laughter. Over our coversuits, everyone wore overpants with a sewn-in "bump"—a thick pillow at our bottoms coated with a durable layer of rubbery cloth. On top of this, I wore my bright red kangra wool coat.

We emerged from a series of low sloping tunnels into the sunlight, bright but not harsh. The cold felt different without the wind, brisk, not biting. In front of us, the ground dipped like a giant scoop of ice cream had been removed. All around the top, several snow cave openings yawned at no one in particular. Maddy, Alf and I seemed to be the entire populace.

Alf patted my bump with a smirk. "You're gaining weight, Caz."

"And this padding is for…?" I cocked an eyebrow.

"For this," said Alf, giving me a playful shove.

I crashed backward to the ground and spun down the slope into the center of the snowy bowl. As I spiraled to a stop, I saw Maddy and Alf flop down and slide after me, laughing with their arms in the air.

"I can't believe you did that to me in my weakened condition!" I balked.

Alf rolled his eyes. "You can still break me in half with your bare hands if you want to."

The memory of our first day working together at Lamond came back, and I echoed his words with a mock scowl. "Don't make me kill you. I don't want to do that."

He laughed, and I shoved him hard on the shoulder, sending him in a wide arc up and back down the slope to bump into me.

"It's a very efficient mode of transportation, isn't it?" Maddy's eyes gleamed with good humor. It warmed me inside to see him happy again after his mother's death.

I shrugged. "It works." I stood up and took in my first real view of Tye, the third inhabited world in the Granbo System, and my final destination for the Cycling Ceremony of the Gypsy Pearl. *I'm actually here!* My stomach fluttered with excitement.

"Well, Maddy? Now what? Where are we, and where do we go next?"

"My lady, we now sit at the top of Tye. Welcome to Wandel Hav."

I gritted my teeth to stay polite. "Call me Caz, *please*. And what do you mean?"

"We're near the edge of the polar ice cap. 'Top' meaning a long way from the middle, which is where we need to go."

"Ikekane South," I muttered.

Maddy nodded, unsurprised by my memory. That's how my brain worked now, thanks to the Gypsy Pearl.

"Icky Connie," said Alf. "Why would anyone name a colony that?"

I rolled my eyes at his childish word play. "Where is everyone?" I asked. "It's so quiet."

"It's early yet," said Maddy.

Not quite directly overhead, two half-moons peeked through an unending expanse of pale blue gauze. "But the sun must have been up for hours," I said, pointing. A piece of me thrilled to note that I marked the passage of days by the sun and the phases of moons, something impossible to do from space where the blackness outside is constant.

"You've lived only in equatorial regions on Caren and Craggy," said Maddy. "We're thousands and thousands of kilometers away from Tye's equator. Days start much earlier and end much later this time of year."

"Why didn't we fly directly to Ikekane South?"

"Wandel Hav has the largest and most private landing strip," said Maddy. "We thought it best to come here just in case anyone back on Craggy revealed that you had survived the second assassination attempt."

"Is my identity safe here, or am I still in hiding?"

Maddy shrugged. "No one here is going to know anything about what happened on Craggy, but we don't need your presence to be noticed much, just in case word leaks back through a gypsy connection or something. I'm not really very concerned at this point."

Alf harrumphed. "I hope you're right. What do you know about the people here in Wandel Hav? Are there gypsies here?"

"It's a wonderful group. Despite the climate, they were one of the first colonies because it's the largest flat land mass on the planet. Shuttles from orbit can land and move equipment around easily here." He gestured and we trudged back up the slope, kicking the toes of our boots into the snow with each step to create footholds. Maddy paused, squinting in the sunlight.

"They used to make boots with little claws coming out of the toes for gripping, but too many of the children sliding on their bumps ended up gouging their playmates when they crashed."

"Ow!" I winced at the vision. "So, do we fly out from here?"

"No, planes are fairly rare up this far north."

"Why?" asked Alf.

"Only because of the fuel required to fly them. They're practical for speed, but the synthetic petrol they use is very expensive. Most travel on Tye is by boat."

A distressed gurgle fell from my lips.

Maddy frowned at me with a mixture of pity and humor. "Still afraid of water?"

"Not in love with it." I mulled over the memory of the first time I'd ever set foot on any planet. I had plunged into the shallows off the coast of the Rik Peninsula on Caren. Well, they were considered shallows to everyone else, but I had gone underwater totally unprepared. The thought of getting salt brine in my eyes and mouth again still terrified me. I took a deep breath and stretched my muscles, feeling them thrum with the light exertion. "Oldest colony on Tye, yet they only have a handful of snow caves?"

Maddy turned to face the way we'd come, and I followed his gaze. There, on the back of all of the snowy domes, bright red circles guaranteed no one could miss the cluster of structures in the middle of the whiteness that stretched in every direction.

"There are hundreds of these little groups of snow caves nearby. They're called hubs," explained Maddy. "See? There's a blue one, and to the right, a greenish-yellow one."

Alf and I shielded our eyes with our mittens and turned slowly to survey the expanse. Sure enough, I could see many groups of colorful lumps in the snow.

"In another month, they'll be able to clear away the snow in some of these patches between for the planting season. The caves are built where there's a rock base below to keep the snow year-round. Small glaciers. Some of the clusters are just homes, and others are specialized areas of labor like you'd find on an ICS or in a city. People work on everything from developing technology to recording and studying history."

Alf looked back. "What's the hub we've come from?"

"The Committee of Elders meets there as needed, and there are places for visitors—usually traders—to stay. Most of the Elders came in from their regular hubs two days ago when we airdropped."

"Airdropped!" My eyes popped wide, and I shook my head. "No. Don't tell me. I've already been dropped from a ship once. I don't need to live it twice."

OOO

"I'm so glad you're better," said a wrinkled woman with a broad smile. "And walking already!" She sat on her bump, wrapped in a thick, bright green and yellow blanket. Beside her were the other seven men and women who served as the Elders of the Wandel Hav Colony.

A shriveled man with thick glasses and a fuzzy hat nodded. "No doubt your father used some pearl powder at the scene of the accident."

"The accident?"

"When you fell," he said.

Ah, the cover story. Right. An accident. I glanced at Maddy. Yes, we could easily pass for family. Maddy gave me a side hug. "Glad it worked. Thank you all for helping us. She needed a safe place to recover."

"We're glad to help," said the woman. She winked at me. "Next time, stay further back from the open hull. I can't imagine falling into a cargo bay like that. You're lucky you weren't killed."

I chewed my lip, eager to change the subject since I didn't know which cargo bay I had imaginarily thrown myself into. "How in space do you all manage in this cold?" I blurted.

The talkative woman smiled, unfazed by my question. "It's simple. We made the Decision to Survive."

The other Elders nodded and murmured, "The Decision to Survive."

Alf scoffed. "You can't just decide to survive."

Another man, as old as the others, but rounder and more inclined to smile with his mouth hanging open, spoke up. "Of course you can. Oh, there are very rare instances when death comes suddenly and instantaneously, but for the most part, it can be prevented or fought until Nature's time. You simply must decide." He gestured with both hands as if handing us the answer.

I blinked. "You mean don't give up."

"Exactly!" The round man beamed.

"Once you make the Decision to Survive," said the first woman, "you live accordingly. Your determination sets you in action, and you do what you need to do. You won't curl up in a ball and wait to be rescued, or sit in a corner and complain about the difficulties. You'll get up and start solving problems."

"We can solve problems for others, too, because we need each other to survive," I added.

Everyone in the room agreed, and Alf squeezed my hand covertly.

A moment of giddiness distracted me, but then I turned back to the Elders. "And how were you chosen to lead?"

The most shriveled woman of them all, barely visible as more than a tiny head sticking out of a mound of thick blue and orange blankets, squeaked with laughter. "No one chose us. We got *old*."

"So the 'Elders' thing is literal?"

"We've been here longest," said the round man. "We've seen the most sunrises—and believe me, up here, they are *long* sunrises—so we know from experience what to expect."

A serious, squinty man added, "And we know from study and research what more we can hope for. We got lucky in that each of us specialized in something different." He pointed to each of his peers in turn. "We have a doctor, a mechanical engineer, a nutritionist, a game and wildlife specialist, a linguist and historian, a horticulturist, and—"

"I am Wandel Hav's leading authority on Happiness," announced the round man with a straight-faced delivery.

Alf snickered. Maddy and I both gave him a light punch on the arm, which only made the round man laugh aloud.

"You don't want to be happy?" he asked Alf, his eyes sparkling with humor.

"*I* want to be happy," I said. "Is that a decision, too? The Decision to Be Happy?" The Elders nodded, and Maddy grinned beside me.

"Is this a joke?" asked Alf.

The round man gave an exaggerated frown. "No. Happiness is serious work!"

I leaned my elbows on my knees and copied his mock scowl. "Please teach us about the ever-elusive, always-coveted thing called Happiness."

"We choose optimism or pessimism, gratitude or greed. We choose to love and be grateful, or to fear and complain. We can't always choose what happens to us, but we can choose how we respond."

The round man and the others went on in a lively discussion for almost an hour. Certain things, they said, increased Happiness: putting the needs of others first, smiling, singing, creating things of beauty, accomplishing a difficult task, and developing self-control. There was more, but I'd let the Rik leaves remember it. I just soaked it all up by auditory osmosis and enjoyed a welcome sense of safety. Someday their theories might prove useful, after all. Who *doesn't* want to choose to be happy?

OOO

"Are you sure we're not lost? We've been walking for an hour," Alf whined.

Maddy had obtained new comlinks for each of us, and we used these periodically to check our global position in relation to a hub with ski-bikes we could borrow to get to the Edge. It felt good to have some real technology back in my hand, and I rolled the egg-shaped device in my pocket as we walked. Despite the boring landscape, I felt happier than I could ever remember. Exertion, purpose and friends do that.

"The old man's right," I said, my voice muffled by the thick wrap across my lips.

Alf looked at me with raised eyebrows. "Huh?"

"About Happiness." In my mind, it should be capitalized, like an esteemed person or place.

"Never thought about it much before," said Alf. "I just knew I *wasn't* happy."

I stopped walking and stared at him. "Not even now?"

He spun and continued walking backwards so he could face me. "This is probably the closest I've ever been." He shrugged. "Maybe I'm not choosing hard enough."

Isn't he as happy to be with me as I am to be with him? I trotted to catch up, casting a glance at Maddy. On cue, he slapped Alf's back. "Tell us, Alf. What would make it easier for you to choose to be happy?"

Alf didn't answer right away, and he lowered his gaze from the horizon to his feet.

I nudged him. "Alf? You in there?"

"Yeah," he said. "I guess I'm getting used to being a part of something, but I wish I were a *meaningful* part."

"What do you mean?" asked Maddy.

"Well, Caz is the future savior of a species and ruler of the Granbo System, and you're her guide. I'm just..." He shrugged. "Trailing along like space debris."

"Alf, that's not true. You're hugely important. We need you."

He shook his head. "No you don't. I don't belong on this quest."

"Yes, you do!"

His voice grew melancholy. "I never really belonged anywhere. Growing up, people didn't talk to me much, and I didn't feel the need to make them. It wasn't until I'd been at Lamond Reformatory for over a year, and Caz took my spot in the cafeteria that anyone ever reached out."

"Ha! I remember that. I wasn't reaching out," I said. "I wanted to see what would happen if I messed with the patterns all the inmates had established."

Maddy laughed lightly. "That sounds like you, my la...Caz. Trying something new to see what happens."

"Call me a scientist. Or a gypsy. Either way, I'm curious."

"And it's that curiosity and boldness that might bring peace to the Worlds." Maddy meant well, but that was the absolute wrong thing to say. Alf practically retreated into his personal gloom, probably feeling left out again. I wasn't really fond of the subject, either. Helping King and the faneps was one thing, but the whole gypsy queen bit still didn't feel one hundred percent right.

I was just about to ask Maddy how upset the gypsies would be if I opted out of that part of the Cycling Ceremony when he called out, "We're here!"

Gold mounds rose from the ground ahead. In the open spaces between the caves, people stood talking to each other. One of them caught sight of us and began waving with both arms. We waved back, and Maddy ran on ahead.

Grabbing Alf's sleeve, I stopped. "Alf, I want you to be happy, too."

Something softened in his eyes. "I'm sorry. I don't mean to be depressing." He tugged at the scarf, freeing his mouth to the air. "It's great that you have something important to do and people who love you and—"

I gripped his shoulders. "Alf, *I love you*."

A smile spread across his face before vanishing quickly. "You're the only one."

Am I not enough? "You *are* part of something big. I couldn't do any of this without you."

"Sure you could. You're the superhuman." He pulled his hood snug. "I'm an afterthought." He followed after Maddy, leaving me unable to speak, but my heart cried out plenty.

Can't you see you're irreplaceable to me? You're the best friend I've ever had!

OOO

Alf rode his ski-bike as if he'd been born for speed, darting back and forth in front of us, laughing and sending up sprays of powdered ice. Clearly, choosing to be Happy was easier now.

I, on the other hand, developed an instant hatred for the motorized beasts. The skinny frame balanced on a single blade that vibrated so much I felt like I'd been put in a food processor. My bones took a beating with each patch of uneven ground even with the heavy padding of my bump. Twice, I sent the ski-bike soaring almost a meter into the air before crunching back down. I expected to sever my tongue at any moment.

A rise loomed ahead, and I slowed down so I wouldn't launch myself into the atmosphere, but Alf charged ahead, screeching like a fanep. A moment later, he caught air. Too much air! As I saw him plummet, my heart sank through fear's clutches.

"Alf!" I screamed, feeling my own ski-bike slide out from under me. I couldn't hear anything over the whirring of the motors. Maddy popped lightly over the rise, and I yelled after him to hurry. Running up the slope, I felt my legs buckle and freeze beneath me. Panic had poisoned me with adrenaline. I scrambled with my arms, dragging my own dead weight behind, and peered over the top of the rise at what I assumed would be the bloody, crumpled body of my best friend.

OOO

34 FISHING

I'm going to kill him. As soon as I get my legs back. I planted my face in the snow and breathed out a sigh of relief.

Alf and Maddy had dismounted their ski-bikes and stood talking to a bundled figure. Scattered nearby, several other people worked with poles doing something to the snow.

"Alf!" I shouted, feeling as foolish as I'd been frightened. "Alf!"

He turned back and waved me to come.

"I can't! I…" Ugh. *If every time my adrenaline spikes, I become a useless lump of flesh…* I stared up at the sky. "I'm ready for that third Power any time now!" I groaned through gritted teeth.

Alf reached me quickly, dropping to his knees. "Did you crash?"

I propped myself up on my elbows. "No such luck. I thought you had, and I sort of panicked."

He glanced back at my legs. *"Again?"* I could hear the frustration in his voice, and I felt it doubly. "Caz, you can't worry about me. I'm fine."

"I know, but—"

"I was having fun."

I dropped my forehead onto my arm and muttered into the snow. "I know. I'm turning into Felly. Need a naggy big sister?"

He rubbed my shoulder. "You're not my sister, Caz. You're my…"

I looked up. *How will he finish that sentence?*

Alf's dark eyes shone. "You're my everything."

Giddiness plastered a ridiculous grin on my face, and I wriggled my toes. *I wriggled my toes!*

Maddy trudged up a few minutes later, by which time I'd been able to roll myself over and sit up, flexing my ankles. "What's going on up here?" he asked, squinting back down the slope to where I'd left my ski-bike. "Did you fall off?"

Snorting, I shook my head. "No. I hit the 'Eject Brains' button."

Maddy threw back his head and laughed. "Are they floating out in space right now?"

I knocked my knees together, accepting the sensations that prickled up my legs. It meant I'd be walking soon.

"I'll grab them up before we go. Who are those people down there?" I asked, stalling for those healing moments.

"Fishers," said Maddy.

"How's that?" I rolled back over and crawled up to see. "There's no water."

"Of course there is. Under the ice." Maddy took aggravating pleasure in watching me discover things for the first time.

A new kind of numbness crept into my body, and I grabbed onto Alf's shoulders for support and balance. "Speaking of ice, I'm pretty sure I've become one with the ground here."

Maddy smiled. "The cold will do that. Keep moving." He pointed to the fishers below. "If you watch, they always have their feet shuffling. It's part of surviving the temperatures up here when you're not sitting on a revved motor."

Alf helped me up, and I leaned on him, ready to walk down.

"No, no," he said, tugging me back down. "Take the fun way."

Seconds later, we swirled to a stop, our bumps having carried us swiftly into the center of the action. A few of the fishers glanced in our direction, and one reached down a hand to lift us up.

"I know we're just passing through, but can we stay and watch for a little while?" asked Alf. His face looked like a little child begging for a treat.

"This is your first time in Wandel Hav?" asked the fisher.

"Yes."

A furry hood wrapped the man's head but left his face uncovered. "Take a look around. Just don't fall down a hole," he added with a wink. He gestured for us to follow, and Alf and I plodded after him. My joints still felt stiff, but no one here moved quickly anyway, so I fit right in.

"Want me to go back and get your ski-bike, Caz?" suggested Maddy.

"Yes, please. Thank you."

"Are you taking those all the way to the Edge?" asked the man.

Maddy stopped. "That's the plan. Why?"

The man pointed towards one of the workers. "She isn't feeling so well. Any chance she could take one of them back to our hub? We'll gladly give you some fish."

Maddy glanced at me. "Would you mind sharing a ski-bike with me? You can just sit behind me and hold on."

And not have to drive? "Sure. She can take the bike."

Maddy went to retrieve my ski-bike while the fisher showed us the apparatus they used. The poles were actually resonance blasters that emitted a high-pitched sound to crack through the ice.

"You want to try?" he asked.

Alf's eyes widened with delight. "Yes, sir!"

"Have fun with it. I'll be right back. I should check on my friend before she heads back to the hub." He left us with an encouraging smile.

Alf and I looked at each other. "Well, it isn't squishing bugs in a duspy field, but we can learn, right?" I giggled. We triggered the device several times, and eventually, the sound dug a hole all the way through the ice shelf, about six meters down.

"Whoah! Would you look at that?" Alf flopped to his stomach and stared down the hole. It was only a little bigger in diameter than his skull, so for a moment, his head disappeared from view as he hollered triumphantly into the icy tunnel we'd created.

"You're going to scare away the fish, Alf."

"But look!" he insisted.

I did and found myself mesmerized by the play of light and shadow in the shaft. Blue and white ricocheted with bits of gold down to the blackness of the water. Sound, too, volleyed back and forth like whispered children's laughter, as if the sea below couldn't contain a long-held secret any more.

"So how do we get the fish?" I asked. My voice echoed in the space and I couldn't resist. "Hellooo? Here fishy fishy fishy!"

I glanced at Alf who stared at me like I'd lost my mind. "You're going to scare away the fish, Caz," he said, mimicking my earlier tone.

"What? You have a better idea?" I asked.

He shook his head and sat up. The fisher had returned and stood chuckling at our antics. "It really is your first time, isn't it?"

I gave him an embarrassed grin. "How do we know if there are fish down there?"

"Because there always are," he said. "The smallest ones tend to swim near the top of the water, just below the ice. Those are the ones we'll skim off of the shoal."

"Leaving the bigger, stronger ones to breed more," added Alf.

I stared at him. "Where'd you get that?"

"Logic," he said, tapping his mittened hand to his forehead.

"He's right," said the fisher, clearly impressed. "Here, you'll need these." He handed us more equipment and explained what we'd have to do next. One tool mimicked the cries of certain underwater creatures. We would lower weighted transparent nets into the water and then activate the call. The first time we felt movement, we were to start pulling on the nets. We could expect to catch at least two or three at once.

"It takes a lot of strength, though," he said looking at my comparatively scrawny frame. "They weigh five to ten kilos each. You should probably let him do the hauling."

Alf and I exchanged winks, and I handed the netting to him. The other fishers each worked alone, holding the nets in one hand and the calling device in another, but I wanted to help. Gripping the transmitter, I pressed the buttons I'd been shown, and we heard a mournful song resonate through the tube.

While the fisher went and chatted with Maddy, Alf and I waited. Huddled close over the opening, our ears brushed against each other.

"Thanks for saving me back there," I said. My words echoed a little through the tube of ice below us.

"What do you mean?"

"You counteracted the adrenaline."

"What? How?"

I shifted slightly and could feel his breath on my cheek. My lungs started dancing around in my chest. "You calmed me down," I said, my voice cracking.

"I guess I'm not very exciting."

Tell that to my heart! I nudged him playfully, and our eyes locked. Despite the cold, I felt warm all over. He brushed my scarf from my face with a finger. I closed my eyes as he leaned in.

"Whoah! I got something!"

Back to the fish...

Alf burst into movement, pulling hand over hand on the long cords. I pocketed the transmitter and joined him. Before the net broke the surface of the ice, I let go with surprise and watched Alf finish. There in the net flopped a slithering pile of dark, rubbery things. They tumbled out of the net and slid onto the ice, flopping and gasping for air. Their blue-green scales caught flecks of snow with each movement, and the water and ice played against each other until they stilled.

A nearby fisher shuffled over. "Five! Good haul!" She stooped to help us gather the fish. Others called out, commending him for his speed and strength.

I sat back on my bump, watching with awe and a hint of sadness. *This is what Alf wants to be: a fisher.* The cold didn't touch him as he worked and laughed and ran back and forth with the dry cases in which they would transport the fish.

At last he sank to his knees beside me, grinning. "That was fun!"

I smiled. "That was gross."

He gave me a funny face before retying his scarf to cover all but his eyes, glistening now with action.

"Do you want to stay here?" I asked quietly.

He tilted his head. "The fishing is fun, but I'd rather have it a little warmer."

"Are you doing another net?"

"No time," said Maddy, stomping up to us. "I've arranged passage on a supply ship. We can't afford to miss it. It leaves the Edge in an hour, so we'd better hurry."

OOO

The top deck of the *Equation* came almost perfectly level to The Edge—

the cliff drop where the ice stopped and the sea started. With my eyes closed, I shuffled across the broad plank, clinging to Maddy's elbow like a child balking on the first day of school.

Once out of the sunlight, normalcy embraced me. It felt a little like my home on the Arxon ICS. The enclosed, metallic, boring spaces were oddly reassuring—especially since I knew I could step outside onto the decks and breathe fresh air.

Maddy opened the door to our dorm, called a cabin. It managed to be luxuriously stark. The comforts included three soft, ample berths and a private washroom. Only one of us could see out of the small circular window at a time, and I claimed the first long gaze.

Activating a vid screen on the wall, Maddy showed us a map. "Between here and Ikekane are five colonies, each several days apart."

"You mean we're stuck on this boat for weeks?"

"It's a full-sized planet," said Maddy with a smile. "The island groups are small and very far apart on this side of the globe."

I pressed my nose back to the glass window. "I suppose I'll have memorized the view by then." Sighing, set to work unpacking our meager supplies of clothing and hygiene items. "What are the other colonies like?"

"They're all quite different," said Maddy. "Most of the islands are volcanically formed. Some are mostly rock, others mostly lagoon in the middle of an atoll. We'll be traveling southward in a wavy diagonal line." He pointed on the map to specks in the blue.

I nodded at the vid screen. "Can we get news on that thing?"

"I would imagine so," said Maddy. "The satellite system for Tye is very sophisticated. You could even call the Arxon if you wanted."

Something somersaulted inside me, and I fumbled in my pocket for the comlink. Pressing the required controls, I sat down on one of the berths and watched the inverted cone of blue light bloom. Alf signaled that he would check out the news on the vid screen, but kept the volume turned down, standing close to listen.

"Caz!" My sister's excited voice kicked all the tears from my eyes. "Oh! Are you all right? Why are you crying?"

"You idiot, Felly! I'm happy to see your ugly face." I groaned. Felly's ultra-straight hair framed a face that resembled Mom's. Beautiful, actually. Trust Felly to get Mom's looks while I get the wanderlust.

"Let me call Dad. Wait a minute." She shifted so that her 3D blue self faded to a vapor at the edges. I used the time to wipe my eyes and rake my hair smooth with my fingers. Maddy flopped back on the bunk adjacent to mine, and Alf stood transfixed, watching the vid screen.

A moment later, Dad and Felly both appeared, huddled together so that I could see their faces. Dad smiled. "Caz, my little star-hopper! You're moving!"

Alf signaled to me, but I waved him away. *This is family time, and my dad is actually being nice!* "Yes, Dad. Thanks! I heard you coordinated with the medics."

"You're upright. May I assume my diagnosis was correct? How much strain have you been under?"

"Not much. A little scare, but it only stopped me for a few minutes."

He nodded in that doctorly way of his. "My guess is that the Earlie syrup has shifted your system in such a way that you can only metabolize a limited amount of stress hormones. However, if the parts per million of adrenaline reach a certain level, your body moves you into your dorsal vagal system in an extreme way—"

"Uh, Dad? Just the pertinent facts, please."

"Don't get too scared too fast, and you should be fine."

Alf hissed at me, pointing to the vid screen.

"In a minute," I grumbled. Turning back to Dad, I plastered a huge smile on my face. "Now that no one is trying to blow me up or drop me from shuttle crafts any more, I think I'll be especially fine." I was laughing, but he was not.

"Well, I'm glad to know the sedation worked." His face did that twitch he used when holding back criticism, but his voice came out kinder than usual. "Too bad you didn't get my message not to take the Earlie syrup into your body."

I shook my head. "Dad, I would have done it anyway. It's part of the whole deal. I'll just have to stay calm."

"Caz," said Alf more urgently.

Felly was laughing at what Dad had said, and I nodded at the irony. "I know. If it were either of you, there'd be no trouble. I'm the comet chaser of the family."

"No, that would be Brita," said Dad. *He didn't sound sad. First time!*

"Caz!"

I glared at Alf. "Stop interrupting, Alf! This is important."

Dad continued, "She sent me word that she's heading out after you with someone."

My heart almost leaped from my mouth. *She survived the troops sent to the Sumayar valley!* "That's great news!"

Maddy shifted to sit up suddenly. "Caz, I really think you better see this," he said sharply.

I looked up at the vid screen and gasped.

A female reporter sat in front of a picture of Mom and spoke with the sterile detachment of an ICS dweller who couldn't care less about Surface life. "...Governor Jipps insists that the threats on her life were not what led her to resign, but rather that she wishes to return to family back on Caren. She is reported to have landed in the Rik Peninsula Bay and is heading to the North Mountains. This was the first anyone knew of her family connections to Caren, and it casts into doubt the validity of her bid for Governorship three years ago where only natives of Craggy are allowed to run. Emergency elections to fill her post will commence in Garvey…"

I fumbled with the comlink. "Dad! Dad, what's this about Mom going to…?" The connection had broken.

Alf turned off the vid screen as it switched to other news. "What does this mean, Maddy?"

I bobbed my head. "Yeah. I'm getting conflicting reports. Dad said she's coming here."

"I thought so, too," said Maddy.

"The Gypsy Network Headquarters are in the North Mountains," said Alf.

Normally, that might make perfect sense. Why wouldn't a gypsy check in at HQ after interplanetary travel? But in light of recent events…My chest tightened. "That's where Saloma is." *Saloma.* As head of the Gypsy Network on Caren, she saw herself as the logical one to cycle a Gypsy Pearl and assume control of the entire Granbo System, uniting three worlds' worth of colonies and the entire Interplanetary City-Station system under her voice. But King didn't choose her. He gave me the Pearl. Painfully. He'd named *me* Queen, even though I'm just a teenager—and a troublemaker at that. I didn't want the job. I just wanted to help King and the faneps. I'd figure out the rest later.

Alf's eyes narrowed. "Does Saloma know we're alive?"

"No," said Maddy.

"How can you be so sure?"

"Brade said Saloma was already celebrating over your death when the watchtower blew up."

"She *was* behind the attack." Alf's voice came as a growl.

"I know you trust Brade," I said. "But what if he's misinformed?"

Maddy shook his head. "I don't know."

"What do we do?" asked Alf. "If her mom is coming to Tye, that's one thing, but if she's going to meet with Saloma…" He frowned. "Why would she even do that?"

"If Saloma sees she survived the tower attack, she might assume you did, too." Maddy's voice trailed off into a moan.

Alf sat heavily beside me, as if weighed down by the sudden worry. "If she finds out you're still alive, we won't be safe anywhere for long."

OOO

I quickly reacquainted myself with proper hygiene in the washroom. Soap is a marvelous invention, and I will never take it for granted again.

Smelling artificially fruity is so much better than the alternatives my body creates. There were no water rations on Tye for obvious reasons. A mechanism in the belly of the ship desalinized water directly from the ocean, extracting the salt for cooking and the water for cleaning.

As I patted myself dry with a real towel, I poked my head out of the door, keeping my body hidden. "I need my clothes."

"Oh, those are being burned," said Alf with a wicked grin.

Maddy tossed a pillow at Alf and stooped to get something from a drawer under his berth. "I have fresh clothing for you that's more appropriate for this part of Tye." He handed me a bundle of material, some blue and some creamy yellow.

I closed the door to change. "This is quality fashion, Maddy. Even I recognize it from the holocube reports on the Arxon."

"I'm glad you approve, my lady."

"*Caz*, please. You know I don't like the formal stuff." Pondering how I'd approach the subject of *not* being a queen, I pulled on the thick blue pants that fit more snugly than my usual coversuit but left my feet open for air. I slid the soft, flowing blouse over my head and stopped to pose in front of the mirror. My dark, chin-length hair still framed my boyish face, but I looked older. The Gypsy Pearl also seemed to have accelerated the more feminine changes of my body, and I could swear I'd gotten taller. I smiled at this and stepped out of the washroom.

Alf clucked his tongue admiringly. "Very glamorous."

"Alf, do us all a favor and take your shower!"

He laughed and dragged himself and a change of clothes into the washroom.

Maddy had shed a few layers while I was in the shower and now wore two layers of multi-colored vests over an outfit much like mine.

"Let's take a quick walk while he washes up," he said, sliding his long boots over his pants and buckling them swiftly.

I pounded on the washroom door. "We'll be back soon. Don't use the whole Karlis Ocean to get clean. We need the water to get where we're going."

Alf gave an exaggerated fake laugh back, and Maddy and I headed out into the hall. We climbed a flight of narrow steps and opened a sealed door that reminded me of an airlock. Instantly, the salty mist of the ocean covered my face. I shivered. "Maybe we should go back and get coats."

"Just for a minute or two?"

I grunted with indecision but opted to brave the deck. About six meters separated us from a railing over which I could see the ocean. Tucking one hand under Maddy's arm, I ventured forward a few steps. "It's as big as space!"

"When the sky is overcast, it blends into the horizon."

"It looks like we live inside a giant ball." I willed my body to warm up, grateful again for the Gypsy Pearl. "What's that?" I pointed to a peculiar cloud that kept shifting closer.

He squinted for a moment and then grinned. "It's a flock of belltroes. They must have found a shoal of kelpies."

"Uh-huh. And for those of us who don't know—ooh wait. I remember this. Or the Rik leaves do, anyway." Back on Caren, I'd studied an archive about the sea life of the Karlis Ocean, and now the Rik leaves did their memory boost. I straightened up as if giving a report to my teacher, Mr. Virgil. "Belltroes are a very common aquatic bird native to Tye. They dive for their prey and can swim underwater for several minutes before coming up for air. Kelpies are small fish that swim in swarms—shoals, excuse me—for safety. They provide protein for many of the larger sea creatures. They follow the underwater warm currents." I gave a self-satisfied nod.

Maddy threw back his head and laughed. "Excellent, little girl. You may advance to the next class!"

A flash of movement caught my eye. The belltroes had flown close enough to hear their angry cries. As I pulled back towards the sealed door, three of them plunged from the sky and splashed into the sea, sending up a tall spray of water. Others followed in rapid succession, and I held my breath in awe.

"They dive into the shoal in different places trying to break up the kelpies," said Maddy. "The fish are easier to chase when separated." He crouched a little beside me, pointing. "There. See those ones? They've come up with their catches. It's a very effective strategy."

"Divide and conquer," I murmured. "One of the oldest."

OOO

35 SCILLY

Three days passed with no news or incidents that caused us concern. For once in my life, the confinement on a vessel did not frustrate me. Sea air refreshed my lungs whenever I went up on deck, filling me with a peace more enduring than any anti-anxiety medicine.

Another call to Dad answered our questions about Mom, too.

"I spoke with her yesterday, Caz," he said. "She's coming your way. Caren was just a detour. She'll get to you in a couple of weeks if she takes the express."

"What about you?" I asked. "Can you get away for the Ceremony?" It was the first time I had suggested it, and I think the question surprised us both.

He chewed his lip thoughtfully. "I don't suppose you have the event scheduled? I would only be able to take a very short leave, so I'd have to time it right."

Maddy did his best to guess our arrival time in Ikekane South, but that didn't mean anything without King. It wasn't as though we could start without him. We decided to hold off on planning Dad's trip until we knew more, but the very fact that he even thought about coming to the Surface to support something so gypsy encouraged me.

"Everything's coming together for you," said Alf as we shuffled along the deck in our kangra wool coats.

A crisp breeze tossed our short hair around our ears, making us look like a black and white sea anemones on two walking red rocks. I leaned in close to his chest and found myself stupidly admiring his strong features and tender eyes.

With his hands still in his pockets, he nuzzled his nose against my forehead. "What are you looking at?"

"Did you just snot in my hair?"

He rubbed my head with a mittened hand and tucked me under his arm. "Caz," he said.

"Yes?"

"I think I'm figuring out this happy thing."

"It doesn't take much after all, does it?" I said, thinking of the choice.

"It just takes you," he said.

My already chapped cheeks camouflaged the blush, but I couldn't hide the smile. "Yeah?"

"Yeah."

"It's not just that you're on a boat and free?"

"That helps, too."

We walked the deck, talking to other traders along the way. Everyone dressed for the cold, but no one complained about it. Those with the round faces of people from Wandel Hav greeted us with vigorous slaps on the back, which, whether intended or not, served to warm us up.

As the sky exchanged its dull horizon hues for something more daring, someone shouted, "Land in sight!"

Alf and I grinned but tried to look as if this experience were commonplace. We needn't have played it so nonchalantly. Everyone reacted with renewed energy. People pressed forward to the railings to catch a glimpse of the first break in the blue monotony since leaving The Edge.

I held back behind Alf's shoulder, and Maddy soon appeared and sandwiched me protectively from behind. Whispering, he said, "That'll be the island of Scilly. A tiny but interesting colony."

"Are there gypsies?" I asked.

Maddy shook his head. "Not living there regularly. There isn't any unused land where we can camp, and there's only one inn. Trading is good, though." He chuckled to himself, as if at a personal joke. "The people of Scilly are very concerned about family bloodlines. Before you can do the most basic business, you have ask after family members."

"That's just being polite, isn't it?" I said.

"Ah, but then you have to *remember* who to ask about the next time you see them."

"Oh." I rolled my eyes. "That could get exhausting fast, trying to keep it all straight."

"To say the least. There are almost six thousand people," said Maddy. "And if you make a blunder, it can damage trade relations."

Alf gestured between us. "What's our story now? Are we siblings? Your children?"

Maddy chewed the inside of his cheek. "That won't work. I've been here before. They'll know I don't have children."

"Can't we be your friends?" I asked with an arched brow. "Like maybe the truth would work?"

"Or at least part of it," said Alf. "Associates in training."

Maddy laughed. "All right. The truth it is, then. With obvious omissions about you being delinquents on the run." He raked his fingers through his hair. "Really, you have no idea how long negotiations go when you have to ask and then hear about everyone's aunt and second cousin."

I shrugged. "I'll remember it all, thanks to the Rik leaves."

OOO

I watched with mounting anxiety as passengers stepped through a gate in the rails into tiny watercrafts suspended on cables. These "life boats" swayed and knocked against the hull for over a minute before reaching the bottom. The dangling death trap awaited us, but I couldn't separate my white-knuckled grip from the railing.

And the water! After all that endless nothing of the open sea, this water raged like an angry toddler, beating white foamy fists on the rocky shore.

Maddy declared it only mildly dangerous. "This surf is fairly typical. Not stormy."

The steward glared at me. "Either board the lifeboat now, or return to your cabin for the duration of our stay."

I spun and faced Maddy. "That's an option? I could stay?"

Alf hooked his arm around my waist and heaved me unceremoniously into the lifeboat. "I'm not leaving you alone, and I'm not missing this. Come on, Caz. This is the adventure you always wanted."

"Of course. Throw *that* in my face." I focused on breathing slowly while Alf made funny faces at me. By the time our lifeboat smacked against a partially submerged rocky platform, I was laughing.

A spray of icy saltwater flew over our heads and drenched us on its way back down. Shrieking at the cold, I scrambled after the other passengers out of the boat. My feet felt the immediate sting of ankle-deep ocean water pulling at me, as if trying to drag me back over the ledge. Before I could panic, Maddy ushered me inland out of the water and onto a gritty surface that clung to my wet boots.

"What is this stuff?" I asked.

"Sand," whispered Maddy. "Pretend like you've seen a lot of it before. It's very common on Tye."

Alf splashed up to us, carrying our waterproof backpacks. "Where to, Maddy?" He handed Maddy and me our backpacks.

"Up to the top," said Maddy, leading us.

My feet sank into the sand but released almost as easily, sending thousands of tiny, glistening crystals flying with each step. I ducked quickly and scooped up a handful to examine as we walked. *Sand.* Each tiny grain, so insignificant, and yet together, it covered an island.

Now distanced from the spitting, hissing water, I could see the beauty of my surroundings. Tall grasses poked up where the sand blended into rusty brown rock. Steps carved into the steep slope zig-zagged their way up to another green area that faded from view above us. I loved the feeling of my leather boots on the stone steps as we climbed. The rich aroma of solid earth delighted me, and I could almost taste the plants in the wind. We went slowly, enjoying the varied vibrant flowers that sprouted at ridiculous angles from the rocky wall beside us, like colorful three-day stubble on a man's cheek.

Panting, we reached the top step and stood on an enormous rolling plateau. Dark green grasses moved like waves in the wind, and the belltroes now flapped in the air below us because we were so high up.

A well-beaten path led up to an enormous wall made of the native stone. Through a wide opening, we could see movement. *A city!*

"A fortress against the elements," said Maddy. "The storms here are brutal, but city walls provide good shelter. The original colonists blasted away part of the island to create enough rubble to build this city."

I nodded appreciatively. "It's very solid."

Alf smoothed his hand over the stone. The impressive outer wall probably stood almost twenty meters high and at least two meters thick. The individual buildings inside looked like stone cylindrical canisters with flat tops and lots of windows. They lined up more or less in rows, creating thoroughfares of activity.

"What about agriculture?" I asked. "What do they eat?"

"There are vegetable gardens on many of the rooftops," said Maddy. "And they also harvest plants from the sea. There are also some crops and livestock on the other side of the city. It's all very well organized."

A group of men and women emerged from the opening in the wall clad in the strangest coversuits I'd ever seen. They jogged past us, veering right along another path.

Alf and I stared after them.

"Those are some of the local fishers," explained Maddy. "Most fishing is done on boats, but with the belltroes above, that means there's probably a shoal of kelpies washing in."

"What's with their weird coversuits?" Alf was already trailing after them.

I winked at Maddy. "We might as well follow. He'll be of no use to us until he's seen what they're doing."

Sure enough, Alf became animated. "Is that rubber up over their heads?" asked Alf.

"The wetsuits are protection against the cold of the water," explained Maddy. He led us to a railing that enclosed a natural balcony overlooking the water below. Several little children in purple coats huddled there and watched eagerly. We stood behind them, still able to see where another submerged platform of rock jutted out into swirling black waters.

"There he is!" cried one of the children. "That's my uncle on the left."

"The one that's marrying my sister?" said another. "He'll be my brother soon!" The children gripped the railing, resting their chins on their wrists.

Maddy pointed over their heads to a dark patch in the water below. "I was right. See? That's the shoal of kelpies. The belltroes won't dive after them here because they'd crash on the rocks."

Alf smirked. "I bet the kelpies love the shallows."

"That they do," grinned Maddy. "And so do the fishers."

Somewhere between the top and the bottom of the cliff, the fishers had acquired a rectangular net which the eight of them carried flat as they jogged toward the submerged platform. Suddenly, the first two bolted forward at high speed, plunging into the knee-deep water on the flat stone. As they ran, the net extended with them. A second later, the next followed after them, further pulling the net open telescopically. This continued in perfect rhythm, unfolding a much longer net than I'd imagined until they stood covering the length of the platform. With one smooth movement, they dropped the nets, twisted and lifted. All along the net, the weight of hundreds of kelpies bulged.

"Amazing!" Alf gaped in awe.

I did, too. The fishers now shifted their grips, turned, and began marching back up the sands to the cliff-side steps.

The children cheered. "That's a good haul!" cried one.

"Did you see how fast they were? Someday, I want to do that."

"I know! And that was *my uncle!*"

Alf craned his neck to see the strange serpentine procession make its way up from the surf. "They probably earned a week's wages in those few minutes!"

Maddy chuckled. "Perhaps more. But the kelpies rarely come in such numbers. They were lucky they could get ready that fast."

"They're obviously well-trained," I said as the fishers reappeared on the plateau, glossy and dark to match their catch. They showed signs of strain from the exertion. Without thinking, I moved forward to help. Alf, too, ran to their aid.

"One of you has a nephew who's very proud of what you just did," I said.

A young man about Alf's size grinned and waved at the purple-clad children. "That's my Dog!"

"Dog?"

"He follows me like a puppy, so I call him Dog."

The fishers continued walking, unbothered by my intrusion.

I thrust my fingers through the weave of the net and added my strength to the march. Alf did the same on the other side, a little further up the line. We threw off the rhythm of their pace for a moment, but those closest to us nodded thanks and shifted themselves to give us room. The Gypsy Pearl made it light work for me, but I matched grimace for grunt with the others so as not to arouse suspicion. Even so, the uncle said, "You're strong. What do you trade in? Building blocks?"

The fishers laughed and stopped walking as a large flat-bed cargo cart rolled up. Alf and I stepped back to watch them hoist the net tube of fish onto the cart, doubling it back against itself and fastening the mesh to hooks on the cart. At last they slapped their hands clean on their wet suits, and the cart drove away.

"You really know what you're doing," said Alf.

"Practice," said Dog's uncle. The others walked after the cart, stretching and punching each other proudly on the back. "We practice every week. Then we just add the fish!" He held out his hand. "I'm Hugh."

Alf shook his hand. "I'm Alf, and this is Caz. We hear you're getting married."

Hugh nodded. Releasing blonde, curly hair from the tight wetsuit hood, he said, "That's right. My Mary has consented to be a fisher's wife. I'm a lucky man, indeed."

Alf's eyes flickered at me, and I bit back a rush of warmth. My current age and task list didn't leave room for too much romance, but that didn't stop me from imagining the future.

Maddy sauntered up. "Is that Hugh Woolway?"

The fisher leaped forward and embraced Maddy. "You're here, too, Maddy? Do you know these two traders-cum-fish-haulers?"

I gaped at Maddy. "Do you know everyone *everywhere?*"

"Maddy is a well-known trader," said Hugh. "He always has the best goods, and he trades fairly."

With a wave, Maddy changed the subject. "Are you going to introduce us to any new additions to your family?"

"You mean anyone interested in trading, no doubt," joked Hugh. "The newest additions are still gumming milk bars."

Hugh and Maddy dove into a cheerful and complicated exploration of the condition of Hugh's family tree, though he clearly wanted to talk about Mary most of all.

Alf nudged me. "Seems like Maddy is a goodwill ambassador as much as a gypsy merchant."

"He is," I agreed. "And he's pretty wonderful, isn't he? If everyone could know a gypsy like him, people everywhere in the system would love gypsies."

"Maybe that's the key to building better relations between the different groups. Get the friendly, honest people out there making contacts?"

"Instead of the politicians?" I winked.

We shifted our packs and trotted to catch up with Maddy and Hugh. Scilly's layout definitely appealed to me. The buildings felt both ancient and alive, and the pale yellow, sandy streets bustled with activity. Slow-moving flatbed carts pulled by simple one-man control seats dominated the transportation. Some carried fish, others chairs, bolts of cloth, and even a group of children all in purple coats, dangling their legs off the edge and waving at pedestrians. The buildings varied in height but most had about the same circumference. I couldn't identify the purpose of all of them, but I saw a fish-drying shop, a school, a clothing manufacturer, and a place to buy food, both cooked and raw.

The people wore red, pale greens, and vibrant purples dyed from sea snails, according to Hugh, though I didn't want to know the process. No fear of outsiders worried the citizens here though I noticed they were all mostly pale-skinned and light-haired.

"You fit right in here," I said, nudging Alf with my elbow. I cast him a sideways glance, wondering if he'd opt to stay here instead of continuing on with me. His eyes sparkled with interest at everything around him, but his fingers tangled themselves with mine.

"Here's home!" Hugh pushed open a door in one of the buildings and led us inside. My jaw dropped in wonder. The place hardly seemed architecturally feasible. The massive cylindrical outer walls formed the frame, but inside, ramps swirled up to different levels. Curved walls rolled on tracks to form new spaces or open up a room, and a central core of power banks supplied energy for technology as sophisticated as anything I'd ever seen on the Arxon: holographic displays, food processors, even health-monitoring apparatus.

We learned quickly that this tower housed four generations of the Woolway family, totaling thirty-nine people if I counted correctly. Everyone buzzed with excitement about the upcoming addition of Mary to the home.

Dog—everyone called him that—handed us a hot beverage to drink. With a serious tone, he said, "When Hugh and Mary have children, I'll have more cousins than any of my friends.

"And how will they all fit?" I asked, not knowing what else to say.

"Grandma Nathani will drift away soon," said Dog. "She's passed her Age of Purpose."

Alf stifled a surprised snort, and I pressed my lips together to hide a smile. *Was that a euphemism to say she's really old?* Deciding not to pursue the matter, I listened to Maddy and Hugh exchange stories about shared acquaintances for over an hour. Other members of his family, many of them with similar bold yellow curls, came and went, shifting walls as needed and utilizing the equipment for entertainment, study and food preparation. I felt like we were inside of a living machine. Several members of his family piped in comments from wherever they were as if the conversation included them. Apparently it did. No one minded eavesdropping because no one expected privacy. Cozily intrusive or intrusively cozy—it was the only thing that irked me about the place.

Hugh turned to me. "So, Caz. It's wonderful to see a new face here on Scilly, especially one as beautiful as yours. Tell us about your family. Do you come from a southern isle, too?"

A low rumble sounded, and I shot Alf a glare. *Are you seriously going to growl with jealousy at a simple compliment?*

The rumble grew louder, and it didn't come from Alf.

"Ah, we'll have to wait on that answer," said Hugh with a patient frown. Cupping his hands to his mouth to amplify his voice, he called, "Batten the hatches! Disconnect!"

Instantly, the motion in the home accelerated. The curved partitions on their tracks slid to lock against the outer walls, blocking the windows. An aunt and two children scrambled to pick up items from the floor and clear a table bolted to a moving wall. Hugh and his older brother went to the central core and began powering down the various devices until we could only see dim shadows.

"What's going on?" I asked, a twinge of fear cracking my voice. Though they all moved with calm precision, their urgency unnerved me.

The rumbling grew louder.

"Storm coming," said Hugh. "That's probably what drove the kelpies here. Would you rather be up or down?"

When I scrunched my face with confusion, Maddy whispered, "Would you rather be down below, or go higher in the building to watch?"

"What's safer?" I asked.

"The whole house is safe. It's a matter of preference," said Hugh.

Dog and another little one tumbled down a ramp, and each grabbed one of Hugh's hands. "Come on!! You're going to miss it!"

Hugh chuckled and let the boys drag him up the ramp to the next level.

Alf tucked his arm in mine. "Let's watch!"

I swallowed an objection and allowed Maddy and Alf to lead me up three flights of ramps to a circular room that filled the entire top floor of the building. People lay back on enormous pillows, peacefully watching through the only remaining exposed windows of the house. The room provided a panoramic view of the city and sky. I could see many circles of green on the rooftops where gardens flourished. No evidence of electricity winked in the city below, and only a few straggling people ran between the buildings, ducking against the driving rain.

The real spectacle, however, moved overhead. Clouds rolled and billowed with black and silver, advancing furiously with intermittent roars that seemed to shake even the solid rock island. Suddenly a web of white light cracked the darkness into a hundred pieces, and all the children squealed with delight. Some of the adults murmured appreciatively.

"Aren't these storms dangerous?" I hissed at Maddy. I had experienced only one in my life, back on Caren while I was still at Lamond Reformatory. It was the day I tried to save a bully named Ora when a bough broke from a tree and fell on her. It was before I knew the strength of the Gypsy Pearl inside of me or became so acquainted with death.

"Storms help Scilly," explained Maddy softly. Alf tucked in closer and listened, too. "Most of the homes have been fitted with lightning rods to capture the power of the storm," continued Maddy, pointing at the ceiling.

"You mean we're in a building that's *trying* to get hit?" A sudden fatigue threatened to engulf me.

Alf stroked my hair. "Stay with us, Caz. Calm. Calm."

"It's all right," said Maddy. "We're perfectly insulated here. On any roof that doesn't have a vegetable garden, they have special reservoirs to catch the fresh water. These storms bring power and life."

I tried to take comfort in what he said, but each flash of white only lit the memory of the dark blood seeping from Ora's side. Trembling, I pressed my face into Alf's shoulder and focused on breathing normally. The booming thunder grew louder, and the enthusiasm in the room baffled me.

"Caz," whispered Alf. "You're digging a hole in my arm. Take it easy."

I let go of him, apologizing but not daring to open my eyes. *This storm is different. I'm sheltered. It's safe.*

"Caz," said Alf, his voice warm. "You can't calm the storm outside, but you can calm the storm inside of you, yeah?"

I smiled despite my fear. *Calm the storm inside.* I thought of working in the duspy field with him, now a fond memory. And I thought of the time he kissed me on the snowy pass on Craggy. And I thought of King and the faneps dancing. A faint, happy melody crept into my mind and settled there. Something in its tenderness tied me to the people I loved, and I let the peace lift away the fear.

OOO

36 NATHANI'S PURPOSE

Night fell, and the home echoed with cheerful, windy music. Rich aromas floated up the ramps to where we still sat on the top level. The rest of the house resumed its activity, but now Maddy, Alf and I sat with Hugh and his grandmother, Nathani, who dozed on a giant pillow across the room. Despite what Dog had said, she didn't appear ready to die any time soon. Old, yes. At the brink of death, no.

"Where's your family, Caz?" asked Hugh.

"Uh. They're all in transit, actually," I said. "Any chance I can charge my comlink?"

Hugh's face showed I'd breached island etiquette.

"Her family trades in pharmaceuticals, like our teas and powders," said Maddy smoothly. "It takes them all over the System. They can be hard to track."

With a wave of his hand, Hugh indicated where I could connect my comlink to the central power core—powered by lightning!—and then he leaned back on a pillow. "So where were they the last time you talked?"

Maddy gave me a warning cough, so I improvised an evasion. "My father is a really good healer, and my sister stays with him to take care of the home. Her name is Felly, and she gets top marks in school." It was the kind of comment I'd heard the others make, so I hoped it sounded right.

Hugh nodded. "And your mother?"

"I-I'm not sure where she is right now. She went to visit more family on Caren, I believe."

Hugh frowned. "How strange that your family has divided itself between planets. Why not stay together and help each other grow well?"

"We...uh..."

"It's the gypsy way, Hugh," said Maddy complacently. "You know how we are. Bound by love, but we often separate for brief periods of time to do business. We always come back together."

"Don't you ever leave the island?" asked Alf. "Travel around? For fishing ventures at least?"

"It's not our custom to go off alone, without our families," said Hugh. "Not until we pass the Age of Purpose, like Grandma Nathani over there."

That strange phrase again. I raised an eyebrow but said nothing.

"Your comlink's ready," said Maddy, pointing to my silver egg. "They charge quickly here." Moving to stand, he glanced to Hugh for permission.

"May we call to find Caz's mother?"

"Yes, yes," said Hugh. "Then it'll be time to eat. We can hear about *you*," he added with a smile at Alf. He ambled down the ramp leaving us alone with the sleeping grandmother and my comlink.

"Who should we call first?" I asked. "Maybe Brade?"

Maddy nodded, his lips pressed in a thin line. "He's still on his way back to Caren, but he can probably find out whether your mother is there without raising suspicion."

I handed Maddy the comlink and let him enter the connecting coordinates. A moment later, the blue cone of light sprang up, and Brade's face stared wearily out at us.

"Maddy? Is that—?"

"We're all here, Brade," said Maddy, reaching to Alf and me to cram us into the line of sight for the sensor. He glanced over at Nathani before continuing. "What's the word on—?"

"Discretion *highly* advised," said Brade, firmly gesturing for us to back away from the sensors. Alf and I stepped aside and watched from a safe angle as Brade continued. "The governor and president have met in private council. It's unclear if King was present, too, but developments do not look promising for the queen."

Governor, president, King, queen. All the grand titles for Mom, Saloma, the fanep and myself.

"What do you know?" Maddy leaned closer to the comlink, lowering his voice.

Brade sighed. "The queen should proceed with caution until the reason for the governor's trip can be verified." The blue image blurred suddenly, re-forming a second later. "I need to disconnect. Not all connections are secure."

"Brade!"

"Both the governor and the president are on their way to Tye now."

The comlink swallowed Brade's image, and I was left with a lump in my throat. *Mom and Saloma are both coming to Tye—together?*

"Do you think it's safe to get back on *The Equation*?" asked Alf. "So many people on board. Who knows if any of them have connections to Saloma?"

Maddy sighed. "If Saloma knows Caz is still alive, she'll use any resource she can to—"

I held up a finger to silence him and shuddered involuntarily. "Where is King in all of this? Dead? Is he captive with Saloma because Mom turned him in? Everything depends on him. What if he never shows up?"

Alf sighed. "Too many questions, Caz. Pick one."

Tears stung my eyes, but I braced myself with reason. "All right. Let's be practical. How else could we get to Ikekane South, if not on *The Equation*?"

"I could take you."

We all startled and turned to the feeble figure across the room. Grandmother Nathani sat up and rubbed knuckles in her eyes as she yawned.

How much did she hear?

Maddy moved to Nathani, offering a hand to help her up. "Nathani, good to see you again. You've been sleeping since we arrived."

"Off and on, yes," said Nathani. "Did I hear you need passage south?"

Maddy darted a concerned glance at me. "We were wondering if there are any other ways to travel but the supply ship," he said casually. "But your people here on Scilly don't leave the island except as families, and we can't inconvenience that many people."

Nathani turned slowly to the blackness outside the window. "No, we don't venture out much anymore. But I did when I was your age." She tapped a gnarled finger on the glass. "I still know how to get to Menorca Colony. It's easy to navigate with the technology, anyway. It's just managing the boat that's hard."

Maddy shook his head. "Nathani, it's too far for you."

Nathani grunted. "Only too far for the faint of heart."

I stared at her.

Maddy placed his hand gently on the old woman's arm. "Nathani, I don't know if your health could—"

"Please." Her voice stirred a strange pity inside of me. She moved to my side and clasped my hand.

I tensed. "What do you mean?"

She fixed her gaze on me. "Everyone thinks I'm past the Age of Purpose, but this voyage will give me a new one." My confusion must have been clearly etched on my face because she continued. "It's our custom, once a body is too old to work, to get in a small rowboat and set ourselves adrift."

Hence Dog's comment about her drifting away. We collectively dropped our jaws in disbelief. "But why?"

"You see how small the island is. We cannot sustain too many people. Those who are past the Age of Purpose must make way for the new lives. It's what we do. It's expected."

"But—"

"Hugh and Mary will start their family soon. I'll be in the way."

How different this culture is from Wandel Hav, where the people revered the Elders as leaders!

"But the voyage could kill you," said Alf with uncharacteristic gentleness. "The storms. We have so far to go."

Nathani smiled at Alf. "I'll die at sea anyway. If I can help you on your way, I'll at least have one last purpose." She turned again to me. "Please."

264

○○○

Mary embraced Nathani. "Good-bye, and thank you," she said warmly. "You have made way for the next generation."

Hugh wrapped his arm proudly around Mary and nodded. Her beautiful, long, wavy hair shimmered gold next to eyes as bright as the sky. Dog beamed up at them happily, and Nathani's children—all adults—dabbed at their eyes with sleeves and fingers. The solemnity of the occasion unnerved me. They expressed sorrow, but totally accepted her choice. I saw none of the grief that had weakened Maddy so much when his mother died. No one begged her to stay, even if just until the wedding.

If we hadn't needed Nathani so much, I would have been outraged that they let her go without protest. A tear slid down my cheek as I considered her lost humanity. Surely she had once been as strong and agile as any of them. This should be a time for her to rest from her labors and rejoice in her posterity. Instead, everyone accepted her decision to float away to a sure and solitary death. The way of Scilly. It made no sense to me in light of the emphasis on family, and yet they all treated it like a business transaction. The colony registrar made the necessary records, and she received permission to take an old fishing boat from her youth since it went unused now.

Nathani had said nothing to her family about taking us with her, so we didn't offer up the information. It puzzled me that they did not wish to see her off, but it did simplify our inconspicuous departure. While Maddy made a show of negotiating some trades of southern silks for food supplies, Alf and I begged a chance to go explore. Once outside, Nathani led us slowly through the city to another large opening in the city wall.

We stepped through to a vastly different scene. A grassy expanse rolled downward gradually, marked with orderly low walls dividing it into even squares, each a slightly different color. Crops, no doubt. Between these, paths lined the way like a grid of circuitry.

The sky rested like a giant silvery dome over our part of the ocean. The air was as thick and misty as the steamy shower rooms on the Arxon, only cold.

I stopped and brushed the dampness from the stubble that now blurred Alf's tattoo. He leaned into my hand, making my heart flutter. "Strange place, isn't it?" I said. "They get so much right, and then this…discarding the old."

"Let's take extra good care of her," said Alf.

I hugged him. "Thanks for being so good."

"Me, good?" he teased. "I'm a fugitive of justice."

It seemed funny to think that we had escaped the Lamond Reformatory on Caren, but in the aftermath, none of the authorities worried about us.

Only a free gypsy leader pursued me—not to bring me to justice, but to murder me.

We walked for almost half an hour before the scenery changed. Dotted about the fields, two different species of animals munched and plodded aimlessly against the breeze. One resembled a sleeker version of a kangra, its broad bulk and gentle eyes seeming at odds with each other. These, Nathani called bovines.

"They give milk," she gave a wry look. "And when they pass *their* Age of Purpose, they give us meat."

"Ew." I'd never stopped to think much about where meat came from since we didn't eat it often.

"The other creatures are ovis," said Nathani. The ovis stood like white balls of fuzz about a third as tall as the bovines. "Their coats can be shaved off periodically and used for weaving cloth. Go ahead and touch one. They're perfectly tame." She stopped and sat on one of the low stone walls, tossing a leg over to stand on the inside perimeter of one of the fields. When a few of the ovis approached, she showed no fear. "They probably think I've brought them a special treat."

On the other side of the path, one of the bovines stopped chewing and looked at us. Alf reached out his hand and nuzzled its enormous nose with his palm.

"He won't bite?" I asked.

Nathani chuckled. "*She* eats nothing but grass and the occasional felly flower."

"Felly! I have a sister named Felly." I stepped forward, daring to touch the bovine. It turned, blinking with ridiculously long eyelashes and let out a soft moan. I jumped back as if electrified by the sound. "Did I scare her?"

"She's saying hello," said Nathani. "Go ahead and pet her. That part between the nostrils is particularly soft." She continued to dig her fingers affectionately into the back of the ovis' neck.

Alf gave me a half grin and stroked the bovine's nose. His eyebrows slid upwards, and his full smile grew, hiding his tattoo in his dimple. "She's so soft."

"You like big noses, huh?" I teased.

Nathani cupped her hands and called out a strange long note that rose and fell. The scattered ovis raised their heads and shifted their attention. "That's how they call them in when it's time for shearing," she said. "Let's see if any come."

Sure enough, several more ovis trotted over, their long ears bobbing up and down as they returned Nathani's call. My stomach tightened as they surrounded her, nearly knocking her over. I pinched my nose at their dank smell, and stifled a yelp at the same time. But once they positioned themselves at the wall to watch us, they simply looked at us expectantly, showing no sign of aggression.

Alf laughed. "They're like little children crowding around their teacher."

"Yes, without the purple coats," said Nathani.

"I saw that. Why do all the children wear purple coats?" I asked.

"The wool is dyed with sea snails, and it makes the material more resistant to water and stains." She shrugged. "It keeps them dry and somewhat cleaner, which is helpful at that age."

"Very practical," I said.

"That's Scilly. Practical." Nathani's tone hinted at bitterness. "Shall we continue?" She climbed back over the wall and began to walk again.

Alf and I followed, surprised to find that the group of ovis and the bovine came, too. At least as far as the wall would let them.

I pointed back at them. "Are they going to sail with us?"

Nathani chuckled. "They're not the brightest animals. They follow their leader, whoever it is, wherever he goes."

"What if the leader is lost?" asked Alf.

"They get lost together," said Nathani. "Not much of a problem on an island this size."

As we neared the waterline, the terrain became steeper and rockier. Nathani halted. "I forgot about this." She swept a hand through the air. "The original colonists left these boulders as a barrier to prevent livestock from wandering down onto the beach and drowning." She chuckled.

"Practical again," said Alf.

"Ever practical," agreed Nathani. "But not if you want to get to the shore on old legs." She appraised Alf's physique. "I don't suppose you can carry me?"

"You're helping us, ma'am. I'll do anything you ask."

His gentleness engraved a grin on my face.

Alf mistook my smile. "Don't think I can carry her? You want to try?"

Nathani's eyes widened. "Nonsense. You're much bigger."

"Ah, but she's stronger."

Fortunately, Nathani took it as a joke and reached to Alf. I carried his backpack and scouted ahead for the surest footing. The ovis, now out of sight, called to us mournfully. I thought about how some people need to follow, and others need to lead. Others simply *want* to lead, whether they should be followed or not.

OOO

"This is my little ship," said Nathani proudly when Maddy joined us an hour later. "My brother and I used to go out with our friends to fish almost every day in the summer." An ancient fire ignited her eyes and her movements carried more energy. "She can get us where we need to go. The

Sea Callabus is a good ship."

Maddy eyed the little boat. "That's a fishing boat?"

"An old one, yes," said Nathani. "It's fully mechanized. The hull is still intact."

"There's a sail," countered Maddy.

"Automated boom and rigging," said Nathani calmly. "We can do this. It carries eight plus a day's haul hooked to the sides."

"But it has a sail," repeated Maddy.

"What's a sail?" I asked.

Nathani's eyebrows shot up even as Maddy ran his palm over his face. I'd made an obvious blunder.

"The big roll of cloth there," said Maddy pointing. "It attaches up there to catch the wind. That's how the boat moves. With the wind."

I shrugged. "So?"

Maddy inhaled deeply. "There's no motor—no engine to propel the boat."

I swallowed. "I thought it was fully automated."

"Oh, there's a solar-battery that powers the gears and pulleys, but..." Nathani took a step closer, eying me. "You're a spacey, aren't you?"

Before my heart could sink, a sense of confidence trickled into my brain. "Yes, ma'am. I am."

"So am I," said Alf.

She looked at us steadily. "But you defected?"

I couldn't help chuckling. "In a way, yes."

"What are you doing here on Tye running from dangerous people?"

Maddy sagged against the boat and rubbed his eyes. "It's a very long and complicated story, Nathani."

"Like yours?" Nathani asked, touching his cheek. "Everyone who knows you knows you're no killer, despite the mark." She shifted to Alf. "What's that mark on your cheek? I've never seen just a *C*."

Alf fingered the fuzz that did not quite hide the green tattoo. "I fought in defense of a friend. My victim recovered, but only after they'd started branding me. Instead of prison, I was sent to a reformatory on Caren." He glanced at me. "And after a rotation, I escaped."

Nathani showed no sign of alarm or distrust. "Just like I'm doing." She turned to me. "And you? Why are you with him if he's a fugitive and people are after him?"

"They aren't after him. They're after me." I surveyed the boat lying sideways on the sand. The sea kept creeping closer as if to touch it, but then retreated with feigned apathy. "Help us get to the next island, and I'll explain everything."

ooo

The *Sea Callabus*, barely ten meters long, felt very small in the midst of so much water. The mechanisms all positioned themselves hydraulically while Maddy checked over the sail. It had blotches of mildew in several places and a few holes. I refrained from making the obvious joke about the sail looking past its Age of Purpose and positioned myself where I didn't have to smell its moldy stink.

Nathani spoke and moved little except to direct our actions. She navigated by turning a wheel like the kind on an airlock door, but once she'd set our course, she mostly just held the wheel steady. Meanwhile, I recounted the major events from the time of my first meeting with King up to the present.

Raised on Tye all her life, Nathani knew of faneps and some of their customs. She also remembered my grandmother, Levia. "Queen Levia. I didn't know her personally, of course, but I admired her. Many of us did. She really understood people and how to help them." She winked over at Maddy. "She was a good gypsy."

"You don't, by any chance, know what the three Powers are, do you?" I asked. "I've only seen two."

Nathani shook her head. "I didn't know she had any special abilities. She was just wise and kind."

I smiled, proud of my heritage. "I hope I can live up to her legacy. At least the character part, if not the leadership."

"It'll be interesting," said Nathani, "to see what happens to the faneps. If they truly are restored to a higher state of intelligence or communication, that will be fascinating. They're already advanced, from what I hear."

I couldn't help grinning. "You're the first non-gypsy I've met who likes faneps."

"Faneps are amazing," she said. "For one thing, they create cities *inside* the rock of a volcano, even as it extends below the water."

Maddy nodded. "They swim very well, too. They can hold their breath for a really long time."

"I bet they could build habitats on the ocean floor." Nathani warmed to the idea. "There may be no stopping their progress."

I shuddered at the idea of living underwater and then frowned at a thought. "Do they need to communicate to do all of that? They already work telepathically. I saw it in their cavern on Caren."

"But they'll have to assert their rights with humans," added Nathani. "They've always been seen as a subspecies. Who will advocate for them? I mean, besides you?" She gazed out at the horizon, loosely gripping the wheel. Her eyes watered, whether due to the breeze or emotion, I couldn't guess.

"Why wouldn't humans want to be able to communicate with the faneps?" My heart thrilled. "Think of all the things we could learn from them. They have so much knowledge that's hidden to us."

"Knowledge is wonderful," agreed Nathani. "But it isn't the same as wisdom."

Alf yawned. "What do you mean?"

She tapped her forehead. "Knowledge is up here, and it's all facts and figures and skills. It's *what* and *where* and *how*." Spreading her palm across her chest, she said, "Wisdom is the *why*. It's compassion and selflessness. If knowledge grows faster than wisdom, it ceases to breed kindness. Who knows what will happen to humanity if we try to understand the fanep abilities too quickly."

I considered her sacrifice of giving up her final days of life to help strangers instead of being with her family. "Is it wisdom for the people of Scilly to set their elders adrift?"

Nathani sighed, and the rest of us watched her closely. Even the breeze hushed, waiting for her answer. But none came.

OOO

"We've got trouble coming," said Nathani.

I saw no approaching ship. "What is it?"

"Quickly," she said, moving back to the wheel. "We need all hands at the ready."

"But you—"

"Something's coming."

"What do you mean, 'something'?" The boat suddenly lurched. Grabbing the bench, I squatted. "Did we bump into a rock or something?"

"Something bumped into us," said Maddy.

"A shoal of kelpies," guessed Alf.

"Close," said Nathani. "Gouldings. Bigger and more aggressive in their own defense."

"Defense?" I held tighter as the boat started to tilt back the opposite way. "What are they defending? We're not attacking them."

The boat heaved again, and I went sprawling at Nathani's feet. She almost fell on top of me, but caught herself on the wheel, which then spun to one side. Again the boat moved.

"Set the sail!" she shouted. "Caz! Maddy! Somebody!"

Maddy hurdled the bench and got to work. Thick twine net covered the floor space. I dropped to my knees and crawled awkwardly across the nets as the boom shifted overhead and caught the wind. With white knuckles, I gripped the edge of the boat beside Alf and peered over.

"They move like one big creature," marveled Alf, not looking scared so much as impressed.

"One big creature that can capsize us," said Nathani, yanking the wheel.

"'Capsize'?"

Her voice trilled. "They're trying to knock us over."

I tried to gulp back the mounting fear inside of me, but nothing in my experience told me this was supposed to be a calm moment. The dark mass below the surface of the water shifted purposefully, and through the jumble of nets, I heard a rapid thudding and clicking sound. "Now what?" I felt dizzy and tingly, but I wasn't sure if it was adrenaline or the vibrations coming through the bottom of the boat.

"When gouldings see a predator coming, they all begin biting it at once," said Nathani. "The predator either leaves to avoid being harassed, or dies from blood loss."

I jerked back from the edge and felt the strength in my legs give out. "The gouldings are *killers?*"

"No, no!" cried Nathani, her eyes examining the swells of water around us. "They're protecting themselves. They won't attack if they sense no danger."

"But they *are* attacking, and we're not predators," said Alf.

The boat tilted so sharply that the ocean seeped over the side into the boat. In the churning water, thousands of gleaming eyes and teeth met my gaze. Just as my heart felt like it would leap out of my throat to appease their fury, an unexpected peace muffled my senses. Though my legs were numb, I reached to the water.

As if from a great distance, I heard Nathani warn me. "The gouldings might bite."

"The boat's going to tip!"

"We needed to rebalance!"

And then I heard something else: fear, but not my own—a collective urgency to survive.

Stretching my hand out, I touched the water that slapped angrily against the boat. The sea bubbled, and I became aware of Alf holding on to me, keeping me from going overboard.

We're not here to hurt you. Don't be afraid.

The gouldings brushed against my hand in the water, scraping my fingers with their scales. Their mouths were open in silent cries, and I answered them in kind. *Don't be afraid. We're just passing through. We're on a journey. We won't hurt you.*

The boat rocked violently back into an upright position, and Alf pulled me into his arms, gasping.

Sound returned to my awareness. Nathani's voice cracked. "I've never seen anything like it!"

"They just swam away!" Maddy panted.

My eyes ached in a sudden light, and I closed them, feeling exhausted. "People are like gouldings," I slurred. "Sometimes they gather together and attack out of fear."

Though the water had reverted to its gentle swells, my body still rocked with turmoil. No, it was Alf. He held me, swaying side to side in a tight embrace. With my ear on his chest, I could hear his voice amplified.

"It's like she *talked* to the fish!"

Maddy murmured something in reply.

Alf's hand stroked my hair back. "I wonder if that's the third Power. Talking to animals."

"It would hardly make sense coming from the Earlie syrup. Craggy has no native life forms," said Maddy.

Alf's lips brushed against my forehead, warm but trembling. "Since when did any of this pearl cycling stuff make sense?"

I shook my head. "It didn't feel new. It felt familiar, like when I communicated with the faneps. I don't think it was the third Power."

"But if it *was*," insisted Alf, looking at me with an intimidating amount of awe, "then you'd really be able bring peace to the Worlds—all the planets, all the species. It's amazing!"

"I don't know why you're talking about peace amongst the Worlds. They aren't at war."

"No, but they aren't unified, either," said Maddy.

"Do they have to be?" The words tumbled out because I was tired, but the question hung like a knife, ready to cut the future of the Granbo System in two very different ways. I didn't want to be the one wielding the blade.

"Why does Cycling the Gypsy Pearl have to mean being a queen, Maddy? Why does it have to mean everything has to rest on my shoulders? Why can't I just help the faneps?"

Maddy's mouth dropped open, but he didn't answer.

I stumbled over my words to erase their rudeness. "I just wonder how anyone could ever keep all the Worlds and the ICS system unified in purpose."

Nathani's lips twisted. "You mean like Age of Purpose?"

"No. I mean making sure they use their resources wisely and keep some sense of order."

Nathani breathed out a skeptical laugh. "Unity is a vague term, isn't it? What does it really mean? Can humanity ever really be united? What would it take? What would we have to give up to achieve it?"

Her words punched me in the stomach. As my mind spun through memories of the different cultures in the Granbo System I'd experienced, I doubted more than ever that I'd be able to reign over the whole thing—with or without a Gypsy Pearl.

ooo

37   DABBLING IN DIPLOMACY

The sunset lit up the horizon like a campfire, and we all sat there, lulled by the colors and the salty breeze.

"That'll mean good sailing tomorrow," said Nathani, sipping milk she had warmed on a shipboard heating disc.

"Are you sure the boat knows where it's going?" asked Alf.

"It's on autopilot. Straight lines aren't hard to follow." She winked.

"What if a storm comes?" he persisted.

"It won't. Look at the sky," said Nathani. "A true sailor knows as much as the tech instruments. Read the sky, day or night, and it'll tell you many things." She went on to explain how different cloud formations and colors of sky foretold different weather systems, and how the stars formed constellations that could guide a ship even without comlinks or global positioning units. Unlike Mr. Virgil, who could make a planet sound boring, she drew her words with magic and romance. I watched her for a long time, my mouth unable to move from its starry grin even though my body had regained most of its mobility.

The sky faded gradually into the familiar blackness of space, and I considered the stars from this new perspective. Alf and I had grown up seeing the constellations from aboard our homes in space, of course, but never like this. Never breathing them in. The *Sea Callabus* gently rose and fell, water lapping her sides like a mother kissing her baby to sleep. As each new star appeared, Nathani would tell us its name and a story that connected it to the sea. Alf listened with rapt attention, and I knew he wouldn't need Rik leaves in his blood to help him remember it all.

ooo

"The Menorca colony is coming into scanner range." Maddy tapped the instruments on the navigation panel. "They get a lot of trade because they have a landing strip for planes and several convenient harbors."

"'Harbors'?"

"Docking bays for boats," said Maddy.

"The agricultural families will be hard at work planting," said Nathani. "When I was about your age, my brother and I would sometimes come all the way down here and watch them work."

"'Agricultural families'?" I sighed heavily. "Do I have to tell these people all about my family, too?"

"No, no. The term 'families' is much looser in Menorca," said Maddy. "They're more like groups of families. Each group owns part of an island."

"They *own* the land? It's not community property?" I couldn't even imagine.

Nathani smiled, and the creases of her face almost swallowed the glinting blue of her eyes. "I suppose on an ICS, no one can own a part of the ship or it would run the risk of falling into disrepair and thus endanger everyone."

I nodded. "Exactly. We're assigned living quarters based on our family needs."

"Right. There's limited space, and all of it must work perfectly. It's not unlike Scilly."

"Most island groups on Tye allow private land ownership," said Maddy.

"There's more than one island, right?" Alf knocked his bare feet together with suppressed enthusiasm.

"Are you just a little excited?" I teased. "Maybe they won't let you come ashore. You stink."

"We all stink," said Nathani with a laugh. "Isn't it fun?"

Maddy gestured to Alf and flipped open an image on his comlink. Pointing at the 3-D image, he explained. "There are three large islands and over ten islets and atolls spreading out west for the next 400 kilometers. Take a look."

"While you're at it," said Nathani, "try to glean some local vocabulary so you don't stand out like a bulbous squid worm in a flock of butterflies."

Huh? "What's a butterfly?"

Maddy and Nathani laughed and ordered us to study the archive. Alf and I settled with our backs against the side of the boat to watch the vid. Only three of the islands of the Menorca colony could be seen from space. The largest of these bore the colony's name. Limnos loomed next to it with half the area but twice the elevation and a semi-active volcano. In the satellite pictures, Flinders, the smallest of the main islands, was nothing but a scratch of white sand on the blue ocean under Limnos. It boasted the most beautiful beaches and the fewest regulations for visitors, so that's where we headed.

Alf and I got up on our knees and looked at the horizon. The summit of Limnos grew up from the expanse of ocean, a lone bubble in a simmering pot of blue soup. Nathani steered us in a wide arc for another few hours. The land mass was huge compared to Scilly. We moved around the island to where we could see a gold and green streak blocking the horizon: the island of Flinders.

The semi-enclosed water between these two islands bore the name Sleeping Bay, and I could feel why. As we glided across the teal tranquility, I ventured a peek overboard. For another hour, Alf and I sat shoulder-to-shoulder in pure delight. The view of the clear shallows teeming with colorful fish and the feel of his warm skin next to mine thrilled me. This was better than anything I had ever dreamed of while staring at Tye from the cafeteria window of the Arxon. Occasionally, a really large creature would slither beneath us, as if inspecting our boat, but then it would wander off. Hundreds of small boats like ours glided across the bay. Most used sails, but a few had motors, and others appeared to be propelled by men slapping sticks into the water.

A long howl tore the bay's dreamy restfulness, scaring several belltroes into flight.

"What was *that?*" My eyes widened.

Before anyone could answer, it sounded again. Over Nathani's shoulder, I saw a large sailboat approach. It caught the wind with two bright red and gold square sails.

"That must be Governor Pollenca's ship," said Nathani.

Men and women ran around on deck tugging at ropes and doing things our tiny automated craft did for itself. They executed the tasks efficiently, though, and soon the ship rested alongside the one vacant dock in front of us.

"I doubt we'll be allowed to dock opposite her," said Maddy.

I waved my fingers in front of Alf's face. "You're drooling, Alf. Let's get this thing up on the beach so you can go kiss the pretty boat."

He backhanded me playfully, and Nathani chuckled. She tucked her arm around Alf's waist. "Nice to find a kindred spirit."

Alf ruffled her hair. If she found it disrespectful, she showed no sign.

OOO

"Is it me, or is she really fat?" Alf watched Governor Pollenca stride down a plank onto the dock.

"I believe that's called really pregnant," I corrected.

Pollenca walked with out-turned toes and small steps, her fists pumping at her sides. Long brown hair flowed down her back like a grand cape. An entourage of three women flanked her, but as she reached the end of the dock where it connected to the land, she waved them off. Two men stepped forward eagerly. Even from our distance, it was clear they each wanted to be close to her, yet far from each other. They constantly repositioned themselves to catch her gaze, which shifted distractedly around the harbor. One stood tall and broad with lighter hair hanging over his ears. The other, bald, oily and unkempt, waddled rotundly beside her.

"That one looks like a predatory sea snail," said Nathani. When I barked a laugh, she winked. "Two representatives of agricultural families in dispute, no doubt," said Nathani.

We left off watching the spectacle and set to the task of bringing the *Sea Callabus* up onto the beach where the breakers disappeared into shining sheets of water. Maddy jumped overboard as we bumped gracelessly to a stop, the flattish bottom of the boat couching itself in the sand. The abrupt stop sent me rolling over the railing, and I landed on my back in the wet sand. A wash of salt brine reached rudely past me. Fortunately, my head didn't go under, but the force of the water dragged me in a half circle before I could regain my feet.

"I recommend feet-first disembarkation in the future," teased Maddy. He hauled a large coil of rope to secure the boat to a tree that pushed up through the sand. I guess it was a tree, anyway. Scrubby and squat, with several branches writhing in different directions, it shot up sprigs of green spikes. For a large insect, it would be a gloriously secure fortress, impenetrable by belltroes or children's hands. As a pulley, however, it lacked credibility.

Alf helped Nathani out of the boat so she could stay dry, and she waited patiently while he retrieved the supplies.

"Where are we going to stay?" I asked. "And will they mind that I'm dripping all over their floors?"

Maddy gestured inland. A road lay parallel to the shore with sea-facing buildings made of broad wood planks. It still amazed me that Surface dwellers used wood to build houses when even the smallest piece of carved wood was worth a great deal in space.

Space. This world was so different from anything on an ICS.

I nudged Alf. "Don't you love how we don't have to go through quarantine every time we move from place to place, no matter how gross and dirty we are?"

"I love everything about this world."

The short climb up to the road proved tricky because the sand grew deeper and finer, pulling us back down half of every step we took. I didn't mind, but in the end Nathani couldn't continue.

"I guess it's my turn to carry you," I said cheerfully.

"Do you really think—?" Her voice faded to a surprised squeak as I folded her over my soggy shoulder indecorously and marched up the sandy hill.

Maddy roared with laughter while Alf fretted that I'd hurt her. Nathani grunted and giggled until I set her down on the solid footing at the edge of the road. She reached over and slapped my rear end.

"Excuse me? A spanking?"

"I'm getting the sand off of you," she said with a sly wink. "It clings when you're wet like that, you know."

People went back and forth here on the strange ground. Like stone, but much smoother and more regular, it provided a perfect surface for the wheeled carts that the Menorcans pushed or pulled along.

The natives wore long-sleeved shirts and loose, flowing pants, with wide-brimmed hats to protect their eyes from the sun. Maddy and Alf both shed their gypsy vests, and Nathani rolled up her sleeves. My comlink registered a local temperature of 21 degrees Celsius—room temperature on the Arxon. *Perfect.*

A clattering caught my attention, and we turned to see something resembling a bovine, but with a longer neck and leaner body. Its feet beat the ground rhythmically, and it raced by, huffing with effort.

"Poor thing!" I cried. "Someone tied a cart to its neck! No wonder it's running." I remembered the boys who tied toys to the cat's tail in the Arxon rec hall.

Maddy and Nathani laughed, and Alf shook his head.

I pouted. "What? What don't I know now?"

"Everything," said Alf grinning. "That's a callabus, as in the *Sea Callabus*? People ride them and use them to haul loads all the time. They have them on Caren, too."

I groaned at my own ignorance. "I can't wait for the pearl cycling thing to be over so I can get on with exploring every stretch of land on all the planets. I feel like an idiot that I don't know any of this."

Alf dismissed my embarrassment with a wave of his hand. "You know it now. And you'll never forget it with that Rik brain of yours."

"The thing about Menorca," said Maddy, "is that people are fairly relaxed about visitors coming and going. Visitors provide new business. And for those not engaged in commerce, they provide new targets."

"Targets?"

"For thieves, yeah?" Alf swept his hand wide to indicate the bay and the dock. "A docking area sees so many people coming and going that it'd be easy to steal something and get away without anyone noticing."

Maddy chuckled. "Why Alf, you have the mind of a corrupt gypsy!"

Alf laughed and shook his head, his hair tumbling in his eyes and over his ears. As gritty as he was, he seemed to shine with radiant strength.

Maddy cleared his throat, and I looked up to see his eyes twinkling. *Had I been staring at Alf all stupid?*

I coughed and changed mental directions. "How are we going to find out what Saloma and Mom are up to?"

Alf lowered his voice. "Do you think they're in contact with the Gypsy Network HQ here on Tye?"

Maddy shook his head. "I don't know how to find out safely without revealing our location."

"How many routes are there from Wandel Hav to Ikekane South?" I asked. "I mean, Mom probably knows that's where I started because Dad would have told her. Wouldn't she deduce the logical path?"

"There are a few ways to get there by boat," said Nathani. "Or one could fly. It really depends on which colonies one prefers to use for stopping points."

"Is there one gypsies prefer?" asked Alf.

"Yes," said Maddy, stiffening. "We're following it." He ran his hands through his long dark curls. "I didn't even think of that precaution. We should switch courses, but I don't know if the *Sea Callabus* is going to be the right craft to get us off this route. She's so small."

"Fly? Get a bigger boat?" suggested Alf.

"Both very expensive options," said Maddy. He turned to me. "Oh my lady, I'm so sorry. I hope my lack of foresight doesn't cause us any trouble."

"No one knows we're here, do they?" Alf shrugged. "This is the perfect place for getting around unnoticed."

Another caballus lumbered by, slower this time. Behind it, a small two-wheeled cart with a seat and a covering against the sun rolled along.

Nathani clucked her tongue. "That was the governor! She really shouldn't be riding in her condition!"

ooo

The next morning, an uproar from down the hall woke me up. Maddy had rented us two tiny rooms next to the kitchen in an inn owned by a man named Jagaro. We'd all settled in for naps and ended up sleeping through the night. Now shouts emanated from the kitchen area. A moment later, Maddy and Alf pounded on our door.

"What? What happened?" I groused, letting them in with a yawn.

They slid inside, and Maddy leaned against the door. "Why did I pick this inn?"

"Because the food was good, and they didn't care that I was soaking wet?" I yawned again.

"This is terrible," he moaned.

"What? What happened?" I looked at Alf and mouthed, *Am I repeating myself?*

"Guess who's in the luxury suite upstairs," said Alf.

I blinked and let out a panicked yelp. "Saloma?"

"No, no. Not *that* bad," said Maddy. "But Governor Pollenca stayed here last night, and there's a big fancy breakfast with disputing representatives here in less than ten minutes."

"And...?"

"And there will be reporters covering this because she's up for re-election in two months. This will be highly publicized on Tye," said

Nathani flatly. She tossed aside her covers and sat up wearily.

"Oh." *Oh.* "Not good."

"Let's make sure you're not caught in the vids, yeah?"

"Can't we just hide out in our rooms?" I asked, eyeing my bed longingly.

Nathani shook her head. "These kinds of things can go on for days. We'd have to come out to eat or use the washrooms, and then some reporter might stick a recorder in our face to ask us what we think."

"I guess security isn't very tight on Flinders," I said.

"No, it'll be nothing like the Arxon," admitted Maddy. "We need to get out of here. At least move to a different inn. The place is already filling up with curious people."

We quickly grabbed our belongings and pressed our way through the crowded hall towards the front entrance. Sweaty smells mingled with artificial perfumes and someone stepped on my toe. As I stopped to wriggle it free, I felt a hand on my rear end. Instinctively, I grasped the attached wrist and wrenched it upwards. "Hey! That's private property!" I barked. To my astonishment, the hand belonged to a girl about my age, and her hand clutched my comlink. Surprise switched to defiance in her eyes until I glared her back down to fear. The death grip I had on her arm probably helped, too. I snatched back my comlink before letting go of her.

She jostled her way through the crowd in the opposite direction, but the delay had cost me. Before I could reach the door, a crowd of reporters swarmed into the common room with their lighting and recording devices. I turned my face towards the wall and tried to sidle behind the other people, but the crowd was too thick. They began shouting questions as Governor Pollenca waddled down the stairs from the upper level with the two agricultural family representatives.

"No questions yet," she called. Her voice resonated deeply, filling the room with authority. I glanced over my shoulder and saw her raise her hand strategically to block the vid recorders. She said something to the taller of the two representatives. He shook his head angrily, his hand moving to something on his hip.

"He's got a gun!" shouted a reporter.

A clamor of yelling ensued, and Pollenca let out a horrendous roar, freezing me to my spot against the wall.

"Governor, are you all right?" asked several reporters.

"It's time!" she shouted.

"Time for justice!" cheered the greasy man.

"No, it's *time!*" Pollenca's knees buckled, and she dropped out of my line of sight.

I scanned the faces of the crowd, hoping to find my friends, but I saw only agitated strangers.

Pollenca groaned loudly, and a woman's voice shrieked, "Get back! Give her room! Can't you see she's about to have her baby?"

Nathani?

"Everybody out!" shouted Jagaro, the innkeeper.

The crowd dispersed reluctantly as the Governor's entourage encouraged them forcibly out the door at gunpoint. I had been standing near Jagaro, but started to follow the crowd out with my head down. Hearing a grunt, I turned and saw Pollenca, now reclined on Nathani's lap.

"Out!" shouted a man, grabbing my arm.

"No, wait!" called Nathani. "She's with me! I need her help here."

The man glanced at Pollenca, who nodded. My mind raced. *What is Nathani doing? Why would she single me out?* I raised a hand to the side of my face, blocking it from the view of the departing reporters. A moment later, the inn common room was empty except for Pollenca, Nathani, me and Jagaro.

With calm efficiency, Nathani ordered Jagaro and me to bring pails of hot water and clean towels. She led Pollenca's wilting form back up the stairs to the luxury suite. I acted as a runner, carrying things back and forth while Jagaro directed his staff to keep everyone else downstairs. Each time I entered the room with more hot water or towels, Pollenca looked weaker and Nathani looked stronger.

"You're a doctor!" I whispered.

"A mid-wife," she nodded, soothing Pollenca's brow with a damp cloth.

Pollenca tensed, her teeth grinding.

"Bear down," murmured Nathani. "Breathe like I showed you." She looked up at me. "Come here and hold her hand."

"What good—?"

Pollenca exhaled a pained moan and grabbed for Nathani's arm. She squeezed the old woman with white knuckles, and I feared she'd do harm. Reaching in, I pried her fingers loose from Nathani and felt the vice close around my own hand. *Better me than Nathani.*

"Don't squeeze her back," warned Nathani.

Right. I might break her hand.

A give-and-take of breathing and pushing and soothing continued for an hour or more, and though I mostly just sat there being clawed at and mumbling encouragement, I found it exhausting. Nathani, however, was in her element, and her self-assurance kept me from fear. It most certainly empowered Pollenca, who regained her strength the closer the moment came. At last, in a rush of water and blood, the baby emerged looking wrinkled and alien, but perfectly whole.

OOO

With Nathani, Pollenca and baby all resting peacefully, I descended the stairs, stopping when I noticed the two representatives sulking on opposite sides of the common room. I don't know how they'd slipped back inside, but they didn't look ready to leave any time soon.

"We've waited long enough," said the greasy one. He heaved himself out of a chair and wiped his hands on either side of his belly. "Come on, Catalan. Let's get this over with."

"You really think we should disturb the governor, Toro?" asked Catalan. He sounded hopeful, but did not move.

Toro approached the staircase, but Jagaro hurried over from his desk and waved his hands in warning. "No, no. She must have time to rest. She just had a baby, after all. Tomorrow. Come back tomorrow."

"We've waited for ten months," said Toro. "She went and got herself pregnant to get out of talking to us. She *will* hear me." He stuffed his hand into his loose pocket and pulled out a gun.

"No, no!" cried Jagaro. "Let her sleep. It's bad luck to disturb a new mother."

"Bah!"

Toro shouldered past Jagaro. I stood, my feet on the bottom step, and folded my arms across my chest. "I'm sorry. It's bad luck to bother a new mother." The superstition didn't matter to me, but the gun did.

"Out of my way, girl," said Toro. "I need to talk to the governor."

I reached my arms out to touch the walls on either side of the stairs. "No. Come back tomorrow."

"I will not!" boomed Toro.

"Put your gun away."

"Don't patronize me, child," said Toro. "This is official business."

I spoke with stilted deliberation. "I'm not asking you to do anything hard. Do *I* have a gun?" I frisked my form-fitting pants for his benefit. "No. I'm not asking you to do anything that I'm not. Put the gun away. There'll be no killing here."

Toro glared at me and raised the gun to my face. Adrenaline should have spiked, but instead, I felt the Gypsy Pearl sharpen my senses. As Toro took a step closer, I knocked the gun off course with my right palm even as I brought my left forearm in to connect with his elbow. The crack of his bone sounded like a laser snap.

Cradling his arm, Toro backed away shouting. Catalan retrieved Toro's fallen gun and held it up over his head in a gesture of surrender.

I tilted my head to Jagaro. "Give the gun to him."

Catalan complied and then actually went to Toro's aid.

The two looked ready to unite against a common enemy, so I raised both hands. "I'm medically trained, and since I know what I broke, I can help you set the bone." I waved my empty fingers. "No guns."

Toro hesitated, then nodded and sank into a chair.

"Don't even think about disturbing the governor," I said. "Or I'll break your legs." I went to gather something I could use as a splint and bandage, wondering if this would get me sent to another reformatory for violent offenders.

OOO

"So what's the big conflict between you people, anyway?" I asked, securing the last fold of a sling on Toro's shoulder. He hadn't called for any authorities to cart me away, so I suspected he'd violated local laws when he threatened me with the gun.

Now he lay back on a sofa built for two, his head and feet curving upwards at either end. Not a predatory sea snail, anymore. A giant sea cucumber. "Catalan took our land," he whined.

Catalan scowled. "It's been in our family for three generations."

"Well your grandfather took it from my grandfather."

"Forty-seven years ago," stated Catalan. "Before you were born."

Toro looked at me seriously. "That family took over seventy square kilometers of our land!" He tried to sit up, but when he leaned on the injured elbow, he barked a few vulgarities and flopped back down. "Where's that drink, Luis?"

Jagaro clapped his hands, and a young boy ran in with a small glass of something pink and bubbly. Toro drained it with one gulp while Catalan sneered.

"Seventy square kilometers! Are you hearing me?" Toro hiccupped and turned his eyes back to me. "You're a pretty thing, but you should let your hair grow."

I mentally counted to ten before giving him a curt nod and turning to Catalan. "Seventy square kilometers?"

The topic clearly wearied Catalan. "The Toros left the land fallow."

"I'm sorry… 'fallow'?" *I really need to boost my vocabulary.*

"I know. Can you believe it?" He eyed Toro's empty glass and signaled Luis to bring him one, too. "Fallow. Barren. Useless. Like the whole Toro family. They did nothing with the land."

"It was *our land!*" shrieked Toro. "Who cares what we do with it? If we want to leave it—"

"If you want to leave it, then why do you care who owns it?" Catalan barked. He leaned forward on his knees, appealing to me with a reasonable expression.

"Hmm. Yes." I nodded sagely. I had no authority to redeem the situation, but sometimes people just need to feel heard. Until Maddy and Alf came back with a new transportation option, I had nothing better to do, so I sat back in my chair and did my best to look attentive.

"My family took the land. It's true," said Catalan. "And since then, we have turned it into the second most productive farming region in the entire colony. We've planted sixteen fruit orchards and two separate fields of duspies."

"Duspies! I know them well!" I brightened, happy to sound knowledgeable for a change. "How do you keep the insects away?"

"We're out in the rows every day," he said proudly. "Something the Toros would never do. They only want the land back now because of the orchards. They're easy to maintain because they're fully grown and prospering, but the fruit is ours. *We* planted the trees. *We* did all the work." He leaned back, stretching his legs belligerently out in front of him. "Everyone knows Toros are lazy."

Toro snorted and lifted his glass for another sip before he realized it was already empty.

"Why didn't you petition this forty-seven years ago?" I asked.

"He wasn't born yet," said Catalan.

I doubted *he'd* been born yet, either, but no one argued that point. "Wasn't there a formal complaint lodged?"

Toro shrugged and reached for the drink Luis proffered Catalan. Luis hesitated, shifting between the two men nervously. Catalan harrumphed and said, "Oh, give it to Toro. He needs a transfusion. He was running low on fuel."

I chewed the inside of my cheeks to keep from laughing, and Luis handed Toro the drink.

"So you want easy income?" I was goading, I knew, but Toro presented no threat at this point, slushy and injured as he was.

He slurred something under his breath and dropped the glass onto the floor. It must have been made of something very sturdy because it didn't break. What a wise invention for holding alcohol.

"What do you do with the land you have?" I asked.

"The official stance is 'tourism'," said Catalan, answering for Toro.

"It *is* tourism!" Toro shifted his body so that his head lay on the flat part of the cushions. That meant that his knees crooked over the armrest. I feared he'd fall asleep before I learned the whole story.

"And is that profitable?" I asked.

"It's too much work," he grumbled. "Visitors expect fancy accommodations like this place, and the upkeep is expensive."

I thought about the walls of Jagaro's inn with gaps big enough to peek through. A single, unshaded bulb hung in our room over a single stark shelf and two lumpy beds. *Fancy?*

"Do you have other options for income?" I asked. "Surely you can do something useful for the colony at large. Where's your community spirit?"

Toro shook his head and closed his eyes. "You sound like some fool spacey."

We sat in silence for a few minutes while I pondered these men and their positions. Then the Rik leaves tickled my brain with something. "Aren't there spiral reefs nearby?"

"Yeah, a few kilometers off the shores of our district," said Toro.

"They're one of the great mysteries of the Karlis Ocean."

"So?"

His disinterest reeked, but Catalan raised an eyebrow at me. "What about it?"

"Don't they attract all kinds of beautiful marine life to the area?"

"Yeah, but they're under water," said Toro. "Can't see much unless you want to go swimming."

"What if you rent boats to people to go out and observe all the animal life?" Suddenly I doubted myself. "Would that be interesting to anyone?"

"Sure. The rich ambassadors that spend all their time in space," said Catalan with disdain.

"Exactly. The *rich* ambassadors who would then have positive things to say about Tye, and about Menorca and Flinders in particular." I shrugged. "Maybe if the view is good enough, they won't complain about the accommodations."

Toro frowned. "You still can't see that much from above the water. And those rich spaceys don't know how to swim."

You got that right! "What if you made the boats out of that glass there?" I pointed at the empty glass on the floor.

Toro scoffed. "Pretty small."

Catalan, however, sat up straighter. "Glass-bottomed boats so people could see underwater."

"Yes," I said, warming to my own idea. *Maybe I could be an inventor!*

"That's brilliant!"

I blushed. "Why thank you, Catalan."

Toro grunted and flailed his legs until he'd righted himself. "Now wait. Those spiral reefs are in *our* sea space!"

"Of course," said Catalan. "But you'll need boats."

"I got boats."

"You'll need *glass-bottomed* boats." I could almost see machinery whizzing inside Catalan's brain. He grew more animated. "We can build them for you. We have the glassworks factory, too."

"Oh, so this is all about *your* profit again," said Toro, spitting as he spoke.

"We'll build you a hundred boats if you'll let us keep the disputed land," said Catalan, rising to his feet. "You won't have to do anything but minor repairs on your inns, and you'll be able to charge twice as much because a stay includes a marine biology tour."

Toro scraped his uninjured hand across his chin and belched. "A hundred boats? What if I need more?"

Catalan paused, so I jumped in. "Why don't you wait and see how lucrative the venture becomes? Then you can negotiate the details further."

"I think it's a fine idea!" said Catalan. He crossed the floor and grabbed my hand, pumping it up and down enthusiastically. "I doubt Governor Pollenca could have come up with a better solution."

OOO

38 ALTERING THE COURSE

"We need to leave now," said Maddy. He had sneaked in through the kitchen's back door.

"I'm staying," said Nathani. "I think I proved I'm not past my Age of Purpose. Governor Pollenca said I can take care of the baby while she works." She winked at me. "Though, it sounds as if you did some of her work for her!"

"That's why we need to leave," said Maddy. "The reporters found out about the deal Caz helped close, and they want to get vid of her as the hero of the day. If this makes big enough news—and I imagine it will, seeing that she's so young—she's going to be very famous very soon. We can't have that."

"Won't it make her all the more credible as the rightful gypsy queen?" asked Nathani.

"Then we can let the story leak out later—after the Cycling Ceremony," said Maddy. "Until then, we can't risk Saloma finding out where she is."

"What if we use the exposure to publicize that we're taking a nice casual trading tour along your established route?"

"And then we speed out the other way," said Alf bobbing his head. "Yeah. That could help."

"Let me check something," I said. I connected with Dad using the comlink. After rushing through the pleasantries, I jumped into business.

"Brita's en route to Arecife," said Dad.

Maddy nodded from across the room. Dad couldn't see him mouth the words, *The gypsy trade route.*

"Did she say why?" I asked, keeping my expression neutral.

He looked at me like I was a little child. "She's hoping to catch up with you, of course."

How can I tell him I'm not sure if I trust Mom? "All right. We're heading out now!" I said.

"Send our love to her," he insisted.

I nodded without promising and disconnected quickly. *He still loves her.* I knuckled a tear from my eye.

"That settles it. We'll break the route," said Maddy. "We can avoid the stops in between until we get to Ikekane North. There just isn't another connecting point." He stopped and stared at me. "What are you doing, Caz?"

"Calling Ruddie and Sasa," I said, working the comlink.

"Hello?" Sasa looked amazing, her hair grown and fluffed. Her jaw dropped. "Caz, is that you? I swear you look worse every time I see you!" She said it with a friendly laugh, and I knew she meant nothing unkind by it.

"That's me. Windblown and carefree." I chuckled for show, and then squirmed with how direct I'd have to be. "So...I know you don't owe me anything, but..."

Sasa leaned in, ready for action. "What's up?"

"I need information. I don't suppose you have any?"

Her eyes widened with exaggerated indignation. "You know I don't deal in information anymore."

Sasa had been sent to Lamond for her blackmailing habit. "Right. I thought maybe you could do a pro bono job for me?"

She threw back her head and laughed. Regaining composure, she whispered. "How delicate? Will I need to work Ruddie's connections?"

"You'll need extra discretion," I said. "Lives are at stake."

"Lives I care about?"

I gave her a heavy-lidded look. "Mine?"

Sasa's face grew serious. "Still?" She had helped us with information back on Craggy, but probably assumed things had settled.

Exhaling a long breath, I shrugged. "That's what we need to know."

"What's the information?"

"The current whereabouts of Governor Jipps and any information on her traveling companions you can get."

Her lips pressed into a thin line. "Caz, what's going on?"

"Are you worried about digging into that?"

"Government officials don't like—"

"She just resigned," I said. "Please, Sasa. If I make it through all of this, I promise I'll make it worth your while somehow."

Sasa's smile relaxed a degree. "I'll get back to you as quickly as I can. Is this the comlink to use?"

"Yes, for now."

We said our good-byes, and I put in a similar call to Fizer on Craggy. The colonists in the Sumayar territory had returned to normal life. I didn't want to alarm him or get him chatting—Fizer could talk for a day without breathing—so I kept it simple. "Any word on Mom?"

"I haven't heard anything about your mom, Caz, but those armed men never came back after she and Pathankot went out to meet them. Pathankot said they'd struck some kind of bargain involving King, so I guess it's all fine. There was some strange stuff in the local Garvey news, though. We picked it up on one of our wireless receptors. Some armed transit was heading off-planet for something, but I don't know if it had anything to do with your mom. Hey, you should see the Earlie trees. They're coming up really fast on the east slope—"

"That's fantastic news, Fizer! Thanks for the update! I'll be in touch, but...my battery is about to die."

"Oh, right. I understand!" He grinned and waved. "We'll talk more next time. I've got so much to tell you about the lab. It's all—"

"Good-bye, Fizer! Have fun learning!"

I disconnected and looked up at Maddy. "The smartest, but possibly most aggravating boy I know. Kind to a fault. Talky to a fault."

"He won't talk too much?" asked Nathani with a pointed look.

"No. He wouldn't say anything that would put us at risk. Besides, I didn't tell him where we are."

"Even though he's a friend?"

"It's better if we play it safe," I said with a heavy sigh. "I sure wish that third Power would show up. Something like armored skin would be nice."

"You really don't think it was talking to the fish?" asked Nathani.

I shook my head. "No. There's more. I just don't know what it is."

OOO

Governor Pollenca's gratitude toward Nathani and me turned out to be quite profitable. She procured a newer, larger boat called the *Snow Storm*. It had a lower deck for sleeping and a motor that ran on wind turbines. Pollenca was also more than willing to help us keep the reporters away. After all, she didn't want to lose face as a negotiator, and I didn't want to claim credit for the success with Toro and Catalan.

We bade the isle of Flinders farewell, waving and shouting for anyone who might hear, "Off to Arecife!" A few kilometers past the tip of Flinders and back out in open sea, we veered west instead of southeast. The *Snow Storm* felt completely different from the *Sea Callabus*. Even in the unchanging scenery, I could tell we were moving much faster now. A *V* of white churning water stretched behind us.

"Will that be visible from the air?"

"Only at a very specific angle. And no one will be looking for it out here."

"Why not?" I asked. "Is there something dangerous about being out here?"

"No."

"Then why doesn't anyone go where we're going?" I asked.

"Because the only colony out in this direction is Apia, and..." Maddy frowned. "Outsiders are not very welcome there."

That got my attention. I turned on the comlink, expecting to access data banks about Apia, but a call was coming in from Sasa.

"Jipps flew on an armed express transit from Caren, courtesy of someone from the Rik Peninsula region," she said. "I couldn't find out who. Sorry. Does that help?"

Saloma. Who else would have that force available? I sighed. "Yes, Sasa. Thanks."

"Did I just confirm a disaster?"

I smirked. "Since when did disasters stop me?"

Sasa's smile, ironic yet warm, made me wish for an end to the chase. "All right, Caz. You'll just have to make it through again."

"Give Ruddie a hug from me. The kisses are up to you," I teased.

Sasa winked. "Saving yours for Alf?"

I gurgled with embarrassment. "Bye, Sasa!" I closed the connection.

Alf grinned. "You didn't answer her question," he said with exaggerated innocence.

The heat rushing to my face had nothing to do with the sun. "So what were you saying about Apia, Maddy? Are there archive vids?"

"There won't be anything current," he said, snickering at our exchange. "The people of Apia have *no* technology."

I squinted at this thought. "Then how do they teach their children?"

"They don't," said Maddy. "At least not in a way that we would ever imagine." He shook his head. "It's very isolated and very ignorant."

OOO

By the end of the day, I had officially died of boredom. Only a few random flocks of birds and passing through a massive colony of giant amoeba floating in puddles of milky white on the surface broke up the monotony for me. It was almost as bad as Solitary. Without even a sail and its rigging to mess with, we had nothing to do, and no Nathani telling us stories. We couldn't use the comlinks too much because we had no way of recharging them, so we had to entertain ourselves. Maddy taught us how to tie several different kinds of knots, and once we'd mastered them, Alf and I made up a game where we each took opposite ends of the same rope and began tying knots one-handed as fast as we could to see who would reached the middle first. When he was about to win for the third time in a row, I gave a frustrated tug to the rope. He'd been kneeling intently over his work and pitched forward to land on me.

Suddenly my heart pounded louder than the motor. I couldn't remember the last time he'd been this close to me, but somewhere along our journey he'd acquired an electric touch that sent jolts of heat all through me and stopped my breathing. His face hung just above mine, the longest of his locks brushing my cheek. The corner of his mouth twitched. "No fair distracting me," he said, reaching his hand behind my head.

I closed my eyes, ready for a kiss but afraid to move in case I ruined it.

"Done!" he shouted.

My eyes snapped open to see him holding the last knot in his fist, a triumphant grin on his face.

"Gaaah!" With a frustrated—or disappointed—grunt, I propelled him up and off of me...and overboard. Thus began his first swimming lesson.

After that, at least three times a day, Maddy stopped the boat, tied one of the thinner ropes in a tether around Alf's waist, and gave him lessons on how to float on his back or stomach, how to scoop the water with his hands to move himself forward, and how to kick his legs right. At least I appreciated the view from my perch. Both Alf and Maddy grew browner and brawnier in the sun.

If I'd been more adventurous, I'd have tried swimming, too, but I just wasn't ready to brave the deep water yet. I considered the fact that all the water on the planet couldn't drown me if it didn't get inside, but I remained unconvinced, and consequently stinky. The boys could go overboard and wash off the sweat from the heat of the day. I just got to dump the occasional bucket of sea water over my head.

"Can't I learn to swim somewhere where the water isn't so deep?"

"We'll find you a rain puddle when we get to land," teased Alf.

"There are some diving masks, Alf. Do you want to try?" asked Maddy. "We hold our breath for however long and explore. If we run out of air, we pop up to the surface and then go back down."

"Hold your breath? You'll be up and down every fifteen seconds." I put extra effort into my skeptical tone. "This will be an exercise in wasting time."

Maddy bit his lower lip in that self-deprecating way of his. "I can often go for more than three minutes underwater. It's a gypsy diver skill."

Three minutes. I stopped breathing to see if I could hold my breath that long, but the Gypsy Pearl and Rik leaves would give me an unfair advantage. "That's you. What about Alf?"

"Toss me a mask," said Alf. "I'll give it a try."

A few moments later, they both sported the most ridiculous goggles I'd ever seen. "Are you working with volatile chemicals, or trying to scare away the gouldings?"

Alf didn't care. "Whoah!" His jubilant, dripping face pricked me with jealousy. "It's amazing! You can see really far!" He tugged the mask up. "Caz, it's so peaceful and quiet down there."

I rolled my eyes and indicated the horizon in every direction. "It's noisy and crowded up here?"

To my dismay, he went back to practicing longer face plants in the water so that he could increase his lung capacity. I discovered I could admire and resent him at the same time. Sulking down into the sleeping berth, I tried not to think about Alf underwater and everything that could go wrong.

That night, Alf flopped back exhausted in his bunk after he'd set the autopilot. Maddy said we'd made good progress on distance traveled. As Alf drifted off to sleep, I rolled on my side and watched him. He smelled like sunshine and sea and Happiness. *I really need to get over my fear of water.*

ooo

"Is that a fire burning?" I pointed at the lowest and widest of the massive rocks that barred the way to the island of Apia. It looked like a lumpy overturned bowl.

"Could be," said Maddy evasively. "It might be a cloud."

"That's smoke, Maddy. Why would there be smoke on a rock? Surely no one lives on it." He cleared his throat but didn't answer. "Wait. What's wrong? Who's on the rock?"

Maddy sighed and cut power to the engine. We drifted to a halt. Turning to me with a grave expression, he said, "They really don't like outsiders here."

"That's nothing new for me. I lived on the bigoted Arxon ICS. Despite the city-station's purpose, you never saw so many people who disdained 'outsiders'."

"And yet your father married a gypsy," he countered gently.

I nodded. "They fell in love."

"And it opened the gene pool."

Alf and I digested this morsel.

"You mean these people have been intermarrying for generations without *any* new bloodlines?"

Maddy's squeamish look said it all.

"The place must be dead. If everyone here is descended from the same original colonists with no new blood coming in, there must be all kinds of birth defects by now."

"Exactly." A look of repulsion and sadness clouded Maddy's face. "The mainland Apians banish every person with a major defect to the rocks. Most die as infants. Some, whose defects are noted later in life, are sent as children."

My eyes ached with an inability to blink away the evil. "That's worse than setting elders adrift. Don't they know how to prevent genetic mutations? Can't they just—?"

Maddy shook his head. "No."

"What?! That's common knowledge!"

"Not if they've rejected all knowledge from outside of Apia."

"Why would they reject it?" asked Alf. "I mean, I didn't love school, but I can't imagine refusing to learn *anything*."

"When the first Tye colonists arrived, groups were assigned by lottery to different islands or archipelagos," explained Maddy. "Apia was smaller than many. The group assigned got so angry that they refused to have anything to do with the Granbo Charter or anyone else."

Alf's mouth hung open for a moment. "They threw a tantrum like little kids losing a game."

Maddy nodded. "Right, and they consequently lost everything."

"Is it even safe to go there?" I asked. "Will they be hostile?"

"Gypsies have come here in the past without too much conflict. Since we live outside of the Charter, too, I guess they don't feel threatened by us. It's a stopping point where we can fish and camp and scrounge some vegetables or fruits."

"Something fresh would be great," I agreed. "We need the vitamins. I assume there's a fresh water source?"

"Several streams, yes," said Maddy. We all stared at the low mound of green earth, teeming with strange trees that grew without branches until they fanned out and spiked the sky.

"Scilly was much smaller," I said dully. "With none of this lush vegetation."

"The Apians didn't know what they had." Alf's dark eyes narrowed. "They weren't grateful, like that old man in Wandel Hav said. They didn't Choose to be Happy."

"And so they were miserable."

We dropped something called an anchor into the sandy shallows. In theory, it would hold the *Snow Storm* stationary while we ate. I stared at the turquoise waves that pestered the huge rocks like children climbing on a tired grandparent. One rock looked like a fat, disembodied hand dipping its fingers into the water. Birds raced through the crevices of its fingers as if playing a game of catch-me, and I became transfixed by their agility. They darted and dove for several minutes in the distance then swooped towards us as if ready to attack. At the last second, they changed course and flitted in a horizontal path to pass so close that I could feel the flapping of their wings.

Startled, I dropped back on my heels, bumping into Alf. I hadn't realized he was sitting behind me. He smiled and steadied me, his hands sending a rush of giddiness down my arms.

I gulped back a blush. "I want to meet the outcasts."

"Defects. The Apians call them defects." Maddy said with a scowl. I wasn't sure if he found the people or the title distasteful. Perhaps both. "If you really want to. Brace yourself emotionally, though."

"Is there any chance the natives will get curious about our boat?" asked Alf.

Maddy squinted at the shoreline. "I don't think they'll notice us here, but maybe you should stay and guard it just in case?"

"How will you get over there?" asked Alf.

"I can swim her over," said Maddy. He wrapped a length of rope around his waist and jumped overboard. "Alf, can you lower Caz down so she doesn't plunge?"

"I can do it," I swallowed a lump of anxiety and swung one leg over the railing. Slowly, I let my whole body down until my ankles sank into the water.

"Let go," said Maddy.

"I don't want to," I growled. Closing my eyes, I focused on my breathing. *1…2…3—*

Maddy's arms caught me even before my head went underwater, but then he forced me away at arm's length. "Hold still and grab onto my shoulders—not my neck!"

Digging my fingers into his shoulders, I let my legs drift where they would.

"Now, as I turn around, you stay here and reposition your hands so you're riding my back. You can dig into the rope. Understand?"

I shivered at the comparative cold of the water, but made the switch. He began to swim. I'd watched him for days, but it was different to feel the water move around me. Remembering what he'd taught Alf, I kicked with my legs.

"Good! Thanks, that helps!"

"Am I drowning you?"

"No, no," he grunted. "But let yourself float more. Hold on with your hands, not your arms."

I straightened my arms a little so that I dragged more in the water and less on his back. The water lifted me instead of pulling me down, and I laughed.

"You're swimming!" shouted Alf from the boat.

Maddy's body dropped away from me suddenly and a wave pushed me so that my chin smashed into his shoulder blade.

"You can stand now," he said. My feet searched for a sense of down even as another wave rocked me against Maddy's ribcage.

I took in a mouthful of salt brine and in my frustration, stood up to spit it out.

"There, see?" he said brightly.

We stood thigh-deep in bubbles that couldn't make up their minds whether to push me up onto the sand or drag me back out to sea. Maddy held my hand tightly until we reached the base of the rock, which sat amidst many smaller boulders. I eagerly grabbed for this immovable support and pulled myself out of the water.

"Ew. What is this stuff?" A white, crusty film covered much of the ledge I had grabbed.

"That would be from the birds."

A handful of belltroes meandered in an undefined pattern above us. As if to illustrate Maddy's statement, one of them released something from its nether region.

Sploit! It landed a meter away, adding to the accumulated grossness.

"Is this some kind of defense mechanism?" I asked.

"No. Digestion," said Maddy. "Tread with care."

Something in my throat curdled. Probably the bovine yogurt we'd eaten earlier.

Climbing felt really good after all that time sitting on a hard bench. We had to maneuver from side to side to find ledges that afforded sturdy footholds, but it wasn't as bad as the cliff Alf and I had scaled on Craggy. Maddy improvised with the rope whenever he could loop it around something jutting out, and that sped us up vertically.

"This last climb should get us to the top." He tossed the rope with a practiced hand, and it flew out of sight. Tugging, he confirmed that it had caught on something, but before he could begin the climb, I jumped up beside him.

"Let me go first. If anything goes wrong, I don't want you crashing down from this height."

"But if there are people—"

"I can handle people, Maddy. I can't handle losing you." As politely as I could, I took the dangling rope from him and scaled the last five meters quickly. "I really like rocks," I called back. "Have I mentioned that before? I like how solid they are."

At the top, I scrambled clumsily up onto a grittier surface, scattering several belltroes. The rope clung precariously to the stubby remains of some kind of shrub. Calling over the ledge, I added my own strength to the supporting pull.

Maddy appeared, panting, a few moments later. His grateful smile changed suddenly into a bark of horror. "Caz, behind you!"

OOO

39 LAPITA

"What's wrong wif *you*?" The voice rasped from beneath a tangle of black hair that covered the face of the dirtiest little girl I had ever seen. She wore a ragged piece of cloth tied up under her arms so that it hung down to her knees.

Her question confused me as much as her appearance. "What? Me? I'm fine."

The girl's eyes widened as Maddy got to his feet and stood behind me. I sensed that she was both very strong and very weak. Strong because of lean muscles. Weak because her breathing sounded like a dirty air-conditioning vent.

"Can you see? You poop all day?"

Definitely the strangest greeting I'd ever heard.

"My name is Caz."

The girl narrowed her eyes at me. "Why you here?"

"To meet you. What's your name?"

Maddy cleared his throat. "She may not have been given a name," he murmured.

"I have name!" The girl's eyes flashed with defiance. "I wasn't baby when I comed. I comed big."

Her words tumbled in my ears for a moment before I sifted out the meaning. "You came here already big? How old were you when you came here?"

She held up four grubby fingers.

"Four years old?" She had to be about eight years old now. "How?"

She shifted her head in the same way I'd seen the belltroes do, to study me with a sideways glare.

Softening my voice, I lowered myself to one knee so as not to appear threatening. "You've done really well."

She slapped her chest, meeting my eyes with an iron glare.

I wanted to take her in my arms and cry. *What nightmares she must have lived through!* For the first time, I understood Felly's maternal instincts and the desire to clean someone up. I rested on both knees and tried again. "May I please know your name?"

She snatched the hair from her face and stared at me. Throwing her head back, she screeched, "Pleeeeeeeease?"

Startled, I scrambled to my feet and backed into Maddy.

The girl let her hair flop again into her face. "Lapita." She slapped her chest again.

"Lapita? That's your name?"

She nodded, and then broke into an agonizing coughing fit.

I stepped away. "Are you sick?"

Lapita screwed up her face. "Bad breathers."

"Bad breathers—you mean lungs?"

She tilted her head to one side. "Maybe." Again she studied us. "What's wrong wif you?"

"Nothing's wrong with us," I said, gesturing to Maddy. "We came to visit."

"Perfects never come."

I laughed bitterly. "I'm not perfect." Then I caught her meaning. "Oh. I don't come from Apia. I come from far away."

Lapita gazed out over the waves and pointed to the bobbing *Snow Storm*. "You comed over water?" Her voice held a childlike awe for the first time.

"That's right," I said. "We came in a boat from far away to visit you."

She made another screeching sound, but this one sounded happy. Tugging her matted hair back, she revealed a beautiful face with exotic skin several shades darker than Maddy's sunbaked shoulders. A smile spread across her face. "Water girl visit defects!"

"I'm Caz visiting Lapita." I gestured as I spoke to show I meant it personally.

Lapita locked eyes with me and nodded. Something told me she found great significance in my simple statement.

OOO

Lapita led us on calloused feet to where a fissure opened downward into the rock. It only dropped about a meter before revealing a cavern as big as my room on the Arxon. Sunlight warmed the center, but the edges remained in shadow, protected from the elements. It was a decent shelter for camping, but not for a permanent home. The remnants of a small fire smoldered to one side and I wondered how she had managed to start it. The haze of smoke still lingered.

"I bet the enclosed fires aren't helping her lungs," I murmured to Maddy.

"At least she has fresh water," he said.

Rain must have fallen often enough to erode the rock directly under the fissure because a small depression held clean water.

Even as we looked at this, a small boy shuffled forward on his hands and knees and cupped the water to his lips. He wore what looked like a giant diaper, and he sat back on his heels considering the ground between me and Maddy.

"What's wrong wif you?"

This time I laughed. "Is that how you greet everyone around here?"

Lapita grew animated. "They comed from water, Tanu! They comed to visit us. They not perfects."

Tanu's face broke into a smile revealing his tender age by the number of teeth left. Six or seven years old. Still he watched with a glassy vacancy.

Blind!

He stood and came forward, his hands outstretched. Maddy shrank back, but I held my ground as he touched first my arm and then moved up to my shoulder, my neck, my face. His fingers searched every bump and hole eagerly, and I pressed my lips tightly closed to keep him from probing my mouth. Satisfied at last, he threw his arms around my hips. Dropping to my knees, I took Tanu's hands to keep him from fingering every part of me. This apparently pleased him greatly, and he settled his movements.

"Tanu like you," announced Lapita.

I patted the boy's long scruffy hair. "I like Tanu, too." I searched the shadows. "Are there more of you here?"

"Two babies died last moon," said Tanu.

"Two babies died? How?"

"No milk," said Lapita simply.

"There's no food at all. How have you survived?"

Lapita looked away. "Bird eggs, fish, candy root."

I gave Maddy a questioning glance. "It's a tiny tuber that grows on some of these sea rocks," he said. "If you're willing to dig, you can find them in the patches of green."

"Candy root sweet," said Tanu. He beamed up in the direction of Maddy's face. "You got some?"

"Uh, no. Sorry."

"But that isn't enough nutrition to keep you alive for years. How—?"

"Babies died because no milk." Lapita seemed determined not to answer my question. "One just sleeped and died, but other turned blue and shaked to die."

Emotions crashed into me, waves of anger, compassion, sadness. Determination won out. These "defects" needed medical attention and love, not a life of literally scraping for their existence and living in a hole in a rock.

I stood. "Maddy, we need to get them to the island. They need proper nutrients. They need baths and medical attention."

Lapita stomped her feet and shook her head. "Perfects hate us." She pointed at Maddy, accusing. "They afraid."

"How could they be afraid? You have birth defects, not contagious diseases." I reached for her hand, trying to make my voice soothing.

"Lapita, let us take you back there, and we'll get you help. Clothing, food."

She pressed herself back into the darkness of the cave. I moved to go after her, but Tanu grabbed my leg, his sharp, untrimmed nails poking me even through my pants.

"Lapita take food and cloth from perfects at night sometimes. If she go day, perfects beat Lapita."

"You steal food from the perfects?"

She cowered as if I would hurt her.

"Lapita give me food," said Tanu earnestly. "I live because Lapita."

I saw her fear and felt heat rise in me. "Good girl, Lapita. You're right to take care of Tanu. The Apians took away your future. You go ahead and take their food. I'll help you."

OOO

Lapita and Tanu climbed down with alarming agility, both having memorized the best way down. No ropes this time. Lapita must have made the climb with her hands full and in the dark on countless occasions. Neither of them seemed afraid of the water at all, though Tanu had to hold on to Lapita's arm so as not to get turned around by the waves.

They had never ventured out past their rock into the open ocean, but when Maddy showed them how he could tow them along with the rope as a tether, they saw it as a fantastic game instead of something to dread. Their courage bolstered mine, and I stayed at the end of the rope attempting my sloppy swimming kicks and concentrating on encouraging them.

The swim to the boat cleaned them up a little, but Lapita's frequent coughing fits shook me every time she had to stop. I thought she was drowning, but listening closer, it sounded more like asthma. Tanu's sightless gaze broke my heart, but his innocent nature seemed eager to love and be loved. Their biggest handicap was the neglect they'd endured.

Alf now stared uncertainly at the two very beautiful, but very unkempt children huddled on the lower bunk. "You want me to watch them while you *what?*"

"We'll need to scout out the situation," said Maddy. "If the Apians are open to caring for the children…"

He sounded entirely too skeptical, so I jumped in. "We've got to make them see reason. They can't simply dump unwanted children on a rock. Look at how these two made the Decision to Survive! Who's to the say the others couldn't have made it also, if they'd just been given some love and care?" A sob choked me, and Tanu reached to offer me comfort. He was comforting *me!*

Alf saw this and visibly melted with the tenderness of the boy. "They should take care of these little things, yeah?"

"They also need to stop interbreeding and creating so many defects," said Maddy.

"Don't call them that," I snapped. My spine stiffened with anger even as hot tears streamed down my cheeks. "These children have been strong enough and smart enough to keep themselves alive for all this time. Years! There is *nothing* defective about them."

Lapita began to cry, and I worried that my raised tone had frightened her, but she looked at me with such…hope? I knelt at the edge of the bunk and touched her little feet. "You don't have to live on that rock if you don't want to."

"What if they won't take the children back?" asked Maddy under his breath.

"Then we take them with us," I said firmly. "Take care of them until we get back, Alf."

"It's getting dark," protested Alf.

"Then feed them dinner and put them to bed." I softened when his jaw dropped. "Please, Alf. We'll be back by morning. Keep a light on so we can see you from shore."

"I go wif you," announced Lapita.

Part of me wanted to object, but she and I were made of the same stubborn cosmic dust, so there'd be no point. I looked at Alf and then put an arm on Tanu's shoulder. "Tanu can you stay here with Alf? He's my best friend. He won't hurt you." I watched Alf's face, desperately willing him to show kindness. "He can tell you all about this boat. Would you like that?"

Tanu's response was to latch onto Alf's arm and begin running a hand over Alf's chin and cheeks. "He fuzzy!"

Alf chuckled and then had to close his mouth to avoid fingers. This made him snort, and that made everyone laugh.

I winked at Alf, and his smile in return kicked my heart into a higher gear. Grabbing Lapita's hand, I headed up on deck. Maddy followed with obvious reluctance.

"This doesn't feel right," said Maddy even as he lowered himself into the water. "So many things could go wrong."

"They usually do," I said. "And yet we make it through. We've made the Decision to Survive—you and me and Lapita."

"Yes, but that's all the more important now, my lady."

I knew why he added the *my lady* bit. The Cycling Ceremony. If something happened to me before I'd completed that, everything—all our efforts—would be lost. Yet would that matter if we couldn't find King? And how could I think to rescue a whole species if I couldn't rescue a little girl and a blind boy?

OOO

As we waded up onto the beach, the sun made its own dive into the sea. We'd only have light for about twenty more minutes.

"Which way?" I whispered.

Lapita, already so tiny, crouched down and pointed to our left. We followed her lead, jogging lightly over packed sand, still damp enough not to cling to our boots. Once under the cover of the trees, we paused. Lapita wheezed but did not cough, and I watched her intently. The multiple dips in the sea and the long blouse I'd given her to wear over her skirt had transformed her considerably.

"Try breathing this way," I said, forming a fat straw with my fist and sucking in air through it slowly. "Control it. Slowly if you can."

She glared at me, but tried anyway. Whether or not it actually helped her lungs, it calmed her breathing. A surprised smile spread from behind her fist.

I raised my hands and placed them on the back of my head. "Now do this," I said. "It'll open up your breathers to get more air. When you hunch over, it squishes them."

Lapita mimicked my action and then brought one hand down to continue breathing through her hand straw. It was a funny little pose, and her expression was so serious underneath her long cape of black hair that I almost laughed. But I felt as though I were witnessing a miracle. Maddy and I waited and watched as her breathing settled, still audible, but not as rough.

With a new fire in her eyes, Lapita wordlessly signaled for us to continue. She slipped ahead of us through the trees with confidence in her direction. Maddy tapped my shoulder. "I'm sorry I doubted. She *is* remarkable."

I beamed. "She is, isn't she?"

"And so are you."

"Oh, I'm a doctor's kid. Those are tricks for dealing with an asthma attack or hyperventilation. I figured it wouldn't hurt to try."

We navigated through the trees. No visible landmarks presented themselves except for one clearing and a little stream of fresh water. Lapita instantly dropped into the stream and drank deeply with cupped hands. She began to cough again, but straightened and tried the asthma tricks again. They worked, filling us all with visible relief.

After a few more minutes of walking, we crouched behind a fallen tree. Something the size of my thumb crawled over it, and I stifled a scream, backing away quickly.

Lapita stabbed me with an icy look, and I froze, my hand still over my mouth. The crawly thing from the tree skittered over my foot. *I must not be scared. It's just an insect. A really big insect.* Lapita snatched it up and popped it into her mouth. I squeezed my eyes shut and reminded my esophagus to keep the gravity rule.

When I opened my eyes, Maddy straddled the fallen tree in readiness to go after Lapita. Her retreating head bobbed out of sight as she brushed through a plant that clutched after her with hundreds of soft, green fingers. I got to my feet and joined them, wincing at the feel of plants on my face but enjoying the sweet, spicy aroma.

We entered a clearing of cultivated earth, an impressively large vegetable garden, still visible in the waning twilight.

"I get food here," whispered Lapita.

"Is there a city nearby?" I asked.

Lapita squinted at me. "City?"

"A village," suggested Maddy. "Many houses together."

She nodded vigorously.

"I see you, gypsies," boomed a man's voice. "You're lucky to have landed before we all went to sleep."

Lapita squeaked with fear, but Maddy stood and gently slid her behind his legs.

"Don't worry. We don't always eat gypsies," said the man without humor. "We get them once or twice a year. Come. Let's get you housed for the night. We don't want you camped by our garden, or it'll be plucked clean by morning." His voice sounded friendly, but his eyes did not match the tone. Something in the way he gripped the long, pointed stick in his hand told me it was not a gardening tool, but a weapon. When we hesitated, the man confirmed this by holding it as if ready to throw its sharp end through one of us.

"Have you come to trade, or what?"

Maddy raised his hands in an appeasing gesture. "Trade," he said.

I reached behind him and took Lapita's hand, wishing I could will her breathing to normalize completely. She really could pass for a gypsy—at least one of the stereotypical grubby ones.

"What's wrong with her?" asked the man, gesturing with his stick.

Standard greeting in these waters. "She caught a cold," I said. "A mild respiratory infection. Nothing serious."

He narrowed his eyes. "Is it contagious?"

"Not any more. She's taking the necessary medications."

"Well, keep her back. I don't want her getting anyone else sick."

The man shouldered his stick and gestured for us to follow. Resigned, Maddy tromped after him, but I held back for a moment and whispered to Lapita. "Don't speak to anyone here. He probably doesn't recognize you because you've been gone so long and you're dressed differently. Maybe we can pretend you're my sister."

Lapita squeezed my hand but remained as if her feet had grown roots into the soil.

"What's the matter?"

A tear escaped through her long, dark lashes. "That man my father."

OOO

As we entered a larger clearing, Lapita's father removed a second stick from his belt and held it to a fire that burned brightly in a metal basin. With this flaming stick, he guided us down a beaten path through two rows of tiny buildings made of wood and woven leaves. Occasionally, a portion of a structure resembled a boat or an aircraft adapted to a new cause. Maybe they had salvaged pieces from the original transports that brought the colonists here.

He led us to the largest structure. Its doors opened wide, and a pungent odor assaulted us from inside. Though I couldn't see much in the dark, I got the impression we were surrounded by several small ovis. The man pushed through these and stood at the base of a ladder.

"That's the grain loft," he said. "You can sleep up there for the night, and we'll see what you have to trade in the morning." He frowned at Maddy. "Didn't bring much, did you?"

Maddy fingered his small backpack and the coil of rope. "Not as much as usual."

The man left without a backwards glance, tossing his last words over his shoulder. "Don't try to steal any ovis, or you'll be the one served at the next feast."

I grabbed Maddy's wrist and hissed. "They're not seriously cannibals, are they?"

"I don't want to find out," he said.

We climbed up into the grain loft where we found sacks covering most of the floor. The low ceiling forced us to crawl, but we would be lying down anyway. The sacks sufficed as pillows, and we each bedded down for the night. With so much to discuss, I didn't know how to begin. Until I saw the Apian home group in action, I couldn't formulate a real plan.

"So these people throw away children and eat intruders?" I asked Maddy once I heard Lapita's breathing fall into the steady rhythm of sleep.

"Rumors like that are hard to verify," he answered.

"Ever the diplomat, aren't you, Maddy? You've missed your calling in life." I closed my eyes and thought about how to negotiate for the children's care. "They really don't have *any* contact with the rest of the Granbo System?"

"Think about it. Have you ever heard of Apia?"

I shook my head. Even the Rik leaves couldn't help me. I'd never been taught because the colony didn't officially exist. "That's crazy."

"That's stubborn."

"Their stubbornness could fill the Karlis Ocean," I said with disgust. It numbed me mentally when I tried to fathom a willful lack of curiosity.

"As far as the Apians are concerned, their system is perfect."

"Tanu said if Lapita got caught, the perfects beat her. It must have happened at least once. Do you suppose her own father is the one who caught her? Could he not recognize and protect her? Does he have no heart?"

He shifted. "It's her father? Did she say so?"

"Yes. Can you imagine?"

"Worse than having no father at all," he said, his voice suddenly hoarse with emotion.

It occurred to me that I'd met Maddy's mother but not his father. "Do you have a dad, Maddy?"

"Not one that would claim me." The rare bitterness in his tone was enough to change my line of discussion. Alf was in the same situation, his parents having disowned him when he was sent to Lamond. As strained as my relationship with Dad had been over the years, at least he still wanted me.

I reached out in the darkness and found Maddy's shoulder with my hand. "Someday you're going to be the best father anyone ever had."

The smile returned to his voice. "I hope so. I'd like that."

OOO

Ofato-Pele was the oldest man in this "home group", yet I gauged him to be no more than about fifty years old. Another side-effect of a small gene pool. His taut facial muscles gave the impression that a smile would break his head in half. No wonder Lapita cowered behind Maddy. This man shouted disdain with every glance. His words dripped with the pride of his people. As guardian of their oral heritage, he told stories for a living, but his tales only vaguely orbited reality.

"Unless you have gypsy remedies with you," said Ofato-Pele, "we have little to discuss. We want nothing of your technology."

Maddy glanced grimly at the first aid kit on his lap. I doubted he'd part with his vial of pearl powder. I also doubted the Apians had anything we could possibly want in trade.

Clearly hedging for time, Maddy asked, "Are there other home groups that might feel differently?"

Ofato-Pele stiffened and speared his morning roasted meat with a sharp stick that he used as an eating utensil. He flipped it over on his broad wooden plate, splashing a greenish sauce that spattered onto my arms. I was about to wipe away the sauce from my wrist when Lapita grabbed my hand

and licked it up.

The storyteller sneered down his nose before looking away. "Your daughter acts like a defect. Is her mind stirred by the winds you follow?"

My jaw flopped open, but I snapped it shut. This was the opportunity I'd wanted. "About that," I said. "I understand you've…" My voice trailed off as I looked for the tactful way to broach the subject. "Your good people have had terrible misfortunes with the health of some of your children."

His eyes narrowed at me. "What have you heard?"

I swallowed and set down the plate of meat he'd reluctantly offered us. It was mostly fat anyway. "I only mean that you have had to expel a fair number of …"

"It is no misfortune. It is the way to preserve the best of the people. Livestock breeders keep only the best animals for breeding. Farmers keep the seeds of the best harvest for planting. The same is done with the offspring."

I shuddered at the clinical coldness of his statement.

"This problem doesn't exist elsewhere in the Granbo System," said Maddy cautiously. "At least not as often."

Ofato-Pele flared his nostrils. "The climate here is hard on the people. The air warps the womb of many of our women and causes problems with the newborns. The Granbo Charter didn't care enough to give us decent land, but we're strong. We've managed fine without them." He spoke with his head held aloft, barely making eye contact with our inferior selves.

I realized that he didn't recognize Lapita as one of his own people because he couldn't be bothered to look at her. Like he wouldn't look at reason.

"You have done admirably," I said stiffly, figuring flattery was invented for people like him. "You must be *very* strong."

"We are perfect," he announced matter-of-factly.

I kept my voice free of skepticism. "And how many of you are there?"

"On the whole island, or in our home group?"

"Both," I said.

"We have one hundred and eight here in this home group, and I believe the island population is close to a thousand."

"How have you kept the population up with such a high infant mortality rate?"

"We get rid of the defects so they will not contaminate the rest of us."

I rubbed my eyes, feigning a yawn so he would not see my frustration.

"Do you never marry people from other parts of Tye? Strong ones, of course." I didn't know how to approach the subject scientifically without sparking his defensiveness against Granbo System knowledge. "It might help with the… breeding."

He nodded. "It's true that when the children of leaders from two different home groups marry, their offspring are hearty."

"Right. Exactly. Could you do that more often? And not just the leaders?"

Ofato-Pele's expression became thoughtful, and he focused his gaze on me directly for the first time. "Yes, if we had new people in our home group, it could strengthen our children and our numbers." He nodded and leaned forward. "For example, if you two stayed and married into our home group."

I coughed and Maddy let out a strangled objection. "I'm already married," he lied. "Caz is my daughter. And her, too," he added, pointing at Lapita.

"Where is your wife?" asked Ofato-Pele.

"She's..." Maddy faltered.

"She's not here, is she?" Ofato-Pele arched his back in a stretch and gave Maddy a knowing glance. "You will stay here and take one of our women." His eyes grazed over me, and I felt as though he were looking right through my clothing, appraising me. "You will stay, too. Maybe I will take you myself." He stood up. "Yes. I will go tell the others we need a new shelter built."

"But we—"

The man's hand shot out to Maddy's collar with a fierceness that made Lapita squeal. "You will not leave. No one will miss a gypsy family, but you look strong enough to be of help around here."

OOO

40 A LONG, LONELY NIGHT

"Can we at least get the rest of our supplies from our boat?" I asked.

"You would just run away," he said, his dark eyes boring through me. He bellowed a strange signal that reminded me of a bovine's moan. Four very large men ran up clad only in leggings made of ovis fleece. It made them look half-animal, and the glazed stupor in their eyes heightened the effect. "Take the gypsies to their boat and retrieve anything of value to us. We'll salvage the boat for building supplies. Go."

The men slapped their chests in the same kind of a salute that Lapita had used earlier. Turning to us, they gave us a look that said *Lead us to your boat or we'll eat you.* Well, maybe the eating part wasn't as clear, but I could feel low-grade panic settling in.

I looked down at Lapita. Her eyes shone with tears behind the protective curtain of hair.

"Don't worry," I whispered. "We'll keep you safe. Take Maddy's hand and show him how to get back to the boat."

Lapita reluctantly let Maddy take her into the front of the procession. I followed right behind, wracking my brain for some way to escape. The only hope was to outrun our escorts. Otherwise, they'd dismantle our boat and leave us stranded.

I don't have time for this. Time. Countdowns. "Maddy, T minus 10 and counting."

He flashed me a raised eyebrow but continued at the same pace. Only the tightened grasp on Lapita's hand showed he knew what I meant.

Ten steps later, he swept her into his arms and began to run. The men behind us shouted, and two of them threw their sticks. One struck a tree right next to where Maddy ran, and I felt the sharp sting of a glancing blow on my right arm. The shock of it spun me around, and I grabbed at sticks they'd thrown. Holding the two together in my hands, I broke them in half over my knee. The sticks were big enough that I knew it would surprise them, and I thanked King again for the Gypsy Pearl's strengthening Power. The two who still held sticks hesitated, so I used the time to kick out with the heel of my foot at a tree next to me. As I'd hoped, it cracked. The top began falling back over me, so I turned and ran. Hopefully the fallen tree would be a temporary barrier.

Panting, I caught up with Maddy and Lapita. "How much farther?"

Lapita coughed and pointed.

"There they are!" The men were running after us again.

"Split up!" I hissed. "Take her to the boat. I'll meet you there."

Maddy reached in his pocket and handed me the comlink. "I'll contact you from the *Snow Storm*." He took off running straight ahead.

Glancing over my shoulder, I braced myself for a long sprint and darted off at a 45-degree angle. The men chasing us divided, and I could hear only two of them behind me. If worse came to worst, I could fight them off, as long as I didn't let adrenaline overtake me.

My foot splashed down into a stream, and I paused for a split second. *Which way is the water running?* Following the current, I made my way along the shallow bank and soon came out onto the beach where the fresh water met the sea. For a moment, I thrilled in the chase—not with fear, but with the fact that it led over rugged terrain and water instead of through the sterile corridors of an ICS. If I got caught, however, I would get more than a lecture from Stationmaster Lew.

I scanned the rocky formations in front of me, trying to get my bearings. A few hundred meters to my left, I saw Maddy break the cover of the trees and race towards the sea with Lapita in his arms. He had to be heading to the *Snow Storm* anchored out of view, which meant the big rock in front of me was the upturned hand. Plunging into the surf, I fought the drag it created with each step. I had outrun my pursuers this far, but now I heard them shouting after me. Their cries tumbled over the waves.

"Come back!"

"Get away from there!"

I grunted and pushed forward up to my waist. The coldness of the water didn't bother me as much as its tendency to lift me off my feet and shove me back. My foot struck an unseen rock painfully, and I almost doubled over, but I used the graceless move to crawl up onto the submerged boulder. Through the swirling foam, I could see the uneven ground between me and the main rock. To the side, however, if I sought shelter under the "hand", smooth sand invited me.

I made a snap decision to get out of the Apians' line of sight. Jumping back into the water on the sandier side, I fought my way around the rock, cursing each wave that tried to smash me against it. At last, I reached the first opening and pulled myself inside, using the walls for support. I could span the gap with my arms spread wide to prevent being tossed around, but the water here moved in more erratic swells.

Finding a toehold in one wall, I began a painful climb up out of the water, each side of my body flexing to keep myself wedged in place. Since I didn't know how much longer the incoming tide would rise, I continued climbing until the space narrowed and I found a ledge near the top. Bracing my legs against the opposite wall, I shuddered down at the churning brine several meters below. Hopefully the men would not follow me here. Maybe they would give up.

I gathered my thoughts, finding one that surprised me: my limbs had not gone numb. *Don't I have adrenaline coursing in my veins?* I tried to take a mental inventory of my internal systems. Although I'd run away from the Apians, the fight-or-flight surge had not been a panicked spike. The Gypsy Pearl gave me strength, but it also gave me a purpose. I simply didn't have the option of remaining on Apia indefinitely. I ran away not for fear of what they'd do, but because I had something more important to do.

However, I *did* have a bleeding arm. Assessing the damage was tricky without a mirror, but the salt water had probably done more good than harm. I ripped the stained sleeve of my shirt off and used it to wrap the wound. *Good thing I just learned how to tie all those knots one-handed!*

The watery confusion below me fit my mood as I tried to process all my concerns: the Cycling Ceremony and those who might try to sabotage it, the prolonged absence of King, and the uncertainty of Maddy's and Lapita's fate. But the things I'd learned in each colony so far played in my mind, too. Already I was not the same girl who landed on Tye, and definitely not the same one who left the Arxon half a rotation ago.

I watched the deepening water crash and twist. The salty mist drenched me a little more with each hour that passed. Uncomfortable, cold, battered, hungry and alone, I watched the ocean rise and knew in my heart that it would not swallow me because I was meant for something more.

OOO

My comlink light winked through the material of my pocket, waking me up. *Had I fallen asleep after the sun set? How did I stay wedged up here without falling?* I cradled the blinking metal egg in my hand, and a blue cone shot up from the miraculously waterproof little device. *Of course. We're on Tye. Everything needs to be waterproof.*

"Alf!" I squeezed the comlink tighter. "Where are you?"

"Out here wondering where you are," he said. "Maddy and Lapita came back, and we had to pull up anchor fast. Are you still on the island?"

I grinned. "I'm in the hand, safe and sound."

"The hand? Is that a gypsy thing?"

Laughing, I explained where I'd hidden myself, and I could see him consulting with Maddy.

"You're going to have to stay there until just before dawn. We can't risk being seen, and yet we'll need a little light to navigate the rocks. Is the tide going to come all the way up to where you are?"

"It'll be close, but I don't think so. Maybe that's why they didn't follow me out. They probably figure I'll drown, trapped in the rock's fingers."

"Can you hold on for a few more hours?"

"Do I have a choice?"

His face grew serious. "Hold on *tight*, yeah?"

The connection closed, and I rolled the comlink in my hands, careful not to drop it. Whether the Rik leaves or boredom directed me, I got a sudden brain flash to try something a friend on the Arxon had once done. He called it a comlink sweep, and it scanned for any random signals in the area instead of locking onto a specific communication device. Perfect for espionage applications if anyone in the Granbo System felt so inclined. The boy had been sent to Solitary for four weeks because he had stumbled across a sensitive transmission from a powerful ambassador.

My memory sifted over the details of the trick, and I adjusted the controls. At the last second, I remembered to mute and block my own sound and image. I held it out in a wide sweeping motion. Nothing. Tucking the comlink into my waistband, I shifted my weight to reach over to the opposite wall. After a few extremely awkward maneuvers, I managed to get to the far end of the crevice. There, with each foot wedged on a different wall and one hand gripping an overhead outcropping, I retrieved my comlink. This time, when I held it back out in a sweeping motion, I could hear something. Static white noise first, and then voices in patches, always too garbled to understand.

I gave up for a while but tried back periodically through the night until I caught a new signal. Focusing the comlink in the direction that provided the clearest audio reception, I listened.

"…a vessel due west."

"A cargo ship?"

"Too small."

"Fishing?"

"…get a visual?"

"Down there."

Down? They're in the air?

"…seen us?"

"…think so…too many aboard. Probably a family with children out…"

"…at this hour? It's too early for…"

I almost dropped the comlink. They must be talking about the *Snow Storm!* It took me a few seconds to recapture the voices.

"… count four people…"

They found Maddy and Alf. I closed my eyes, fighting the ache in my muscles from pushing myself in place.

"…sign of her?"

"Could be below…"

"…if what Governor Jipps said is true …"

Mom!

"I think we'd better attack."

OOO

41 PEOPLE CHANGE

Dawn seeped through the cloud cover but failed to penetrate my misery. *If Mom was behind an attack… If Alf or Maddy—or the children—had been killed…* What future was there for me with all my loved ones gone or turned against me? I ached with a loss that I couldn't even confirm.

Below me, the water retreated, and I followed it at a distance, finding new ledges on which to sit and brood. All night long, I'd been unable to reach the *Snow Storm* on the comlink. Surely it had been shot to the ocean floor by now. My eyes, swollen with weariness and too many tears shed, could barely see the controls to keep trying.

A distant drone caught my attention, and I let myself drop into the now hip-deep water. My rear end thanked me for releasing the rocky pressure, but the cold water jolted me awake painfully. Sloshing toward the murky sunlight, I peered around the rock at the featureless sky. No sun, moon, or stars. Not even a belltroe.

The humming grew louder than the surf, like the urgent whine of a child. I searched the horizon again, and my heart sank. In the distance, a small plane dropped lower as if coming in for a landing. Skimming the breezy white-capped waves, it settled down on fat feet and sputtered to a stop about two hundred meters away. I could make out a figure opening the side door. He jumped into the water and began swimming in my direction.

"Caz!"

My heart leaped. "Maddy!"

"Caz! Are you all right?"

I waved enthusiastically. "You're alive!"

His warm laugh rippled across the water. As soon as could stand, I rushed forward and threw my arms around him, sobbing with relief. Maddy held me tightly, smoothing my hair and letting me shake away all the emotions of the long night. "And the others?" I croaked.

"Everyone's safe."

I could have floated away with gratitude. "Where are they?"

He gestured at the plane. "In the sea-runner."

"Didn't a plane blow you out of the water?"

"Yes."

"Are you going to tell me what's going on?"

"As we get closer to Ikekane South, it's going to be harder to *know* what's going on."

"What does *that* mean?"

Maddy's eyes locked with mine. "Will the truth frighten you more than the mystery?"

"You mean about my mom being behind the attack?"

His eyes widened. "How—?" He shook his head. "We're all fine. We all survived."

"Let's go. Tell me on the way."

"I think I'd better let Kinny do that," said Maddy.

"Kinny? Who's Kinny?" After a few deep breaths, I needed clarification. "Kinny, the Kinny from the Ipko, Kinny? Kinny who pretended to be my ally, but then tried to kill me and Alf on Craggy? That Kinny?"

"Kinny, who worked for Derven, who in turn worked for Saloma," said Maddy. "That's the one."

"This had better be good." I took a few more deep breaths, then kicked and paddled faster, doing my best imitation of swimming.

The sea-runner leaned precariously when we pulled ourselves out of the water and onto the landing gear. I vaulted inside, hands up and ready for action. To my surprise, I found Alf sitting in the middle of the cabin facing the front and holding a laser pistol. Behind him, the children sat munching on spacey food. Kinny sat benignly in the pilot's seat.

Alf answered my questioning glance about the gun. "He gave it to me as a token of goodwill, to show he means us no harm."

I smirked. "Does it even work?"

Alf took aim and promptly burned a hole in the back of the passenger seat. "I guess so."

Lapita screamed, but then laughed. She had probably never seen anything like it.

"Alarming. But reassuring." Folding my arms across my chest, I stared Kinny down. "So what's the trick this time?"

Kinny's face wrinkled with tension, and he seemed to exhale his whole air supply in one puff. "No trick. Well, except shooting the boat."

I lunged forward and grabbed his collar, forcing his chair to swivel towards me. "You attacked a tiny little boat with helpless children on board? What kind of alien are you?"

He blinked so many times I could practically feel a breeze coming from his eyelashes. "I struck the boat on purpose. It looks bad—"

"You bet it looks bad! It looks like murder. *Again*. How much is Saloma paying you to fix the botched job you did last time?"

"Not enough," he whimpered.

"What?" I shoved him back so hard that the chair wrenched free of its bolts and toppled backwards, denting the inside of his door. I leaned on the back of the still smoking passenger chair and watched him right himself.

"Caz, hear him out," said Alf, aiding Kinny's cause by welding the bolts back in place with the laser pistol.

I'm not sure how my eyes stayed in my head, but Alf calmly passed another protein bar to Tanu, as if his life hadn't almost been terminated by the man cowering next to me.

"What? How can you say that?"

"My lady…"

"Maddy, you didn't see what he—"

"He bought us time," said Maddy. "He targeted the roof of the boat on purpose because it smokes. It looks terrible from a distance, but it—"

"Sinks it in the middle of the ocean!" I screeched. "With islands as far apart as they are, it's a death sentence." I glared at Kinny. "Don't like killing us quickly anymore? Prefer to see us suffer?"

Kinny cleared his throat. "Please…"

Something in his eyes unhooked my rage and set it aside. Good thing, too. My heart was pumping fast, busy at work numbing my extremities and sapping my energy. I took a deep breath and sat myself imperiously down beside him. If I lost mobility, at least I'd look good and domineering.

"All right, talk. And while you're at it, start flying south."

Kinny's face lit up, and he quickly started the plane. "Yes, that's what I wanted to do."

"Do *not* take us to Saloma," I said through clenched teeth. I couldn't feel my elbows on the armrests.

"No, no. Of course not. She thinks you're dead now."

I craned my neck awkwardly, trying not to shift enough to let my arms flop. That would totally ruin my tough girl image. Alf slid the door to the cabin shut, and Maddy harnessed the children into their seats. They had begun to whimper, and Tanu grabbed at Maddy's arms. We all felt the tug of gravity pulling us, and the children screamed. Maddy and Alf each sat in front a child on the floor and gave them extra support in their seats.

"It's all right. We're just flying again. Remember? Like the birds."

"Don't be afraid of the noise. It's not an animal. It's the plane."

Kinny leveled out the plane, and we rumbled noisily barely ten meters above the water.

"Do you really know how to fly this thing?" I demanded.

"I grew up on the other side of Tye flying shuttles between colonies."

"That was before you took up with Captain Derven as a hired assassin."

"Yes," he said. "Please let me explain."

The motor's rattle drowned out the noise of the children and Maddy talking. Apparently he'd found the right words to calm them because their hysterics died down.

Alf came forward and knelt between Kinny and me, the gun loose in his grip. When his shoulder brushed against my forearm, and he smiled at me, I felt a tingle. Not romance. Better circulation. But I loved him for the effect.

"Saloma *is* on Tye, on a cruiser not far from Ikekane South. Once she found out you were alive, she planned to get rid of you before you could get there for the Cycling Ceremony."

"You know about—"

"Governor Jipps apprised her of your plans," said Kinny.

My breath caught, and tears burned in my eyes. Alf took my trembling hand gently, and I could almost sense the warmth of it over my instant grief. *Mom betrayed me!*

"Who were you with when you shot down the *Snow Storm*?"

Kinny glanced at me sideways. "I flew alone. In this plane."

I shook my head. "I heard you talking to another man."

Kinny nodded. "We flew in two planes about ten kilometers apart, searching for signs of you. I'm glad it was me that found the boat. I shot the cabin roof on purpose because I knew it would send up smoke without killing everyone on board. As soon as my partner confirmed a visual on the smoke, he went on ahead to alert Saloma. He thinks I stayed behind to watch the boat sink. I'm supposed to call in on the radio before too long to confirm no survivors."

"Did the boat actually sink?"

"Of course not."

Hoarse with mixed emotions, I asked, "Why did you do that?"

Kinny's tears matched my own. "I kept picturing the way you defended your friends, protected them. You risked your life to save Alf. I remember your face when Derven made me drop the tether so you'd both fall. I…" He ran his sleeve across his face. "You're better than Saloma. You…"

Alf and I watched him, but he had no more to say.

"Make the call," I ordered. "Tell Saloma we're dead. If I think you're speaking in code, I'll throw you out of the plane."

OOO

The brightness outside the window surprised me as much as the fact that I'd recovered my limbs so quickly after my nap.

"Why don't we trade places, Maddy?" I suggested. "You could probably use a soft spot for a while."

He must have been sore because he didn't hesitate. We swapped positions, and Alf slid onto the floor beside me. With our backs resting on the child-occupied chairs behind us, we sat close.

"How do you feel?" he asked.

"About what?"

"Everything."

"Still choosing to survive." I winked. "It's going to work out."

"How?"

"I have no idea."

He slid his hand over mine and squeezed it, and we sat for a moment with our fingers entwined.

"What happened to your arm?" he asked.

"Oh, that." I used my free hand to pry the makeshift bandage away. "Wow. The Gypsy Pearl does it again." I tugged the cloth completely off my arm, and we wiped away the crusted flakes of blood. Not even a scar. It was the same place where King had sliced my arm and inserted the pearl.

I leaned my head on Alf's shoulder. As he shifted to put his arm around me, Lapita plopped down onto the floor and nuzzled up against me like I used to with Dad. I wrapped my arms around her gingerly even though I was annoyed at her for interrupting a sweet moment with Alf.

"Were you able to save our supplies?" I whispered.

"Yeah. Kinny even helped," said Alf.

I glanced at our pilot. "Very civil of him. I don't suppose you could find my brush?"

Alf crawled on his knees to where our packs hung on hooks along the wall. He tossed me the brush and crawled back. I worked on untangling my hair.

Lapita stared at me. "What you doing?"

"Here, let me brush your hair." This would be a good task to fill the time. Thankfully, I remembered how Felly dealt with my hair when it was longer. She always started with small clumps and worked from the ends up, so that's what I did, being extra careful not to tug at Lapita's scalp. Her initial surprise faded into visible contentment, and I soon developed a rhythm.

Alf and I exchanged several smiles during this process, and I felt myself blushing for no reason. A happy blush. The color of giddy laughter instead of embarrassment.

"Want me to wrangle your hair next?" I teased.

He combed his fingers through his pale blonde locks. They'd grown down to his collar now, and strands clung to his stubble. "No, I'm good."

I winked. "If we've got scissors or—"

"Every centimeter of growth is a month I've been free," he said. "I'm proud of this mess."

I tousled his hair. "My albino gypsy." He grinned and brushed my wrist with his lips, sending flutters through me.

Lapita broke into a coughing fit, her wiry body withering with the effort. I held her tight, trying to muffle the sound so as not to wake Tanu, but he didn't notice. He must have slept through her coughing spells thousands of times.

At last she settled a bit, clutching her fist-straw to her lips and breathing deeply.

"Don't we have any of that pearl powder solution? I bet that'd help," said Alf.

"Alf, you're a genius! Ask Maddy. I know there's some in the first aid kit."

Maddy consented, and Alf brought over the finger-sized vial. "How much should we give her?" He popped open the lid. "I'm guessing it's pretty potent."

I shrugged. "Lapita, we have something that might help you stop coughing so much, but you can't drink it all, no matter how thirsty you are. Just a little sip. Do you understand?"

Lapita eyed the vial dubiously but let me press it to her lips. If she let more than a few drops in, I'd be surprised, but her face didn't register any bitter flavor or strange sensation. "Better now?" she asked.

"Better soon, I hope," I said, sealing the vial shut and handing it back to Alf. "Why don't you rest more while I finish brushing your hair?" Maybe the gypsy remedy wouldn't cure the asthma, but surely it would help a little. The pearl powder wasn't taken seriously by people outside of the gypsy culture, but those who used it in cases of injury or really bad health found it did something to stimulate healing. In my case, having a whole pearl in my body made me ridiculously resilient.

Lapita settled down on my lap while I continued to brush her hair. "How about you, Tanu?" I asked. "Can I untangle your hair?"

"What's that?"

Right. He'd never seen a brush. "Here, touch Lapita's hair." I guided his hand to her head, sure that he had fingered her often.

His sightless eyes widened. "Lapita?" He checked the shape of her face to confirm. She giggled, and he resumed touching her hair. "You soft, Lapita!"

"Girls usually are," said Alf, giving me a sly grin.

Tanu's hands went to Alf's head, and he sorted the strands with newfound interest. "Your hair short."

"Compared to yours, yeah." Alf leaned away, and extracted Tanu's fingers from his ears. "You want your hair shorter, too?"

"Like you?" Tanu squealed with excitement. "Like you! Like you!"

"I'd take that as a yes." I kept brushing Lapita while Alf found the scissors in the first aid kit. "I hope they're sharp enough," I muttered.

"How do I do this?"

I chuckled. "You cut. Start in front of his face so we can see his pretty eyes."

Alf lifted the clump of hair that blocked Tanu's face. The boy's eyes filled with tears, and his mouth hung open. Alf hesitated. "What? You don't want a haircut after all?"

Tanu reached forward and wrapped his arms around me, knocking

Lapita to one side as he did. I rearranged my arms to hold them both. "What's wrong, Tanu?"

"Pretty eyes."

Unsure of what he meant, I echoed his words back. "Yes. Pretty eyes."

Tanu gripped me tighter. "I have pretty eyes?"

My heart squeezed emotion from my own tear ducts. "Yes, Tanu. You have pretty eyes. Very pretty eyes."

"My eyes don't see," he said doubtfully.

"But *I* can see your eyes, and they're pretty. Big and brown."

Maddy, who had been watching in silence, came and knelt beside us. "I bet he's never heard a kind word about his eyes."

"Never a kind word, period." I frowned, but hugged Tanu tighter. When at last he released me, I brushed his hair from his face. "You want a haircut now?"

Tanu nodded his head vigorously.

Alf held the scissors towards Maddy. "Do you want to do this? I'm pretty sure I'll mess up."

I snorted. "Alf, the Adventurer. He'll travel the whole system and face untold danger, but giving a kid a haircut scares him."

"Says the girl who's afraid to swim." He winked and handed the scissors to Maddy.

"Uh." Maddy didn't look any more confident, and he sat with the scissors in one hand and the other hand raised uncertainly over Tanu's head. The boy turned towards the sound of his voice, and Maddy placed his free hand on Tanu's shoulder. Tanu immediately clasped Maddy's wrist with both hands in a gesture of trust and anticipation. That was all it took. Maddy got to work.

Fortunately, Tanu's blindness meant he had no fear of the blade, and the disappearance of his hair was a hilarious novelty for him. He and Maddy spent a long time just playing with the pieces that had been cut off. I finished brushing Lapita's hair and fastened it in a simple braid, which delighted her to no end.

All things considered, we were a more presentable pack of wild things coming in for a landing.

OOO

42 IKEKANE NORTH

We pressed our noses to the windows and peered down at the jumble of jagged rings poking up out of the ocean like broken drinking glasses placed carelessly in a row.

"Ikekane North," announced Kinny.

We touched down inside one of the fatter atolls and buzzed along the water toward a shoreline that showed signs of advanced civilization.

"There's the municipality of Haikou," said Kinny. "It has an excellent hospital with both pharmaceutical and natural remedies. It'll have all the diagnostic tools anyone could ever need. May I suggest you take the children there?"

"What about the expense?" asked Alf. "We don't have any local currency."

Kinny smiled. "That's not the way here. At least not when it comes to health. They're a very hospitable people. If someone needs medical attention, they'll not think twice about helping."

The floating runners chuffed against the sand, and we all disembarked with our supplies while Kinny kept the motor running. I jumped back aboard and sat opposite him for a moment. "Thank you."

"You're welcome."

"I trusted you once before as an ally, and you betrayed me."

His eyes darkened but did not let go of my gaze. "For which I am ashamed."

"Betray me again, and I'll have to kill you. I don't want to do that."

A sad smile played at the corner of his mouth, but not one that incited concern. "You won't kill me. It isn't in you." He placed a hand on my shoulder. "And I won't give you any reason to."

He wasn't lying. I could feel it. "Thank you. Now hurry back to Saloma before *she* finds reason to kill *you*."

His laugh held no humor. "Go now, Caz. The welcoming committee has arrived."

I jumped out to see two men and a woman approaching us with brightly colored oblong boards tucked under their arms. They wore very little clothing to protect them from the sun, and their browned skin revealed the perfect contours of their athletic bodies.

"Heya!" shouted the woman, clapping her hands. "You ubbs need boards?"

317

I blinked and resisted the temptation to clean out my ears. "What language are they speaking?" I whispered.

Maddy didn't answer me but clapped his hands. "That'd be great, thanks. We found some poor shipwrecked kidders who need a check over."

The woman opened her arms wide. "Oh, you poor kidders. Come with me and my ubbs." She clapped again, and it finally clicked into my brain that this was a greeting. "We'll get you to the hospital. It's right over there."

Too fascinated to protest, Lapita and Tanu let the beautiful natives hoist them onto a board. The two young men carried this between them front and back, giving the children a ride. I watched with pleasure to see that Lapita didn't cough once.

"I'm Alegre," said the woman, staying with us. She appeared to be about Maddy's age. "Me and my ubbs are on lagoon patrol today, so lucky for us. Nothing much ever happens, so this'll be an adventure, right? A shipwreck! Tell me while we walk."

Maddy introduced us and explained things as if we'd found the children beached on a rock. He didn't mention Apia or the fact that it was our ship that had been wrecked. I couldn't understand half of what he and Alegre said, but enjoyed her right away.

Alf did, too. I really couldn't blame him for staring. Her sleeveless orange blouse and short pants certainly flattered her figure and coloring.

"She's not wearing shoes," observed Alf.

I giggled. "She looks like that, and you notice her *feet*?"

He blushed. "Well everything else made sense. Doesn't she find the sand hot? I can feel it through my boots."

I shook my head, laughing.

"What?" He wagged a foot at me. "It's hot."

The sand ended quite abruptly at the edge of a paved road. Alegre's "ubbs" entered through sliding doors into a shining white stone-and-glass building that stood taller than any structure I'd ever seen before.

"The children won't need identification to get help?" I asked. "We don't have anything, of course."

Alegre's face puckered into a frown. "I think we'll have to assume the worst if they were all alone when you found them. Not to worry, though. We got plenty of fams right here in Haikou or across the way who'd be more than willing to thin the soup and add another kidder."

"You mean, adopt them?" *Could they really find homes that easily?* "But…the girl's very sick, I think, and the boy is blind."

Alegre cocked her head to one side. "They look all right. Just scrawny. Probably half-starving."

She saw nothing wrong with them. "What about keeping them together?"

"Oh, the bosses'll keep 'em together. Poor little kidders don't need more trauma, now do they?"

"No," I agreed.

Alegre nodded emphatically. "No, that's right. But this is Haikou. Happiest place on Tye. We'll take good care of the kidders." She put her hands on her hips and flashed a winning smile. "Now you ubbs need some care. Even upwind, I can smell you. And let's get you into some proper ropes. You'll melt in all that!" *Ropes?* "Let me run in and see that the kidders are checked in right, and then I'll beg off duty and get you cleaned and roped up."

I didn't ask. I just followed her inside.

OOO

Ropes turned out to be clothes, except here in Haikou, they were nothing like the neck-to-sole coversuits I'd worn all my life. I was relieved to find something that left my torso somewhat hidden behind a shimmering gauzy thing that hung from a "blouse" that covered my shoulders down to a few centimeters above my navel. I opted for a skirt because it fell to my knees, whereas anything with legs holes basically didn't cover the legs at all. Alegre found me a pair of "sallies", shoes only in the academic sense. They had a rubber sole with small twine straps that crisscrossed over the tops of my feet. By their texture, they'd been constructed from seaweed and dead … something gross. But they protected my feet from the heat of the pavement, so I thanked her profusely.

Now we stood with Alegre outside the hospital. The children were going to stay there overnight for observation and treatment, and then we'd be back in the morning to determine where they might find more permanent, loving homes. I realized in retrospect that there was a chance Lapita or Tanu would reveal their true origin and thus the lie we'd told about finding them shipwrecked. Hopefully that would not deter the natives here from feeling compassion for them.

"We're only five kilometers from my home," said Alegre. "I called my fam on the satfone, and Mama says new ubbs are always welcome for supper."

"Where is it?" I asked, ready to eat.

Alegre pointed out across the water of the lagoon. "There, almost straight across. The stretch called Kohala."

Alf's eyes traced the ragged arc of the atoll. "That's no five kilometers. It's almost twice that."

She laughed. "Well if you're gonna *walk* it, sure. You too tired for swimming? We got boards."

I stared at her. "You're going to *swim* across?"

"Well sure! It's not that far!"

When my mouth fell open, she laughed. "Oh, you're a wave *watcher*, not a rider? That's all right. If you walk fast, we'll get there the same time."

Maddy smirked pleasantly. "You swim that fast?"

Alegre grinned up at him with obvious attraction. "I'll race you!"

While Maddy laughed and clearly considered the option, Alf and I exchanged glances. "So, it's all right if Alf and I take the pretty way?"

Alegre gave me a skeptical smile. "If you think the road's pretty." She nudged Maddy with her elbow. "You got a diving mask? You've been here before, right? I think I've seen you. Nothing matches the view down there."

Maddy took the bait. Pulling me aside, he whispered, "Do you feel safe walking with Alf to the other side? You can see the people here are very friendly, and I'm sure you'll blend right in now that you're dressed native."

"How will I know which home it is? It's a big circle. I'll get lost going round and round."

He tossed his chin at the building behind us. "The hospital is the tallest, whitest thing on the island. Just keep going until it's straight across from you and then stop to wait down on the beach. We'll come along eventually."

"Don't drown with fatigue out there," I warned, only half-joking.

"I'll take a board."

"What's with the boards?" asked Alf.

"They're used for sport out on the waves or for transporting across the lagoon where it's calm. I can swim and push it along, and if I get tired, I climb aboard for a rest. I can also put things on top to keep them dry."

"You know, I did see wheeled transports go by. I'm sure that could get us there in a matter of minutes."

Maddy shook his head. "No one uses wheels for anything pedestrian. It's only for transporting people in emergencies or for those who can't walk on their own. Or if they have to carry a very heavy load. The rest of the time, islanders in this part of Tye swim or walk."

"Seriously? And you're up for that kind of exercise?"

He shrugged. "If I had to call any part of the Granbo System home, it would be the Ikekanes North and South. Both archipelagos are a lot like Haikou here. This is my native culture, I guess."

I smiled. "That actually explains a lot."

He chuckled. "Alegre, can you give Caz your satfone number, so she can call you when she gets to the other side?"

She did, and we parted ways holding the new device he'd given us and a handful each of local currency tokens. Alf and I shouldered our backpacks while Maddy and Alegre grabbed bright boards from a communal storage rack and waded out into the water, laughing.

"I think Maddy's in love," said Alf. "Our gypsy dad might get us a mom soon."

The word *mom* stung me back into reality. Mom had been connected with the attack on the *Snow Storm* and even now lurked only a hundred kilometers away in the Ikekane South archipelago with Saloma.

I closed my eyes. *Will Kinny betray me again? When will I get that third Power? And where is King?*

OOO

The road really didn't have much wheeled traffic, but other colorfully-clad, brown-skinned beauties sauntered by every now and then, some just walking, others pushing carts from which they obviously sold food or other wares. Everyone called out, "Heya" and clapped in greeting even though we were strangers to them. We got good at clapping back without laughing self-consciously.

"You can tell everyone here swims all the time." I sighed. "Even that vendor over there looks like he could fly across the lagoon." I affected a flirty tone I'd heard Felly use once. "Be a diplomat and buy a queen something to eat?"

Alf threw back his head and laughed. "That doesn't suit you, yeah? Too feminine."

"Ouch. Thanks a lot."

"I didn't mean it like that, Caz." His hand cupped my cheek gently. "You're the most amazing woman I know."

I reached my hand to his face, and a moment later, his lips met mine in the sweetest kiss. The kind I'd dreamed about almost every day since we'd escaped Lamond. The breeze tossed birds back and forth above us, and the surf pounded on the outer rim of the island, but for that moment, Alf was my whole world. Surface or space didn't matter.

"Heya! You ubbs want something, or are you already eating?"

We broke apart to see the vendor grinning and holding up two thin sticks that held unidentified fruits skewered on them. No clapping to announce his arrival. How rude. Alf licked his lips and pulled out the tokens, displaying them on his palm.

The vendor glanced at them. "You paying me for food or to go away?" If the man's grin got any wider, his head would split open at the ears.

"Both, yeah?"

Laughing, the man took two of the tokens and carefully handed us the sticks. "They're sweet, but maybe you'll save the girl for dessert, huh?"

Alf carefully plucked a piece of food off the end of the stick with his teeth. His eyes gleamed with pleasure. "I don't know. It's going to be hard to decide which is sweeter."

"Oh ho!" The vendor guffawed and trotted back to his cart, clapping now.

I sampled a nibble and had to agree. Alf and I strolled hand-in-hand to a point past the vendor's cart and stood in relative solitude looking out at the Karlis. The view of the ocean felt very different from here compared to sitting on top of it in a little boat. In every direction, the light danced a little differently across the water, and the swells looked more even, like lightly wrinkled cloth lying across a vast bed. Behind us, the teal lagoon lay perfectly smooth, its hues growing darkest in the middle where the mysteries of the underground volcano lay. Out on the open sea, however, a bigger energy pulsed with the tide.

"It goes on forever, doesn't it?" Alf sighed happily and took another bite.

"No. Space goes on forever. This'll bring you back home if you go around it far enough."

"Home," he said thoughtfully. "Where is home?"

"Are you ever going to go back to your parents?" We'd never really talked about his post pearl-cycling plans. Youth who had been sent to Surface reformatories were notoriously shunned by their ICS of origin, so if he felt banished from that particular box in space, that would be normal under the circumstances.

"They don't want me. I don't think they ever did. The assault was just a convenient excuse to get rid of what they deemed an inconvenience."

My brows knit. "They thought of you as an inconvenience?"

He frowned and brushed his hair from his eyes absently. "Maybe I wasn't socially charming enough. They liked to entertain—you know, have people over to our quarters to dine—but I never performed well in that setting. I just ate. I guess I didn't earn my keep."

"Well, you've earned your keep as far as I'm concerned. I want to keep you forever."

He nuzzled his nose against my forehead, sending ripples of joy through my whole nervous system. "Then someday we'll have to make a home together, when you're all done saving the Worlds and I've earned enough money to buy my own boat."

I chuckled at the dream. It wasn't a bad one, and I had a feeling I'd let my imagination wander with it often.

Movement below caught our eyes, and we watched several people out in the water.

"Are they *standing* on the boards?" I gasped. Those crazy people treated the waves like a rec hall as they raced back and forth through the giant curls of green and white.

"I want to try that!"

Shouldering him, I pouted. "You would."

"Those wave riders are good, huh?" The vendor reappeared behind us. Persistent fellow. And he still forgot to clap. "Want any more pina?"

I did, but I didn't want to spend more currency yet. "No, thank you.

We've got a dinner appointment. We're just watching for a minute."

"You're a wave watcher, then. Not a rider?"

"Huh?"

The vendor grinned and shrugged apologetically. "You think all the time and take no risks, am I right?"

Alf snorted. "Oh, she takes risks. Just not with water."

"But you like the water, huh?" The vendor eyed Alf's lean physique.

"Very much!"

"Maybe I find a way to sell you some," he laughed. The vendor smiled and wandered back to his cart, munching on the stick of pina.

"That's the second time someone called me that. A wave watcher, not a wave rider." I frowned. "I guess it means they think I'm boring."

Alf tucked me under his arm. "You're not a wave watcher, Caz. You're the *wave*. You carried Nathani to Menorca and the children here. And me, clear across the Granbo System to this hilltop on Tye."

I stared up at him, overwhelmed with gratitude that he would see something in me that I hadn't seen myself—something good. Squeezing him around the waist, I sighed. "And this is why I keep you with me."

He ruffled my hair. "We'd better keep moving if we're going to beat Maddy and Alegre to the other side."

We resumed our course, faster now. I began thinking aloud. "You know, since I have to stay calm or go numb, I've noticed that there's something to this choosing thing. Deciding to Survive. Deciding to be Happy. I have to Decide to Be Calm every day. It's not like that's my normal way of approaching life, but I'm getting better, don't you think?"

He grinned at me. "As long as you don't die of apathy."

"I won't. I actually feel really good."

Alf squinted. "Have you turned philosopher?"

"Like an old woman."

He grunted with mock disgust. "Well, old woman, you probably have it right. No peace between the Worlds without inner peace."

"Exactly. That'll be my slogan when I'm queen."

His laugh turned a little sour. "That's soon, yeah. You feel ready?"

"No. Not at all. I hope King shows up because I have no idea what I'm supposed to do. I'm fine with helping the faneps, but who wants to rule the Worlds?" I took a few more steps before I realized Alf had stopped walking. I turned back. "What?"

"You know, you got pretty."

I doubted the breeze could cool my blush. "Now? In these old things?"

He rolled his eyes. "Well, after all that time you spent dressed like a mining boy, anything's an improvement."

I slapped his arm playfully. "You're not so bad yourself now that you're finally clean again."

"You're glowing."

"Now you're being ridiculous."

"No, Caz. Something in your pack is glowing." He tugged it off my shoulders and opened the front pocket. "It's the satfone thing. Do you know how to work it?"

We fumbled for a few seconds and brushed some control.

"Are you there? Can you hear me?" Maddy's voice sounded desperate.

"Don't tell me you already swam across!"

"Stop wherever you are. Don't come any further."

"What? Why?" I held the thing to my ear and hoped he could hear me speaking.

"Alegre's family contacted her. There are some suspicious visitors in the area—from Craggy."

"What do you mean?"

"Some men are coming by all the houses and asking if anyone has seen a dark-haired spacey girl and a blonde boy with a partial tattoo on his cheek."

My eyes bulged. "What should we do? We can't hide much here. We're out on the road in plain sight. Who is it? Who's looking for us?"

"See if you can take cover on the outer shore. If not, maybe you can take some boards and get over to the next island."

"But if we ask for boards, the people will be able to identify us."

"Just pick up some from the community racks. They belong to everyone. Head out to the next atoll."

"What? On the open sea?"

"It's right there. Less than two kilometers away. Can't you see it from where you are?"

The sun had passed overhead by now and glared angrily at us, daring us to see past its rays. "Yes." The next island was actually closer than crossing the lagoon. "But the water's a lot rougher."

"Alf will help you. I'll head back to the hospital. Alegre's mother said she'd take the children indefinitely, so we need to get that sorted quickly in case something happens."

"How will we find you?"

I could hear Maddy talking to Alegre in hushed tones through the earpiece. "Uh. I think we're going to need to rendezvous at the final destination. North side of the smallest island. You should have enough currency to get there by legal means, but don't let anyone know who you are. Try to blend in."

"A native who can't swim." I huffed. "No one will notice."

"Just keep that tattoo covered. You don't look like spaceys anymore with all the sun you've had, but be careful what you say. You've got to hide. Saloma has gathered a force to stop you."

"But she thinks I'm dead. Kinny wouldn't betray us again. I just know it." I swallowed hard.

"I think you're right, but how else—?"

"You said they're from Craggy. That's Mom's jurisdiction."

Alf swore beside me. "Let's go. Let's go!"

We disconnected the call. With no one on the road, we took the opportunity to climb up the ridge to our right and down the slope that led to the beach on the outer rim.

"That's going to be hard to get down in these sallies," I groaned.

"We don't have a choice." Alf held out his hand. "Too bad we don't have our Wandel Hav bumps to slide on."

Wiping sweat from my eyes and making the Decision to Remain Calm, I ran down the steep hill, hoping my ankles would hold. Part way down, we came to a ledge and a significant vertical drop. "Guess we go back to rock climbing for this part." I turned and began to let myself down, feet first, searching for a toehold.

"Alf, there's a cave here!" Angling my body carefully, I lowered myself into the opening. I crouched to avoid knocking myself out. A moment later, Alf dropped down next to me, and we surveyed the dark space.

"How far back does it go? Could we hide here?" Alf's sallies crunched on the fine, gritty surface as he walked doubled over. "This is big. Come on back."

I shuffled inside, glancing back to make sure we'd left no discernible footprints. Holding my backpack to my chest, I closed my eyes and sank down to my knees. "I need to calm down for a second."

"You scared?"

"I don't know. Yes, I...No." I shivered involuntarily.

"What's wrong? Don't go numb on me, yeah?"

"I'm not. I just..." Something crumpled inside of me unexpectedly. Still squeezing my eyes shut, I choked back a sob. "Alf, it's my own mother who sent them looking for us!"

"How would she even know where you were?"

"If she's with Saloma—"

"Who thinks we're dead..."

Tears streamed down my cheeks, and my body shook beyond my ability to will it still. "Betrayal is the worst kind of loss. Worse than death."

"I think we're safe here for the night," he said gently. "Why don't we make the best of this?" He wrapped me in his arms, and I focused on settling myself emotionally. The salty air and the smell of his skin helped. I felt tears streaming down, but some of them were tears of gratitude for such a wonderful friend. I snuggled closer and fell asleep.

When I awoke hours later, we watched the sky unfold ribbons of pink and gold along the horizon until the deep purple night slid down and crushed the sun.

OOO

43 THE DIVE

"Hello, children," I said, smiling at the small faneps sleepily. "May I join your dance?"

The triangle expanded with neat precision, each fanep child shifting without instruction to a place that kept the symmetry and absorbed me at the same time. They moved with an uncanny rhythm, synchronized like a graceful, living machine. Trusting, knowing, feeling, I closed my eyes.

"Thank you for letting me be one with you," I said.

They sang their replies in a language that touched my heart more than my ears. We danced as if we had done so all our lives. And when they balanced effortlessly on one hand, I likewise floated upside down, my fingertips grazing the ground for comfort, not support. I saw only blue and green and white swirling around me in fluid motion, up, down and around, with a guiding pale light always above.

"It's like looking at the sky from underwater," I mused.

I let go, only to fall through the air in slow motion. But it wasn't air. It was water. A pale circle of light above me shrank. I reached upwards even while falling back. The circle disappeared into a pinpoint of white light and then fell into my palm.

The pearl.

Salt air and the gentle lapping of water almost lulled me back to sleep. Funny how after so many nights rocking in the boat, even the cave floor swayed.

"Caz." Alf's whisper came close to my ear along with the sound of a light splash. A belltroe diving, no doubt. "Don't open your eyes."

I smiled. "Did you bring me a surprise, or are you just too grubby to look at this morning?"

"Focus on that whole inner peace thing you talked about yesterday, yeah? Calm, happy thoughts. We've got a long day ahead of us."

I played along. "All right. Five more minutes?"

"Five more hours, if you want."

What? I opened my eyes. "Where's the cave?"

He squeezed my hand. "Close your eyes, Caz." His voice trembled urgently.

Tired of the game, I sat up and screamed. Instead of sitting in a dark cave, we lay out in the middle of the ocean. Beneath us, a large transparent plastic square rested on top of hundreds of dirt-colored balls that kept us afloat just barely above the water. It was like a big, bumpy mattress.

"What the—?"

Suddenly, one of the lumps near my hand rose up from under the edge to reveal a face.

"King!"

The fanep pulled himself lightly out of the water and perched on my knees. Soaking wet and clothed in seaweed, the miniature man with the fuzzy head, huge eyes, and razor teeth grinned at me. His gravelly voice filled me with joy. "King found Queen."

Hugging him tightly, I laughed. "Yes, you did. It wasn't a dream? I was really with you!" I looked around, feeling especially tiny from the surface of the ocean. Even in the *Snow Storm* or the *Sea Callabus*, I'd felt a little bigger. "Now where are we?"

Alf stared at me. "You're not scared?"

"King's here. What's to be afraid of?" This, after all, was King's world, and he had powers far beyond my own.

"Have you noticed our mode of transportation?" He gestured as if trying to balance horror and relief.

"Is that—?"

"Faneps help Queen," said King.

"What? How?"

"Swim you safely."

"We're sitting on top of a bunch of fanep heads." Alf's eyes crossed. "I told you to go back to sleep."

"How did I not wake up during all of this?" But even as King's smug grin taunted me, I realized the dream had conveyed me part of the way. "Alf, when did you wake up?"

"A couple of minutes before you did. I have no idea how they moved us, but what happens when they need to come up for air?"

"Faneps breathe slowly," said King matter-of-factly.

"But it's really far!"

"Faneps swim fast."

I gingerly patted the bumpy raft and tried to imagine all those creatures working together to keep us from sinking.

"They're like the gouldings," observed Alf. "Moving as one."

"And probably next to invisible from the sky." I nodded appreciatively at King. "That could be handy. No sensors are going to pick up *this* boat!"

"Queen safe now."

I pulled him in for another hug. "Where have you been all this time? I've had so many questions."

"Start with why you gave her the Earlie syrup when it can kill her." Alf's old animosity returned, and I tried to cut it with a glowering look.

"Syrup not kill," said King.

"What are you talking about?" yelled Alf. "Every time she—"

"Syrup make still."

Alf rolled his eyes. "Now you're a poet?"

"Stillness helps Queen," insisted King. With a serene blink, he lifted off of my lap and sat levitating in the air at face level.

"Want to explain that one, King?" I asked.

"Stillness uncovers Power."

I tensed eagerly. "Three Worlds, three Gifts, three Powers? *That* Power?"

King nodded.

"So what is it? What's the third Power?" I moved to lean forward, but felt awkward placing my hand on some poor fanep's head. Then I remembered my butt sat on some poor fanep's head. Try sitting comfortably with that thought. Especially in the middle of the ocean with assassins after you.

And yet there I was. Mostly pretty calm. "What's the third Power, King?"

"Power inside Queen."

"Power not showing," I said with a sing-song copy of his three-word pattern.

King chittered, a sound I'd missed, and he shook his head, still smiling. "Power shows clear."

Exasperated, I flopped back on my bed of heads. "Ooh, sorry!"

I felt a rippling of movement under me, and all of the faneps at the end of the square farthest from us came up gasping for air at once before disappearing completely. Seconds later, the tops of their heads appeared on the opposite side. A rolling movement took place under us as everyone scooted over to make room while still holding the plastic square in place.

"Did they just rotate their breathing?" asked Alf, his expression betraying that he was impressed. "You little rat-men are astral!"

"Alf!" I hated it when he called the faneps rat-men. "They're people, too. That's what this is all about, isn't it?" Speaking to the tops of their heads, I said, "If he calls you that again, you have my permission to open up a hole in the boat and drop him through."

"Don't miss and drop her," said Alf, grinning. He grew more serious and turned to King. "You really are an amazing species."

King acknowledged this with a gurgle. "Faneps free soon."

I drew a deep breath. "Right. About that. What exactly does this Cycling Ceremony entail?"

King dove from his airy perch into the water and rose again a moment later holding a watertight sack.

"What's that?"

He held it out to me, and I pulled it open. My mouth gaped as I gazed upon the wide bands of blue-green cloth that shifted the sunlight like the water around me. I'd seen cloth like this once before, back on Caren when I first learned that I was appointed to be a gypsy queen. It was when Maddy changed roles from friendly gypsy to a special guardian and guide. It was when my whole life switched from escape mode—escape the box in space, escape the Lamond Reformatory guards—to one of direction: Cycle the Gypsy Pearl and become Queen of the Granbo System.

"This is the ceremonial wrap." The outfit consisted of stretchy leggings to pull on and then two wide, incredibly long ribbons that wrapped over my torso and arms. "Uh. It's not the kind of thing I can put on all by myself, but maybe I can get the first part?" I glanced at the water thinking I could find a way to change underwater away from watching eyes. Then I remembered how many more eyes there were down there. As if to punctuate that thought, the next row of faneps took their breath and rotated under. "All right, boys," I said with a Felly-tone. "Turn around. A girl needs her privacy."

I got as far as I could, thankful that my body wasn't wet while I dressed. Truly, nothing in my life had ever been stranger than sitting half-naked on a plastic sheet in the middle of the ocean with at least a hundred creatures holding me up while I tried not to kick or elbow them in the head.

"Do queens really grunt that much?" teased Alf.

"Shut up and turn the other way or I'll break your ribs again."

Alf wheezed with suppressed laughter, but otherwise behaved himself. I did what I could with the wraps up my torso, but eventually I admitted defeat when I got to the shoulders.

"King, I could use some help."

He bounded over and surveyed my work. With nimble, sharp fingers, he prodded my arms out of the way and tightened a bit here, loosened a band there. Then he deftly wound the ribbons down each arm and tucked them invisibly but securely at the wrist.

Alf whistled, and his eyes drank me in. I wished the wrap covered my face, too. "You look like something from another world," he whispered.

"No alien jokes, please."

He shook his head. "You're beautiful. Like you're made of the ocean. Like you belong here."

"Queen belongs here," agreed King. He bowed deeply before me, even as I sat on the heads of his fellow faneps.

Flushing with embarrassment, I reached a hand to each of them. "Thanks, both of you. I guess I do belong here. Whenever *here* is with you."

OOO

"It doesn't matter how deep the water is. You only swim on the top."

"Shut *up*, Alf." I shook away the numbness in my legs, proving only the cold, not adrenaline, gripped me. "Please," I added with a contrite smile.

He laughed, showing no sign of offense. "You'll feel warmer in a minute."

As far as I could tell, the water teemed with more faneps than salt, and they swirled around me. The plastic square continued to float with a fanep at each corner, holding up our backpacks.

After half an hour, I could tread water properly, and Alf wanted me to try swimming along the surface unaided by any tether. Guilt at making the faneps work so hard to carry me had motivated my self-imposed swimming lesson, but now I entertained second, third and fourth thoughts.

"I can't swim all the way to Ikekane South."

"No one's asking you to." He kicked away from me about two meters and held out his hand. "Just swim as far as my hand."

I grumbled and leaned into the work of pushing the water away. Though I could feel myself moving, his hand stayed out of reach.

"Are you cheating?" I gasped. "Why can't I—*stop swimming away from me!*"

Alf roared with laughter, which would have annoyed me, except that I secretly felt proud that I'd gone further than expected. With one powerful kick, I reached forward and caught his hand, tugging him close enough to shove his head underwater with my other.

He popped back up, spluttering. "Oh, I don't think you want to play that game with me, Caz!"

"I'm sure I don't. So swim away before I catch you!" Making a game of it, I pushed forward a little more each time, confident that the faneps would not let me drown. Many of them swam below me, giving my eyes the impression that the bottom of the sea was much closer.

Even with the Gypsy Pearl inside of me, I eventually tired. I could also see that Alf had pushed himself farther than usual for my sake. The faneps willingly re-formed the "raft", as King called it, and we broke into the last of our food supplies, which thankfully included dried pina. I lay on my stomach, trying to spread myself wide to disperse the weight for the faneps below me. It also minimized the chilly breeze on my wet skin. Alf and King flanked me, and before I knew it, I'd fallen asleep.

OOO

"We are here!" King excitedly shook us awake, and we slid off the raft and into the rushing tide. The sound energized me, and the welcome solidity of the earth beneath me granted me instant peace. For a moment, the water churned as hundreds of faneps sloshed ashore. They moved in unison without exchanging a single word, and led us up a series of ledges back and forth for at least an hour. With still more to climb, they all stopped, and King came to adjust my wrap.

"Ceremony starts soon," he said.

"Already? So soon?" I hadn't had a chance to contact Dad and Felly to have them join me. How had I forgotten? I swallowed my disappointment. "What will I need to do?"

"Dive in lagoon."

"I what? You never told me *that* part."

"Queen rest now."

"But—"

"Queen must rest."

I sagged beneath the weight of my questions. *What is it going to be like? Will it hurt? Will I have to do anything under water? Will the faneps all be able to speak? Can't it wait until Dad and Felly get here?* But King's tone had been final, so I focused my thoughts on my breathing and on how happy I was that it was almost over.

All around us, the gleaming eyes of the faneps blinked at me. I could feel their anticipation.

I dared one last question. "When do we start?"

"Dive at dawn."

OOO

We reached the outer rim of the crater as the murky yellow haze appeared on the distant horizon. The light did not yet touch the interior of the crater, but I could tell it was only about half as big around as the one at Haikou. We stood at the highest point where a bubble of land reached out toward the sea, creating a second smaller pool.

"Pearl is home," said King.

"You mean this is where it came from? This very lagoon?" I guess I should have known that, but it amazed me to think that the little sphere had traveled so far, and that I had been a part of that journey.

The faneps swarmed over, picking their way down easily, disappearing into the shadows. King remained with us, leading us along the surest path toward a wide rocky outcropping that jutted out over the water. By the time we got to it, the faneps had disappeared further down, presumably to the water's edge.

A palpable mist filled the bowl of this crater.

"Clouds?" I asked.

"Morning fog," said Alf. "I saw it a few times on Caren. It'll burn off when the sunlight hits it."

"Eerie, isn't it? I can't see where the water starts. How far down do you think it is?"

He took a step closer to the edge. "Not sure. I hope there aren't rocks down there."

"This is it." I sighed. "So, I jump in the water, and then what happens? Maddy's down there, right?"

King didn't answer, his focus drawn away by some movement below the fog that only he could discern. In the stillness, I shivered.

"We're being watched," said Alf.

"Of course, with all those faneps." But I shuddered again at a present sense of danger. Closing my eyes, I measured my body systems, willing them to work with steady precision. No need to startle myself unnecessarily. *A cloud can't hurt me.* Nevertheless, I stepped away from the ledge.

A sound behind us jerked me around, and my veins couldn't decide whether to burn fire hot or space cold. Mom stood there, wrapped in the same ceremonial clothing I had on, her black hair tucked in at the neck.

My body convulsed with a confusion anger, surprise, love, regret, and several other emotions that I could not begin to name.

"Mom." My voice sounded as thick as the fog.

Alf and King stared. Mom came closer, slinking through the fog, glorious in the gypsy queen garb. Her face, smooth and expressionless, filled me with a sense of longing.

"Aren't you going to say anything?" I asked.

"I need to make the dive," she said.

"You've come to take my place?" Tears flowed so quickly from my eyes that I could hardly believe they were mine. I shook my head and ran to her. "It won't work. Mom, how could you—?"

"I have to," she said, her eyes steady on mine.

"But that's impossible. You don't even have the Pearl."

"It's my place." Her arms folded around me, strong but cold.

"Why?" I croaked. "Because of Levia? Because you were supposed to be next in line?"

"Your turn will come," she said, her voice low. "But not today." She combed her fingers through my hair as she had done when I was little, and I felt a pang of sadness for those lost days and years. The sun broke over the rim of the crater, slicing the fog with a shaft of light. Mom hugged me tightly. "I love you, Caz. Remember that no matter what happens next." Then she shoved me down to my knees and moved to the edge of the precipice. Drawing a deep breath, she raised her arms triumphantly and dove headfirst over the edge and into the fog.

Gunfire rang out from below, shattering the silence angrily. A second later, the splash of Mom's body echoed, and then a commotion broke loose from unseen hiding places along the inner rim.

Wide-eyed, I flattened myself against the rock and called out to King. "What happened? What's going on?"

He turned to me with an urgent fire in his eyes. "Queen must hide!"

But I couldn't move!

OOO

44 IT'S ALL OVER

Alf grabbed my wrist and dragged me to my feet, but my dead weight resisted him. He hoisted me over his shoulder and sprinted over the rise, heading back down the other side of the crater.

"Someone's calling us!" The satfone glowed in his pack right where my face hung.

Alf carefully set me down and answered it. Maddy's voice came through sounding frantic. "Alf! Where's King? Can you see him from where you are?"

I scanned the slope without moving my head. "No sign of him."

"Who's with you?" Maddy choked back a sob.

"Caz, of course. Maddy, what's going on? Why was there gunfire?"

"Caz is *alive?*"

"She's right here, giving my wrist the tourniquet move with her bare hands."

"Sorry." I let go. My hand worked. Just one, but it was something!

"Where should we hide?" demanded Alf.

"She's alive?" Maddy's voice cracked. "Then who jumped? I saw her get hit at least four times."

"That was Mom." *Mom had been shot!*

Another volley of gunfire sounded, and Alf cringed. "Maddy, what the—"

"Get back out to the open water! Swim away. Caz will be nearly invisible with that wrap. Go! I'll signal from shore when it's safe."

"WHAT IS GOING ON?"

"I don't know!" The call ended, and Alf and I stared slack-jawed at each other. Alf hadn't had time to tell Maddy that the adrenaline had frozen me.

OOO

Hours passed, or maybe only minutes. Although my wrap would indeed hide me in the water, Alf wore the sunny hues of Haikou ropes. He'd be seen instantly in the water, an easy target. Besides, he couldn't swim well enough to carry me, too. We decided on an alternate plan.

Alf stayed on land under a shaded spot, hidden from anyone viewing from above. I remained in the water, clinging to a rock. Clinging to hope. Rocking with the waves and mixing my tears with the salt of the sea. I could see nothing but the roiling sky above. I could hear nothing but the belltroes and the waves arguing. I could feel nothing but the slow pounding of my heart. I'd never felt so alone. This was worse than the night I thought Maddy and Alf had been shot down. This time, my mother had been shot down. I didn't just think it. I knew it.

The clicking of my chattering teeth continued until I clasped the side of my face to stop it. That's when I saw the faneps. Hundreds—thousands of them. Their eyes were wild, their claws out, yet I didn't fear them.

"Help me, please!" I begged, my voice hoarse but audible.

In an instant, they swarmed over and around me, pulling me back up onto the sand. They pressed their tiny feet into my body as they ran back and forth. I shielded my face and gasped for air. *What are they doing? They're going to trample me to death! Ouch!*

Ouch?

I could feel again! With a guttural yell, I rolled over again onto my hands and knees. Instantly their movement stopped and they lifted themselves, hovering in a blur above me.

"Where's King?" I asked, brushing the wet sand off of me. "Is he all right?"

"King is here." He emerged from the masses and stood beside me, solemn.

Wrapping my arms around him and lifting him up, I realized my tears had already been spent. "What happened, King? Can you tell me?"

A loud whoosh whistled above, and the beach beside us exploded in a gritty fountain of fire and rock. The faneps glided backwards like a shoal of kelpies averting a belltroe. I scrambled to my feet and stared at the smoking crater.

Shouts drew my eyes upward and my mouth fell open in disbelief. Up on the ridge and coming half way down, at least fifty military personnel pointed laser guns or projectile launchers at the assembly of faneps. The men moved like green lava in their thick coversuits and black boots, clumsily but quickly toward the narrow beach.

"Hold your fire!" An amplified voice ordered, and most of the troops looked to a spot at the front line.

There she stood, regal and commanding, beautiful and deadly. Saloma.

"Identify yourself and bring me the fanep king."

She didn't recognize me? I glanced at King, who looked calmly back at me.

"What do I do now?"

"Queen will know."

I sucked in a deep breath and jumped up onto the rock behind which I had been hiding.

"Has it been so long, Saloma?" I called out. "Don't you recognize me?"

Saloma used the voice amplifier. "Who are you? Identify yourself or die."

I gestured down to the ceremonial wrap I wore and then squared my shoulders defiantly. "I am Caz Artemus!"

"Impossible! Caz Artemus is dead." She signaled to some of her troops and began running down toward us.

Reaching for King, I held him close to me. "I won't let her hurt you."

King did not answer, but the faneps moved in perfect synchronicity, spreading themselves vertically in a great wall behind us. The soldiers stumbled to a stop wherever they were, clearly unnerved by this show of mystic power.

"Nice move, King," I muttered under my breath. "Definitely intimidating."

"Kill them!" shrieked Saloma into her amplifier. "But don't hit the girl...yet! She has the one we want." She continued her descent as the barrage began. Hundreds of tiny missiles traced laser beams through the night, trying to find a target and missing over and over as the faneps dodged and flipped in the air. The wall of creatures may have looked like an easy target, but it was made up of twice as many holes as heads.

Saloma's blaring voice raged up over the snap and whoosh of their guns. "Hard fire!" She led the way, reaching the sand before everyone else, but there she stopped.

This time bullets flew, no tracers signaling their target in warning. Instantly, several faneps fell to the earth, screaming in agony. The deafening noise startled me enough to jump down onto the sand. I shoved King behind the rock and ran forward, hoping to draw fire away from him.

"Caz, no!" Alf leaped from his hiding place and tackled Saloma. Throwing a brutal punch to her ribs, he knocked her down, and the gunfire stuttered out. The troops yelled to Saloma but did not advance. Alf wrenched Saloma up from the sand, and at last she and I stood face-to-face, not two meters apart.

"It *is* you!" she hissed. "How did you...?" Her eyes narrowed. "Who dove from the ledge? Who cycled the Gypsy Pearl?"

King glided between us and met her angry gaze. "Queen cycled Pearl."

"But..." She struggled to free herself.

I nodded at Alf. "Let her go. She can't hurt me now."

He shook his head and jerked his chin at a strap on her thigh. "She's got a knife, yeah?"

My eyes flickered to the weapon. Saloma's face seethed with anger, marring her handsome features. I took a step closer and swiped the knife from its sheath, holding it at a defensive angle across my body, ready to slash down or up as needed.

"Let her go," I repeated.

Alf released her with a shove, and she nearly knocked into me. I made a point of not moving, and it forced her back a step. *Why am I not scared?* I looked into her eyes. *Because she is. Gouldings attack out of fear.*

I remembered our first meeting. She had been so haughty. So surprised. She had called me a child. I sweetened my tone and fed her own lie back to her. "I am so pleased to meet you."

Whereas her smile had never reached her eyes on that first meeting, her fury did now. "This cannot be happening! I have worked for years—for longer than you've been *alive*—to bring power to the gypsies!"

I had no answer to that. Swallowing, I said simply, "Call off your guards."

Saloma's glare tried to cut me in half, but she turned and faced the rocky slope. With a broad hand signal, she commanded, and they obeyed. Every gun muzzle and launcher bowed to face the ground even as a hundred or more eyes watched, alert, ready for action.

She spun back to face me, wiping sweat from her brow. She eyed Alf and King in turn, then sneered at the undulating wall of faneps behind me. "You stupid creatures," she spat. "You should have chosen me. I'm stronger. I've made all the connections. I amassed the resources. I can bring unity to this miserable system of planets and dignity to the gypsies at last. Why would you choose a child?"

Her last words were directed at King, but he turned, rising to float in the air, and deferred to me.

I looked back at Saloma. "Dignity?" My eyes rested on the fallen faneps. "Disregard for life holds no dignity. Forcing, buying, killing your way into power holds no dignity."

"What do *you* know?" she snarled. "You've ruined my life's work!"

I shook my head. "No. Your life's work has ruined you."

With a roar, she grabbed for the knife, trying to wrestle it from my hand. I held it in place as if I were an adult battling a toddler over a toy. Clucking my tongue, I said, "As the daughter of a surgeon, I must warn you that playing with knives is dangerous." I waved my free arm at the wall of faneps. "It'll either result in your gruesome shredding, or I'll just break your spine in half."

She let go, spitting an oath. "It should have been me. You're just a child. You know nothing of leadership."

I pursed my lips. "I know what it is not."

She lunged again, catching me off guard and turning my arm so the blade I held pricked at my torso. Before I could react, Alf grabbed her arms. A sickening crack sounded, and pain flared in her eyes.

"Alf!"

"She would have killed you, yeah?" He let go of Saloma, and she fell in a crumpled heap on the wet sand, cradling her arms against her body.

I stood above her, my shadow falling on her. The faneps lowered themselves to the ground in a semi-circle behind me even as Saloma's men advanced, guns pointed.

Slowly, I bent and scooped her up into my arms as if she were the child. She tucked her chin to her chest, refusing to make eye contact, too pained to fight me.

"Hold your fire!" I called out.

Alf echoed me and stood back so they could see that I held their leader.

They stopped, most close enough for me to see their faces. I looked at as many of them as I could, remembering the gouldings. "Don't be afraid. I'm not going to harm her. There will be no more killing today. There will be no more killing."

OOO

Authorities from Ikekane South ushered Saloma's men back off the island, and she was arrested and extradited back to Caren to stand trial for the murder of my mom and her role in the multiple attempts on Alf's and my life. Vid reports went out through the Granbo System, and I realized that before the next day dawned, everyone who cared about Surface life on Tye would be aware of the strange battle we had survived. I would be famous after all, but no longer in danger.

As a fleet of sea-runners carted away the last of the madness, King, Alf and I looked at the fallen dead of the faneps.

"King, I'm so sorry."

He didn't answer. *What could he say?* The faneps closed around their lost ones, no longer hovering in the air. One by one, they lifted them up, bearing each body on their heads. Silently and with perfect unison of movement, they disappeared into the breaking waves until Alf and I were left standing alone on the beach.

"I guess they release the bodies into the ocean just like we release them into space," said Alf quietly.

"How do you release someone that's still attached to your heart?"

Alf took me in his arms and held me for a long, long time. I was standing on Tye, yet I felt literally millions of miles away, drifting in orbit and exhausted by all that had happened.

I slipped my hands into his. "I guess we'll have to walk, right?" Maddy had called on the satfone and told us to meet him at the same precipice.

Alf looked at the steep slope in front of us. "That's life, yeah? Going up isn't easy, but it gets you where you need to be."

"We've scaled a lot of mountains together, haven't we, Alf?"

He brushed his lips over my forehead and gave me one more squeeze. "It's been better than living in a box in space."

The climb back up to the rim of the crater was just a matter of putting limb in front of limb and pressing upward, but the mental and emotional ascent from the abyss of grief would take longer. I didn't know what kinds of steps to take. My mother, whether she intended to or not, had saved my life. Her motives were no longer important. She was gone, and those brief days I'd spent with her would be memories I'd need to sift through carefully when all was done.

I cleared the outer summit with Alf and nearly collapsed with relief when the familiar, welcome silhouette of Maddy appeared not far below. He had built a large fire, one like the pyre he had made for Ninetta. A proper gypsy funeral. Weary but grateful, Alf and I stepped into the reach of its golden glow. Just beyond it, I gasped to see a line of faces I could never have expected: Dad, Felly, Ruddie, Sasa, Fizer. They erupted with cheers as soon as they saw us.

"How...how did you know to come *here?*"

A jumble of excited answers boiled down to Maddy and Dad having made all the necessary contacts. Alf sank to the ground, tired, but smiling now, and took the food that Maddy offered him.

"Thank you for the fire," I murmured. "You always think of everything."

He bit his lip with uncharacteristic shyness. "And thank *you* for opening my heart to the children of Apia."

I smiled. "They would have torn your heart open and inserted themselves without my help," I said.

He paused. "My lady, now that you have come to your time, will you need me for anything?"

"I'll always need you as my friend, Maddy. Why?"

"I thought I might settle down for a while." My arched eyebrow coaxed a grin. "Maybe rent a place near Alegre and her fam. I want to watch over Lapita and Tanu until I'm sure they're going to be all right." He shrugged.

"I already told you that you'll be a wonderful father. If you're watching over them, they'll thrive."

I went to Dad and Felly, and we wrapped ourselves into a family hug. "I'm so sorry about Mom," I said.

"We saw it happen from down below," said Dad. "It was..."

"Horrible," finished Felly. She clasped my face in both hands. "Caz, don't be that kind of gypsy. Come home to us."

How could I answer that? I made no promise, but hugged her hard.

Ruddie and Sasa came closer, holding hands. "I thought it was you that got shot," said Ruddie.

Sasa grabbed my shoulders and shook me affectionately. "Will you stop dying already?"

"That'll be the last time for a while," I said. "I plan on living life far less dangerously now."

"Promise?"

"Do *you* promise to tell me all about what's happening next in your lives?" I asked, looking pointedly at Ruddie. "Are you going to continue your schooling? How's the new ICS?"

"Small, orderly, in need of good managers," said Ruddie.

"Will they take a future stationmaster with a record?" I teased.

He jerked his chin in the direction of the lagoon. "Stranger things have happened."

Fizer sidled closer, unusually subdued. When I gave him a hug, he cast a glance at Alf. "He won't be mad?" he whispered.

"You saved us back on Craggy. If it hadn't been for you, we'd never have made it through the placement tests. We couldn't have entered the colony in the first place, and I never would have found my mom again. Thanks for everything, and for coming, and..."

"You're talking like Fizer, yeah?" Alf called out playfully. "Take a breath."

"Thanks for being here," I said, giving Fizer a tight squeeze.

Fizer beamed. "How could I miss such an anthropological wonder as the mythical Cycling Ceremony?" he asked. His voice wasn't perky, though. "I'm sorry about your mother. She was scary, but..."

"Yeah, I know."

In my peripheral vision, I saw movement as the faneps arrived. They conformed to the mountainous terrain, surrounding us with a sort of reverent support. I could feel their pulse in my own, and I knew the time had come for them to be freed of their strange, mute curse. Joy burbled inside of me, and I wasn't the only one feeling that way, apparently because a great chatter went up in the assembly of faneps. They swarmed in amongst us as much as they could, and soon we were all settled closer around the fire.

"So, King," said Alf, when the regal little fanep walked up to us. "Does this mean she tries again tomorrow morning at dawn?"

The faneps chittered, clicking their teeth.

King floated before me serenely. "Queen is ready?"

"I'm ready. Tomorrow it is, then?"

He nodded. "Queen returns Pearl."

"Wait, what?" Alf snatched King's tiny little leg and dragged him down onto his lap. "What do you mean '*returns* Pearl'? It's *inside* of her. How is she supposed to return it without dying? If it isn't *in* her anymore, she won't have it to heal her."

I looked at King sharply. "King? Will I lose the Power that goes with the Gypsy Pearl if you take it back?"

King looked at Alf and then at me, unruffled. "Ceremony at dawn."

OOO

"What if it kills you?" Alf held my face in a protective vice grip.

"King's done so much for me."

"But if he takes the pearl back, you won't be able to heal. He's been using you this whole time."

"He's given me everything that I've become."

Alf took my hands. "No, Caz. You've become all of that on your own. Don't throw your life away."

"I'm *giving* it away, Alf."

He fingered the wrap on my arm. "People—*I* have been working all this time to keep you alive. You're going to waste all that?"

"You've been keeping me alive so I could get to this very moment."

"I love you, Caz. Don't leave me."

Tears leaped from my eyes. "I love you, too, Alf. More than anyone. But this is where I'm meant to be."

His grip hurt my arms. "You're meant to be with me! Not at the bottom of some lagoon."

"Please, I can affect the future of an entire species—of the whole System."

"But the ratman lied to you. You won't be a queen. You'll be *dead*."

"I—"

"Can't you make the Decision to Survive?"

I looked up into his steely eyes knowing that I longed to stay with him. "But at what price? I would forfeit the Decision to be Happy if I gave up my destiny."

"Aren't you afraid?"

I rested my forehead on his shoulder. "Does it matter? If I get scared and freeze up, then I won't feel it when he takes the Gypsy Pearl back."

Alf squeezed me tightly to him, giving me a tender kiss, and I held on to the moment for as long as I could, thinking of nothing but him.

Shuddering again, I pulled apart. "Is it cold? I can't stop shaking." It was probably adrenaline. The adventures of the last weeks flooded my mind. I'd lived more in the last few months than in the whole lifetime leading up to them. *I have every reason to be grateful.* The thought calmed me.

The dawn's light crept under the thick clouds and tapped my shoulder, announcing the hour. Faneps trickled with the rain down the mountain and into the lagoon, sinking into its depths with barely a ripple. King went last, pausing to draw three horizontal circles in the air between us. "Three Worlds, three Gifts, three Powers."

No time to remind him that the third Power never materialized.

After tearful but wordless good-byes, my family and friends followed to a vantage point below to watch and presumably retrieve my body when it was all over.

So this is it. I could be angry. I could feel betrayed by King, yet I know it is right. I can feel it. I must give myself, so that the fanep species can be free.

I stepped to the edge of the precipice, my toes curling over the edge, now damp with a soft, drizzling rain. No fog to hide the view today. My head spun with vertigo, and the water thirty meters below looked like it was swirling down an invisible drain. I drew a deep breath and raised my hands, not in some gesture of triumph, but as a last embrace of the Granbo System. Between my palms, I held the galaxy above and all of us in it. I couldn't make a beautiful dive, so I simply took a step forward and let gravity do the rest.

The adrenaline seized me instantly, and I sensed nothing but the blur of a shadowy lagoon through my tears. And then I plunged underwater. Deep underwater. Deep in blackness. Deep in an unexpected warmth. Before me, thousands of pearls drifted in and out of sight. No, not pearls. Eyes. The faneps surrounded me, pulsing in and out with each breath I couldn't take, but drawing a little closer each time.

King appeared out of the murk, luminescent. As if hovering in the air, he bowed with his placid smile and reached his razor claws into my heart. I felt a moment's stinging cold, a grief for something unnamed, and then I felt nothing. I drifted downward even as a stream of blood swirled up like a plume of smoke. High above was a white circle.

A circle of light.

A pearl.

I sank.

OOO

45   THE GYPSY PEARL

"You're crazy, Caz!" Alf's voice scratched with emotion.

I rubbed water from my eyes and shivered with cold. "What did I do now?"

"You rose to the occasion with a most spectacular fall, my queen."

I pulled myself up to one elbow and smirked at Alf. "My, what eloquence."

Alf shook his head and pointed over my shoulder. I turned to see King sitting beside me where I lay now beside the lagoon on a slick, black platform carved directly into the rock of the crater.

"On behalf of the entire fanep species on the planet Tye and throughout the Granbo System, I thank you, Queen Caz, for your willing sacrifice." King's eyes twinkled with mischief.

I squealed and hugged him fast. "It worked! It worked! You're talking! Can you *all* talk? Are you free?"

"We are as free as you are whole, good Queen."

I gasped with excitement and slapped away at my chest. A sizable gash marred the front of the wrap, but peeking inside revealed my clammy white skin and nothing much else of interest. Tugging at the ragged pieces to keep the hole from growing, I lay back and laughed until my sides ached. "Why did I even think otherwise? Of course you weren't going to kill me!" I was breathless with relief.

"No, my Queen, but you were willing to let me, and that is what brought the Power necessary to free us all."

I sat up. King stood there, dignified in a sea-colored wrap of his own. He'd grown a little taller, a little fuller, a little less alien.

"That was the Power? The third Power with the third Gift?"

"Yes, my Queen."

"Explain it to me, King. What happened?"

"The Earlie syrup heals the heart. It strengthens it physically, but it also magnifies the sentiments within."

I rolled my eyes. "Emotions aren't actually stored in the heart, you know. It's a recycling pump for blood."

King leaned in. "With all due respect, my dear Queen. Your Rik leaves can't help you remember things you never knew, things that are more ancient than humanity on this world."

I chewed my lips shut and listened.

"I knew you would react differently—dangerously—to having the Earlie syrup in your system. That very danger—a weakness, if you will—forced you to settle your mind and find an inner strength. It was *that* strength that became your third Power."

"I still don't understand."

"Caz, from the moment I first felt you near me on the Arxon, I sensed your character, untamed yet. You were curious and predisposed to find good in people who were different. Since that time, you used those attributes and added to them courage and loyalty." He touched me gently. "And great compassion for others, human or not. Through your weaknesses, you discovered and developed your greatest strengths. It is why you are the one to unite the Granbo System." He opened his arms to gesture at our surroundings, and I noticed for the first time that my family and friends all waited, watching.

Felly rushed forward and hugged me. A moment later, we panted under a pile of well-wishers.

"Breathe!" I called. "I can't breathe!"

They peeled themselves back like petals on a flower, still tucked close, but giving me room.

Maddy cleared his throat. "Saloma wanted the authority, but her character held too much greed and selfishness. Imagine if that had been amplified by the Earlie syrup!"

"And that's why she ordered the men to shoot Mom…"

"Saloma thought it was you, of course."

My eyes darted to Dad. His eyes, though red-rimmed, showed an almost professional detachment. "Your mother knew what she was doing. It was a calculated risk."

"Did *you* know what she was doing?"

He lowered his gaze. "She meant to protect you and the people she met in that valley on Craggy."

"The Sumayar?"

He nodded. "Yes, the Sumayar. I guess she struck some kind of a deal with the Garvey Colony forces that entered the valley. Sanctuary for the Sumayar people in return for her resignation. But when she tried to join you here, they re-routed her to Caren at Saloma's command. King went along to protect her."

"King and Mom were working together?"

"She loved you," said Dad emphatically.

"Still do," said a hoarse voice behind me.

I turned to see my mother looking haggard. She smiled broadly, and my heart surged with joy.

"Brita!" My father practically leapt over me to embrace her. A moment later, Felly and I joined in a group hug, tears streaming down our faces.

"Caz," said Mom. "My wonderful gypsy daughter." A streaked abrasion on her forehead marked where a bullet had almost killed her. She still wore the wrap, but where the bullets had ripped holes into the material, something black shone through. My finger went to a hole on her shoulder.

"Bulletproof body suit." She gave a smug wink. "A gypsy comes prepared."

My hand went to the wound on her face. "You *knew* they were going to shoot at you?"

"I knew they were going to shoot at *you*. Saloma tracked me all the way here to get to you. This was the only way I could think of to—"

The force of my hug knocked her back onto her rear. "You're a genius, Mom!" The tears flowed so fast I didn't even try to wipe them away. "But you were shot. You obviously got hit. How did you escape?"

"I saw you go down," agreed Maddy. "But you never come back up."

Mom gave him a wry smile. "I'm a gypsy. You don't think I can hold my breath long enough to swim to an underwater cavern and hide?"

"But what took you so long to come out?"

"I had to be sure Saloma thought I—you—had died." She touched her forehead. "And I was dealing with an injury."

I laughed with joy and looked back and forth at my parents. "So now what?"

"Well, you no longer have to worry about adrenaline spikes," said Dad. "With only two of the elements in your system now, you can terrify yourself to your heart's content, and it shouldn't bring you any kind of paralysis."

I looked to King. "So I lost the Power associated with the Gypsy Pearl? I'm no longer a quick healer and physically strong?"

King wrapped his hands around my arm where he had first inserted the Gypsy Pearl. "You have traded it for a far more important Power. The Power of your character." He smiled. "Besides, you know enough about anatomy, medicine, and gypsy healing techniques to keep yourself well and strong, do you not?"

"Yes, yes I do. Though I might ask Alegre to train me to swim across a lagoon."

The others laughed. King hovered beside me at eye level, and the fanep nation surrounded us in the air, now brightly clothed like the people of Haikou.

"Are you ready then, my Queen?" asked King.

I felt a glorious peace. "No."

An uncomfortable surprise shook the assembly.

"No, I'm not ready to be any kind of queen. I'm fourteen."

"Fifteen," corrected Felly. "You missed your birthday a few weeks ago."

I gave her a dry groan. "Fifteen. Hardly ready to reign over anyone."

"You don't want the authority?" asked Mom.

"It isn't really mine to take," I said. "I mean, who am I to go to the people of the ICS system, or the governors of the colonies on the planets and say, 'I'm your new leader because I've had this amazing experience with the faneps'?" I shrugged. "How does that make me a queen of the whole system?" I held up a finger to the protests. "And who would take my place afterwards? Do we really want to open that door?"

Fizer, of all people, bobbed his head eagerly. "Sociologically speaking—I mean in terms of ancient history—supreme leaders and their empires never lasted beyond—"

I burst out laughing and the others gradually joined in.

"If the gypsies want a centralized leader, I guess someday I could try that much of it. The gypsy queen thing," I said. "But I'm not going to tell anyone how they need to do things. Each colony is different for a reason. Each has developed its culture and way of doing things to fit the local needs."

"But—"

I rested a hand on Alf's shoulder to quiet him. "I'm not saying I agree with everyone's ways of doing things, but change has to come from inside, doesn't it?" I grinned at King. "Wasn't that what you just taught me? All the lectures and disciplines and control of the Arxon didn't teach me as much as I've learned on the Surface of these planets. I had to find out for myself what is right and what works. Experience, communication, seeing others in action…" I sighed. "We just need to open our minds and our doors to learn from each other and glean the very best ideas. I can't imagine trying to dictate a single code of regulations for all the cultures. But maybe if we work together better. If we learn from each other and adapt and grow…"

"What about being an ambassador?" suggested Felly, and the other ICS dwellers nodded.

Mom practically glowed with suppressed enthusiasm. "I imagine something could be arranged. It would require a lot of travel."

I tried to frown, but my face betrayed me. "Oh, I suppose that wouldn't be so bad." I gripped Mom's arm.

"You really don't want to be queen?" asked Alf.

"Queen? I'm a gypsy. No one place for me."

"Where will you live? What will you do?"

I tucked my hand into his and squeezed. "Maybe I'll try to spread peace throughout the system by helping others find inner peace."

"Will you need help?" he asked.

Nuzzling my forehead against his cheek, I whispered, "Don't I always?"

Mom, Dad, and Felly came in for a group hug.

"You'll have as much help as you need," said Dad. "We can take turns going with you." He glanced at Mom, who smiled and nodded at him. "And the rest of us will make sure we're watching you from the sky."

I grinned. "That sounds like a Decision to be Happy, if I ever heard one." I looked at Mom. "Ambassador is the wrong word, though, don't you think?"

"What then?" she asked, ruffling my hair.

"Just call me the Gypsy Pearl."

MORE BY LIA LONDON

The Circle of Law ~ Fantasy

The Fargenstropple Case ~ Cozy Mystery / Humor

Her Imaginary Husband ~ Sweet Romantic Comedy

Magian High ~ Young Adult Urban Fantasy

A Maze of Tales ~ Fairy Tales / Humor

Parables & Ponderings ~ Christian Spiritual Growth

For more information about Lia London and her most current writing projects, visit www.LiaLondonBooks.com.

Fun Trivia Facts about *The Gypsy Pearl* and Lia London

The original idea for the story came from a dream in which Caz and Felly were boys back in the 1800s who found a gypsy caravan. Lia shared the idea with a group of writing friends who suggested moving the story to the future and making the lead character a girl.

Originally, the fanep was only going to show up in the opening scene, but readers of the earliest drafts wanted him to play a bigger part. They also came up with the whole idea of cycling the pearl by visiting the various planets.

The girl on the cover is the big sister of a student at the Taekwondo studio Lia attended for many years. As soon as Lia saw her, she knew she was the perfect face of Caz. She asked if she could take a snapshot of her, and from that one photo came the covers of all three books in the trilogy and this cover for the full trilogy edition. (Oh, and Lia earned her black belt!)

About the same time that Book 1 was released, Lia adopted a black cat from the animal shelter and named her Gypsy. The cat was very beautiful, but had an enigmatic personality that kept people guessing if she was going to purr or bite. Her nickname was "Miss Gyps", and she became the inspiration for Caz's mother, Brita Artemus, who took on the name Ms. Jipps on Craggy.

Book 1 took almost a year to write. Book 2 and 3 each took fewer than four months because the story was already mapped out by then.

Lia has always enjoyed traveling to foreign cultures and learning how and why they do things differently. This is part of why she likes fantasy and science fiction stories—because they give people the chance to explore new worlds and ideas in their minds.

In addition to reading and writing, Lia loves to sing, play the piano, swim, practice Taekwondo, eat milk chocolate, spend time in nature, and watch old *Star Trek* episodes with her son.

Made in the USA
San Bernardino, CA
17 July 2016